FOREVER NEVER

LUCY SCORE

That's What She Said Publishing, Inc.

ISBN: 978-1-945631-73-3 (ebook)

ISBN: 978-1-945631-75-7 (paperback)

lucyscore.com

013122

To Linda, Clint, and Cassandra for your Michigan hospitality!

1

*B*rick Callan had no idea that he was one grocery aisle away from his worst nightmare.

Had he bothered straightening to his full six feet four inches and looked up from the canned goods, he would have caught that telltale flash of red. The color of forest fires and the temptations of hell.

Instead, he weighed the options between diced tomatoes with or without green peppers while shopkeeper Bill House complained to him.

"I'm telling you, Brick. That Rathbun kid spent half the afternoon gunning his snowmobile down Market Street like a maniac," Bill hissed, crossing his skinny arms over his chest.

Brick tucked the tomatoes with peppers into the cart next to a bag of yellow onions, two cartons of beef broth, and the pack of batteries.

"Kid scared the hell out of the horses on delivery yesterday," Bill continued. "*And* he came this close to side-swiping Mulvaney's new Arctic Cat last week. You know we'd never hear the end of that."

Brick bit back a sigh. Just once it would be nice to do his

shopping without small talk. "I'll talk to him," he promised. He happened to know a thing or two about the dumb shit boys did to impress teenage girls.

Bill blew out a sigh and adjusted the Doud's Market ski cap he used to keep his bald head warm from November through April. "Appreciate it, Brick."

There was a delicate balance to their little island community, and Brick's job was to help maintain that balance even in the dead of the Michigan winter when only the most hardy of residents remained on Mackinac. It was the same reason he'd promised Mrs. Sopp he'd change the batteries in the smoke detectors of her rental when she'd called from the back nine of a golf course in Florida.

The door to Doud's opened with a jangle of the bell.

Mira Rathbun—mother of said "Rathbun kid"—blew into the little store with a bone-chilling lake wind. Bill clammed up, looking as if he'd swallowed his tongue. The man didn't mind tattling to the off-duty cops on his neighbors, but he was more comfortable doing so behind their backs.

"Shut the damn door!" The order came from the cashier and two customers closest to the entrance.

When the last full ferry of tourists left Mackinac Island back in October, it also took the polite courtesy required for a summer resort with it. The town's 500-ish year-round residents hunkered down for another bone-chilling offseason in the middle of Lake Huron with a charming surliness.

"Yeah, yeah. Sorry," Mira said, impatiently brushing a layer of powder off her bright orange snow suit. The woman was a mile-a-minute whirlwind, which stressed Brick out. It was unfortunate for the community that she'd been the one to teach Travis to drive his third-hand snowmobile.

This was Brick's fourteenth winter on the island. He perversely looked forward to the frigid temperatures and the seasonal closures of most of the businesses. Winter was quiet. Low-key. Predictable.

Bill peered into Brick's cart, eyebrows disappearing under the edge of his hat. "Beef stew again? Don't you know any other recipes? I bet there's a single gal or two on the island who wouldn't mind cooking up a nice pasty for ya."

"I like beef stew." He also liked not being forced to be social while eating it.

Brick made a batch of beef stew every week and ate it for four or five days straight because it was easy and familiar. As for the social aspect, he'd earned his solitary winters and wasn't inclined to set a second place at the table.

"Didja hear the news?" Mira demanded, bustling over and crowbarring herself into the conversation.

Brick was skeptical. News didn't happen on Mackinac in the winter. Which meant this was gossip. Something he preferred to avoid despite the fact that both his jobs constantly put him on the receiving end of it.

"This have to do with the plane that came in late last night?" Bill asked, temporarily forgetting his problem with Mira's kid's accelerator hand.

Her eyes sparkled with the rare nugget of novelty in the middle of a season when every day looked a hell of a lot like the day before. Brick had a sudden desire to walk right out into the cold and avoid whatever bomb Mira was about to drop. Instinct told him something bad was about to happen, and he'd left his gun at home.

"Now, keep this under your hats because rumor has it her family doesn't know yet," she said, leaning in and dropping her voice to a whisper.

Brick had a very bad feeling about this.

"Whose family?" Bill asked, looking bewildered. "I'm not following."

"I'm drawing it out for effect. Jeez. This is the longest conversation I've had with someone I didn't marry or give birth to in three months. Let me have this," she insisted.

Brick nudged his cart forward, hoping to escape the news. But Mira grabbed on tight, stalling his progress. "Remi Ford!" she announced.

His knuckles went white on the handle.

Remington Honeysuckle Ford.

Remi Honey to family. Trouble to him. *Hell.*

"Well, I'll be damned," Bill crowed. "What's she doing back here in the dead of winter without telling her folks?"

Their hushed voices melded beneath the steady hum in his ears. Brick did his best to keep his face expressionless while his insides detonated. The exit was only twenty feet away, but his feet rooted to the floor, knees locked. Over the deafening thump of his heart, he stared at Mira's mouth while she spilled the dirt.

She couldn't be here. Not without a heads-up.

It took him weeks to prepare mentally, to gird himself before being forced to exchange casual greetings across the dinner table.

"Psst!" The cashier, Bill's nephew, waved his arms from behind the register and silently pointed to the next aisle. Brick's stomach dropped into his boots.

No. This was definitely not happening.

Mira and Bill made a mad dash for the cereal aisle. Brick charged in the opposite direction toward the cashier, deciding now was as good a time as any to escape before—

His cart T-boned another just as it peeked around the corner. The momentum took both carts into a tower of oatmeal boxes, sending them toppling.

Fuck. He knew it before he looked up from the vanilla almond and maple bacon massacre on the floor.

And there she was. All five feet two inches of mischievous pixie. She wore her red hair in a long, loose braid over one shoulder of her magenta parka. Ear buds peeked out from the yellow wool cap crammed on her head. Her eyes were the color of the green antique glass his grandmother had once collected. Her mouth was full and wide, and when she turned that smile on a man, he couldn't help but feel just a little dazzled...at least until he got to know her. The smattering of freckles across her nose and cheeks stood out against the ivory of her skin.

She looked different. Pale, tired, almost fragile. The energy that usually crackled off her, raining down like sparks on her unsuspecting victims, was only a dull buzz. As someone who'd spent half a lifetime cataloging everything there was to know about Remi, Brick knew something was wrong.

Their gazes held for one long beat. He couldn't decide if he should say hello or if he could get away with running for his life. Before he could choose, she abandoned her cart and walked straight into him.

Instinct had him wrapping his arms around her even though it was the last thing in the world he wanted to do. She slid her hands under his coat and melted into him. Her scent was still agitating. It always reminded him of a meadow...right after a lightning strike. Without thinking, he rested his chin on the top of her head, his beard scraping over the soft knit of her hat. Something dug into his side, but before he could figure it out, she distracted him by letting out a long, slow breath, and some tension left her. This was not the Remi he knew. That girl would have teased him with a loud, smacking kiss on the mouth just to piss him off before whirling away again to wreak havoc.

He pushed her back, holding on to her upper arms. "What's wrong?" he demanded, keeping his voice low.

"Well, if it isn't little Remi Ford!" Bill declared as he skidded to a stop, Mira on his heels.

"What are you doing home in February?" Mira asked.

Remi slipped out of his grasp and plucked the ear buds from her ears. The smile she sent them wasn't up to her usual wattage, but he was the only one who noticed. "What can I say? I missed the winters here," she said brightly.

That raspy voice was so familiar even after all this time it almost hurt.

Bill hooted. "Now, that's a dirty lie!"

Mira rushed in to give the prodigal a hug. "Are you surprising your parents?" she asked. "I know they missed you at Christmas this year."

Remi avoided looking directly at Brick when she answered. "I felt bad about missing the holidays with them and thought I'd make up for it now with a nice, long visit."

She was lying. He was sure of it. Whatever had put those shadows under her eyes wasn't guilt over a missed holiday.

"You're such a good daughter. How's big city living?" Mira pressed. The woman would drain Remi of every detail if she let her. Then it would be served up to other islanders over school pick-ups and to-go orders.

"It's...good," Remi said.

Brick's eyes narrowed on the hesitation.

"Quick! What's my aura color?" Bill asked.

Remi's cheeks pinked up. "You're looking a nice bright green today just like always," she told him.

There were a lot of things that made Remi different from the average girl. Synesthesia was one of them.

The story went that little Remi Ford caused a fuss in kindergarten when she demanded a pink crayon to write her Es because everyone knew Es were pink. It took a few years, but her parents finally got an answer from a specialist. Their daughter's brain created extra connections, tying colors to things like letters, words, people.

But the thing he found most fascinating was the fact that she could see music. Back in the day, before things got complicated, he used to quiz her about the colors she saw for songs.

"Are you still at the museum?" Mira asked.

"Actually, I'm painting full time now," she said.

That was news. He was surprised her parents hadn't mentioned it.

Brick glanced into her cart and spotted three boxes of Marshmallow Munchies cereal, coffee, sugary creamer, and a package of honey buns. Not a protein or a vegetable in sight. The woman was stress eating.

"Houses or paintings?" Bill teased.

"Mostly just paintings," Remi said with a wink. "But I'd paint a house for you, Bill."

The man turned a shade of scarlet Brick had never seen. Such was the power of Remi's charm.

She tucked a stray hair behind her ear, an old nervous habit, and that's when he caught a glimpse of pale orange plaster between her thumb and index finger. Her right arm was in a cast.

Brick's gut clenched as questions revolved through his mind.

It wasn't any of his business. And he knew what would happen if he let himself get curious. Remi Ford was no longer his concern.

"Are you seeing anyone?" Mira asked. "Did you bring a boyfriend for Valentine's Day?"

Brick clenched his jaw. "Excuse me," he said, gripping the handle of his cart. "I've got to get going. Welcome home, Remi."

"Thanks. It was nice to see you, Brick," she said with a sad little smile.

He gave her a tight nod. With heroic effort, he walked instead of ran to the checkout, leaving her, the rest of the items on his grocery list, and his unanswered questions behind.

2

*W*ell, that hadn't gone horribly, Remi decided, as she looped her bags over her good arm and stepped back out into the biting morning cold.

After a long, sleepless night, she'd survived an unexpected encounter with Brick. And accidentally hugged him in a way that screamed *woman in distress*. But she'd at least managed to swear Bill, Mira, and the rest of the store's occupants to secrecy until she surprised her parents.

Which gave her about an hour before her mom got a call from someone spilling the news.

An hour to figure out her official story and wipe the fatigue from her face.

An hour to try calling the hospital again.

She walked far enough so that she was past the grocery store's windows before dumping the bags on the sidewalk. Using her teeth to yank off her glove, she redialed.

"Northwestern Memorial Hospital, how may I direct your call?"

"Hi, I'm calling to get an update on a patient's condition," Remi said.

"Patient's name?" The voice on the other end sounded like there were a lot of other things she'd like to be doing besides answering phones, but at least it was a different operator than yesterday.

"Camille Vorhees."

"Your name?"

Remi hesitated. "I'm...her sister."

"Name?"

Fuckity fuck fuck. "Alessandra?"

"You're not on the list."

"It's because I'm the black sheep of the family," she tried.

"You're not on the list. According to HIPAA—"

"Yeah. Thanks. I got it." Remi disconnected the call and kicked at the support column holding up the porch roof of the next building. "Damn it," she muttered.

"Remi."

She jumped clear out of her skin. That voice. That fucking rough, low, gravelly voice that still haunted her dreams.

"Jesus, Brick!" He was crossing the street, coming toward her like the tide. Inevitable. Unapologetic.

It was annoying that her heart still sang whenever she saw him. But she couldn't really fault its taste considering Brick Callan was one giant hunk of man. Her appreciation for him had started probably somewhere around the broad shoulders and wide expanse of chest. But it hadn't taken long for her to realize those serious blue eyes, now with faint crinkles at the corners, had hypnotic, panty-melting superpowers.

The cowboy hat he stubbornly wore despite the much warmer alternatives in headwear added to the rugged appeal. Especially when mixed with his heavy winter coat and the jeans that showed off muscled thighs.

The beard was new and glorious. The intensity was the

same and annoying. The deep blue aura pulsed around him. *Steady. Dependable. Strong.*

Twelve years ago, he'd torn her heart in two. Seven years after that, he'd shattered it into pieces. She'd yet to forgive either of them for it. But that didn't mean she couldn't still appreciate him being the poster child for testosterone.

She bent to pick up her bags, but he beat her to it, adding her groceries to the ones he already carried. He smelled like leather and sawdust and horses.

"You don't have to do that. I'm perfectly capable of carrying my own groceries."

"What happened to your arm?" He asked the question briskly like it annoyed him to want an answer.

Of course he'd noticed. Brick Callan didn't miss a goddamn thing, except for the most obvious one in the world.

"It's nothing," she said, reaching for the bags. He lifted them over her head in what she determined to be an unnecessary—and hot—display of strength. "A small break."

"How did it happen?" The familiar, gravel edge of his tone settled in her belly and pooled there like warm honey.

He cared. Maybe not in the way a lovesick teenager had once hoped he would. But to the wounded thirty-year-old, it soothed.

"Car accident," she said. "Seriously. Give me my groceries."

"Where? Were you driving? Was anyone else hurt?"

She faced him on the sidewalk as the lake wind did its best to slip icy fingers beneath her layers. "No offense, but Chicago is out of your jurisdiction, Sergeant. And my life is none of your business. Remember?"

He laid one of those long, broody looks on her, the meaning of which she'd never decoded.

A vibration from her pocket startled her. Forgetting the

man mountain in front of her, she dug frantically for her phone.

Pain in My Ass.

Shit. The hope that had bloomed in her chest disintegrated. She hit ignore like she had on his last four calls and stuffed the phone back into her pocket. Brick was frowning at her now. At least some things never changed.

"Where are you staying?" he asked, finally. "I'll walk you."

It wasn't an offer. He was too much of a gentleman to let her play lame pack mule for a few blocks in hypothermia weather, and no matter how big of a fuss she made, he'd insist.

"Red Gate," she said.

Brick looked down at his boots, then off into the distance where the sky kissed the water. He blew out a puff of breath.

"Oh, don't go all tortured cowboy over it," she said, rolling her eyes. "It's not like we're gonna be running into each other all over the place."

Red Gate Cottage was perched on the southern tip of the island, pinned right up against the water. It also just happened to be directly across the street from Brick's house. She still wasn't sure if that had been a factor in her decision.

"*You're* the reason Mrs. Sopp has me changing the batteries in the smoke detectors?"

"No reason to be an ass about it. Gimmie the batteries, and I'll do it myself."

"Yeah? So you can fall off a chair and break your other arm?" He started down the sidewalk, shaking his head and muttering uncomplimentary phrases.

She jogged to catch up as he strode past inns and souvenir shops shuttered for the season. "Does this crabby cowboy routine actually charm any girl out of her thermal underwear?" she asked.

"Shut up, Remi."

Feeling marginally more cheerful now that she'd annoyed him, she fell into step and stuffed her hands into her pockets. It was a sunny, ten-degree morning. The light coating of snow on the road was groomed by snowmobiles, the island's primary mode of transportation for the season. Snowmobiles, horses, and feet were a resident's options for traversing the four miles of hilly, forested island.

To some folks, Mackinac Island was a novelty. An entire island without cars? A community with a shelf-life of about four months before the interminable, brutal winter set in?

But to Remi, it was home. And home meant healing.

They made the rest of the walk in silence. She hurried ahead of him to unlock the gate, painted a brash, lipstick red. Tall hedgerows protected the white brick cottage from prying eyes on the sidewalk, but the rambling two-story Victorian across the street could look right over it.

"You painted," she said as Brick brushed past her with the groceries. The house had once belonged to his grandparents, who had opened their home to two troubled grandsons. Back then, it had been white on white on white. Now, the cedar shakes and board and batten sported a deep navy. The wide front porch centered on a red front door, a color combination Remi approved. He'd kept the low picket fence along the sidewalk a pearly white.

With the snowy front yard and low-growing evergreens, it was picture perfect.

He grunted—because Brick had a daily word allowance of about fifty—and headed around the side of the cottage to the front door. Rather than a porch, Red Gate had a low cedar platform. In the summer, there was a table and chairs with an umbrella for sitting and appreciating the unbeatable view. In the winter, the deck held neat stacks of wood for the small fireplace in the bedroom.

Remi unlocked the door and barely suppressed an eye-roll when the mountain of a man insisted she go in first. Grumpy chivalry held a limited charm.

The cottage, on the other hand, was overflowing with it.

Agnes Sopp—Mackinac's real estate mogul—had redone it with wide plank pine floors and creamy stucco walls. In the living room, an off-white sofa with deep cushions faced the gas fireplace. The kitchen was tiny, with white cabinets and glossy butcher block. But a small, stainless steel island on wheels added storage and counter space. The windows on the front wall had all been replaced to make the most of the view.

And what a view it was.

The inky, gray waters of Lake Huron stretched out to infinity in front of the cottage, constant and dependable. Just like the man prowling her space. He stalked into the kitchen, taking up all of the space with his cowboy shoulders and grumpy competence.

And *that*, she realized as she shed her boots and coat, was why she'd come back. To be just close enough to feel safe again. Despite his protestations, Brick Callan cared about her. There was something in his spirit that demanded that all the people he cared about be safe. She envisioned him running around like a cattle dog, nipping at the heels of the people of Mackinac, keeping them all from harm's way.

She let out a sigh. Nothing good ever came from mooning over the ungettable man. Besides, she had bigger, more dangerous problems on her hands.

He produced a blister pack of batteries from one of the bags. She watched as he efficiently popped the cover on the first smoke detector without needing a chair or stepladder and wished she could curl up on the couch and sleep while he was here. While she was safe.

She climbed into one of the blue velvet swivel armchairs

in front of the window. Turning her back to the lake, she pulled her knees up to her chin and watched him grudgingly take care of her.

Covers clipped back into place, he pitched the packaging and old batteries into the trash bin under the sink.

"Do you do a lot of maintenance for Agnes?" Remi asked.

He turned to look at her, and when those long legs of his ate up the space between them, she scooted back in the chair. She didn't know what she'd expected him to do, but it certainly wasn't to take her right hand gently in his and push up the sleeve of her oversized sweater.

She had hugged, kissed, poked, prodded, and leaned into him about a thousand times over the years. There was a spark of something special every time they touched. It fascinated her. Comforted her. Confounded her. But the very thing that attracted her to Brick seemed to repel him from her. She could count on one hand the number of times the man had voluntarily touched her first.

"How the hell did you do this?" he demanded. His voice was stern, but the way he held her hand as he examined the plaster was almost tender.

"It wasn't *my* fault," she insisted, not sure if that was indeed the truth.

"Does it hurt?"

"No, it feels great. Of *course* it hurts. It's a broken arm," she snapped.

"How did it happen?" he demanded grimly.

She tensed, unable to control the visceral reaction to the memories. *Blindingly bright lights. Metal collapsing in on itself. Falling into the dark.*

"I told you. It was a car accident," she said, trying to pull her arm away. But he held her arm carefully, firmly in his grip as his fingers explored the tangerine plaster of her cast.

Those blue eyes focused on her as if they were peeling back the layers.

"What happened?" he asked again. His voice was rough and low, but his touch warm. That blue, pulsing light that surrounded him seemed to envelop her, too.

She was horrified when her eyes filled with tears.

This time, she was able to yank her arm free and turned away to face the windows and the water beyond. "I don't want to talk about it."

"You always want to talk about everything."

"Not anymore," she murmured.

"How much does it hurt?" he rasped, sounding as if he were in some pain himself.

She rested her cheek on her knee and willed the tears away. "Not so much anymore."

"You do remember that I can tell when you're lying," he said, spinning her chair around and forcing her to look at him. She saw storms in his eyes. More gray than blue now. She wondered what he might see in hers.

Would he look past the bravado and see what lurked beneath the surface? The thing that hadn't existed before. The thing that had changed everything.

"That was a long time ago," she reminded him quietly. "We're both different people now."

He rose, straightening those mile-long legs of his and returned to the kitchen. "You're gonna need to stock up on some essentials," he observed as he loaded up his bags. He was leaving. She was relieved and sad. As much as he annoyed her, his presence chased away the shadows. And that pissed her off.

"I'll get around to it," she told him, quickly wiping a tear away when he wasn't looking.

Groceries collected, he paused and gave her another once-over. "You look tired. You should rest."

"Good-bye, Brick," she said pointedly. He headed toward the door, and she waited until he'd opened it. "I like your beard," she called after him.

With a clench of his jaw and one last smoldering look, he was gone.

3

"*R*emi Honey?" Not much surprised Chief Darlene Ford. Born and raised on Mackinac, she'd served the island as a cop for nearly thirty years. But finding her youngest daughter—who was supposed to be working and living in Chicago—standing on the front porch seemed to be enough to put a hitch in her step.

"Surprise!" Remi wrapped her mom in a too-tight hug and held on for dear life. The name badge clipped to the front of Darlene's offseason uniform sweatshirt bit into Remi's shoulder. She may have inherited the woman's green eyes, but she hadn't gotten any of the extra height.

"Well, holy hell!" Darlene breathed, squeezing her hard. "Why didn't you call and tell me you were coming? I could have gotten your room ready. How are you? Are you taking your prescriptions? Is something wrong? How's your painting going? Have you sold any?"

The motherly interrogation made Remi laugh as she released her. "I wanted to surprise you and Dad. I don't need my room because I talked Agnes Sopp into renting me a place. And everything else is just fine."

"Well, I'm just tickled!" Still gripping her shoulders, Darlene looked over her shoulder and bellowed. "Gil! Get your ass down here."

"What's wrong? It's too cold for spiders," Gilbert Ford called back from the second floor.

"It's not a spider," Darlene shouted.

Darlene Ford had been born fearless...except when it came to spiders. It was the one area in which she allowed her mild-mannered, English-teaching husband to ride to her rescue without complaint.

"Well, come on inside before we heat the whole neighborhood." She ushered Remi across the threshold into the house she'd spent her teenage years escaping.

Small details were different. The rug under her feet was new. There was a sturdy desk in the cluttered study on the left. The old one, a rickety-ass card table, had finally collapsed last year under the weight of high school essays and half-empty coffee mugs. Across the hall, the living room boasted a bigger, newer TV.

But it still smelled like home. Coffee and furniture polish.

Her landscape of Mackinac's shoreline, one of her first paintings, still hung in the hallway that led to a sunny kitchen and dining room. And her parents still yelled from room to room.

"Remi Honey!" Gilbert Ford was one inch taller than his wife and a little less athletic. His dark red hair was always slightly mussed, clothes just a little mismatched, but he had a way of really listening to people that made them forget all about his disheveled appearance.

In his excitement, he missed the last step and nearly bowled both women over at the foot of the stairs. He flashed a sheepish grin before wrapping Remi up in a tight hug.

She closed her eyes and let herself be loved. "Hi, Dad."

"What a wonderful surprise," he said, swaying them side to side. Gilbert was an expert-level hugger and just the right medicine for what ailed his daughter at the moment.

How was it possible, Remi wondered, to be homesick while standing in her childhood home wrapped in the arms of the first man to ever love her?

"You didn't know either?" Darlene asked her husband, shooting him a calculating look.

He shook his head, releasing Remi. "I had no idea," he insisted, giving her hands a squeeze. "Didn't you?"

Her parents were notoriously busy and often forgot to relay messages of varying importance to each other.

"I didn't tell anyone I was coming home. I wanted to surprise you both," she assured them.

Gilbert's smile faded a bit, and his eyes narrowed behind the tortoiseshell glasses he'd been wearing for twenty years. "What's this?" He gave Remi's wrist a gentle squeeze.

"Oh, that. That's a cast," Remi said.

"A cast? As in you broke your arm?" Darlene barked.

"I was in a little fender bender. It's just a baby break. No big deal."

Her dad's brow furrowed. "Can you paint with the cast, sweetie?"

"I haven't really tried yet."

So many little white lies, and she hadn't even made it past the foyer. It was a record.

"Well, come on back. You can help yourself to some coffee and tell us all about it," Darlene insisted. "How long do we have you?"

"I thought I'd stay for a couple of weeks. Take a little vacation," she said, following her mom into the kitchen.

It was her favorite room in the house. After spending two straight weeks arguing about stains, her parents had gone rogue and painted the cabinets a hunter green. Glossy blue tiles made up the countertops. An odd-shaped island angled its way between the workspace and breakfast nook, a booth with deep cushions and a rich maple table built into the bay window.

"Did you get fired?" Darlene asked.

Remi snorted as she opened the mug cabinet over the coffeemaker and dug through the contents until she found her favorite. A chunky, bright yellow mug that said Don't Worry Be Happy. "No, Mom. I didn't get fired. I'm actually painting full-time now."

"You are? Well, isn't that—Holy crap! Is that the time?" Gilbert squawked, checking the microwave clock. "I have to get to school!"

"Well, shit. I have a call I can't miss this morning," Darlene noted as she glanced at her own watch.

Remi jumped out of the way as both parents dove for the coffeemaker to top off their travel mugs.

"Family dinner for our starving artist," her mom decided, screwing the cap on her mug.

The starving part of that description was something Remi had, until recently, looked forward to dispelling. But now she couldn't reveal the good news without breaking the bad.

"Tonight?" Gilbert shoved the now empty carafe back on the burner and frowned. "Do I have a thing or do you have a thing?"

"Double shit," Darlene groaned. "You have the fundraiser at the basketball game tonight, and I have a town council meeting."

"It's okay," Remi insisted. "I'm in town for a while."

"Tomorrow night," Gilbert announced, pointing both index fingers at her. "I'll call your sister."

Darlene grabbed the bag of coffee beans and shoved it at

Remi. "Make yourself a fresh pot and pull a roast or something out of the freezer. Oh, and since you're here, mind switching the laundry over to the dryer?"

Her parents sandwiched her for noisy, rushed cheek kisses, and then they were gone. She heard the old Yamaha snowmobile fire up on the street and watched through the front window as her dad climbed on behind her mother. Chief Ford would drop Mr. Ford off at the K-12 school and then loop around into downtown to start her day at the police station on Market Street.

She felt the tiniest sliver of disappointment that they hadn't had time for coffee together. But that's what she got for popping in on them unannounced on a Thursday. The kitchen was too quiet, so she switched on the ancient radio her father used to catch Wolverine games.

As something quiet and classical poured forth from the speaker, soft yellow and gold clouds billowed around the room, keeping her company. Who'd have thought that the little girl with skinned knees and pink E's would find her place in the world painting things that only she could see?

"Coffee first," she decided.

She started a fresh pot, then ducked into the tiny laundry room housed between the kitchen and dining room. Not much had changed there besides the amount of clutter. Since there were no longer two teenage girls in residence, the space was tidier. The little clothesline strung between two walls was no longer laden with bras. Now, it held unmatched socks clipped with wooden clothespins.

She opened the lid of the washer and began stuffing damp clothes into the dryer. Everything took twice as long as it should with only one good arm. She wasn't looking forward to four to six weeks of being without full use of her dominant hand.

Something red and lacy caught her eye. Digging it out, Remi gingerly held up a fancy thong.

"Dear God. What is this?"

She grabbed her phone and snapped a picture.

Remi: Please tell me this is Mom's and not Dad's.

She saw three dots appear then disappear. It took a solid five minutes before her sister responded.

Kimber: What are you doing digging through our parents' underwear, perv?

Remi: I came home to surprise everyone. By the way, surprise! Mom and Dad abandoned me and gave me a list of chores.

Kimber: Some things never change. Except Mom's underwear apparently.

Remi: Are you home? Want to hang out?

Her sister didn't respond, so Remi finished loading the dryer and pushed the start button. The tinny vibration on top of the appliance signaled a new message.

Mom: Don't forget to clean the lint trap! That's how fires happen.

Remi: I know, Mom. I'm not 10!

Guiltily, she stopped the dryer and emptied the lint trap before restarting it. Then just for fun, she pinned the thong to the clothesline where her parents would definitely see it.

Dryer running, fire averted, and mug full of fresh coffee,

she headed into the basement. The wooden steps were scuffed and worn in the middle from decades of trips up and down. Paint splatters on the risers told the story of her earliest artist days.

With its low ceilings and lack of natural light, the Ford basement hadn't been the best studio. But as long as she covered the chest freezer with a tarp before she started painting "happy little trees" with Bob Ross, no one cared how messy she got the concrete floor and block walls.

The lid of the freezer opened with a haunted house creak, and she peered into its frosty depths.

Remi: Dad, you have 1,000 roasts in the chest freezer. Which one am I defrosting?

Dad: It's a special occasion! Bust out the turkey breast. We'll have ourselves a Thanksgiving redo! Now, time to go break the spirits of my class with a pop quiz!

She broke out into an honest to goodness smile for the first time in what felt like forever. It was good to be home.

She took the turkey breast back upstairs and submerged the bird in a sink full of cold water.

After topping off her coffee, she decided to take a little homecoming tour and headed upstairs. Her parents' bedroom was in the back of the house. The door was closed to keep the heat in just like every other winter. Life on Mackinac was expensive, and winters were cold. Most folks worked more than one job and sacrificed balmy indoor temperatures for lower heating bills when possible.

Growing up, Kimber and Remi each had rooms in the front of the house.

She pushed open the door to her childhood bedroom and

sighed. They'd made changes in here. Gone were the deep purple paint and the posters of Usher, Alicia Keys, and Zac Efron. They had kept some of the art prints she'd collected, though. The colorful pieces popped off the clean, beige walls.

The bed was the same, with its wrought iron headboard, but the kaleidoscope of scarves she'd woven between the bars was missing. Ivory bed linens made the room feel tranquil instead of moody.

Remi couldn't help but wonder if this was the version of her that her parents would have preferred. Toned down. Restful. No longer a "hurricane of color and chaos."

She couldn't blame them. She was well aware that Remington Honeysuckle Ford was a lot to take.

Alessandra Ballard, on the other hand, was whimsical and interesting. At least, that had been the plan. But now, standing in her old bedroom, Remi wondered exactly where outgrowing the past and ruining her future left her.

Not that she could afford to think about that yet. Not when there were more pressing matters.

She took out her phone and opened her email. Ignoring her overflowing inbox, she started a new message—slowly and painfully due to the restricted movement of her right thumb.

C,

I hope you're okay. Please be okay. They won't tell me anything. Please tell me you're okay.

R

She stared at the top of her inbox for several long minutes, willing a response to appear. When one didn't, she flopped down on the bed and stared up at the ceiling, letting thoughts and memories rise.

She was home. Home was safe. As long as no one in her other life figured out where to find her. This was where she would exorcise a few demons, heal a few broken bones, and come up with a plan to fix everything before it was too late.

God, she hoped it wasn't already too late.

4

"Come on, Brick. I was just having a bit of fun."

Maybe it was the measly thirty minutes of sleep he'd managed the night before. Or maybe it was the whine in Duncan Firth's voice as they stood over the mangled frame of the Polaris after it had done battle with a split rail fence and a stop sign.

Whatever the reason, he wasn't feeling particularly fond of fun in the moment.

"That's Sergeant Callan to you when I'm in uniform," Brick said, handing over the citation. "Next time you think about ramping your vehicle, try aiming it away from the fences and street signs."

"Yes, sir," Duncan said, morosely stuffing the ticket into the pocket of his snowsuit. The man was in his early sixties, a grandfather of three, and a bit of a daredevil. He was the first islander to test out the ice bridge that connected the island to the mainland every year. The longer winter stretched on, the dumber his decision-making got.

"Pops! Pops! Didja see the video?" Duncan's seven-year-old grandson jogged over holding a phone over his head.

"Lemme have a look-see," Duncan said, pulling out a pair of reading glasses.

With a shake of his head, Brick decided it was time to leave before he had to add any other charges to the citation. Knowing Duncan, there was a six-pack of beer buried somewhere in the snow nearby.

His horse, one of the few left on the island for winter, stamped an impatient hoof at the fence. Like his owner, Cleetus was quiet, dependable, and bigger than most. He stood sixteen hands high, his dark coat glossy in the Friday morning sun. Brick stashed his gear in the saddlebag and gave the horse a pat on the rump before heaving himself into the saddle. "All right. Let's get you some breakfast, bud."

The big, black horse tossed his head in agreement, and together they headed toward town.

It was the kind of morning that took a man's breath away. The sun threw thousands of diamond glints off the snow, blinding in their brilliance. Meanwhile, the lake wind worked its way under layers of gear, reminding anyone who stepped out under that brilliant sun that it was still February, still a long haul to the spring temperatures of May.

Brick appreciated the rugged beauty of winter. The long, dark nights. The blanket of quiet. Work was slower, easier. The focus shifted from policing thousands of tourists to keeping an eye on the few hundred neighbors who called Mackinac home all year round.

It was peaceful.

At least it had been until yesterday.

The lights at Red Gate had stayed on all night. He knew that because he'd checked every hour or so, standing in his old bedroom at the front of the house and staring across the street at the cottage.

She'd always been a night owl, always been on the

forgetful side. She'd never really had to deal with the consequences since there was always someone walking along
behind her to turn out the lights.

But his instincts were telling him this wasn't just a case of
Remi being too lost in paints and adventure to pay attention.
Something was off. *She* was off. He'd seen it in the shadows
under her eyes, the way she startled when he'd caught her
outside the grocery store.

The snow-covered road stretched out in front of him,
woods to the right, glimpses of water views through the trees
to the left. The little downtown where most of his adult life
had played out was straight ahead. He'd made this place
home. Carved out a spot for himself. He wasn't going to upset
the balance by getting too close to her. Not again. He had his
reasons, not the least of which was the fact that Remington
Ford had been born with wings, not roots.

It was better, simpler if it was just him, Cleetus, and
Magnus, the stray cat. He had his house. Work that he loved.
Good friends. And a place at the table of a family he'd often
wished was his own. Wanting more was greedy. And in his
experience, greed greased the road to hell.

Cleetus picked up the pace when the white clapboard
stables came into view. His hefty hooves were muffled by the
few inches of snow on Market Street.

Brick did what he did best, focused on the tasks at hand
and let all the what-ifs and what-could-bes go. With his mount
fed and tack stowed, he shouldered the saddlebags—his
version of a briefcase—and headed up the street. He ducked
into the coffee shop conveniently located halfway between the
stables and the station where he picked up the usual, a box of
assorted pastries.

The small talk between the staff and the two other
customers reminded him that no matter where he went on the

island, he wasn't going to escape mention of the troubled redhead.

Yes, he did hear that Remi Ford was back.

No, he didn't know how long she was staying.

Yes, he supposed she did look just as pretty as the last time she'd been home.

While he'd made a place for himself here, she'd been born into one. The entire island looked forward to her visits because everything was just a little bit brighter, a little more fun with Remington around.

She was the kind of girl that when she gave a guy a nickname, the entire town was still using it over a decade later.

He kept his shoulders hunched against the gusts of wind that funneled between buildings and hurried the final few hundred feet to the station.

The white, two-story building on Market Street always reminded Brick of a church. However, instead of Sunday sermons, it was home to the Mackinac Island Police Department, town hall, and town court.

Slipping in the side door, he took off his hat and coat, hanging them both on designated pegs. There was only one other parka on the rack so far that morning. In season, the tiny department swelled to include dozens of cops policing the streets of Mackinac on foot, bikes, and horseback. But off season, only a handful stayed on to serve the full-time residents.

He took the pastries into the break room, where he found the boss pouring a fresh cup of coffee into her *It's Called Snow, Get Over It* mug.

"Morning, Brick."

Chief Darlene Ford was a formidable woman. A lifelong resident of the island, a windchill of eight degrees didn't faze her. Not much of anything did. She was tall and athletically built. Her auburn hair, streaked with silver, was scraped back in its usual short, serviceable tail. Her eyes were a cool, assessing green. The rangy build came from a rigid adherence to daily weight training. She could do more push-ups in one shot than most of the rest of the small force.

Brick excluded, of course. He made it a point to be able to out-work, out-ride, and out-shoot any other officer.

"Morning, chief." He poured his own mug.

"What did Duncan do this time?" Darlene asked, perusing the pastry selection. She selected a bacon-topped bear claw then offered him the box.

He shook his head, heading for the fridge instead, where his protein shake waited. "Ramped his brand new Polaris into a fence and took out the stop sign on Huron Road."

"Dang fool is gonna get himself killed one of these days," she said.

"Anything happen overnight?" Brick asked, taking a hit of coffee.

"Remi's home." She glanced down at the protein shake and didn't bother hiding her shudder.

"I heard. She okay?"

Those green eyes landed on him and held. "Seems to be. Surprised us on the front porch yesterday morning. Got herself a broken arm from some fender bender. Looks tired, but who isn't this far into winter?"

Brick grunted, swallowing the questions he had.

"That reminds me. Family dinner tonight. Seven o'clock. Be there." Darlene started for the door. "And don't bother telling me you're too busy or you don't want to intrude."

Damn it. There went both his best excuses.

"I'll be there," he said.

"Good. Bring bourbon. Gil's moved on to Manhattans," she said over her shoulder. "And eat a damn pasty to wash down that shake. A man can only have so much discipline before it's unhealthy."

He settled in at his desk, a dented, green metal throwback that he'd grown attached to over the years. While his computer booted up, he downed half of his shake and fired off a text to Darius, knowing full well his partner at the bar wouldn't be awake for a few hours yet.

Brick: Won't be in tonight.

It wasn't his night to work anyway. But he liked checking in. The more in tune he was with the bar, the fewer surprises there were.

Refusing to think about spending an entire evening across the table from Remi, Brick got to work. Wincing at the 10 a.m. slot on the department's calendar, he logged Duncan's accident, then perused the afternoon's welfare checks. Community policing involved more "driving seniors to church on Sunday" tasks than chasing down criminals.

He enjoyed the adrenaline of the high-season with all the challenges one million tourists brought with them. But he preferred the winters when he felt he was doing his part, not just keeping the island safe, but making sure everyone had what they needed.

He plotted out a route for the welfare checks and found nothing pressing in his email inbox. By the time he hit the bottom of his shake, he'd run out of willpower.

With his gaze on the chief's office, he typed the name he'd been trying his entire adult life to forget into the database and sat back while the engine populated results.

Remington Ford had five traffic violations. Not a surprise.

She'd also been arrested twice.

He'd known about the first. Hell, he'd been the one doing the arresting.

The second arrest was more recent. He skimmed the report. It stemmed from a protest in Philadelphia three years ago. The charges had been dropped. Also not surprising.

What did surprise him was the fact that there were zero motor vehicle accidents listed. An accident with injury warranted a report and a victim name.

He glanced toward the chief's office again. Darlene was on the phone, boots propped on the desk as she shot the shit with a few members of the chamber of commerce on a Zoom call.

Since the boss was still busy and he was already looking, he decided to dig a little deeper. He expanded the search and skimmed the rest of the results.

Pay dirt.

Four days ago Remington Honeysuckle Ford, 30, was transported from an apartment in Chicago to the emergency department of St. Luke's Hospital for a "severe asthma attack." Edging closer to the screen, his elbow caught the empty shake bottle, sending it tumbling to the floor. Snatching it up, he shot a guilty look in Darlene's direction then shifted his attention back to the monitor.

The emergency responder report ended there. Without a warrant, he wasn't going to get anywhere with the hospital's records department.

Had she passed out from the asthma attack and broken her arm in the fall? If so, who had been at her apartment to call 911? And why would she lie about a car accident?

The side door burst open, and Brick sent his shake bottle flying again.

God damn it. Less than two days on the island and the woman had already frayed his nerves.

"It's a beautiful day in the neighborhood," sang Carlos

Turk as he wandered into the bullpen, hands on his hips. The corporal was obnoxiously and permanently cheerful. Every day was beautiful. Every work shift was fun. Every burger was the best he'd ever eaten. It was hard to dislike a man for being happy all the time, but Brick still made the attempt.

"It's fourteen degrees," he countered.

"A beautiful fourteen degrees." Carlos paused and gave Brick the once-over. "You look like shit, man."

"Beautiful shit?"

"I wouldn't go that far. Reasonably attractive shit?"

"Good enough. Pastries are in the break room," Brick said, exiting out of his search. He'd worry on the problem later.

"You caffeinated enough for this morning?" Carlos asked, rubbing his palms together. "I believe it's your turn to be the bad guy."

THE STYROFOAM BAT caught him mid-thigh as a six-year-old screeched for help.

"Nice work, Becky. Hit him again," Carlos instructed cheerily from the sidelines.

Brick bit back a sigh as he monster-walked toward the little girl with lopsided pigtails.

She shrieked as she wound up then let the bat fly, hitting him in the gut.

He should have had that bear claw.

"Look, guys! He's going down," Carlos called, winking at the perky kindergarten teacher.

Taking his cue, Brick lumbered down to his knees and then slumped onto the floor, growling and moaning dramatically.

His partner blew the whistle as the rest of the dozen

kindergarten and first graders erupted into cheers. "Now what do we do?" Carlos yelled over the din.

"Run away and go get help!" the kids shouted in delirium.

"Great job, kids," the teacher said. "Now that we know how to handle stranger danger, who wants a snack?"

There was a small but terrifying stampede to the back of the room, where cookies and juice awaited.

Carlos helped Brick back on his feet. "Decent death scene. You're really improving," he said.

"Thanks," Brick said dryly.

Becky skipped over to him and held up a napkin-wrapped cookie. "Thanks for letting me hit you real hard, Mr. Brick," she said, showing off dueling dimples in her round cheeks.

He accepted the cookie. "Any time," he said. "Thanks for the cookie."

"You're welcome," she bellowed, beaming at him before sprinting back to the snacks.

Deciding he'd earned the sugar, he took a bite.

His cell phone rang in his pocket. He pulled it out and nearly dropped it and the cookie when he saw the screen.

Remi Ford.

"Yeah?" he answered gruffly.

"Brick, it's Remi."

"I know," he said, sounding more exasperated than he'd intended. "What do you need?"

"Good morning to you, too, sunshine," she said lightly. "I was wondering if you were using that room on the back of your place for anything?"

Once an accessible space for his wheelchair-bound grand-father, Brick now used the room to store horse and fishing gear.

"Not really," he hedged.

"If you're not using it, I was wondering if I could rent it

from you." Her words came out in a rush. Like bubbles in a glass of champagne. The cadence was so familiar it built an ache dead center in his chest.

"Uh."

The woman wanted to rent space in his own house. How in the hell was he supposed to stay away from her if she was under the same roof?

"I need space to fling some paint at a canvas, and the cottage is a little small and a lot clean."

He envisioned her wielding a brush in one hand, another clamped in her teeth as music blared and turpentine and oil paints splattered everywhere. It was a guaranteed disaster.

He should say no. It was the only answer that made any sense.

"Uh. Yeah. Shouldn't be a problem," he lied. It was a big problem. A huge one. The last thing he needed was Remi under his roof. Distracting him. Annoying him. Worrying him.

"Really?" Her voice rose like it always did when she was excited. "Brick, you are my hero. My own personal hero. Thank you! Let me know when I can come over and look at the space and we can talk rent."

"I don't want your money, Remi," he said.

"Money or something else. We'll work out a trade that doesn't piss you off," she promised sunnily.

He looked at his watch. "Fine. Meet me over there in an hour."

5

"The room isn't for rent," Brick said. "The *room* isn't for rent. The room isn't for *rent*."

He was a big man who preferred to move slowly, methodically through a task. But with only a few minutes before a visit from a woman who had no problem snooping through other people's things, he kicked the decluttering into high gear.

He wasn't a messy person by anyone's standards. He also didn't feel like being anything close to vulnerable around Remi.

So his breakfast dishes went into the dishwasher, the stack of opened mail into the breadbox. The sweatpants that he kept next to the front door in case someone came knocking unexpectedly went into the coat closet. Last night's pizza box fit under the sink. He buried the issue of *GQ*—the one from six months ago with the redhead on the cover who vaguely reminded him of Remi—under a couch cushion.

He flicked on the lights in the room in question and let out a breath. With windows on three sides, the natural light was good. There was an attached bathroom. Also good because it meant she wouldn't have to traipse through his house while he was there trying to pretend she didn't exist.

Magnus the cat wove his way between Brick's feet.

"You already had breakfast," he said sternly but still bent to pick up the sleek brown and black beggar. He was a skinny, picky pain in the ass that had appeared in Cleetus's stall at the stables last winter with a chunk missing from one of his ears and an eye swollen shut.

Brick's bleeding heart had taken the mangy beast home and nursed him back to health. It had cost him $400 in vet bills, five sets of his grandmother's drapes, and half a dozen distinct claw marks skating down the back of the leather armchair in the den upstairs.

Eventually, they'd brokered a truce with Magnus going out at night to prowl and Brick providing enough scratching posts inside to prevent any further property destruction.

Glancing at his watch, he put the cat down on the counter. Remi was always late, which meant he had another ten minutes before she got here. He veered off into what his grandmother had called a mud room. He'd turned the space into a large pantry with open shelves, an upright freezer, and a second refrigerator.

Supplies on the island in the winter were at the mercy of the weather and deliveries. Islanders stocked their freezers and pantries with staples leading up to the long winter. Something Remi had probably given no thought to before jumping on a plane.

She'd live off candy marshmallow cereal if left to her own devices.

Just because he wanted to make sure she stayed fed didn't mean he was overstepping his bounds, he decided.

Brick dumped a few pounds of chicken, ground beef, and vacuum-sealed bags of beef stew into a tote bag. Glancing up, he spotted the neat row of blue and yellow boxes on the shelf. Kraft macaroni and cheese. When they'd been alive, his grandparents kept it stocked just so they could make her some whenever she stopped by. He'd continued the tradition, even though she hadn't set foot in the house since his grandmother's funeral.

The doorbell rang, sending Magnus skittering for a place to hide. Brick also felt the urge to hide. But he was a very large, very strong man, he reminded himself. Hiding from a tiny redhead was not an option. Besides, she always found him. On a sigh, he grabbed two boxes of the pasta, stuffed them into the bag, and went to answer the door.

"Hi," Remi said.

The sun was hitting her from the back, making her long hair shimmer fire and gold. She was wearing another hat—a bright green knit he recognized from her high school days—purple leggings and a pair of stylish-looking boots with fur sticking out of the top. Clutching a travel mug in her mittened hands, she managed to look both tired and irresistible.

"Hi," he said after a long moment.

She'd painted her lips today. A kind of deep pinky red. He should probably stop staring at her mouth. And he should definitely not picture those red lips wrapping around his—

"Can I come in or are you just going to stand there glaring at me?"

He hadn't realized he was glaring. *When had he lost control of his face? Oh, right. The second he'd heard her name yesterday morning.*

"Come in," he said woodenly and stepped back farther than necessary to let her pass.

She entered and took a deep breath, then sighed it out. "It smells different in here, but it looks the same."

What the hell was that supposed to mean? Did his house smell?

Was it better or worse than how it smelled when his grandparents were alive?

Magnus dashed across the hall behind him.

"Was that a cat?" she asked.

"That's Magnus. Pretend you didn't see him. He thinks he's invisible," Brick said, finally finding his words.

Remi shrugged out of her parka, revealing a tight, white turtleneck that hugged full breasts. The woman was covered from neck to toes, and he was still uncomfortably turned on.

He would not get an erection talking to her, he decided. This was a test of his self-control. There was no reason why a casual conversation with a woman dressed for warmth should make his flag fly. He was a man. An adult. He could control his baser reactions, damn it.

She put her coffee down on the entryway table and then gripped his arm. He wasn't expecting the contact and almost yanked it away until he realized she was using him for balance as she removed her boots. She was wearing fuzzy socks with red cherries on them. *Socks were not erotic.*

"So the room—" he began.

"Lead the way," she said, looking up at him with a soft smile. Her hair fell away from her shoulder like a curtain, and his hand itched to stroke through it, fist in it. It distracted him from telling her he'd decided not to give her space in his house.

Socks and hair were not erotic, he reminded himself. *Stay focused.*

"Okay, *I'll* lead the way," she said, stepping around him when he made no move.

He followed her down the hallway. Which turned out to be a mistake. Her tight little ass in those damn purple pants hypnotized him with its sway. His dick stirred behind his fly, further distracting him from his purpose as she poked her head into each room as she went.

"I'm disappointed. I thought I'd see more bachelor clutter," she announced, turning away from the kitchen.

"Bachelor clutter?"

"You know. Pants you don't feel like wearing. Pizza boxes. Magazines with mostly naked women on the cover."

"That's a very stereotypical picture. Besides, how do you know I'm still a bachelor?"

She gave him a pointed look over her shoulder. "I knew within ten minutes of the ink drying when your divorce was final. This island does not keep secrets. If you had a girlfriend, everyone who's lived on Mackinac in the past fifteen years would have gotten a text, an email, or a phone call about it."

They'd reached the glass door that led into the back room. He needed to say something now. He couldn't show her the room and then say something like, *"Sorry. It's not for rent. Take your tight ass and the hair I want to wrap around my fist and get out of my house."*

"So. Listen," he began.

But it was too late. "Oh, Brick. It's even better than I remembered," she said, opening the door. Magnus skirted past their feet and skulked inside. "Look at all the light."

She wasn't seeing the clutter of outdoor gear. The kayak in the middle of the floor. Or the cobwebs hanging from the rafters. Remi only saw the good. Three walls of the room were all windows looking out into the fenced backyard and garden he'd tried hard to maintain to his grandmother's standards.

Wide plank pine floors matched the timber beams in the cathedral ceiling above.

"I forgot you put in a bathroom," she said, peeking into the small room. "This is better than the space I have in Chicago."

Fuck.

She bent down as Magnus came out from under a folding table laden with fishing gear to sniff her socks.

"Hey, buddy," she said, letting the cat nose at her fingers.

Of course the stupid, picky cat loved her. Everyone did.

He couldn't stop staring at her ass. *Was she wearing anything under those leggings?* Barely concealing a groan, Brick turned away and pretended to study the kayak on the floor.

Get a hold of yourself, man. Your dick does not control you. Tell her she can't be here.

He took slow, quiet breaths and thought about cold water and fish bait.

Under control again, barely, he turned and opened his mouth to tell her that he wasn't going to let her have the space. But stopped when he saw her.

Her arms were crossed over her chest, shoulders hunched as if she couldn't get warm.

There was still something weighing her down. Normally, she'd be chattering on, words spilling directly out of her brain. She'd skip or spin or move in a way that suggested dancing rather than something as boring as walking. This subdued version of her was quieter, more repressed.

It worried him.

"Can you paint? I mean with your arm in the cast," he asked, suddenly needing to break the silence.

She opened her mouth, and a short sigh drifted out. "I haven't really tried," she admitted, not looking directly at him.

Again there was no elaboration. No chipper announcement of what art form she'd be tackling until she could get back to painting. No silver lining or funny anecdote.

"When does the cast come off?"

"Four to six weeks."

"Maybe you can finger paint till then?" he suggested.

This time she did look at him, and he was relieved to see a little spark in those green eyes. "Maybe," she mused.

"I can clear out most of the outdoor equipment to give you more space," he said when she got quiet again.

What. The. Fuck? Christ, five seconds with the woman and all his carefully made plans tumbled like a house of cards.

They would both be better off with as much distance as possible between them. But he was worried about her, and until he figured out what was wrong and how to fix it, he'd have to suck it up and deal with the proximity.

"You don't have to do that. I just need a little corner with good light. Besides, this is just temporary until I figure out... some things."

"Are you okay?" Sleep-deprived Brick had the self-control of a four-year-old. He wanted to kick himself for asking the question. He wanted to keep asking questions. To keep pushing until he had real answers. Something was wrong, and he didn't like it.

Why wasn't she in any accident reports? What had caused her asthma attack? Why had she suddenly materialized on Mackinac? Why did her lights stay on all night? Why was she lying?

Things weren't adding up, and he was starting to get the feeling that Remi was in trouble. And if there was anything more irresistible than Happy, Playful Remi, it was In Trouble Remi.

Her gaze skated away from him. "Sure. I'm fine." She said it with a little, careless shrug and then turned to look out one of the windows.

It was the opposite of convincing. She could look anyone in the world in the eye and lie to their face. Except him.

"Would you tell...anyone if you were in trouble?" *Would she tell him?*

He watched her cover up the fatigue, the worry with a

facade of bravado. Her smile, while still a punch to the gut, didn't come close to her eyes. "Now, when did you go and get a big imagination, Brick Callan? Everything is fine. I'm fine."

Remington Ford had never once in her entire life been fine. She'd been wonderful. She'd been devastated. She'd been on top of the world. She'd been shattered. But never something as flat or normal as fine.

If he was going to find out what the hell kind of trouble she'd gotten herself into and fix it, he was going to have to keep her close. Or he could just step back and let her deal with it herself.

Fuck.

"Remi—"

She cut him off. "If I do paint," she said, looking down at her cast. "I don't like anyone seeing my work before it's done. I'm superstitious about it."

He almost said he'd respect her privacy, but that would be a lie. Maybe he wouldn't peek at her work, but he sure as hell would be digging into whatever the hell was going on with her. So he nodded instead. "I can get you a couple of tarps. For the floor, and you can use one to cover your work."

"That would be great."

"I can lock the door to the house, too," he offered. Maybe a locked door between them would help his sanity.

"Now you're just being silly."

He was never silly. Rarely ever even funny.

"So is that a yes?" she asked. "You'll rent me the space?" She made a show of pressing her palms together under her chin as if she were begging him.

"Yeah. You can use it," he said wearily.

Some of the tension left her shoulders. "Thank you, Brick. Once again, you're there with exactly what I need."

He decided the best reply was a non-committal grunt.

"Oh. One other thing," she said. "I paint naked. I hope that's not a problem."

He turned away from her so swiftly he jostled the table behind him, sending a tackle box to the floor. On an indignant yowl, Magnus sprinted toward the door. *Fuck.* There was no amount of fish bait he could think about to relieve the swelling in his cock. Short of untucking his uniform shirt, there would be no hiding it from her.

"Geez. Tough crowd. I'm kidding, big guy. I'm not going to prance around your house naked," she said behind him.

For fuck's sake. Stop saying naked!

"I'll get you a key," he said as he focused all his attention on bending over to pick up the tackle box without cutting off circulation to his stupid, throbbing erection.

"Need a hand?" she asked.

Hand. Mouth. Hot, wet pussy. Fuck fuck fuck.

"Nope. I got it," he rasped. He stood, holding the box in front of his crotch.

"So I guess the only thing left to do..."

His mind went wild for a moment, fantasizing about folding her over the table and dragging those leggings down her thighs. He imagined what it would be like to see his handprint pink on one of those ivory globes.

She was looking at him expectantly as if she'd said something that required his response.

"Sorry. What?"

"The only thing left is to agree on the rent."

"Rent," he repeated. Looking at her was only making him harder.

"Yeah. You know how rent works, right? You give me space? I give you money?" Her smile, though small, was a little warmer.

He shook his head, aiming some of his annoyance at her. "I'm not taking your money."

"Don't be so old-fashioned. Name a price."

"I mean it," he said sternly. He set the tackle box down and tried to pretend that a hard-on wasn't hell-bent on tunneling its way out of his pants.

"Now you're just being—"

Of *course* she looked down. Those green eyes locked onto his zipper and her pink lips parted in a sexy little O.

"Now I'm just being what?" he prompted.

"Just being...grouchy?" She was still staring. And he was starting to like it.

"You're asking me if I'm being grouchy?"

"What?" She gave a little head shake and dragged her gaze away from his pants. "I mean. Food. Cooking. Well, baking. I'm pretty good at baking things."

She was looking at the ceiling now, cheeks flushed, eyes bright. He wanted to order her to look down again, then realized he was being a masochistic idiot.

"Fine. Baking. I'll walk you out." *And wrap his hand around his dick the second he shut the door behind her.*

He led the way, in a hurry to get her out of his house, out of his head. At the front door, he spotted the bag on the floor and grabbed it.

"You look tired," she observed. "Are you okay?" She was looking at his crotch again. Only this time, her tongue darted out, and she licked her lower lip.

His cock twitched in reaction, and she made a strangled little noise. A man could only take so much torture.

"Fine. Great. Good." He held the bag out to her. "Here."

"What's in the bag?" she asked, looking as if she was addressing his dick.

"Meat. It's for you. Pickings are slim this time of year. Figured you haven't had time to stock up."

He held out the handles and tried not to jump back when her fingers got tangled in his. Normal people could touch other people's fingers and not get hard-ons. Not spontaneously erupt in their uniform pants. He needed to be normal.

"Mac and cheese? You remembered." She looked up at him with a real smile, and it hit him dead center in the chest. *Ah, fuck. This was a huge mistake.*

"Everybody likes mac and cheese," he said gruffly.

"This is really sweet of you, Brick."

"Yeah. I'll get you a key." He ripped the front door open. "I'll see you around."

"Is it okay if I put my boots on first?"

Fuck. "Yeah. You can let yourself out. I have to..." He pointed over his shoulder with his thumb. "Get back to work." Yeah, that was it.

Without another word, he turned his back on her and headed for the back of the house as if he was running toward an emergency. By the time he got to the bathroom door in what was now Remi's new studio, he already had his dick in his hand.

Before he slid the pocket door closed, he was already giving his shaft a violent stroke.

He barely had time to brace one hand on the vanity, barely had a moment to imagine himself peeling down those leggings and bending her over before he was already coming. It was an unrelenting torture, being this close to her and still fucking his own goddamn hand. That first wrenching spurt dragged a groan out of his throat as he painted the countertop with his release, wishing it was Remi's tight little ass.

"God damn it," he panted, stroking his way through it.

The woman reduced him to this. To an emergency jerk-off session in the middle of the fucking work day after a simple conversation. *Was this what it would be like with her here?*

He grabbed the hand towel off the hook.

"'Here's a bag of meat.' Idiot."

6

Fourteen years earlier...

*B*rick paused on the porch outside the screen door that led into his grandparents' kitchen to brush the dust and dirt from his jeans and peel off his boots. It was a new routine that came with a new life. One he wasn't sure he was adjusting to.

It had been a good day of hard work. He'd picked up some odd jobs as a handyman but most recently had landed a full-time position at one of the stables. Being able to continue working with horses was the highlight of the move to Mackinac Island with his little brother in tow. The rest of it basically sucked. Because as much as he enjoyed working in the stables, he still had to return to someone else's home. To people who were strangers to him. To a grandfather who looked at him and saw nothing more than a reflection of his father.

But he could deal with it. He'd bear it as long as it took for Spencer to feel comfortable here. Then Brick would be free to move on with his life. At twenty-four, he felt like if he could get far enough away from his father's shadow, there might still be good things in store for him.

He bent and peeled off one boot when a cheerful voice carried out to him.

Remi Ford. He knew it without peering through the screen. The wild child redhead who lived two blocks away was in his grandparents' kitchen. He debated slipping around to the front door and hightailing it upstairs. There was something about the girl that made his palms sweat.

She looked at him like she had plans for him. But then he heard his name from her lips and paused.

"You must be so proud of Brick," Remi said.

He dared to sneak a glance inside. His grandfather, an old man with wispy hair and a wheelchair, sat at the kitchen table with his back to the door. Remi sat next to him, spooning up something bright yellow and holding it to the man's thin, chapped lips.

It should have been sad, devastating even. The withered old man whose life had whittled down into a handful of rooms and a wheelchair being fed by the vibrant, bubbly teenager. But Remi was the wild card. There was something almost beautiful about it. About her.

"William," his grandfather muttered gruffly in his painful, post-stroke speech.

"*I* call him Brick," she insisted, scooping up another spoonful.

"Dad prison. Same name. Same blood," his grandfather rasped.

Brick shrunk back from the doorway, away from the truth of the words. Apparently Mackinac wasn't far enough to escape a father's sins.

"Well, that's just silly," she chided. "Brick's as far away from a criminal as you can get. I've never met anyone with a bigger heart."

"Big," his grandfather wheezed.

"Can I tell you a secret?" Brick could hear the smile in her voice. "That's why everyone thinks I call him Brick. Because he's so big and strong. But really it's because he's impermeable. Indestructible."

His grandfather chuckled then opened his mouth nice as you please for another spoonful. Brick shook his head. His grandmother was at her wit's end trying to get her stubborn husband to eat. And all it took was a pretty girl who didn't make him feel like an invalid. He couldn't blame the man.

"While we're on the subject, what did Brick and Spence's dad do to end up in jail?"

Brick closed his eyes and leaned against the wall, willing the dread away. It didn't matter what she thought. She was a teenager. The eight years that stood between them might as well have been an entire generation. She was the youngest of a tight-knit, loving family. He was the oldest of a splintered, scattered faction that didn't have things like Christmas morning traditions or family cookouts.

His grandfather struggled with the words. She waited with what looked like patience and interest, just the right amount of both to defuse Pop's automatic rancor at his condition.

"Hang on!" She lit up like the world's greatest idea had just landed in her head. "Why don't you write it down? I'll get you a piece of paper."

That sneaky little redheaded manipulator. Gram had mentioned to her in passing last week that they couldn't get Pop to do his physical therapy. Which included writing.

"Here. I got you a pen, a pencil, and a marker," she said, dropping the items in front of him on the sheet of paper.

Brick watched in amusement as Pop picked up the pen, then discarded it in favor of the thicker marker.

"I'll get the cap for you," Remi insisted. "There you go."

Pop took the marker and, with a shaking hand, guided it to the paper. She leaned over the table, red hair falling over her face like a curtain of fire.

"Oh! He was a con man!"

At his grandfather's harrumph, she rolled her eyes. "Well, it's not like he's out there kidnapping and murdering people."

"True. Still. Lazy," Pop wheezed.

"Well, yeah. I mean, obviously, if he's just taking someone else's money and not trying to earn his own. But Brick's nothing like that. I mean, all you have to do is look at how happy-go-lucky Spencer is. That's all his big brother's work there. I'm sure you know Brick didn't have to come here. He's a grown man. But he feels responsible for taking care of his brother. It's obvious he's done a heck of a job there. Spencer seems happy and well-adjusted to me, and I've known my fair share of teenage boys. There's only two places that could have come from. His big brother and his mom."

His grandfather's shoulders slumped. "Should be with them," he rasped slowly. The words seemed to exhaust him, and for the first time, Brick glimpsed the bone-deep disappointment Pop had for his only daughter.

She *should* have been with them. But, like William Callan II, their mother had chosen another life. And just because her choice wasn't illegal or unethical, it still left the same bitter aftertaste. Both parents had chosen something other than them. Than *him*. He never wanted Spencer to feel the weight of that.

Remi patted Pop on the arm. "I know. But if she were, they might not be here. It might be just you and Dolores in this big old house, and Brick and Spence might never have found their way to our little island. You gave them what they needed most. A home, a place to finally plant some roots. And they fit right in like they were born and raised here. That's your doing and Dolores's doing."

That manipulative, little redhead. He saw exactly what she was doing. A smile tugged at the corners of his mouth.

Pop struggled to say something, his lips working uselessly to form the words that wouldn't come. He gripped the marker and moved it over the paper.

"Pink s-h-o-r—" Remi broke off laughing. "Spencer's pink shorts! They *are* terrible, aren't they?"

To Brick's amazement, the stubborn Pop gave a shuddery chuckle. The man had never once laughed in his presence.

"Okay, maybe he doesn't fit in quite as well as Brick does. But his grades are up."

The old man nodded once.

"I tell you what," she said. "If you eat the rest of that mac and cheese, I promise I'll spill something really bad on those pink shorts the next chance I get."

Brick watched as Pop raised his trembling right hand and managed a shaky thumbs-up.

"It's a deal. Let me just warm this up a little bit for you so you don't have to eat cold mac."

Remi snuck another scoop from the pot on the stove into the bowl on her way to the microwave.

Her head lifted, and her eyes found him in the doorway. "Well, hey there, Brick. How were the horses today?"

Busted.

He pried off his other boot, dropped his cowboy hat on the bench outside and warily stepped into the kitchen. "Fine," he said, shoving his hands in the pockets of his jeans.

"You want some mac and cheese? We made a whole pot of it," she said brightly.

He eyed his grandfather, looking for a reaction. Pop reached for the paper and dragged the marker over it in a familiar pattern.

Brick stared down at the large hash mark, and Pop pointed to the chair Remi had vacated.

An unexpected invitation. Unsure, he glanced over at Remi, who flashed him a wink.

"I should shower first," he hedged, hand on the back of the chair. He'd been under the impression his grandfather hated the idea of his dirty grandsons on his antique furniture.

"Quality time doesn't require soap. Hang out with us now, shower later. Besides, I kinda like the smell of horses. Don't you, Pop?"

Pop didn't answer. Instead, he drew a crooked X in the top right of the hash mark and then slowly, painfully nudged the paper toward him.

Brick's throat tightened. There were a lot of reasons in the moment. The ravages that time and age took. The unexpected invitation. The absolution of a father's sins. The acknowledgment of how fucking hard he'd worked to give Spencer as much normal as he could.

The girl with the wild red hair lighting up the room and making it all possible.

His toes curled in his socks, gripping the floor, but he did as he was told and sat.

Just as he carefully drew his first O, Remi leaned over and placed a bowl of neon yellow noodles in front of him. She smelled like sunscreen and summer, and he knew he'd never forget the scent. Or the memory she'd made for him there that day.

He and Pop were in the middle of their third game when Spencer burst into the kitchen in a V for Vendetta t-shirt and the infamous, god-awful pink shorts. His hair was getting lighter thanks to the island sun. Mackinac seemed to agree with him, to Brick's relief.

"I caught the *biggest* freaking fish today!" he announced.

Remi whirled around from the open refrigerator with a squeeze bottle of ketchup. An arc of tomato red noisily squirted out, raining down on his brother's shorts.

"Oh, man! My shorts!" Spencer whined, looking down at the damage.

"I'm so sorry! I was just going to have Pop try mac and cheese with ketchup, and the next thing I know, it's raining condiments!" she said, all wide-eyed and apologetic.

"Who eats mac and cheese with ketchup? These are my favorite shorts!" Spencer moaned.

Brick got the wash rag out of the sink and started to clean the excess ketchup from the cabinets and floor. Pop let out another wheezy chuckle that he covered with a cough. Remi earned another trembling thumbs-up as Spencer bemoaned his wardrobe's fate.

"I feel *awful*," Remi said with theatrical horror. "Run on upstairs and take them off. I think with ketchup stains you're supposed to let them set for a few hours before washing it out. Right, Pop?"

Pop gave one enthusiastic nod, the corner of his mouth still lifted.

Spencer thundered up the stairs cursing all tomato-based condiments.

"What on earth is going on in here?" Brick's grandmother, Dolores, demanded from the doorway. Her sterling silver cap of hair had been set in fresh curls. "It looks like a crime scene in here."

"I swear it's not blood. No one's been maimed," Remi announced, grabbing the roll of paper towels off the counter and joining Brick on the floor. "It's just ketchup."

"Well, what's it doing all over my kitchen?" Gram demanded.

"It was an accident," Brick volunteered.

Remi gave him an impish grin.

"Pop and Brick were playing tic-tac-toe, and we were all enjoying some macaroni and cheese, and I was telling them about how my friend Tammy Kim likes to eat it with ketchup, and they didn't believe me. So I was going to have them try it, and then Spencer came in, and I guess I just lost my grip on the bottle—"

"Pop and Brick were playing tic-tac-toe?" Gram interrupted.

"And eating," Brick added.

His grandmother nearly went misty-eyed on them as she crossed the kitchen to put her hands on her husband's thin shoulders. She took in the bowls, the paper and marker, and dropped a kiss on the top of Pop's bald head.

"Hair looks...nice." Pop formed the words slowly.

"You old charmer," Gram whispered.

Brick felt like he was intruding on a private moment and itched to give them their space. Remi must have had the same notion because she nodded her head toward the hallway.

"I'll help you take the trash out, Brick," she announced brightly.

She waited while he hefted the bag from the bin, then led the way to the back of the house. She held the door for him, and together they stepped out onto the back patio.

"I've never seen someone do that much good by telling that many lies," he told her when they were out of earshot.

"I'll take that as a compliment," she said cheerfully, plucking the metal lid off the trash can. He dropped the bag inside. "Teamwork makes the dream work," she said, closing the lid and wiping her hands on the back of her shorts.

"Thanks for that in there," he began. "All of it. Gram's been worried about him."

"I hardly did a thing," she insisted. "Sometimes folks just need to remember there's a whole lot of life left to live."

He dipped his head and glanced down at his feet. "Well, thank you for reminding him."

"Think Spence will forgive me for those damn shorts?" she asked, not sounding like it bothered her a bit.

"Eventually. Probably."

"I guess I'd better get back home. I have to write an essay I told my dad I finished Friday."

Not for the first time, he found himself at a loss for words around her. *Remington Ford was a handful of trouble and sunshine.*

"I guess I'll see you around then," he said.

She wandered into the backyard toward the gate in the fence. "You know, if you enclosed this whole porch thing, it might be a nice big living space for Pop," she mused.

He grunted.

"Well, I'm sure we'll be seeing lots of each other. Bye!"

He said nothing as he watched her stroll around the side of the house and let herself out through the gate.

7

*D*espite the ever-changing outside world with its dark deeds and charming monsters, Mackinac remained solidly, stalwartly the same. There was still a chair for her at her parents' table. Still a jar of butterscotch candies on the counter. And her father still didn't want her getting in his way in the kitchen.

"Ouch!" Remi rubbed away the sting of the dish towel he'd snapped at her.

"Move away from the oven, Remi Honey," he ordered, glasses steaming as he opened the door to peer at the turkey.

"Dad, I think I know how to be present in a kitchen when the oven door is open," she said, plopping down on a stool and unwrapping a candy.

"Need I remind you about the time I told you the burner was hot, and you still lunged for it like it was a floor tater tot?" Gilbert chided, closing the door and wiping down the meat thermometer.

"I was *two*. Just like how long Mom was in labor with me, you're not allowed to hold stuff I did at two against me."

He reached across the counter and ruffled her hair. "Sleep

okay last night in your fancy lakefront cottage? You look tired. How are you affording the rent on that place, anyway?"

There were a few things it was time to tell her family. A few things pre-broken arm she'd been excited to share. But then everything had gone to hell.

She was saved from having to answer—or lie—by the timely arrival of her sister.

"We're here!" came the call from the front door over the noise and fuss of coats and kids.

Remi slid off the stool at the sound of her sister's voice and bounced toward the front door.

"Coats and boots, you little heathens."

Kimber Marigold Olson was born to be a mother. It struck Remi every time she saw her big sister with her son and daughter. Kimber had managed to inherit both their mother's implacable calm and the everyday delight of their father. It was a perfect mix of good parenting genes. Meanwhile Remi seemed to have exploded from nowhere. The running joke was that she'd been left on their doorstep by a traveling circus.

"What did you do with Hadley and Ian?" Remi asked, feigning confusion as she leaned against a gold-toned wall and crossed her arms. "Trade them in on two taller models?"

"Aunt Remi!" Seven-year-old Ian bolted toward her with one boot on and one bare foot. He wrapped thick little arms around her and squeezed, dislodging his glasses.

"Hey, buddy! I missed you," she said, managing to pick him up so that his feet dangled just off the floor. Her arm twinged in protest, and she plopped him back on his feet. She shoved a hand through his thick mop of chestnut hair and studied his sweet, round face.

"We missed you! Can we paint with you?" he asked. "I got a new app that analyzes and identifies the exact mixture of colors." Her nephew was a little, round genius. He'd been programming his parents' universal remotes at age four.

"Of course," she promised him. She could handle that at least. *Couldn't she?*

"Hi," Hadley, ten, said quietly. She was whisper-thin and leggy. Ethereal was the word that came to Remi's mind. Her niece had stick-straight hair that toed the line between blonde and brown, a mix of both her parents. But the eyes were all Ford. Jade green. She was going to be a stunning woman in no time at all.

Remi opened her arms, and Hadley, after the briefest of hesitations, walked into them. "Hey," she whispered to her niece, who no longer smelled like markers and Play-Doh but of dryer sheets and hairspray.

Hadley ended the hug first and took an awkward step back. On a sigh, Remi let her escape. She'd hoped there were a few more years before little kid enthusiasm gave way to teenage apathy. But time stood still for no aunt.

She waited until Kimber had finished precisely arranging gloves in pockets before demanding a proper greeting.

"Hi," her sister said, leaning in for a hug almost as an afterthought. "It's nice to see you."

Remi hugged her back firmly. "I missed you. How are you? What's new?" she asked.

Kimber extracted herself from the hug with a perfunctory smile, and Remi felt an unexpected distance between them open up into a yawning chasm. "Everything's fine. Just busy with the kids."

Kimber looked exhausted as she retrieved the two casserole dishes she'd parked on Gilbert's desk. Remi could empathize.

"Where's Kyle?" she asked, glancing over her sister's

shoulder to the door, wondering if her brother-in-law had been left on the porch.

"He's not coming. He worked late and didn't feel up to being good company." Kimber gave the explanation as though it were a speech memorized long ago.

"Where are my grandmonsters?" Darlene bellowed from the top of the stairs.

Hadley flashed a ghost of a smile toward her grandmother while Ian shrieked in mock terror and sprinted for the kitchen.

"Thanks, Mom," Kimber said with an eye-roll. "No running in the house," she shouted after her son.

They convened in and around the kitchen, the grandkids catching up the grandparents on school and social activities. She found it telling that neither of her parents asked Kimber where Kyle was. She also noted that her father didn't feel the need to tell her nephew that the stove was hot.

"Here are the sweet potatoes and the broccoli casserole," Kimber announced, placing the dishes next to the oven.

"You guys could have told me to bring a pie or something," Remi said, feeling a little guilty that she hadn't contributed anything other than her wobbly presence to the meal.

"Don't be silly," Gilbert said. "You're the guest of honor."

"Yeah. Besides, we want food that's editable." Ian smirked.

"Edible, you little jerk," Remi said, screwing up her face at the boy. "I'll have you know I'm an excellent baker." *At least she was when she paid attention to the recipe and the oven timer.*

Removed. It was how she'd always felt within the ranks of family. Her parents and sister had things in common. No one had much in common with the asthmatic synesthete who was always getting into trouble. Though thanks to the aforementioned reasons, she'd been at the center of the circle. Not part of the ring, but the gravitational force they'd all had to orbit around. Doctor's appointments. Schemes. Parent-teacher conferences. Trips to the emergency room.

Raising her must have been one long, exhausting battle, she realized with sympathy.

Now that they were all adults, the distance was all the more pronounced. They shared a day-to-day existence that she had no part in. Kimber was a parent. Her parents were grandparents and busy with island business. It was as if the circle had closed without her, leaving her on the outside. Just because she was the reason for the family meal didn't make her feel more like a part of the family.

"I'll put away the extra plate," Remi volunteered, hooking a thumb toward the dining room, suddenly wanting to be in motion.

"It's not extra," Darlene told her, looking up from the stovetop where she was showing Hadley how to whisk gravy. "Brick's coming. That boy has been living off beef stew for months now."

"At least it's homemade, Mom. You make it sound like he's eating cold ravioli out of a can," Kimber teased over the veggie tray she was arranging.

Well, shit.

"I didn't know he was coming," Remi said. Now she definitely needed to move, to burn off some of this nervous energy.

After this morning's awkwardness, he wasn't exactly someone she wanted to spend an evening making small talk with.

"It's family dinner," Gilbert said, as if that was a reasonable explanation for the invitation.

"Brick's not family," she insisted. If he was family, well, she was going to need to talk to a therapist about a lot of things STAT.

She'd been convinced the man was going to tell her no on the studio space when he'd opened the door. Then he'd asked most sincerely if she was okay, which had nearly undone her wobbly defenses. And then. *Then!* She'd just happened to notice the baseball bat of wood he was sporting in those tight uniform pants. Dear Josephine Baker in heaven. She couldn't have been more hypnotized by that obscene length of dick if he'd taken it out and swung it back and forth in front of her eyes.

After he'd ditched her at the front door with a bag of meat, she'd indulged in a little fantasy where Brick had to take matters—matters meaning a monster of an erection—into his own hands and pleasure himself thinking about her.

It had to be her, right? What else would have riled him while they were alone in his house talking about natural light and macaroni and cheese?

The man had *finally* had a single moment of weakness. On one hand, it was a long sought-after triumph. On the other, it was an unnecessary complication. For years, she would have reveled in Brick's attention and enjoyed torturing him. But right now? She just needed him to mind his own damn business so she could handle hers.

And speaking of handling her business, she'd also discovered the frustration of fantasizing about an old crush without the use of her good hand. She absolutely did not need to be sexually frustrated for an evening with Brick Man Mountain Callan.

"Why doesn't Aunt Remi think Uncle Brick is family?" Ian asked from his perch in the breakfast nook where he was expertly folding cloth napkins.

"Aunt Remi and Uncle Brick don't get along," Kimber said wearily.

"Why not?" Ian wanted to know.

"We get along fine," Remi insisted.

"You look flushed," her father interjected. "Are you feeling okay?"

Her face burned.

"You do yell at him a lot," Hadley piped up from over the pot of gravy.

"I yell at everyone a lot," Remi said, feeling defensive.

"So does Mom," Ian said.

"Ian!" Kimber snapped.

"See?" the boy said smugly.

"Let's keep the yelling to a minimum tonight," Gilbert suggested, precisely arranging his bartending paraphernalia on the counter.

"Kimber, you mind heating the corn?" Darlene asked. A pro at redirection, she hurled two bags of frozen veggies at her eldest daughter.

"So, what are we making tonight?" Remi asked her dad as she snooped through the ingredients on the counter.

"Manhattans. Brick said I can try my hand at some bar shifts this summer."

"He did, did he?" *Great.* Her own family had replaced her with the man who'd chased her off the island in the first place.

"Remi Honey, we finally got that Bluetooth speaker thing you got us out of the box last night," Darlene announced. "Why don't you play some music for us?"

8

*H*e stabbed at the doorbell as he'd done a thousand times before, knowing full well that Chief Ford would complain about his insistence on formalities. But he wasn't the type to just stroll into his boss's house on a Friday night.

"Get in and get out," he reminded himself, shifting the paper bag to his other arm. "No need to linger. Don't think about her naked."

"Uncle Brick!" Ian threw open the door and launched himself at Brick's right leg.

"Hey, kid," Brick said. Reggae music, most likely Remi's doing, poured out of the kitchen. He heard voices coming from the back of the house and smelled roast turkey. But the siren song that lured him inside was the promise of Remi's presence.

Not that he'd be doing anything about it. After the earlier disaster, he'd recommitted himself to not being attracted to her.

He plopped his hat on top of Ian's head then shed his coat, perversely hanging it on top of Remi's parka.

"Hi, Uncle Brick," Hadley said from the foot of the stairs.

Most confused her quiet demeanor for shyness, but the kid was a natural observer, lurking in corners and committing everything she saw and heard to memory. If the girl ever witnessed a crime, Hadley Olson would be able to tell the cops the perp was left-handed, how many tattoos he had, and what color his eyes were.

"Help me leg cuff him, Had!" her little brother demanded. "We can get him this time!"

Ian had the brain power of an adult, but he still played like a typical seven-year-old.

"It's gonna take more than you two scrawny mosquitos to stop me," Brick said, knowing his role by heart. Since they were toddlers, it had been their favorite game with him. In another few years, he probably wouldn't win.

With a roll of her eyes that was too close to teenage angst for Brick's liking, Hadley reluctantly sauntered over and grabbed his left leg.

"Is that Brick I hear?" Gilbert called from the back of the house. "Come on back, bartender."

Carefully, Brick made his way toward the sound of adult voices, a kid attached to each leg.

"It's not working, Ian," Hadley observed.

"Try to weigh more," Ian insisted.

Brick couldn't help but crack a smile as he rounded the corner into the Ford family's airy kitchen, a space that had felt like home to him for the last decade and a half. Like *a* home, he corrected, not *his* home. Growing up, home had been a never-ending series of rentals that rotated every few months depending on which parent was following their dream or scheme at the time. They bounced around from places like Reno and Las Vegas to Oklahoma, Kansas, Montana, and even a stint in Florida when his father got a hot tip on a land deal.

Sometimes he had his own room.

Sometimes he and Spencer didn't even have their own beds.

He'd envied kids who went home to the same house every day. Kids whose parents came home every night.

The Ford girls had grown up with both of those things.

Darlene, still in her Mackinac PD sweatshirt, was bent over a saucepan on the stove. Gil, in corduroys and a sweater vest, was peering at a printout of what was probably his new drink recipe. Kimber was tucked back in the breakfast nook by the fireplace, arranging neatly sliced vegetables on a tray.

Remi was nowhere in sight. But he still *felt* her.

He reached down and plucked Ian off his ankle, throwing the kid over his shoulder. "Delivery for a Kimber Olson," he reported officially.

Kimber accepted her wriggling, giggling son with a series of noisy kisses on his face. "Just what I always wanted," she said.

"Ew! Mom!"

She was an attractive woman by anyone's standards. Thick russet hair shades darker than her sister's framed a lean face with a full mouth and straight blade of a nose. She had her mother's unflappable calm and leggy height. She loved fiercely, without fuss, and could always be counted on.

In Brick's never voiced opinion, Kimber could have done a hell of a lot better than Kyle Olson. A man who appeared to be absent once again.

Hadley disengaged her leg lock and took Brick's contribution to the meal—a bottle of decent bourbon—over to her grandfather.

Kimber turned her wriggling son loose and greeted Brick. "Nice to see you, Sergeant Callan."

"Hanging in there this winter?" he asked. It was a natural

question for anyone who lived on Mackinac through the winter. Isolation, loneliness, boredom, depression. Everyone was susceptible sooner or later, regardless of who they married.

"Like a champ," she said. The smile she flashed was a tired one that didn't quite climb to her eyes.

"Mom's learning French this winter," Ian piped up. "Say something French, Mom!"

Living this close to Canada for so many years, Brick had known enough Quebecers to loosely translate some of the sentence Kimber said into colorful four-letter words.

"What's that mean?" Hadley asked, forehead furrowed.

"Can you tell me where the library is?" Kimber lied without a hint of dishonesty on her face. Maybe the sisters had more in common than he thought.

"What are we making tonight, Gil?" Brick asked.

While his oldest daughter spent her winters learning to swear in foreign languages, Gilbert Ford mastered cocktails.

As the man launched into the history of Manhattan recipes, Brick's Remi radar sent out an alert. A buzz of energy nearby, a low-level threat. It made him sweat.

As much as he would have preferred not to be anywhere near her, it was better to keep an eye on the threat rather than have it sneak up on him.

"Brick? Can you grab the gravy boat in the dining room?" Darlene asked. "I asked Remi to find it, and she hasn't been seen since."

He headed toward the dining room with the enthusiasm of a death row inmate. The familiar recipe of dread, anticipation, and adrenaline mixed in his gut.

The dining room was tucked away in the back of the house, across the hall from the kitchen and past the laundry room. He ducked his head in the doorway and spotted the long maple table dressed up like it was Thanksgiving Day. The long interior wall held a small electric fireplace and sturdy built-ins. A petite redhead was swearing—in English—as she stood on tiptoe on the sliver of butcher block that served as a counter. Blindly feeling inside one of the cabinets with her bad arm, she used her good hand to anchor her in place.

The woman was a goddamn danger to herself.

He hadn't even completed the thought when those fingers slipped from their hold.

"Oh, fuck." She didn't even have the decency to sound scared as she tipped backward.

He liked to think that he took a moment to consider letting her fall, letting her suffer the consequences. But he didn't. He never would. Instead, she landed neatly in his arms as if he'd been created with the sole purpose of catching her.

Those green eyes, mesmerizing like sunlight shining through bottles on a window sill, looked up at him. Boring into his soul. Tunneling his focus until the only thing that existed was the woman in his arms. *How could one sister make him feel nothing but brotherly concern and the other make him feel everything but?*

He wanted to dump her on the floor.

He wanted to toss her over his shoulder, take her home, and shake some sense into her.

He wanted to—

"Hi, Brick," she said on a soft breath. The fingers of her good hand brushing the skin on the back of his neck, scorching him, torturing him.

Without a word, he set her on her feet and opened the lower cabinet. He grabbed the gravy boat and its platter off the shelf and held it out like a shield. "Here."

"Well, hell. Since when do they keep it there?" she complained.

Her hair was pulled on top of her head in a fiery knot. Loose strands escaped as if even her hair refused to be tamed. She was dressed casually in another pair of long tights and a cropped sweatshirt the color of fresh grass. It was loose-fitting, the hem flirting with the high waist of her pants. He knew he'd lose sleep that night thinking how easy it would be to slide a hand under it.

She reached out to take the dishes, her fingers brushing his, and he wished for things to go back to the way they'd been before. Before she'd come home. Before she'd walked into his arms. Before he'd seen the shadows.

Before he'd jerked himself off so violently he still felt the damn vibrations of it.

He should be letting go of the dishes. He should be taking several steps back. Not obsessing over the feel of her fingers against his.

Breaking out of his fugue, Brick took the dishes back. "Stop falling off shit," he snapped.

"Stop telling me what to do." Her gaze flicked to the doorway and back again. "And stop fighting with me. Everyone thinks we hate each other."

"Don't we?" He hadn't meant it. Not really. He hated himself when it came to her. But he could never hate her.

Old Remi would have punched him in the shoulder and called him an asshole. But this new Remi was an entirely different creature. Watching the hurt bloom in those moss green eyes made him feel like a fucking asshole.

"Remi, wait—"

She shook her head and stepped out of his reach as he juggled the gravy boat. "I'm too tired for the hot-cold routine. Let's leave it at cold and leave each other the hell alone."

"What hot-cold routine?" he demanded, trying to keep his voice low. He knew exactly what she was talking about but didn't want her running out of the room until they were back on an even keel.

"You know what I'm talking about, you monumental ass," she hissed. "One second, you're stocking my freezer with your cock hard enough to cut off the circulation to your lower body. The next, you're telling me you hate me."

"I don't know what you're talking about," he lied.

"Fuck off, Brick." She flipped him off on her way out of the room.

He swore under his breath and followed. It was going to be a painful night.

9

"What color is this song, Aunt Remi?" Hadley asked from across the table.

Remi shifted away from Brick yet again. Usually he sat as far away from her as possible. But since she was furious with him, the chances of her flirting with him were nil. She was still dangerous, but it was a safer kind of danger.

Remi cleared her throat as she looked up from the moat of mashed potatoes she'd been poking with her spoon. "It's all bright yellows and oranges with little explosions of red," she told her niece.

She didn't sit in chairs like a normal adult. There was no straight-backed posture for Remi. She hugged one knee into her chest, her other foot swinging as if she couldn't tolerate stillness for even one meal.

"So, Remi Honey," Darlene said, changing the subject. "How long are you renting Red Gate?"

Remi didn't look up from her plate. "Just a couple of weeks. Agnes doesn't have a reservation until spring."

"A couple of weeks?" Kimber's eyebrows shot up. "That

can't be cheap even in the dead of winter. Where'd you come up with that kind of cash?"

Brick listened raptly as he hefted a fork of turkey to his mouth.

Remi shrugged. "Pretty sure she gave me a 'practically family' deal. I forgot how cute that place is on the inside. She had the kitchen redone a year or two ago with new cabinets and appliances. And between the furnace and the fireplace, it's downright toasty."

There was her trademark misdirection. Enthusiastic info dumps that dazzled the listener into forgetting what the original question was.

"Can we come see the cottage, Aunt Remi?" Hadley asked.

"You better come visit, or I'll be deeply offended and not buy you any Christmas presents for two years," she teased.

"How's your asthma? Have you been taking your prescriptions?" Darlene asked.

Remi shifted in her chair. Her gaze stayed fixed on her plate. "It's been good," she said. "I thought I'd have more problems last spring with all the pollen and the air quality alerts. But I really didn't."

The lies that came out of this woman's mouth.

Brick marveled at her ability to spin a tale without batting an eyelash. If he hadn't seen the EMT's report, even he might not have picked up on the lie. It had been a while since his Remington Bullshit Detector had a workout.

"That's wonderful," Gilbert said. "I'd always said you'd probably outgrow it."

"Fingers crossed," Remi said with a smile that wavered around the edges.

"Aunt Remi, how'd you hurt your arm?" Ian asked, eyeing her cast as he dropped a piece of turkey in his lap.

Without missing a beat, Kimber handed her son a napkin.

Remi wrinkled her nose. "I was in a very small car accident."

"Like a Matchbox car?" Ian asked.

"Not that small. The accident was small. The car was normal-sized," she assured her nephew.

"In *your* car?" Darlene asked.

Remi drove a Chevy Suburban, and Brick still wasn't certain it was big enough to keep her safe.

She shook her head. "No. My friend was driving."

The hand that reached for her drink was shaking. And all he wanted to do was pick her up, carry her out of the room, and interrogate her.

"A boy friend or a girl friend?" Hadley wanted to know. Brick's grip tightened reflexively on the knife in his hand.

"Girl," she said, managing a smile for her niece. But he watched as she curled in on herself even tighter.

Operating on instinct, he spread his legs wide enough that his left knee pressed against hers. Remi didn't move away from the touch, and he wondered just what the hell that meant.

"Like girl friend or girlfriend?" Hadley pressed.

Remi choked on her Manhattan and managed a laugh. "Are you asking if I'm a lesbian?"

"Or bi."

"Pansexual," Ian added.

Kimber coughed into her napkin. "I let them watch *Schitt's Creek*," she admitted.

"Oh, I *love* that show," Gilbert said, his enthusiasm heightened by his third Manhattan.

"So, *are* you?" Hadley asked.

Remi's smile was genuine this time. "I seem to be straight. Just boys for me so far."

"My friend Alicia? Her older sister Megan is bi," Hadley announced.

"Uncle Brick, do you like boys or girls?" Ian asked as if he were conducting a prime-time interview.

Brick felt the harsh burn of an invisible spotlight. "I, uh. Girls?"

"You don't sound very sure about that," Kimber teased.

"Girls," he said again, more forcefully.

"Mom and Grandma say it's a shame you haven't dated anyone since your divorce," Hadley recited to the table.

Remi snorted into the bottom of her drink then coughed. "Excuse me. I think I need a refill."

"Remind me never to say anything in front of your big ears again, traitor," Kimber said, feigning a glare at her daughter.

"Sorry, Uncle Brick," Hadley said with a small smile.

"It's. Uh. Fine. So what about you? Girls or boys?" he asked.

She shrugged daintily. "I'm not sure. I haven't met the right one of either yet."

"Take your time," Darlene advised with a sage poke of her fork in her granddaughter's direction. "There's no rush. Your Aunt Remi was boy-crazy when she was a teenager."

Remi had just reappeared in the dining room door with a full glass in time to hear her mom's comment. "Nope. Not enough alcohol," she muttered under her breath and disappeared again.

She returned a minute later with a full glass and the cocktail shaker.

Her hip brushed his arm when she sat. He ignored the lick of fire that blazed through him at the contact. But he couldn't ignore the peek of stomach he saw just below the hem of her sweatshirt. Brick's mouth went dry.

She pulled both knees into her chest and took a long sip of her fresh drink.

"Remi, for Pete's sake, can't you eat one meal with both

feet on the floor?" Darlene said in exasperation. "You're setting a bad example."

On cue, Ian put his socked feet on the table.

"Ian Gilbert," Kimber said in her most threatening mom voice.

"Aunt Remi started it," Ian said, all innocence.

"Remington Honeysuckle," Kimber said sternly.

The sisters exchanged quick grins, and Remi put her feet on the floor, her knee brushing his beneath the table.

While Gilbert and Darlene quizzed Kimber about her latest home renovation project, Brick leaned in as close as he dared to Remi. "What caused the accident?" he asked, keeping his voice low.

She looked at him sideways.

"The roads were icy. Another car accidentally hit us from behind and pushed us into a guard rail. Can you pass the gravy, please?"

He handed her the gravy boat and watched her bobble it with her left hand. Taking it back from her, he poured it over the turkey she'd barely touched. "Must have been going pretty fast if the impact broke your arm," he observed.

"Actually," she said, leveling him with a guileless stare. "I fell getting out of the car, but it sounds cooler to say it was the accident."

She was definitely lying.

"What's your friend's name?" he pressed.

He watched several emotions flit over her face, one after the other, before she lowered her chin. "Leave it alone, Brick."

"Why?"

"A girl might think you cared if you take too much interest in her," she shot back.

It was a direct hit.

"Are you two fighting?" Hadley asked, breaking their stare down.

Kimber snorted. "They're always fighting."

"We never fight," Remi insisted.

"You *look* like you're fighting," Hadley pointed out.

Ian shook his head. "Aunt Remi hasn't slugged him yet. That's when they're fighting."

"Aunt Remi and Uncle Brick have a strained relationship," Gilbert offered from the head of the table.

"Why?" Hadley asked.

"Yeah. Why?" Kimber asked, adding her own curiosity to her daughter's.

Remi gave up on the pretense of eating and crossed her arms over her chest. "Uncle Brick hurt my feelings a long time ago and never apologized, and so much time has gone by that there isn't an apology big enough for me to not be mad at him anymore."

Brick stiffened. This was fucking news to him.

"What if he got you flowers?" Ian asked. "That's what Dad used to do for Mom."

Remi's gaze flitted to her sister's face at the "used to." "Um. No. Flowers definitely wouldn't do it."

"How about a public serenade in a soccer stadium?" Hadley suggested.

"We also watched *10 Things I Hate About You*," Kimber interjected.

"Heath Ledger," Remi said, raising her glass at her sister. Kimber mimicked the toast from across the table.

"Aunt Remi is really good at holding a grudge," Darlene explained with a wink at her grandkids.

"This is true," Remi agreed. Her foot began to jiggle under the table.

Brick cleared his throat. He felt the weight of everyone's

attention. That was the problem with not being much of a talker. When you did speak, people paid entirely too much attention. "I've been thinking," he said, frantically searching for a topic. "The welfare checks the department does."

"What about them?" Darlene asked, scooping up a bite of equal parts, turkey, corn, stuffing, and potatoes.

Yeah. What about them, dumbass?

"What if we did something different?" This is why he didn't talk much. Because when he did, he sounded like an idiot.

Darlene thoughtfully chewed her way through a bite.

"Welfare checks?" Kimber asked.

"The department checks in on some of our older residents. Keeps an eye on anyone we know who lives alone or has been sick or going through a tough time," Darlene explained.

"If it was neighbors checking in on them, it might seem more like a social call," Remi mused.

"Yeah. I was thinking something like that," Brick said, grateful for the inadvertent lifeline she'd thrown.

"That's a great idea, Brick." Gil gesticulated with his glass, spilling a healthy portion of bourbon on the tablecloth. Unlike both of his daughters, Gilbert Ford was a lightweight.

"Actually it was Remi—"

"You'd be keeping a closer eye on the vulnerable," Kimber added, cutting him off. "Freeing up your department for other work. And people might be willing to talk more frankly to neighbors about how they're feeling than someone in uniform."

Darlene steepled her fingers over her plate and nodded slowly. "Why don't the three of you spearhead it? See what you can come up with in terms of volunteers and a schedule."

"The three of who?" Remi asked, choking on her drink.

"Brick will spearhead and, Kimber, you and Remi can help."

Brick wasn't sure which one of them was more appalled by the suggestion.

"Oh," Kimber said.

Remi looked a little wild-eyed. "Uh."

Brick knew better than to hedge. Chief Ford always got her way.

"Sure. Fine," he said.

"Great idea, Brick," Gil said, raising his glass.

10

"*I*'m going to head back," Remi announced, appearing in the kitchen already wearing her coat.

Brick stood abruptly, nearly knocking over the kitchen stool he was occupying. "I'll walk you," he volunteered.

This night was not ending without her hearing his apology.

"No!" she yelped. "I mean. That's not necessary. You should stay."

"*Now*, she's gonna sock him," Ian said in a stage whisper.

"Brick? Make sure our girl gets home safe, will ya?" Darlene asked, swooping in to give Remi a tight hug.

He gave a brisk nod. "I will."

"Mom! It's not even two blocks away. Have him walk Kimber and the kids."

"It's dark and cold, and if anyone can disappear in two blocks, it's you," her mother announced, matter settled.

No. Remi mouthed the word at him over Darlene's shoulder.

Her trademark defiance and the fact that she'd finally been forced to address him directly almost made him smile.

"My turn," Gilbert said, elbowing his way in to hug Remi. "Missed you," he whispered.

"Missed you, too," she confessed, squeezing him harder.

Brick still felt awkward around the Ford family displays of affection. The Callan clan hadn't been big on hugs or I love yous. And once his mother had flitted off in search of a spotlight somewhere, any sporadic affection had gone with her.

The rest of the hugs and good-byes performed, Brick followed Remi to the front door. He put his bulk between her and the exit while he pulled on his winter gear so she couldn't duck out without him. It earned him a glare from her.

"I'd prefer to walk home *alone*," she said through clenched teeth.

"Yeah, well, I'd prefer that we talk."

"I really don't care what you prefer," she snapped, reaching around him for the door knob. The door opened a scant four inches before hitting him in the back. Leisurely, he laced his boots and zipped his coat while she fumed beside him.

"They're definitely fighting," Ian whispered from the shadows of the stairway.

Hadley shushed him.

"Bye, guys," Brick said, grabbing his hat and flashing the eavesdroppers a wink. Remi used the distraction to slip through the front door. She didn't make it very far. He caught her by the hood, arresting her progress on the steps.

"Brick, I swear to God," she said through clenched teeth as he shut the door behind them.

The night air was cold enough that the entire world felt like it was one big ice cube.

"First. Don't run away from me," he said mildly, tightening his grip on her hood until she fell into step next to him on the walkway.

"Or what?" she scoffed.

"Or you won't like the consequence. Second, I'm sorry."

Her boot caught a lump of snow on the sidewalk, tripping her up. He caught her before she could stumble.

"You're what? And stop manhandling me!" She batted at his hands.

"Stop asking to be manhandled. I said I was sorry. I didn't mean what I said before. You know I don't hate you." They were two blocks from home. Not nearly enough time for the conversation they needed to have.

"Do I? What gives you that impression?" she said haughtily.

He stopped her and turned her to face him. "You *know* I don't hate you."

He waited, and when she didn't give him a reaction, he gave her a tiny shake.

"Ugh. Fine. You're sorry. You don't hate me. I accept your apology. May I please walk home alone now?"

"Not happening. Third—"

"There's *more*? Holy Alicia Keys, how much bourbon did you have?" She broke free of his grasp and started down the sidewalk again.

"I know you're not telling the truth," he said, his long stride easily catching her. To slow her down and to give himself something to think about tonight, he settled his arm on her shoulders, his hand dangling in front of her.

"About what?"

"The accident. Your asthma. Why you came back."

She came to a sudden halt. A shiver rolled through her and he knew instinctively it had nothing to do with the cold. She started to speak, but he took his big, gloved hand and closed it over her mouth.

"Before you lie to me again, Remi," he said, leaning down

to whisper the words in her ear, "think long and hard about if it's in your best interests."

He could feel her running calculations, wondering how much he knew, what she could get away with. After a long beat, she pried his hand from her mouth. "Maybe it's in *your* best interests if you don't know. Maybe it's in everyone's best interests."

"That's never going to be the case," he insisted. "So get your head around it. I'll be here when you're ready to tell me. But if I figure it out before you talk, I'm gonna be pissed."

"This big brother routine is not fun," she complained. "What are you going to do, start terrifying anyone I date with your badge and that nightstick you keep in your pants?"

That fucking mouth.

The way she managed to push so many of his buttons at once made him wonder if she knew his secret. If she knew what he really wanted.

"I'm *not* your brother, Remington," he reminded her.

They crossed the road as her cottage came into view. The lake rolled out black and glistening before them.

She huffed out a breath. "Well, I suppose if you *were,* it would make a few of my teenage fantasies really gross and incestuous."

Another button pushed.

But he had one more thing to say. One more question to ask.

"Fourth and final," he said.

"Oh, come on, dude. I'm tired." She tried to slip out from under his arm, but he merely pinned her to his side as they walked along the cottage's hedgerow.

"How did I hurt you?" he asked.

She sighed. "Does it even matter?"

"Look. About Audrey—"

"It was before that," she snapped. She reached for the gate, but he wasn't done yet. He closed a hand over hers.

"Was this because of that day...after you graduated? That was a mistake."

"Christ. You think I'm carrying a grudge because a guy is either too dense to be attracted to me or, worse, too much of a chickenshit to act on it? Real nice, Brick."

"Then fucking tell me," he demanded, choosing to ignore the chickenshit dig. He needed to know. *How could he fix it if he didn't know what it was?*

She looked down at their feet, then up at the night sky where shimmers of the northern lights were visible, a ghostly green against the midnight blue. "You left me. Without even saying good-bye. You just abandoned me."

Cold crept into his chest and took up residence. He blew out a breath trying to dislodge the iciness. "I *never* meant to hurt you. Not then."

He'd *had* to go. There was no choice. Staying on the island with a warm, willing, of-age Remi would have taken a level of willpower he hadn't possessed.

She looked up at him, green eyes stormy. A clench in her delicate jaw. "You forget, Brick. We used to know each other really well. We used to be close. So yeah. You meant to hurt me when you left. We both know it."

She yanked the gate open, but he didn't let her pass. He blocked her with his body, keeping her against the hedgerow that whispered in the wind. They weren't touching except for their hands on the gate, but he felt stripped naked standing this close to her.

"Remi."

He didn't know what to say besides her name. She'd tossed the truth of it in his face. On some level, he'd wanted her to hurt the way he did. It was selfish and cruel, and he'd thought the pathetic slight would roll off her like everything always had.

Now, knowing she'd been carrying that hurt with her made him feel like a fucking worm.

"I'm sorry." *Good god. He'd apologized more times tonight than he had in the last five years.*

She closed her eyes, appearing suddenly weary. "Look. I didn't come back here to be besties. We both know we're better off with distance between us. So let's just move past all of whatever this is or was."

But he wasn't ready to move past it. "When you saw me at Doud's—" he began.

She'd walked into his arms like it was the most natural thing in the world.

"I was caught off guard. It was reflex."

"You came to me because you're scared. Because you know I can help you. I can see something's wrong. Your lights stay on all night. You used to eat like a long-haul trucker at a diner, now you just push food around your plate. What's got you so rattled, Remi?"

"Stop." She slapped a hand to his chest, and before he could stop himself, he leaned into it. Her head tipped back to look up at him. He hated how much he loved that.

"Talk to me," he insisted, his voice hoarse.

She looked down at the hand on his chest. The point of contact he was pressing into until he nudged her chin up, forcing her to look at him again.

Her eyes shimmered under the dim light of streetlights and stars. "You lost the right to hear my confidences a long time ago. Let's leave it that way. It's safer for both of us."

"You know I'm not going to accept that," he warned.

Her lips curved in a sad smile. "I know," she admitted. "But you can't fix this one. Hell. I'm not sure I can."

"Remi."

"Brick." She sounded exasperated, but her smile was a few degrees warmer now. "You're sorry, and I accepted your apologies. Now we both have to leave it alone."

"No." His denial was flat but firm. He wasn't budging on this. She wasn't going to charm her way out of it.

"At least you're consistently irritating," she said lightly. "Some things never change."

He let out a growl of frustration. "Back at you, baby." He felt her soften at his words. Felt her melt just a little bit against him.

A buzzing sound came from her coat pocket. She dug frantically, finally pulling it free. Her expression dimmed when she read the screen. Pain in My Ass read the screen.

She stuffed the phone back into her pocket without answering.

"Don't you need to take that?" he asked, wondering who Pain in My Ass was and why Remi wanted to avoid them.

"Definitely not." Her jaw was set, making his blood pressure rise.

This withholding from him was fucking torture.

"Look up," she said softly. When he didn't, she cupped his chin in her free hand and forced him. The northern lights flickered and glowed above them. "See the lights?"

"Yeah."

"You once asked me what it's like to see music. It's a little like that."

In silence, they both stared into the night sky. "It's beautiful," he said finally.

"It is," she agreed. "Now, go home before Mrs. Early sees us out here and alerts the gossip authorities."

"You know I'm waiting here until you get inside."

Her sigh was accompanied by a cloud of breath. "I know."

She slipped around him, and this time he didn't stop her. He stood there, rooted, until she was inside and the lights came on. And then he continued to stand guard, wondering what lurked in the dark that frightened the bravest girl he'd ever known.

11

Thirteen years ago...

*S*he was *not* going to miss out on Eleanora Reedbottom's Top Secret Party on Round Island. Just because she was grounded for some practically made-up offense did not mean she was going to skip the party of the season.

She and Audrey had already planned their outfits. Extra short cut-offs, coordinated tank tops, and cute hoodies for the boat ride.

Round Island was an uninhabited 300-plus-acre island just to the south of Mackinac's ferry landing. Part of the Hiawatha National Forest, the island was overseen by the U.S. Forest Service. The sandy beach on the far side of the island was ideal for illicit parties. Like the one Eleanora Reedbottom was throwing tonight.

All Remi had to do was convince her parents she was spending the night in her room and not to bother her. *Piece of cake.*

Her mother had been too distracted by the logistics of

some "work thing" that evening to pay much attention. So Remi had picked a fight with Kimber at dinner, whined about cramps to her dad, then took a pint of ice cream into her room with a serving spoon. No one would come near her in fear of PMS wrath.

Brick and Spencer Callan had been over for dinner. Spencer, her totally cute, often clueless sometimes boyfriend, flashed her the thumbs-up during her theatrics. Brick, his muscly, stoic, big brother, had eyed her with suspicion. The guy had an uncanny knack for sniffing out the tiniest fib.

Frankly, she thought his talents were wasted working with the horses on the island. He'd make a good cop. She'd have to mention it to her mother, when she wasn't trying to sneak out of the house.

Though, maybe she'd wait until she was leaving for college to bring up the topic. Odds were, Brick would use his super-powers to do something stupid like arrest her for some harmless fun.

Her pink alarm clock ticked over to 9 o'clock, and Remi gave her hair one last shot of hair spray. Satisfied with the carefree summer waves she'd spent almost an hour perfecting, she turned off the light and removed the light bulb. The pillows under the covers wouldn't fool any nosy family members if they happened to flip on the light switch.

In the dark, she pocketed a mini bug spray and lip gloss, then climbed out the window onto the roof of the porch. The summer air was thick with humidity and possibilities. Adventure and music and fun waited for her.

The shingles were rough against her knees as she stretched her leg back and down for a toehold on the trellis. One of these days, the rickety old thing was going to collapse on top of her. But tonight was not the night.

She climbed down quickly. Swearing under her breath when

the hem of her shorts caught on a splinter of wood. She wondered if she could figure out a way to rebuild the damn thing without her parents getting suspicious. Maybe if she threw one of the street hockey balls through it, saying she was practicing? Or maybe she could just feign a new interest in climbing vines.

Pleased with her ninja-like escape skills, Remi jumped the last three feet, landing in the flowerbed between a petite Japanese maple and a clump of ornamental grass. When she took a step back, she came up against something warm, hard, and leafless.

When two hands closed around her arms from behind, she spun around and assumed the ball-kicking position.

"Easy, trouble," came a low, familiar chuckle.

"Holy Billie Holiday, Brick!" She stomped her foot in the mulch. "You scared the hell out of me. I thought the land-scaping grew arms!"

Silhouetted by streetlights, he made quite the hulking shadow.

"Good," he said. "Get back upstairs."

"You have got to be kidding me. No! What are you even doing here?"

"Keeping you out of trouble," he said, crossing his very large arms over his massive chest and peering down at her.

"Well, what's the fun in that?" she scoffed, refusing to be intimidated.

In the year that she'd known him and his brother, Remi had learned his secret. The man might have been built like a sequoia and had the conversational skills of a brick wall, but Brick was a teddy bear underneath. An extra-large one.

"I'm serious. Get your ass back up to your room and stay there."

"Maybe you're in charge of Spencer, but you have no

authority here, Brick Callan," she said, drilling a finger into his chest.

"You have no business going to Round Island to party, Remi Ford."

Even though she was busy spitting fire, she sure liked how he said her name.

"*My* business is none of *your* business. Besides, Spencer's going! He's waiting for me."

"No, he's not. He's sitting in front of the TV pouting because he's grounded. Just like you will be if you don't get your ass back up into that room. Now."

There was something positively delicious about the way he gave her orders. Not that she had any intention of following them. But still, some previously undiscovered part of her felt like it was waking up for the first time. "Or what?"

She could have imagined the growl she heard rumbling in his chest.

"You're a smart girl, right?" he whispered finally.

Remi narrowed her eyes at the man. She smelled a set-up. "Get to the point."

"What kind of 'work thing' do you think your mom has going on tonight? Do you think it's a coincidence that she's running logistics on some secret operation the same night Eleanora Reedbottom decides to trespass on federal property to host an underage drinking party?"

She gasped. "How did you find out about the party?"

"Because Eleanora Reedbottom has a big fucking mouth. And so does my stupid little brother. He also doesn't have your skill with lies."

She gave a little curtsy. "Thank you."

"Not a compliment, Remi."

"I'm taking it as one anyway," she said with a shrug.

He pinched the bridge of his nose as if he were in the throes of a migraine.

"You ever get your head checked? Seems like you get an unnatural amount of headaches."

"Only when I talk to you," he shot back.

She wrinkled her nose. "Mean. Can I at least come over and hang out with you and Spence?"

"You're already grounded. I'm not busting the chief's daughter out of her house. That's illegal on a whole lot of different levels."

"You're no fun."

"So I've been told. By you. Repeatedly."

She wasn't ready to climb back up the trellis just yet. This was the most number of words Brick had strung together around her, and she didn't want to waste the conversation. "You could have just let me go and get caught," she mused.

"I could have," he agreed.

She tapped a finger to her chin and studied him in the dark. "You came swooping in to save me from having my own mom arrest me."

"I pity the idiot who has to arrest you the first time."

"There you go again with the compliments. You like me. You don't want me to get arrested," she sang.

He winced in the dark before recovering his flat expression.

"I didn't mean that as a shot against your dad, and you know it. Lots of people get arrested. Pretty sure I'm gonna be one of them at some point. Lots of people go to jail. Doesn't mean they're bad people."

He was back to pinching the bridge of his nose. "That's exactly what it means."

"Is it exhausting seeing everything in black and white? Don't you have any room for any other colors?"

"Right is right. Wrong is wrong. Now, don't make me regret sparing your mother from having to handcuff you and send you off to military school."

"She knows better than that. I'd burn it to the ground and lead a rebellion within my first forty-eight hours. Hey, so how's your grandma doing?"

"Stop stalling," he ordered, putting his hands on his hips and staring down at the toes of his boots.

She waited, staring at him until he cracked. "She's fine. The surgery went well. She'll be home later this week."

"Good. Maybe I'll make her a pie."

"Fine. You can give it to your sister to deliver since you're grounded."

"You are infuriating!"

"Right back at ya, baby. Now climb." He pointed toward the porch roof. "Or I'll march you through the front door and deliver you to your dad."

"You *wouldn't*."

"I would."

Realizing she wasn't going to get past the Wall of Good Time Ruining, she accepted temporary defeat in the battle to save the war. "Fine, fun police." She climbed up onto the edge of the porch and reached for the trellis.

"Good girl," he said.

Good girl.

The way he said it, with that rough edge, gave her a delicious, full-body shiver. She wanted him to say it again. She wanted to make him say it again.

"Oh, Trouble?"

She paused mid-climb and glanced down at him, the mountain of a man waiting in the shadows to catch her if she fell.

"Don't wear those shorts again."

"Why not?"

"You know why and because I said so."

It was her least favorite reason. Remi let out a growl and released her hold with one hand to flip him the bird.

His soft laugh followed her back up onto the roof and in through her window.

She waited ten whole minutes, practically a lifetime, before her second attempt.

"Still here," came the gruff whisper.

She peeked over the edge of the roof. "Damn it, Brick."

He edged closer to the porch. "You're gonna fall and break that face, and then I'm going to be pissed."

"I'm not going to the island. I'm supposed to meet Audrey at the dock. I don't want her to get in trouble."

"Then call her," he said dryly. Brick crossed his arms again and looked as immovable as an oak tree.

"I can't. We decided not to take our phones."

"Why?"

"Well, if you must know, nosy. If anyone's parents or annoying big brother called, we could say we forgot our phones."

Obviously not impressed with her ingenuity, he muttered something under his breath. It sounded like it involved the words "be the death of me," but she wasn't sure.

There was a weary sigh, then silence for a beat. "I'll go tell Audrey," he said finally.

"That's fine and all, but if you leave to go tell Audrey, I'm just gonna go liberate Spencer from your house and see what trouble we can get into with the entire police department busy off-island."

"God damn it, Remi."

❧

"I CAN'T BELIEVE you talked me into this," Brick groused, five minutes later.

"Oh, come on," she said smugly, bumping his bulging bicep with her shoulder. "Have a little fun. I'll buy you an ice cream if you cheer up."

"Sneak attack!" Spencer raced past them, a wicked grin on his face. He was a leaner, shorter, happier copy of his brother. Remi didn't know if Brick realized it, but the happy part was due to him. With one parent serving time and one permanently on the road, Brick was the reason Spencer was so well-adjusted.

A musty, cheesy scent reached her nose, and she clamped a hand over her face. "Spence!"

"Did you just *crop dust* your girlfriend?" Brick asked.

"*And* my brother," Spencer announced proudly, jogging backward in front of them.

Brick moved like lightning, putting Remi's own ninja moves to shame. In half a second, he caught Spencer and wrapped an arm around the boy's neck. "I can't believe you're almost allowed to vote. You're just a tall, skinny five-year-old," he said, ruffling Spencer's hair.

"Man! Do you know how much gel it took to get the style right?" Spencer complained.

"I do. You're gonna need a second job just to pay for hair products." Brick released him.

Spencer paused and held up a finger. "I only have one thing to say to that." He farted audibly this time and then took off at a dead run.

Brick chivalrously nudged Remi out of the fart cloud. "You could do a lot better than my idiot brother, you know."

She laughed, enjoying the brush of his arm against hers. She adored Spencer. He was like her aunt's overenthusiastic golden retriever, pretty and always happy to see her. But there was something about his big brother that always had her pulse kicking into high gear. She liked being close to him. Liked talking to him. He was a man of few words and even fewer smiles, but every once in a while, when she pried one out of him, she felt like she was on the first drop of a roller coaster.

"Oh, I know. But he entertains me. Besides, we're not really together anymore."

There was a slight hitch to his stride. "You're not?"

"Well, we're still hanging out. But we're not having sex anymore."

This time he actually tripped. She reached out and steadied him.

"Jesus, Remi."

"Honestly—and keep this to yourself—I think he might have a thing for Audrey. I think they'd be good for each other."

"So, you're not mad?" He sounded confused, concerned. It was adorable.

"What's there to be mad about? You can't fight fate. It's a waste of time and energy when there's a lot of other fun to be had." She shrugged and stuffed her hands in the pockets of her sweatshirt.

He was silent next to her for an entire block, walking half a step behind her. Downtown was bustling that night with tourists, freshly scrubbed up from their days, wandering back to hotels and rentals after dinner out. The shops were closing up, herding everyone toward the bars and ice cream shops that stayed open late.

"Aren't you grounded, girl?" Agnes Sopp, still dressed in her round of golf finery, called from the street corner where she held a towering triple-dip strawberry ice cream cone.

"Hi, Agnes," Remi called back unperturbed. "I think it's

more of a suggestion than an actual order. But I'd be grateful if you didn't mention to my parents you saw me."

"Your secret is safe with me," Agnes promised, shooting her a wink.

"She's gonna tell every person on the island," Remi's grumpy companion predicted.

"She's gonna tell every person *except* my parents," Remi insisted.

"You're exhausting," Brick decided.

She rolled her eyes. "I know I'm a handful. I know I'm a lot. But it's not my fault if people can't keep up."

"You don't need someone who can keep up. You need someone who can lock you up."

"I'm not opposed to either. I assume the right guy will be able to do both," she quipped.

The silence stretched on, and the tension between them mounted. She wanted him to break first. To start a new conversation. To make an effort.

"If it's not Spence, who *do* you like?" Brick asked, finally.

The man sounded disinterested, annoyed. But he wouldn't have asked if he didn't really want to know.

She tossed her hair over her shoulder and shot him what she hoped was a saucy wink. "I'm keeping my options open." Throwing a little extra swing into her hips, she quickened her pace and veered off the sidewalk in the direction of the dock. Spencer had found a group of friends outside the fudge shop, but there was no sign of Audrey.

Remi jogged down the dock, tickled that Brick's footsteps picked up behind her. The man probably thought she was going to throw herself into a boat and take off. Briefly, she considered doing just that in Duncan Firth's spiffy little runabout. Everyone knew he left the key under the life preserver. But the idea was discarded when she remembered she was here to save her friend, not push more of Brick's buttons.

"Psst! Audrey?" she hissed into the dark.

Audrey's head peeked around the weathered shed. She looked pretty and pissed off in cut-offs and a bright yellow tank that looked killer against her dark skin. Remi jogged to meet her, admiring Audrey's new hair cut, tapered on the sides with tight curls at the crown. She was glaring at Remi through purple-rimmed glasses.

"Where have you been? I've been waiting— Oh, heeeey, Brick. Remi, did you bring my...calculus notes with you since we have that test to study for?" Like Spencer, Audrey also sucked at lying.

"It's okay. He knows," Remi told her. "He's being the fun police and keeping us away from the actual police who are raiding Elle's party."

"You're welcome," Brick grumbled.

Audrey's brown eyes widened, and her thick lashes fluttered. "Wow. Thanks, Brick. That's really n...awesome of you."

Remi bit her lip to hide her smile. Brick Callan had that kind of effect on women of all ages.

He grunted in response and, with a pointed look at them, turned to head back toward the street.

"Nawesome?" Remi teased.

"Shut up. He looked directly at me. What was I supposed to do? Form actual speech? Not everyone's as brave as you are, you know," Audrey muttered.

"Come on. Let's go buy the big guy an ice cream cone," Remi said, slinging an arm around her friend's waist. "You can help me plan outfits around these shorts."

Audrey looked down at Remi's legs. "Why?"

"No reason. I just feel like wearing them for the rest of the summer."

12

Remi watched transfixed as the thick, red liquid dripped onto the plastic on the floor, splattering in a macabre pattern over her bare foot.

Radiohead's "No Surprises" blared from a wireless speaker on the table. Pulsing waves of oranges, blues, and rich purples shifted around the interior of the cottage. But instead of feeling comforted as she usually did, she was sick, almost dizzy as the red rolled like blood over her skin. The canvas in front of her taunted with its blinding white perfection.

Red. White. Blood. Snow. The shimmer of broken glass glimmering in headlights. Dark. Dark. Dark.

Despite the sunshine reflecting off the endless surface of the lake beyond the windows, she felt like she was back in the suffocating midnight black of that cold, horrible night.

The brush—a tool once so familiar—felt foreign and wrong in her left hand.

She shook herself forcefully.

"Don't be a fucking baby," she insisted, raising the brush like a wand. A spell to vanquish the darkness. To bleed color onto the canvas and, in the process, exorcise the terror, the helplessness.

Sweat dotted her brow and the back of her neck where her hair hung in a limp curtain. Her breath was weak within the confines of her lungs. A warning that she needed to pause, to breathe.

The bristles inched closer to the surface. One sweep, and the white wouldn't be perfect in its emptiness anymore. She'd learned the lesson early. Void wasn't perfection. Putting her colorful, lawless mark on an otherwise blank canvas was what she did best. At least, it had been.

"This is stupid," she hissed through her teeth as the song started over again for the ninth time. "Just put the damn brush on the damn canvas."

It had been nearly two weeks since the last time her brush had swept through richly colored oils and created worlds where before there'd been nothing. It felt like a lifetime.

But the nothingness, the void, was safe. Pristine.

The tightness in her chest started to burn, and the brush rolled from her stiff fingers.

"For fuck's sake," she muttered, sucking in a breath.

She sank to the ancient, dusty drop cloth she'd reclaimed from her parents' basement and used a corner of it to swipe the paint from her foot.

This whole "breakdown" thing was really starting to piss her off.

Her breath sounded thin and wispy.

"How are you going to live a full life if you can't take a full breath?"

An old question posed by a new friend. And for once, Remi had paid attention.

"I'm not a yoga type person," she'd insisted, eyeing the colorful parade of tights and tank tops and mats as students of all shapes,

sizes, and colors marched into the studio. "I'm more of a 'boot camp that makes you barf at the end' person."

"Mmm. And how is that working for you?" her friend had asked serenely.

"Fine, but next week you come to a boxing class if I hate this."

She hadn't hated it. She'd found something different, something special in the yoga classes that taught her to harness her energy and her breath. To move her body in ways that felt like honor rather than torture.

The breath was an anchor, and she'd clearly lost hers. Now she was adrift. And alone.

The song cut off, and her phone's ringtone filled the living space. *Pain in My Ass.* Ugh. She hit ignore, sending the call to voicemail again.

On a wheezy groan, she switched playlists, cueing up some Lizzo girl power. Pinks and purples instantly billowed around her in pretty, vibrant clouds as she forced herself to sit and breathe in one of the swivel chairs in front of the window.

She glared out at nature's perfection.

It had been premature and stupid to borrow studio space from Brick if she wasn't even going to be able to use it. Thankfully she hadn't tried this little failure of an experiment at his place. The idea that he could catch her in a moment so pathetically vulnerable made her want to barf like a finisher of a boot camp class.

If he caught her in the midst of a life crisis, he wouldn't stop until he'd pried the story out of her. Then, he'd do what he'd always done, ride to her rescue.

And this time, it could get him killed.

There was no rescue. No hero to swoop in and clean up her mess. She'd gone too far. And the consequences due were hers alone.

"I'll end her. And you'll know it was because of you."

The threat echoed in her head, and she did her best to breathe through it.

She just needed to push through. What she wouldn't give for a sweaty sun salutation or a marathon painting session to get her head right again. She needed to find a way through the fear, back to the Remi who wouldn't just roll over and let a monster win.

The tightness in her chest demanded her attention.

She drew in a breath, holding it when she'd hit capacity, then exhaled with control. *Breathe in. Breathe out.*

The familiar scents of her oil paints, the brush cleaner, the bread she'd baked that morning grounded her, blocked out the memories of the metallic smell of blood and smoke.

She wasn't going to sit here, wallowing in the what-ifs, and give herself a goddamn asthma attack.

Breathe in. Breathe out.

She sat still, breathing deeply until the tightness in her chest loosened, until her yoga instructor back in Chicago would be proud.

Crisis averted, for now. She decided to unearth her inhaler and keep it handy just in case. But just as she started to work up the energy to get her ass off the chair and start digging through her hastily packed luggage, a familiar jingle on the street caught her attention.

Remi threw on her coat and slippers and jogged out to the gate just in time to see Mickey Mulvaney and his trusty steeds Murphy and Rupert clip-clop into view, the dray wagon stacked with boxes and bins.

"Mickey Mulvaney, haven't you retired yet?" she teased. The man had been running package and freight deliveries over the island for practically her entire life.

The man beamed down at her from his perch behind the Clydesdales. Brown eyes peered out at her between a wool cap and thick scarf. "Well, if it isn't little Remi Ford!" he crowed. "I'll retire when I'm dead. How's big city living?"

"Not as good as island life. Packages show up there in these things called trucks."

"Those mainlanders don't know what they're missing." He cackled as he hopped into the flatbed to paw through envelopes and packages. Mickey and Murphy were fixtures on the island, running mail and deliveries all year long.

"Got something here for you," he said, triumphantly snatching a thick envelope from one of his satchels.

"For me?" That was a surprise. The only people who knew she was here were the ones on Mackinac. And for them, it would be easier to just knock on the door rather than send a package.

He handed it over. Her name was written across the white envelope in a harsh, black scrawl. Her mind adding a pink shimmer to the E's. There was no return address.

"You planning to fix a little hockey action while you're back? I heard Red Wings are down a couple so far this season."

Mackinac's main form of entertainment in the winter was the two-team street hockey league. Every Wednesday for nine weeks in the coldest stretch of winter, the Mackinac Island Red Wings and St. Ignace Storm faced off downtown on Lake Shore Drive. No skates, no pads, no helmets. Just stir-crazy residents wanting to beat the crap out of an orange ball—or each other—with a hockey stick.

High school sophomore Remi had orchestrated a ruse that made it look like their star forward had a leg injury and couldn't compete in the Bynoe Championship Cup. She'd made $300 on the bet with his "miraculous recovery." Until her mother made her give it all back.

"Not this time around. But I hope to catch a game while I'm here."

"Too bad about that. Well, the boys and me got some deliveries to make," he said, releasing the brake on the wagon. "Glad to have you back."

"Glad to be back," she said, not sure if it was the truth or not. "Bye, Mickey."

With a salute, he clucked the horses into motion, and the wagon rolled off down the road.

Remi tiptoed through the snow and let herself back into the warmth of the cottage. The envelope was weighty in her hand. Maybe it was some kind of invitation?

Inside Lizzo still sang. The sunlight still reflected off the lake water. Red paint still dried on the floor covering. But something felt different. Off.

Glancing down at the envelope, something stirred inside her. A tiny tendril of anxiety.

So she hadn't shredded it open the second Mickey had handed it to her. Didn't that count for something?

She blew out a breath. Ignoring her impulses wasn't relieving any stress at this point. With a rush of impatience, she ripped it open and dumped out its contents.

Inside, she found a thin stack of papers. They appeared to be printouts of blog posts and news articles. The top piece's headline jumped off the page at her, and she cringed. A quick perusal of the others confirmed they weren't much more flattering.

Artist Alessandra Ballard MIA since car wreck.

Rumors of rehab circulate for Chicago artist.

Artist's friend still hospitalized, condition unknown.

City's art community rocked by Ballard scandal.

The last page was a printout of an email.

Her hands started to shake as she skimmed the text. It was the message she'd sent just days earlier.

C,

I hope you're okay. Please be okay. They won't tell me anything. Please tell me you're okay.

R

"No. No. No," she whispered to herself.

Beneath it, there was a handwritten note in the same horrible scrawl as the address on the envelope.

Distance only makes the heart grow fonder. I won't forget about you no matter how far you go. But it seems like you've forgotten our arrangement.

She dropped the papers as if they were on fire.

Innocuous words, but the threat was there, a living, breathing thing in the ink on the page. Like a toxin.

He knew where she was. There was no hiding. So much rode on one man deciding if she was worth squashing or not.

"Fuck," she breathed, flipping through the articles and skimming their contents.

The innuendo and rumors were there, but there had been no official statement from either party. Everything she'd built hung by one tenuous thread, and he held a pair of scissors.

But he'd miscalculated. The asshole assumed she was more concerned with her career, her reputation. And while she had clawed her way to the top, while she'd fought for every success and built something she was proud of, the truth was, she'd burn it all to the ground if it meant saving Camille.

But there was an upside. If he was sending her shitty reminders of their "arrangement," that meant Camille could still be saved.

She blew out a breath and felt just a little steadier.

Maybe it was time to start doing a little threatening of her own.

She dusted off her laptop, spread the articles out in front of her and went to work.

Hours later, she leaned back in her chair to roll her tight shoulders when she realized it was dark outside already. She'd spent an entire day parsing through news reports, gossip blogs, press releases, and her own overflowing inboxes, hoping for something, anything that would light the way out of this situation.

She'd come up empty. This was a fight she wasn't equipped for. And the cost of failure was too high. She wouldn't survive paying.

A shiver crawled up her spine as the gloom of the dark house sank into her bones. She needed light. And alcohol. And people. She needed to forget.

She jumped up from the table and dialed her phone as she turned on lights.

"Hey. It's me. Want to get out of the house and—"

"Yes," her sister cut her off.

"We could talk about that neighbor welfare check thing."

"Don't care," Kimber snapped. "Get me out of here."

"Do you want to go someplace we can take the kids?"

"I want to go somewhere no one will call me 'Mom' or 'babe.' Meet me at Tiki Tavern at seven and try not to be Remi late."

Not the Tiki Tavern. Anything but the Tiki Tavern.

"Isn't there another bar open?"

"Not in February on a Wednesday. Besides, your nemesis doesn't work Wednesday nights."

Hell. Why couldn't there be more than one bar open on the island in the winter?

"Fine. I'll see you there," Remi agreed.

13

*T*he Tiki Tavern was the kind of theme bar that shouldn't work but somehow did. Its vibe was Caribbean rum shop meets country-western bar. The staff wore Hawaiian shirts, denim, and belt buckles while serving barbecue and bourbon next to jerk chicken and tropical drinks with umbrellas.

It was a skinny two-story building clad in white clapboard siding that hugged a busy street corner in downtown. In the summer, the rooftop patio with kick-ass water views and killer happy hour specials beckoned tourists. But mid-February on Mackinac meant local patrons were restricted to a smattering of tables in front of the bar and gas fireplace.

It was the only bar that stayed open throughout the winter, making it a gathering place for the lonely and the stir-crazy.

Remi congratulated herself on being exactly on time when she pushed through the front door, kicking a light powder of fresh snow off her boots.

It smelled like smoked meat, liquor, and sunscreen. A Jimmy Buffett classic about cheeseburgers in paradise bathed the room in a riot of colors she wished she could capture. She'd have to settle for ordering red meat, she supposed.

There were a few islanders hunkered around tables, another handful holding down barstools with beers and piña coladas. Kimber hadn't arrived yet.

"Well, I'll be damned. Look who just walked her trouble-making ass through my door." The voice from behind the bar brought a smile to her face.

Darius Milett put the Tiki in Tiki Tavern. Born in Barbados, he'd moved with his family to Michigan—of all places—when he was a kid. His parents and most of his siblings had long since migrated on to the warmer climes of Arizona and Florida, but Darius had inexplicably fallen in love with the novelty of island winters. So he'd gotten a degree in hospitality and, with the help of a most unlikely business partner, had opened the doors to the Tiki Tavern.

Zipping in just a hair under six feet, he was broad-shouldered and muscular with smooth dark skin and the kind of laugh that was contagious. His head was shaved, but he sported an impeccably trimmed beard.

"Trouble-making?" she scoffed, unzipping her coat. "I am a *paragon* of good behavior."

She had a role to play, expectations to meet in this place. No one wanted to see a trembling, afraid-of-the-damn-dark Remi Ford. They wanted the grown-up version of the girl who'd once filled a seasonal fudge shop server's bed with horse manure after he got too handsy with her friend.

"How many times you been arrested, Remi?" Duncan Firth, grizzled local legend, called from the dart board.

"That was in my wayward youth, Duncan," she shot back with a wink. "Besides, unlike some others, *I* haven't wrecked a snowmobile this season."

The man coughed out a laugh.

Darius delivered the margarita he'd mixed to a man in a Michigan State sweatshirt and ducked under the service bar. In three steps, he had her swept up in a bear hug, the sleeves of his parrot and flamingo shirt threatening to rip under the strain of bulging biceps.

She returned the hug and pressed a noisy kiss to his cheek. "God, it's good to see you!" And it was. No matter what had transpired between Remi and his younger sister Audrey—her former best friend and Brick Callan's ex-wife—the smiling, built bartender had remained friendly toward her.

A resounding crash from the bar had Darius setting her on her feet again. "You break it, you bought it, man," he called, eyeing his partner.

Brick Callan's surly expression as he unloaded clean glasses from the rack was comically juxtaposed against his cheerful parrot and flamingo shirt.

She gave the man a little salute, then turned her back on him to focus on Darius. Of all the tiki bars on the island, she had to walk into his. "I thought he wasn't working tonight."

Darius shrugged muscled shoulders. Remi thought she heard the fabric of his shirt whimper. "Said he needed a distraction. You two aren't gonna get all snippy with each other and ruin my island vibes, are you? When are you gonna outgrow this whole big brother-little sister thing?"

"Ew! We do *not* have a big brother-little sister *thing*." The idea made her shudder. As complicated as her feelings were for the grumpy monument to all things masculine, none of them included anything that fell in the realm of sisterly.

"I've never seen two adults rub each other that wrong for that long," he mused.

It was time for a subject change before she got to thinking

about Brick rubbing her in any way, shape, or form. "I see you've quit the gym and let yourself get all flabby," she said, drilling a finger into his rock-hard stomach.

"Don't you dare say the 'f' word in my presence. I've got a reason to stay in shape."

"A hot *manly* reason?" she asked, interest piqued.

He grinned down at the toes of his sneakers. "Remember Ken?"

"Three summers ago Ken? Hot and heavy all summer long Ken? Call me if you're ever in Colorado Ken? Hmm. Nope. Doesn't ring any bells."

"Smartass," Darius said with affection. "As of last spring, Colorado Ken is now Mackinac Ken. He bought the barber-shop and moved in with a hot bartender." The man blew on his knuckles and rubbed them against his shirt.

Remi slugged him in the shoulder. "Shut up! Are you serious?"

He managed to look both embarrassed and ecstatic.

"We kept in touch. I flew out there for New Year's Eve, and the rest is history."

"Well holy shit, Dare. I'm thrilled for you two!"

"You should be. We're amazing, and you should have dinner with us so we can all catch up. Starting with how that happened." He reached out and tapped her cast, which was visible thanks to the sleeve surgery she'd performed on the thermal shirt in a fit of frustration.

"Yes to dinner. I'll show up with wine, dessert, and a thou-sand questions. You won't be able to get rid of me," she promised.

He grinned down at her. "It's really good to have you back, kiddo."

"It's good to be back." This time she meant it.

"Now, what can I get you?"

"I'm meeting my sister. Can you make me something with all of the alcohol? And I guess a merlot for her?"

"Kimber's still off wine since the migraines," he said, waving to a couple by the fireplace as they bundled up to leave.

Migraines? She picked through her memory banks and came up dry. "Okay. Then one of whatever she usually drinks."

"You got it, kiddo."

Snagging the table the couple had abandoned, she put her back to the bar so she wouldn't have to watch Man Mountain smolder at her all night. She blew out a breath and congratulated herself on not acting like a terrified woman mid-nervous breakdown, then realized her foot was tapping out a frantic beat against the floor.

She jumped at a sudden bark of laughter behind her and pinched her eyes closed.

Coming apart at the seams was *not* an option at this point. Besides, if she was going to have a mini-breakdown, she wouldn't do it in front of Brick Freaking Callan...who was most definitely staring at her right now. She *hated* being so stupidly aware of the man.

"You're here."

Remi nearly fell out of her chair before realizing that her sister had materialized next to the table.

"I thought I'd beat you here," Kimber said, shrugging out of a hunter green parka. She wore an ivory hat over her hair that she'd loosely braided. She hadn't bothered with makeup, but the winter wind had tinged her cheeks a delicate pink. She looked tired, pretty, and annoyed.

Remi comforted herself with the fact that it hadn't been anything she'd done. At least not this time.

"I was on time for once," she said as Kimber slipped into the chair across from her.

"Ladies." Darius of the impeccable timing appeared with their drinks.

"My hero," Kimber said, feigning a swoon.

"Damn. It is nice to see the Ford sisters reunited," he said.

"It's good to be in the same place," Remi agreed.

Kimber's response was cut off by her phone vibrating on the table. Remi caught a glimpse of Kyle's name on the screen before her sister hit ignore and flipped the phone over.

"If you two need anything, wave me down. Specials are on the board," Darius said, pointing at a chalkboard that looked like a third-grader had attacked it with chalk.

Neither man, it turned out, had the artistic talent for lettering. Their barely legible specials boards had become part of the lure of the place.

When he left, Remi sampled her All the Alcohol drink. It tasted like a tropical version of a Long Island iced tea. Delicious and deadly. "So, Darius was saying something about you getting migraines," she began.

Kimber rolled her eyes. "What about them?"

She was out of sync, like she was dancing just off the beat and couldn't quite catch up with her sister's metronome. They'd always been a little out of step, but when they were growing up, Kimber had made an effort to help her catch up.

"I don't know," she said, feeling awkward. "I guess, when did they start?"

"They started about two years ago, and they're triggered by stress, which apparently a boring stay at home mother finds in monotonous household chores and the daily ins and outs of raising human beings. Do you like it when people ask you about your asthma all the time?" Kimber asked pointedly, picking up her vodka and soda.

"Uh. No?" Remi stirred her drink and wished she had stayed at the cottage and suffered through her own company.

"And before you ask me about the kids, let's talk about how even though she may not look it, a woman can be more than the people she brings into this world."

Remi peered at her sister over the rim of her glass. "Okay. What's a safe topic that isn't going to get my head bitten off?"

Kimber let out a small puff of breath. "Sorry," she said. "Things are...whatever. I don't feel like talking about them."

Her sister's phone buzzed again. She didn't look at it.

"You could tell me how great your life is," Kimber suggested. "But then I'd probably resent you. Then I'd drink too much to compensate. And things would get ugly."

Remi had never seen her sister hanging by a thread before. Kimber had been born responsible.

Every Friday, she'd marched home to finish up her homework for the weekend. She had tabbed binders with procedures for things like Christmas and meal prep and entertaining. She had planned every detail of her wedding down to packing a day-of emergency kit with stain remover, bandages, breath mints, and safety pins.

Remi, the maid of honor, had ended up needing both the stain remover and the bandages.

Well, hell. It was just another example of Remington Ford being incapable of taking care of herself or others.

"My life is...whatever also. I don't really want to talk about it," she said finally.

"Too many boozy brunches and first dates with men who find you wildly intriguing?"

Remi choked on her drink, and Kimber winced. "Sorry. I'm shutting up now. Let's move to the bar. Brick can referee, and we can talk about something that doesn't make me feel violent."

"Any hints on what that might be?" Remi glanced over her shoulder to where the man in question stood in front of bottles of bad decisions waiting to happen.

"Like the initiative thing that Mom dumped on us." Kimber rose, collecting her coat and drink, leaving Remi no choice but to follow.

She took her time, gathering her things and trudging toward the bar.

This was why acting on impulse was bad. She could have been at home in front of the fire with a bowl of macaroni and cheese in her lap streaming trashy TV. But *nooooooo*. She was too scared to be alone so she'd put on stupid pants and braved the frigid night air just to be annoyed by her sister and glared at by a bartender.

She really needed to look into making better life choices.

"We thought we could talk about your idea from last night," Kimber was saying to Brick.

Remi busied herself by dumping her coat over the back of the stool.

"Go easy on that," Brick said, nodding toward her drink.

She looked him dead in the eyes while taking several long swallows from the straw.

Darius hooted until Brick shot him a look. "It's on you if she gets out of control," Brick warned the man.

"It's Remi. She'd get out of control on ice water and potato chips," Darius insisted.

"Do *not* make her another one," Brick warned.

"Do *not* start with the overbearing protector routine," Remi complained. She was already feeling a lick of warmth spread through her. Though she wasn't sure if it was the alcohol or the argumentative bearded bear in front of her.

"While you two are bickering, I'll take another one," Kimber said, waving her empty glass.

"What the hell, Kims? Did it evaporate?" Remi asked.

"The initiative," Kimber insisted, more sharply this time.

Brick crossed his arms on the other side of the stretch of wood. "What about it?"

"Let's talk how to organize it while keeping the entire thing as simple as possible," Kimber said.

To be contrary, Remi polished off the rest of her drink with a noisy slurp while her sister and nemesis discussed things like how to drum up volunteers and frequency of visits. Brick looked like he wanted to slap the glass out of her hand. When he left to deliver two sandwiches on plates piled high with French fries, Darius put another vodka soda in front of Kimber and then slid a tall glass of pink, frothy liquid at Remi with a wink.

"What is this?" she asked, sniffing it. "It smells like grain alcohol."

"I call it a pink flamingo," Darius said. "Just don't breathe near open flames."

"You're hauling her ass home when she can't walk," Brick announced, throwing a towel at Darius.

"You said not to make her another Tiki Tea," Darius pointed out.

"Excuse me, gentlemen—and I use that term very loosely. But I can walk my own damn self home," Remi argued.

"No, you can't," the entire bar chimed in.

"Can we get back to how to enlist volunteers?" Kimber asked.

Remi half-listened while they debated screening and enforcement.

"Are we boring you?" Brick asked, his tone neutral, but there was something happening behind those blue eyes of his.

She pointed her straw at both of them. "You're overthinking this."

"Okay, smarty-pants," Kimber said. "How do you suggest we enlist volunteers to do the visits?"

Remi dunked the straw back into her pink flamingo. She was starting to feel pretty darn good. "The same way every organization gets them. We force them into it."

"Elaborate," Brick demanded.

"We get together with a couple of islanders. The ones who lay the best guilt trips. Mira Rathbun. Dad. Bill House. Mayor Early," she said, ticking the names off on her fingers. "We ask *them* to help recruit volunteers. Within a week, we'll have more volunteers than we know what to do with."

"And what will the three of us do?" Kimber asked, her eyes narrowing in consideration.

Remi shrugged. "I don't know? Take the credit?"

Brick didn't quite cover his laugh with a cough. "You never change, do you?"

Um. Ouch. "That remains to be seen," she said haughtily.

Kimber's phone vibrated again on the bar. This time she glanced at the screen. "Since you two have it all figured out, I guess I'll take this." She slid off her seat and headed for the hallway that led to the kitchen, office, and restrooms. "What is so important I couldn't have ten minutes to myself, Kyle?" Remi heard her snap as she disappeared around the corner.

All did not appear to be well in the Olson family.

A plate of cheeseburger sliders, fries, and broccoli materialized in front of her.

Two large, capable-looking hands appeared on either side of the plate. "Eat."

The man just couldn't stand back and let her self-destruct.

"I didn't order these," she said, despite the fact that her stomach was now audibly growling over the scent of fresh red meat.

Brick loomed over her from across the bar. "You've had two

drinks strong enough to put down a full-grown man, and you barely touched anything on your plate last night."

"Stop looking at my plate."

"Start eating."

Remi pretended to rub at the corner of her eye with a middle finger.

"Play nice," Darius coughed into his elbow.

Brick and Remi both paused long enough to glare at him.

Kimber interrupted the glaring contest. "I have to go," she said, sliding her arms into the sleeves of her coat. "Apparently Kyle feels unequipped to feed the kids dinner."

"Are you serious?" Remi asked. She caught the subtle shake of Brick's head and shut her mouth. "I mean. Okay. I'll call you tomorrow."

"Why?" Kimber frowned, pulling on her jacket.

"Because we're sisters, and if Kyle needs an ass-kicking, I want to be a part of it," Remi told her.

Kimber paused, and for a second, the mask slipped from her face. There was something softer and sadder in her eyes.

"Thanks, Rem." Her sister turned to the men behind the bar. "Boys, it was a pleasure as always."

She reached for her wallet, but Remi waved her off. "I've got the tab. You go save the day."

Kimber eyed her as she tugged her braid out of her coat. "You sure?"

"Yeah. Go be Super Kimber."

"You'll get home okay?"

"I'll be fine," she insisted.

"'Cause you're listing pretty hard to the right," her sister observed.

Remi did her best to straighten up and overcompensated, jostling the plate into her empty glass.

"I'll make sure she gets home safe," Brick promised.

"Thanks for taking up babysitting duty," Kimber said.

Remi was too fuzzy-headed to be properly offended. "Do you know what that's all about?" she asked Brick after the door closed behind her sister.

He shrugged and turned around to key something into the order screen.

"A fount of information as usual," she complained, picking up the dredges of her pink flamingo and slurping at the ice.

He turned around and removed the glass from her hand. "Maybe you should have been paying closer attention to things at home."

"Question. Does everyone on this island have a problem with me, or are you and my sister the only members of the Remi Sucks Club?"

Darius elbowed Brick out of the way.

"So, Ms. Artist. Catch me up. What are you painting? Studly nude gentlemen?" he demanded.

She knew he was redirecting her. But the nice man had given her such good alcohol. It couldn't hurt to share just a little bit of the truth, could it?

"I'm painting music. Well, what I see when I hear music."

"Girl! Good for you!"

"Really?" Brick's mouth was still pursed in a frown, but his eyebrows showed his interest.

"I started to dabble with it in art school. Apparently there's a market for what weird brains see."

"What's the coolest place a Remi Ford original hangs?" Darius demanded, leaning in to snatch a French fry off her plate.

"There's one in the mayor's house."

"Chicago or Mackinac? Because one of those is much more impressive than the other," he pointed out.

She grinned. "Chicago. The mayor saw it at a gallery and

liked it." Actually, the woman had "fallen in love with it," according to the gallery curator. But repeating that just felt like bragging.

"I always knew little Remi Ford would be going places," Darius said as he poured a pint of lager from the tap.

Brick disappeared without a word.

Without his disapproval hovering over her, she snuck a bite of burger. It was so good she ate an entire slider in four neat bites.

She did feel pleasantly woozy. Enough so that she'd forgotten about the envelope and the man who'd sent it. Crap. Now she was remembering it.

"What?" Brick demanded from across the bar.

She jumped, slapping a hand to her heart to make sure it restarted properly.

"Jeez. Warn a girl!"

"Why are you so jumpy? And what's wrong with your face?"

"There's nothing wrong with my face, *ass*!"

She could feel the breeze from his exhale across the bar.

"I meant, you made a face like you were upset," he clarified. "Do you want something else to eat?"

She propped her elbows on the bar and put her face in her hands. "No. The sliders are great. And the broccoli is necessary. Thank you."

"It concerns me when you're agreeable."

She dropped her hands. "Brick, I just need to escape for a little bit tonight. Okay? No questions. No worrying about consequences. I need out of my head."

He gave her a long, charged look. "Fine. But you'll eat. You'll drink an entire glass of water between every drink. And you'll let me walk you home."

"And you won't try to pry anything out of me?"

"I won't try."

"Promise?" she pressed.

"As long as you let me walk you home," he agreed.

14

*R*emi Ford was shit-faced. She was one of those charming, adorable drunks who just got happier and more excited to talk to people until she fell asleep.

By Brick's guesstimate, she was about ten minutes from falling facedown on the bar and snoring.

She didn't notice when he took the half-empty glass out of her hand as she questioned the Ashburn twins about island gossip.

"I'm going to walk our little problem home," he told Darius, nodding in Remi's direction. She was so close to Walter Ashburn's face, it looked like she was trying to breathe the same air.

"Sure you don't mind?" his partner asked.

Brick shook his head. "She's less of a pain in the ass when she's drunk."

Unlike Sober Remi, Drunk Remi let him take care of her. Besides, there was no way he was letting anyone else see her home. He didn't trust anyone else to pour her into bed.

He ducked into the office to grab his gear. When he came back out, she had wandered over to a table of two couples on their monthly date night. Apparently they were discussing the craziest things they'd ever done and whether or not they'd do them again. A topic no doubt broached by Remi.

It was yet another thing he appreciated about her. She abhorred small talk. If she walked up to a stranger at a party, she was more likely to ask them about the complexities of their relationship with a parent or what had been the best thing to happen to them that week. They'd had a lot of those conversations in his first year or two on the island.

"Come on, Remi," he said, steering her back to the bar. "Time to go."

She leaned way back to look up at him and then grinned. "Hi, Brick," she said in a singsong voice.

"Hi."

"You're so tall," she said earnestly.

"You're very observant," he said dryly, stuffing her into her coat and zipping it up to her chin.

"It's one of my favorite things about you. Do you want to know what the other ones are?" she asked.

"No."

He searched her pockets and found only one glove. Not a surprise. He put his own gloves over her tiny hands and led her out the back.

"Where are we going? Are we going to go do something crazy?" she asked, bouncing on her toes and looking hopeful. Drunk Remi was also Do Something Crazy Remi, which was exactly why no one else was going to get the chance to walk her home.

"Sure. But first we're going to stop by your place."

"Okay. And *then* we're going on an adventure, right?" she clarified, her green eyes wide and hopeful.

"Yep." She'd be ready to pass out by the time they got to the cottage. He took her hand and tugged her with him down the sidewalk. It was late, and fat flakes of snow drifted lazily toward the earth.

"Have we done this before?" she asked. "This feels vaguely familiar."

He'd walked Drunk Remi home on more than a few occasions. Especially in her early twenties when the wild child in flowing sundresses couldn't help but attract freaking day-tripping fudgies—fudge-shopping tourists—and vacationers with dicks. Men fell for her on sight when she was sober. And when she was half in the bag, the woman was fucking irresistible.

"Brick, your hand is going to get cold," she said, holding up his bare hand.

"I'll survive," he promised her.

"Here. I'll keep it warm for you," she said, stuffing his hand wrapped in her own into his coat pocket. "If you weren't you and I wasn't me, this would be pretty romantic."

"Do you wish I wasn't me?" he asked before catching himself.

"I wish I wasn't me," she confessed. "I mostly like you being you."

"Mostly, huh?" He couldn't help but smile just a little.

She leaned into his arm, resting her face on his sleeve. "You are really good-looking. Do you know that, Brick? I mean. You just have the whole big, bearded lumberjack deal going on."

"Is that a good thing?"

"It's only the best kind of thing. I bet women fall in love with you left and right."

He decided it was wiser not to answer her and was relieved when she lapsed into silence next to him.

He'd known the second she walked into the bar. The atmosphere changed on a dime. The air electrified as if a storm had rolled in. He'd come out from the back and seen her in that green thermal shirt with the right sleeve cut off just above the cast. The denim that hugged her curves in a way that made his palms itch, his fingers curl in on themselves.

She'd been wrapped in Darius's arms. And despite the fact that he knew Darius was in love and that Remi had nothing but sisterly feelings for his partner, Brick had still gotten sucker punched in the gut.

He despised the fact that others could be so free, so easy with her. That Darius could hug her and not have it send his world flying apart. That other men could touch her and not realize how fucking precious that contact was.

Remi stumbled over a seam in the sidewalk. He stopped to steady her. "You okay?" he asked.

"Fine and dandy," she hiccuped, right before she fell off the curb.

"You asked for it," he warned her. Bending down, he tossed her over his shoulder.

"Hey! Everything's upside down! Wow. Are you always this far away from the ground?"

He rolled his eyes and plodded on up the street.

"Brick?"

"What?"

"Did you know your hand is on my ass?"

"I am aware," he said dryly. As if there were anything else in the world he could think about except for the way her denim-clad curves felt under the palm of his hand.

"Is that on purpose or an accident?"

"I don't really know."

"Well, since you're grabbing my ass, it's only fair I get to grab yours." Drunk Remi had her own logic, and it was always, always flawed.

Pondering this flaw, he nearly took a header into a picket

fence when she grabbed his ass with both hands and squeezed. Hard.

"Remi, if you don't behave yourself, I'm going to leave you in Sam Earl's trash can."

"No, you won't," she said, alternating squeezes. "You're very muscular back here. And tense. I think you carry a lot of tension in this area. Have you ever had a massage?"

He was starting to sweat and he still had two blocks to go before he could lock her in her house and run like hell.

"Uh-oh," she whispered.

"What?"

"I dropped your glove."

On a sigh, he turned around and retrieved the glove from the snowy sidewalk.

"Put your hands in your pockets," he told her.

"But then I can't play butt bongos like this," she said, smacking his ass in a rhythmless beat with both hands.

"Remi. Stop," he said, feeling desperate.

"Butt bongo!" she sang, still slapping.

"Remi," he growled.

But her musical assault on his ass continued. He was left with no other option. At least, that's what he told himself as he slapped her on the ass. Hard.

She yelped, levering herself up until she was almost upright over his shoulder. The sting of his palm, the noise she made, both went straight to his groin.

"You spanked me!" she said in a hushed whisper.

"You gave me no choice. And keep it down or the whole island will be talking about me spanking you." It was moments like this that had defined their relationship. Every once in a while, she snuck in under his defenses and made him reveal something he didn't want to about himself. Like how much he wanted to do it again.

"That would be terrible. Because then they might realize that I kind of liked it."

Dear God in heaven.

"You seem really broody right now. Do you want to go somewhere for a drink and talk about it? There's this place called the Tiki Tavern—"

"We're going home," he growled.

"My home or your home?" she asked. "Because my temporary home doesn't have any booze in it. It doesn't have much of anything in it actually. I left kind of in a hurry."

The cop in him wanted to jump on that opening. Why had she left in a hurry? Why was the fearless Remington Ford so damn jumpy? But he'd made a promise not to pry. At least for tonight.

"My head is spinning," she announced. "I can't tell which end is up."

"Join the club," he grumbled.

She was quiet again as he navigated his way across the snowy street past cozy bungalows, crafty Victorians, tidy fenced-in yards. A pristine coat of snow blanketed everything in sight. He still loved this place. It was his first real home. He'd chosen it over the freedom to go wherever he wanted, over his own marriage. Mackinac Island had his heart. And on quiet nights like this, when chimneys puffed white smoke into the inky night sky, he wondered how much of his heart belonged to the island and how much of it belonged to Remi.

"I missed it here," she whispered from behind him. "No other place has ever really felt like home, you know?"

She'd always been able to read him with unnerving accuracy. "I know," he said solemnly as Red Gate came into view. The lights blazed behind the windows, pushing back the night.

He tried the gate and found it locked. If she'd finally

started taking all his security lectures seriously, something was definitely wrong. Carefully, he set her on her feet on the sidewalk. She stumbled and caught herself in the hedgerow. Grinning up at him, she wrapped her arms around his waist and held on tight.

"You're a good hugger," she murmured against his chest, seemingly unaware that his arms were at his sides.

"Gimmie your keys, Rem."

"Hug me first," she insisted.

"Seriously?"

"But first open your coat. I don't want to hug coat. I want to hug you."

It was not a good idea to let Remington Ford through any layers of defenses. Especially clothing. It was too dangerous.

When he didn't move, she attacked his zipper and the velcro closures of his parka. It took her three times longer than it would a sober person, but she finally managed with a shimmy of triumph.

"Okay. Here we go," she said. "Are you ready?"

He was never ready for physical contact with her.

She resumed her original position, arms around his waist, face pressed to his chest. Without the protection of his coat, he felt everything too much.

It pained him to slip his arms around her small frame, to pull her tighter to him. He hated how well she fit. He could rest his chin on the top of her head and breathe in her hair. "Did you have a hat on?" he asked. She'd changed her shampoo somewhere through the years. Instead of a bright lemony scent, it now smelled like exotic oils. Tempting the senses like a spell cast.

"It fell off somewhere," she said cheerfully. "Keep hugging."

On a sigh, he did as he was told because arguing with

Drunk Remi was even worse than arguing with Sober Remi. And Drunk Remi used deadlier weapons. Pouty lower lips, sad eyes. He could withstand her annoyance, her anger, but he couldn't handle her sad.

Peeling her face off his coat, she leaned back to look up at him. "It's snowing," she announced unnecessarily. It was always snowing on Mackinac.

"I see that," he said, reaching up to brush a snowflake off her cheek. She cuddled her face against his palm.

"Your face and my hand are freezing. You should come inside so you don't get frostbite and lose my face."

"I would if you gave me the keys," he said in exasperation.

"Well, why didn't you say so in the first place?" she yawned, burrowing her face into his shirt again.

"Remi?"

"Huh?"

"Keys."

"Oh, right. Check my pockets."

Cursing, he dug through her coat pockets, coming up with two hair ties, her cell phone, and a candy bar wrapper. He found the cottage key ring in the front pocket of her jeans and fished it out as quickly as possible with two fingers.

He noticed she wasn't carrying her inhaler. That would be a conversation for Sober Remi.

"I'm sooooo sleepy," she announced with a dramatic yawn.

"Come on, Sleeping Beauty," he said, opening the gate and wrestling her through it.

She was shuffling her feet like it took too much effort to lift them, so he picked her up again. She wrapped her arms around his neck and then stuck her ice cube of a nose against his throat.

"If I wrote Hallmark movies, this would be a scene. The

sexy lumberjack carries the drunk damsel in distress into a secluded cottage."

He got the front door open and stepped inside. It was warm and bright inside. The fire cast a cozy heat throughout the living space. He was right—she'd turned on every lamp in the house except for the bedroom.

"What would happen next in your movie?" he asked, setting her on her feet and unzipping her coat.

"The sexy lumberjack and drunk damsel would *totally* have sex," she said, swaying into him.

"I don't think you're talking about making a Hallmark movie then," he said.

He took off his own coat and pushed her toward a chair at the little dining table.

"Where are we going?" she demanded.

"Sit." He nudged her into the chair and knelt down to remove her boots. Her socks were mismatched.

She leaned on one elbow and closed her eyes.

"Not yet, Remi. Water first."

"Water first," she repeated without opening her eyes.

He went into the kitchen and filled a glass from the tap. A quick search of the cabinets revealed an old bottle of ibuprofen. With both in hand, he returned to the table where she was now facedown on top of some paperwork.

"Come on, baby. Drink up."

"Ugh. I don't want to drink anymore. Can't you see I'm practically swimming in alcohol?"

"I meant water," he said, pushing the glass into her hand. "And take these."

"Are those Tic Tacs? Is my breath gross?"

"It's for the headache you're going to have in a few hours, and if there's a god, all day tomorrow."

"You know what sucks?" she said as she tossed the tablets into her mouth and nearly knocked over the water.

"A lot of things."

"Hangovers. I turned thirty and BAM!" She slammed a hand down on the table. "It's like getting hit with a three-day flu. I hardly ever drink anymore."

"I find that hard to believe."

"Yeah, well, you think I'm a terrible person, so I can see why you'd think that."

"I don't think you're a terrible person. A terrible pain in the ass, yes."

"Brick?" she looked up at him with sad eyes. Her lower lip trembled.

Damn it. Be strong, man!

"What?" God. What was she going to ask him, and would he be able to say yes? More importantly, would he be strong enough to deny her?

"Will you please make me some mac and cheese?"

His shoulders sagged in relief. "Yeah, baby. I'll make you some mac and cheese."

She smiled up at him. "You take such good care of me."

"I'm glad you think so, at least when you're drunk. Why don't you get ready for bed, and I'll bring you a bowl?" he suggested.

"Do I have to?"

He went into the kitchen and found the boxes of pasta he'd given her in the otherwise empty cabinet. At this rate, he was going to have to drag her ass to the grocery store. "Don't women have to take off their eye makeup before bed?" he reminded her, putting a small pot on the front burner.

"Good point. How do you know that? Oh, right, I forgot. You were married. That was terrible, by the way."

"It wasn't exactly a good time for me either," he murmured.

"If you didn't want to be with me, you didn't have to go off and marry my best friend," Remi said.

He stood there open-mouthed as she shuffled off toward the bathroom.

There was a muffled yelp and a thump followed quickly by an "I'm okay!"

"Are you sure?"

"Is my macaroni done yet?"

He rolled his eyes and turned up the heat on the burner.

She was singing now as water ran in the bathroom. It sounded like she was getting ready to take a shower.

"Psst! Brick!"

He looked up and then immediately glanced away again. She was wrapped up in nothing but a towel. And that towel was only covering one of her two spectacular breasts.

He was a fucking gentleman, damn it. "Uh. What?"

"Can you find me something to sleep in?"

"Can't you find it yourself? I'm making you a snack."

"Oh, right! I totally forgot." She smacked herself in the forehead, laughing. Then stumbled into the bedroom. He listened to drawers opening and closing and a few muttered curses before the telltale sound of her small body hitting the mattress.

He finished the pasta, dished some into a bowl and grabbed a spoon big enough for a drunk to hold. On his way to the bedroom, he stopped by the bathroom to turn off the shower she'd started.

"Remi?" He knocked on the partially closed bedroom door.

It was dark in the room, and she was curled in a ball on top of the covers. At least she'd managed to dress herself. The

Mackinac PD hoodie was huge on her and it was on backward, the hood bunched under her chin. He let out a sigh and put the bowl on the nightstand. "Come on, Rem. Get under the covers before you freeze." He managed to pull back the quilt and sheet and stuff her under them without coming into too much contact with her bare skin.

"Do you want to eat or do you want to sleep?" he asked, smoothing the covers over her.

"Will you turn the lights on?" she asked in a small voice.

"Which ones?"

"All of them."

He paused. "Are you afraid of the dark, baby?"

"Don't tell anyone," she whispered. "I just need to be able to see him coming."

Him.

"Who, Remi? Who are you afraid of?"

Fuck temporary promises. If there was a man out there who scared her, he wouldn't rest until the scales were balanced.

"This is why I came back," she murmured against her pillow.

"Why?"

"You make me feel safe."

He stood there staring down at her, hands fisted at his sides as a wave of possession knocked into him.

He made her feel safe.

She'd come back to be close to him. That made whatever problem she'd gotten tangled up with his problem. And he was going to solve it as soon as he pried some answers out of her.

He turned on the lamp on the nightstand, then did the same with the overhead light before lighting the fireplace to chase off the chill in the room.

She was sprawled out on her stomach like a starfish under the covers. Unable to help himself, he brushed her hair back from her face and spread it out over the pillow.

She was bewitching. Even drunk and snoring, all that fiery red hair, that smooth ivory skin made her seem so touchable.

This is why I came back.

Her words echoed in his head. He knew he was going to get more involved. Hell. He was involved the second she'd turned the aisle in the grocery store. He was going to do the thing he'd promised himself he'd never do: Get close to Remi Ford.

Because there were no witnesses, and because he desperately fucking needed it, he leaned down and brushed his lips over her furrowed forehead. The lines disappeared, and her expression eased as if he'd taken away her worry with the brush of his mouth.

He was so fucked.

He forced himself to walk out of the bedroom before he did something stupid like climb in next to her and cuddle up against that soft, warm body.

Back in the living space, he turned down the fireplace and shut off a few of the lights. He dumped the rest of the mac and cheese into a container, washed the pot, and put it back in its cabinet. Next, he got the coffeemaker ready to go because a hungover Remi required almost a full pot of caffeine before she was functional again. He fished out one of the rainbow of cereal boxes and put it on the counter next to a bowl and spoon.

He heard an insistent buzzing and found her phone faceup on the table.

Pain in My Ass.

It was late. It might be a friend calling with an emergency. Or it could be a guy calling to "Netflix and freeze" or whatever the kids were calling it now. He debated for two more buzzes before his desire to know more got the best of him, and he swiped to answer the call.

"Yeah?"

There was a brief silence on the other end, and then, "You have got to be kidding me. She got a new number and didn't freaking tell me? Unbelievable." It was a man's voice. An annoyed one. Frankly, if he was dialing Remi's number and sounding annoyed, Brick couldn't blame him.

"Who are you looking for?" he asked.

"Alessandra. Well, technically a brat named Remi. I don't suppose you know her?"

"Remi isn't...available," Brick said, choosing his words carefully.

"So this *is* still her number?"

Seeing as how the guy was in her contacts and had called the number looking for her, Brick felt okay with confirming. "It is. Can I take a message?"

He heard the sound of something like a pen clicking repeatedly on the other end. "Just tell her Raj called and she can't avoid me forever."

"Maybe you should take the hint," Brick suggested dryly.

"Maybe you should take the message, Secretary Boy."

"Maybe I see why she has you in her phone as Pain in the Ass."

Inexplicably, this caused Raj to guffaw. "Ah, that ungrateful little twerp," he said with what sounded like affection. "Tell her I called. Tell her to call me back or at least answer her goddamn emails."

Raj disconnected the call without any of the usual pleasantries, leaving Brick staring down at the phone in his hand. His gaze flicked to the bedroom. It had been a stupid move, answering the call. One a sober Remi would have his balls for.

He needed a game plan. One that had her opening up to him rather than him sneaking around behind her back.

The easel set up in the center of the room caught his eye. He wandered over to inspect the blank canvas and wondered why she'd bothered setting it up at all if she was supposed to be using his space for her studio.

An idea struck him. If he could make the studio space inviting enough—instead of just shoveling things to the edges of the room like he'd done—it would give him more time with her. And more time together meant more opportunity to drag some answers out of the woman.

It also meant more time resisting his insatiable physical attraction. But he'd spent fourteen years building a tolerance to it. He could handle a few weeks of proximity. Couldn't he?

After a quick tour to check window and door locks, he was satisfied. Remi was safe. He could go home and for once not stare out his fucking window, wondering what the hell she was doing at 3 a.m. with all the lights on.

Instead, he'd go home and start clearing a space for her.

He was halfway across the street when he realized whose sweatshirt she'd worn to bed.

15

One second, Remi was miserably shoveling rainbow unicorn cereal into her mouth as a replacement for the dinner she'd forgotten to cook or order. The next, the Joy of Painting rerun she was watching went dark, as did the rest of the house. Her spoon flew out of her hand onto the rug.

"It's just a regular ol' power outage," she told herself. "No deranged murderer is out there in this squall cutting the power just to break in and commit a homicide."

Though maybe it wouldn't be a bad idea to have a weapon of some sort on hand. Just in case. The wind that had been whipping the island since yesterday gave a particularly creepy howl outside the windows.

She tiptoed her way around the couch and into the kitchen, where after a brief, blind rummage through drawers, she found a pair of kitchen shears. Tucking them into the pocket of her sweatshirt, she began a search for candles and a lighter. She found one taper candle and a box of matches that had apparently gotten wet sometime in the last five years and were basically useless.

Uneasiness curled in her belly.

The gas fireplaces still worked, so she'd be warm. The toilet would still flush. A big plus. But it was dark. Very, very dark.

~

"THIS IS FUCKING STUPID," she muttered to herself as she dashed across the street in the frigid night air. "There's nothing to be afraid of. It's just a little power outage."

It was so damn dark. The lights up and down the block were out. Except for the house across the street. The lanterns on either side of Brick Callan's front door blazed bright, beckoning her like a beacon. Because of course the man she'd been trying to avoid since her drunken alter ego had made a fuzzy yet certainly embarrassing appearance had a generator.

Her teeth were chattering so hard her jaw ached. It wasn't the cold that had her literally shaking in her boots. Well, it wasn't *only* the cold. The dark was suffocating, closing in around her as the cold burned her bare legs.

She wasn't running to Brick, she told herself even as she picked up the pace, bounding up his front steps. She was merely knocking on a neighbor's door and—

The heavy wooden front door was wrenched open just as she raised her hand to knock.

"Holy Miles Davis!" she yipped, slapping a hand to her chest and taking an involuntary step backward. "Jesus, Brick. You scared the life out of me. Where are you going?"

"To get you." He said the words simply as if they weren't meant to give her solace and hope and make her feel weak in the knees.

His gaze heated her straight through to the bone. He had boots on with pajama pants stuffed into them. On the opposite end, those flannel pants rode low over his hips, revealing the waistband of his underwear. He had one arm shoved through a heavy winter coat and no shirt. The man was shirtless. There was so much to look at.

Her brain came to a screeching halt as she stared at a solid acre of muscular flesh. The comforting bulk of broad shoulders. The taper of his stomach to his narrow hips...and the dangling temptation of an untied drawstring.

"What the hell are you wearing?" he demanded.

Tearing her gaze away from his man chest, Remi glanced down at her middle of the night ensemble. In her panic, she hadn't changed out of her hoodie and shorts before pulling on snow boots and running for her life.

"I don't know what you're complaining about. It's a hell of a lot more than I was wearing five minutes ago," she told him.

He swore under his breath, then grabbed her by the front of the sweatshirt and dragged her inside.

"I swear to God, woman," he said, pulling her further into the house without loosening his grip.

The first few rooms were dark, but the living room was warm and cozy with a fire going in the fireplace and a single lamp casting a glow from the end table.

The light drew her in, instantaneously lowering her pulse from a gallop to a steady jog.

She threw herself on the worn, plaid couch and went to work pulling her boots off. Brick waited until she was done and moved the boots closer to the fire.

On the coffee table, a laptop was open to a search engine. She sneaked a peek when his back was turned.

Remington Ford artist Chicago mayor.

That sneaky son of a bitch was snooping on her.

Under most normal circumstances, it would piss her off.

But in the current situation, it damn near made her panic. He needed to leave this alone. She couldn't let more people get hurt because of her.

While she feigned interest in a blanket on the back of the couch, she noticed him close the computer and move it.

It was quiet, aside from the soft whir from the fireplace fan and the purr of the generator outside.

"Do you want me to turn on more lights?" he asked, his voice low and rough.

She squeezed her eyes shut. "Damn that Darius and his pink flamingos. So I *did* tell you?" She pressed the heels of her hands into her eyes and held them there. "I couldn't remember if I actually opened my big, fat mouth and told you I was afraid of the dark or if I just wanted to tell you."

"Why did you want to tell me?" He hadn't moved any closer. His back was to the fireplace, the coffee table between them. But he still managed to take up all the space in the room.

"Because you used to make me feel safe."

He flinched. An actual physical recoiling like she'd managed to hurt him. Then it was gone.

"Tell me why you don't feel safe now. Why you sleep with the lights on. Why your name doesn't come up in any accident records but you *were* taken to the hospital for a severe asthma attack."

She jumped up from the couch, and something slid to the floor, landing with a soft thump.

"Tell me why you're carrying a pair of fucking scissors in your pocket?"

"You *spied* on me?" It had been a mistake coming here. Coming home maybe. But running to Brick? Definitely. "You can barely look me in the eye but you went digging for information on me?"

She didn't make it two steps before he caught her around the waist. They both went stock-still. She could feel the steady thump of his heart. His heat. His glorious, intoxicating, hypnotizing heat seeped into her bones.

"You're shivering." His voice was a rumble at her back.

"I'm not shivering," she said through chattering teeth. "I'm shaking with rage. Totally different."

For a beat, they stood exactly where they were, bodies touching, breath audible. Then he released her and pointed to the couch. "I don't care if you're trembling with hysteria. Sit your ass down and explain to me what the fuck is going on," he said.

"It's none of your business." It wasn't. She wouldn't make it his. If she couldn't protect Camille, she could at least protect him and the only way she was going to be able to accomplish that was by pissing him off.

"I don't know why you think you can just stick your nose into other people's business and then demand they explain their lives to you," she huffed, working herself up into a temper.

"I'm a cop and a bartender—it's what I do."

"Yeah, well, I'm not a criminal or a patron. So back off."

"Where's your inhaler?" he demanded crisply.

"What?"

"You're starting to wheeze."

She didn't have to work herself up now, she was actually there. For the first time in weeks, she felt strong, not weak.

He blew out a breath. Standing there, hands on hips, he looked formidable. And safe. But it didn't matter. She wasn't his problem. He'd lost the opportunity to make her his problem a long time ago.

"Sit," he ordered.

Stubbornly, she remained standing until he gave an aggrieved groan and took a seat on the couch. "Happy?"

"Not until you tell me why the hell you decided it was imperative that you go digging into my business," she shot back.

His hands closed over his knees, and then he slid his palms up his thighs. "Because you're fucking scared, Remi. And the girl I know isn't afraid of anything. So when you show up here, unannounced, with some bullshit story and a broken arm, and you can't sleep with the lights off, you're fucking right, I did some digging. I know you were hospitalized for an asthma attack, not injuries sustained in an accident. You didn't mention that to your parents when they asked."

Suddenly weary, she stalked to the opposite end of the couch and sat. Pulling her legs up to her chest, she rested her chin on her knees. She couldn't afford to tell him the truth. But he wasn't going to leave this alone. So she had to find another solution.

"Talk to me," he pressed.

She stared at the flames as they flickered in the fireplace. "Why?"

"Because as much as you don't believe me, I care."

"Why?" she asked again.

He rubbed his palms over his thighs. "We're practically family."

She shook her head. "Is that how you really feel? That we're family? That you're some big brother figure to me?"

He hesitated, and the silence filled every corner of the room. Tension built.

"Yes," he said, his voice hoarse.

She stared him down. "You want me to be honest with you. Yet you're willing to sit there and tell me you think of me as a little sister?" she challenged. The man was either lying to her or to himself.

"This isn't about me," he began.

"Do you *see* why I don't feel like showering you with honesty? You can't even be honest about that. Something we both know is true, and you still can't admit it."

Her phone rang from the pocket of her hoodie, and she yanked it out. It wasn't a number she recognized, but the area code was Chicago.

Without an explanation, she bolted from the room.

"Hello?" she breathed, hurrying into the kitchen.

"You want to explain to me why my top client isn't returning any of my calls?" Rajesh Thakur, her annoyingly needy agent demanded.

Remi's shoulders sagged, and the hope that had built inside her deflated like a punctured bounce house.

"Why are you calling me from some random number?"

"Bigger question. Why is Alessandra Ballard answering some random number instead of the last eleven calls from her agent?"

"Did it ever occur to you that I don't want to talk to you?" she hissed, peering over her shoulder to make sure she was still alone.

"Bro, did it occur to *you* that I don't care?" Raj, as he was known in the art crowd, was immune to digs and insults. He dressed like a mob boss, spoke like a recently graduated fraternity brother, and demanded VIP service everywhere he went. As long as he was negotiating his clients' fat commissions, he didn't care what anyone had to say about him.

Brick appeared in the doorway and strolled over to the refrigerator. He leaned against it, arms crossed, and watched her, openly eavesdropping. She would have stepped outside, but it was fucking dark out there.

"What do you want?" she asked Raj.

"To tell you to snap out of this little meltdown funk and get your ass back here. We should be plastering your face all over the blogs."

"I've seen what they're writing. There will be no face plastering," Remi said, glaring at Brick.

He raised an inquisitive eyebrow. She returned it with a middle finger.

"Negative attention is still attention," Raj insisted in her ear. "And in this case, it's paying off big. Ask me how."

She blew out a breath through gritted teeth. "You're the worst. How?"

"First, tell me I'm the world's greatest agent, and you want to up my commission to twenty percent."

"No." As a baby, untested artist, she'd surprised Raj by battling him down from his standard twenty percent to a more palatable fifteen. He secretly respected her for it.

"Your motherfucking genius agent just sold *Once Upon a Dream*."

Remi spun away from Brick's weighted stare. "Wait. What? That wasn't even in a gallery yet."

The piece was huge and complex. Her best yet. It was a wild fever dream of color. It came to being after she'd asked a DJ friend to mix two of her favorite songs together. She'd finished it just before the show at the gallery. Just before the night that had changed everything.

"No gallery, no gallery commission," Raj crowed.

"Raj, that painting was in my apartment." Her apartment was a minimalist, white loft with high ceilings, tall windows, exposed ducting, and wood floors. While it was exactly the kind of place Alessandra Ballard would have been expected to have, it hadn't ever truly felt like home to Remi.

Sure, the light was great for her work. But no amount of comfy furniture or cozy throws ever made it feel warm.

"I've been watering your plants and drinking your booze since you pulled the runaway act. You're welcome, by the way. Anyway, with all this press about the accident, your name and your paintings have been splashed all over the fucking place. So when a tech guru from Silicon Valley in town for a conference came sniffing around for a Ballard original, I took her to your place. Don't worry. I hid your laundry under the sink first."

She'd left the place a wreck. Paints, brushes, drop cloths everywhere. She'd packed in a whirlwind, leaving discarded clothing and toiletries scattered across every flat surface.

"I feel violated."

She sensed rather than witnessed Brick's reaction. When she glanced over her shoulder, he was standing, hands fisted at his side, a scowl on his handsome face. She shook her head at him.

"The price tag will make that go away," Raj said with confidence.

"I doubt that," she said dryly.

"The whole behind-the-scenes, art-in-its-natural-habitat thing added a few pretty G's to the asking price."

"What was the number?" she asked.

"A hundred thousand dollars."

Remi's knees went weak. She took a shaky step toward the table and gave up, sinking to the floor. "*What did you say*?" she asked, rubbing two fingers to the spot between her eyebrows that felt like it was going to explode.

"Your first six-figure price tag, bro," he said smugly. "They only go higher from here."

Her head was spinning.

"Remington," Brick growled.

She ignored him.

"Is that the dick who answered your phone the other night?"

Her gaze slid back to the man in question. "Oh, it better not be." The glare she leveled at him should have made him weak in the knees, should have at least had the survival instinct to cover his crotch kicking in.

Instead, he doubled down and stared back. "Get. Off. The phone."

"Raj, I have to go murder someone."

"I expected a little excitement out of you. But I guess that's what I get for representing temperamental pains in the asses. You're out of good wine, by the way."

Remi disconnected the call and climbed back to her feet.

"Did you answer my phone, talk to someone, and not tell me about it?" She congratulated herself on how deadly calm she sounded.

The man didn't even have the good grace to look embarrassed.

"I did. You were passed out. I thought it might be an emergency. Who made you feel violated? Was it that Rajesh guy?"

"How dare you!" she snarled. "I don't even know what to yell about first. The fact that you keep invading my privacy—"

"You're in *my* house."

"That can be remedied," she said, striding for the doorway.

He stepped in front of her, a wall of muscle and angst. "No. Not until you tell me exactly what the fuck is going on."

She went toe-to-toe with him, tipping her head back so she could look at him. "I don't owe you a goddamn thing!"

"Don't push me, Remi," he warned.

"Or what?" she taunted, poking him in the very large, very hard chest. "You'll storm your way into my business? You'll treat me like a little sister? Oh, wait, I know. You'll go back to disappearing every time I come home—"

He grabbed her by the front of the shirt, and she found herself pinned between a plaster wall and a Brick one. She froze as those massive hands settled on either side of her head. His chest was heaving, nostrils flaring like a stallion about to run. His hips held her against the wall, an obscene length of hard flesh pressed against her belly.

"Shut. The fuck. Up," he enunciated a mere inch from her face.

It was the shock and not the command that had her obeying, she decided.

Then he dipped his head toward her, and she forgot everything. It all slipped out of her head as her attention zeroed in on the man's firm, scowling mouth as it drew closer in slow motion.

Her lips parted as if they were under someone else's control. Heart thundering away in her chest. His breath was hot on her cheek. His body so warm against hers. Every part of her was alert. But this wasn't fear. No. This was *alive*.

The breath she let out was a tremulous one. It had one corner of Brick's mouth lifting in smug satisfaction.

But just when she thought he was going to finally, *finally* kiss her, he tensed against her instead. Those heated blue eyes were no longer focused on her face.

She heard it then. The squeak and swing of the front door. The change in him was instantaneous. Gone was the stubborn seducer and in his place was a battle-ready sentry. Her blood ran cold. No. It couldn't be. Not here.

Brick, eyes blazing, clamped a firm hand over her mouth, dragging her out of her frozen fear. She managed a shaky nod, and he removed his hand. With surprising grace, he whirled her away from the wall and put himself between her and the intruder. Her brain, scrambling to keep up with the ever-changing situation, took a hot second to admire the barricade of muscle.

Footsteps realigned her priorities, and Remi snagged a knife from the butcher block on the counter. The hand that wrapped around the hilt shook, but it felt damn good to take a stand.

He spared her a glance, spotted the knife and mouthed the word "No."

She jabbed the blade in the direction of the hall where it was apparent someone was approaching.

Brick moved soundlessly to the doorway, sinking into a crouch. A lion ready to pounce. She gripped the knife in both hands and held her breath.

16

"*Y*o, Brick! Bricky Tikki Tavi?"

Brick, in the midst of calculations that included where he'd left his service weapon and how to keep Remi in sight without putting her in danger, heard her ditch the knife on the table behind him. At least that meant he wasn't about to get stabbed in the back. Before he could react to the intruder, she grabbed him by the waistband and held on.

"Spence?" Remi called weakly from behind his back. "Is that you?"

"Audrey?"

Remi's hands slipped away from the back of his pants, and he swore under his breath.

He stepped into the doorway and came face-to-face with his little brother, who had no idea he'd just barely avoided an ass-kicking. "Spencer? What the hell are you doing here?"

Spencer took one look at him, shirtless, barefoot, ready to commit murder and blanched.

"Oh. Oh, shit. I'm sorry. Valentine's Day. I didn't realize you two were back together—Shit. Sorry."

"What?" Brick needed a second to shake off the fog of adrenaline...and lust.

Spencer Callan was shorter than Brick, leaner, too. His hair was a light brown that went to blond under the summer sun. He had the kind of look Remi used to call Country Club, dressing as if he spent all his free time on the tennis court or golf course. Now, in fancy, name-brand winter gear, he looked like he'd just strolled off the slopes at some ritzy resort in the Alps.

"I'll go. I just thought—Never mind. It was stupid."

"Spencer Callan, you stay right where you are," Remi commanded from over Brick's shoulder. Well, more accurately, around his bicep.

"Remi?" Spencer went from kicked puppy to elated brother in the span of a single heartbeat. "Boy, am I glad to see you!"

"Not half as glad as I am to see you!" She elbowed Brick out of the way, leaving him to watch as his brother swept her up in his arms.

Jealousy sliced deep. His brother and Remi shared the kind of carefree, affectionate bond he could never be a part of.

"What *are* you doing here?" she asked when Spencer put her back on her feet. Brick had to squash the urge to yank her back to his side.

"The big guy glaring at me didn't respond to my last two texts. Figured I'd fly in, make sure he was alive. Maybe do some tearing around on the ice bridge while I'm at it."

Brick had the sudden urge to find and open a bottle of bourbon and drink until he fell down. His brother had either ruined a moment he'd been waiting for, or saved him from making a huge fucking mistake. "You could have called," he said blandly, turning away from the affectionate reunion and pouring himself a glass of water for his burning throat.

"Since when do I need to call ahead to tell my big brother I'm crashing at his place for a couple of days?" Spence asked, dropping his duffel bag on the floor and wandering into the kitchen to open the fridge.

Halfway through his foraging, he poked his head up over the door like a prairie dog. "Hang on. Are you two..." The unfinished question lingered as Spencer looked back and forth between them, taking in Remi's inappropriately short shorts, Brick's bare chest.

"No." Brick's answer was stony.

"I mean, if you are, I can go find someplace else to stay for the night. It *is* Valentine's Day."

"I know how this looks. But—"

"Don't be silly, Spence. You know your brother looks at me and sees just another sibling. He'd rather pluck out his own eyeballs with a cocktail fork than look at me that way," Remi said sweetly. There was fire beneath that sugary surface, and Brick was afraid it might burn him alive.

"Good thing I never thought about you that way," Spencer said smugly. "Thanks for taking my virginity, by the way."

"Hey oh!" Remi smirked.

They high-fived, his little brother and his...whatever the fuck Remington was to him, in his kitchen as if it were all some hilarious joke. And maybe it was. But not to him. Brick wished he could just lock them both out of the house and go back to his nice, quiet life.

"Well, I should get going. Thanks for letting me soak up some of your lights, Brick," she said, starting for the door.

"No," he said again. And when she didn't listen—because the woman never fucking listened—he had to grab her by the hood of her sweatshirt. "You're staying here."

"You know what that means," Spencer announced. "Sleepover! I brought popcorn and beef jerky. We can light our farts on fire and tell ghost stories."

"Boy sleepovers are gross," Remi observed.

BRICK PLAYED DIRTY. While Spencer went upstairs to change, Brick hid Remi's boots in the dining room so she couldn't sneak out before they'd had their little talk.

He bided his time through the inevitable catching up portion of the evening. Through the popcorn making and the ensuing rounds of competitive Jenga. Nostalgia slapped at him. The three of them had done just this in this exact room. A fire roaring in the fireplace. A movie no one paid attention to on the TV. His grandmother providing the popcorn. His grandfather, the commentary.

His grandparents would have approved.

It felt...right. Like they all belonged here. But anyone could stick around for the good times. That wasn't the true test. And Brick knew from experience that most wouldn't stick through the bad, the hard, the inconvenient. The new, shiny adventure would always beckon to some to shake the dust off their shoes and move on.

Spencer seemed good, happy even. He worked in sales in a complicated position Brick had given up on understanding years ago. He kept them entertained with stories about Detroit and his friends, razzing Remi, reminiscing with Brick. The mood was light like it always was with Spence around.

But every few minutes, Brick would lock gazes with Remi and the smolder there threatened to ignite again. He couldn't ignore it. And if he wanted answers out of her, he was going to have to embrace it.

So he waited until Spencer was snoring in the recliner.

Remi was curled in a ball on the end of the couch under a throw his grandmother had knitted. Brick occupied the opposite end, his feet propped on the coffee table. Something his grandparents would not have approved of.

Remi stirred.

"Do you want me to turn on more lights?" he asked, keeping his voice low.

She shook her head. Those emerald eyes searching his face.

"Are you hungry? Cold?"

"No."

He kicked off the quilt he'd used to cover his legs. "Then come here. I want to show you something."

He towed her off the couch and back into the dark hallway, noting how she drew closer to him in the dark. She might not like him right now, but he damn well made her feel safer. He led her to the door and nudged it open.

"I did a little rearranging," he said, fumbling for the light switch. Finding it, he moved aside so she could step out first.

"Oh, come on," she groaned. "Why'd you go and show me a thing like this when I'm trying to stay mad at you?"

She wandered down the ramp into the room. Where kayaks and outdoor gear had once hibernated, clean work tables and empty shelves stood, waiting. He'd put down drop cloths in the center of the space and built a framework for her to hang larger canvases.

He'd rescued several of his grandmother's glass canning jars from the basement and grouped them on the work tables.

"I changed out the lightbulbs in here to those smart LED ones," he explained, pointing at the pitched ceiling. "You can download an app and change the color and brightness."

She looked up and sighed.

"I also cleaned out Pop's old tool cabinet," he said,

gesturing at the red metal chest. "You can use it for storage. Or whatever."

He watched as she wandered the space, pausing to run a hand over neat stacks of boards. "Those are if you decide to make your canvases." He scraped a hand over the back of his neck, wishing she would say something.

She glanced his way again, a considering look on her pretty face.

"I honestly don't know what the hell to do with you," she said finally. "One minute you're pushing my buttons, the next you're stealing my breath. You make my head spin."

"Talk to me, Remington. Tell me what happened."

"You never give up, do you?"

"Not when it matters."

"Fine. You asked for it." She hopped up on one of the folding tables and let her legs dangle. "There was an accident. My friend and I were driving back to her place after my showing at a gallery downtown."

"You had a showing?"

She bit her lip. "I'm gonna say this, and it's gonna sound like I'm being funny, but I'm kind of a big deal. Or I was. Or I still might be. I don't really know. I've been painting. But not as Remi Ford. To the art community, I'm Alessandra Ballard."

"Why?"

She swung her legs. "Because Remi Ford got arrested for skinny dipping. Because she's a troublemaking screw-up who's always on the brink of disaster."

"That's not who you are."

"That's who people here see me as. I'm the girl who fixed the street hockey championship. Or the one who got in a bar fight when she was nineteen. I didn't want that girl following me into the world. So I'm Alessandra Ballard who wears beautiful clothes, goes to fancy parties, and paints music."

He didn't much care for the idea that Remi felt she had to hide who she really was. But he decided not to derail the conversation into an argument. Yet.

"Anyway, my friend Camille was driving us back to her place. It was late. The roads were icy. We ended up going through a guardrail. I broke my arm, but Camille was really hurt. She was knocked unconscious. And there we were, stuck in the dark. I felt so...helpless. So alone. I didn't know if the car was going to slide into the blackness. I didn't know what was in the blackness. A ravine. A river. A gentle slope. I didn't know."

Not wanting to distract her from the tale, he was careful not to move a muscle. But his arms ached to hold on to her so she'd remember she wasn't alone.

"Anyway, we were finally rescued. I didn't realize at the time that my arm was broken. I was more worried about Camille. She still hadn't woken up. They wouldn't let me go to the hospital with her, and I was rightfully very upset. They had an officer drive me home."

She bit her lip and looked to the side.

"Rajesh—that's my agent—showed up at my place to tell me how the showing had gone, but I ruined his fun with an asthma attack. The cold, the adrenaline. Being upset. Anyway, he called an ambulance, which, for the record, I still think was overreacting."

"And that's when they noticed your arm?" Brick guessed.

She nodded.

"And that's why you're afraid of the dark." Because she thought her friend was dying next to her in the dark and there was nothing she could do. Her pain, her fear was agony for him.

She nodded again, eyes closed.

"Breathe."

He closed the distance between them and took her hands, hating the feel of the cast. She opened her eyes and looked up at him, then took a slow, deep breath. She kept on breathing until her shoulders lowered.

"You look like you could use a breath or two," she observed.

"You could have been killed."

"But I wasn't."

"You broke your arm. That's still too much for me."

"Before you go all big brothery, you might as well hear the rest."

"There's more?"

"Camille is still in the hospital. I don't know how badly she was hurt. I don't even know if she regained consciousness. She hasn't answered any of my calls or emails. So it's hard not to imagine the worst."

"Why can't her family give you an update?"

"Well, that's the other problem. Camille is kind of well-known in Chicago, and so is Alessandra. Together, we got a lot of attention. So there's been some...speculation."

He wasn't going to like this part. He could already tell.

"What kind of speculation?"

"Do a search for Alessandra Ballard online, and you'll find a few dozen articles hinting that maybe I was driving. That maybe I had too much to drink at the gallery and that maybe the accident was my fault. That maybe I put my friend in the hospital."

Brick swore under his breath. He wanted to get on a plane, fly to Chicago and purposely knock the teeth out of every blogger and journalist who dared write lies about her.

"I swear. It isn't true. I didn't cause the accident."

"You think I don't fucking know that?" He reeled it back in. "Sorry. I didn't mean to say it like that."

Her eyebrows were high on her forehead. "How did you mean to say it?"

"You take your lumps. When you screw up or get caught, you apologize and take your punishment. If you had been driving, you would have already apologized publicly and privately about a hundred times."

She heaved a sigh, her fingers tightening their grip on his. "I wish someone would tell her family that. They're inclined to believe the gossip. When I tried to visit her, they had security escort me out of the hospital."

"What about the police report? It would prove Camille was behind the wheel."

"It *would* say that, if I hadn't pulled her out before they got there. The car was sliding, and I thought we were about to plummet off the side of a cliff." She shrugged her shoulders. "It's just my word against a bunch of people speculating about a sexier story."

"So you came home."

"Yeah. I came home. I figured it might be nice to be Remi Ford again." Her eyes filled with tears, and she immediately looked away. "I just wish I knew if she were okay. The news just keeps saying the same thing. Condition unknown. And no one will give me any answers. So I just sit here waiting for her to call, to say she's okay."

He couldn't stand it anymore. Brick pulled her against his chest and held on tight. The muffled sob that escaped damn near broke his heart.

He didn't tell her that everything was okay. Because it sure as hell wasn't. But he'd find a way to make it okay. He'd find a way to reassure her.

"You know another stupid thing?" she asked, sniffling against his chest.

"What, baby?"

"I haven't painted since the accident."

"You broke your arm," he pointed out.

"Yeah, that should just mean I can't paint *well*. But there's this block. Every time I pick up a brush, I just relive it over and over again. The impact. The horrific sound of metal scraping. And then the drop." She shivered against him. "It's like there's no room for music in my head anymore."

"You're healing. Cut yourself some slack. You went through a trauma. You can't just bounce back from it physically or emotionally."

"What if I never bounce back? What if I never paint again? Or what if I do paint again, and it's terrible?"

He cupped her face in his hands, hating the tears he saw there. "You're Remington Honeysuckle Ford—you will fucking bounce back."

Her laugh was half-hearted. "Is that an order?"

"You're damn right. And here's another one. Stay here. Don't try to sneak out and go home tonight. I'll sleep better if I know you're here."

"Just a couple of siblings having a sleepover?" She sniffled, and he handed her a paper towel from the roll he'd put next to the mason jars.

"Remington, sometimes men say stupid things. Not because it's the truth, but because they wish it was."

"That's Brick speak for either you wish I was your sister or you wish you thought of me as a sister," she said, those green eyes sweeping him from head to toe. He felt the heat of her curious perusal like it was a caress.

"I'm not answering that. But you are staying tonight so I don't have to worry about you."

"Fine," she said, noisily blowing her nose. "But only because I *know* you hid my boots somewhere and I'm too tired to tear your house apart looking for them."

"Good girl. Now let's go draw a marker mustache on Spence," he said, plucking her off the table.

She grinned up at him and then froze. "Hey. Did I say anything about butt bongos the other night?"

"Yes. Yes, you did."

"Damn it. I was afraid of that."

He watched her take one last look around the room before she headed up the ramp into the house. He had a lot of complicated feelings. One of them stood out more than the others. She'd told him the truth. But he was damn sure there was more to the story than she'd shared.

17

The power kicked back on just after nine a.m., waking Brick on his own living room floor. He was on his side, facing the couch. His right arm was stretched above him, hand holding on to something warm and smooth. Bleary-eyed he raised his head and realized he was gripping Remi's milky white thigh where it jutted out from the blanket.

Jesus. Even in his sleep he was a possessive bastard over the woman who would never be his. Her skin was so warm and soft.

Her full lips gently curved as if something in her sleep amused her. Her lashes were long and delicate. Skin a translucent shade of pale. She still had that scattering of freckles over the bridge of her nose and cheeks.

He wanted mornings like this. Craved them with a hunger that hollowed him out. He wanted to wake up in this house to watch her sleep. He wanted Remi's face to be the last thing he saw at night before he shut his eyes, the first thing he saw when he opened them. He wanted her laughter echoing throughout the house.

But he couldn't have that. Couldn't have her. He wished

fiercely that knowing that would make the want, the need finally go away.

A twist of red hair fell over her forehead, causing her to frown. In her sleep, she batted it back and mumbled something he couldn't quite make out.

Even asleep she didn't remain peaceful.

She gave another little jolt, jerking her broken arm. Her fingers found his hand on her leg and squeezed.

The intimacy of the moment, of watching her be completely vulnerable and still gravitate toward him, took his breath away.

At least until his brother's snore startled him out of his reverie. Spencer was sprawled in the recliner, sleeping soundly. Brick wondered if his brother had ever met anyone in his life who'd caused insomnia. They were close, but they tended not to talk about serious things.

Sports? Yes. Hot wings? Absolutely. Relationships? That was a hard no.

His brother had seemed almost stunned when Brick told him he was engaged to Audrey.

"I didn't even know you two were dating," he'd said.

Granted, it had been a fast courtship. But still, what did it say about him as a brother that he hadn't even told Spencer he was dating his old high school friend? He needed to be a better brother. Needed to make more of an effort with Spence the man. Just because he was an adult now didn't mean Brick should allow their relationship to just fizzle. They were all they had in terms of family. That alone was worth preserving.

Something stirred at the opposite end of the couch. Magnus uncurled from a cocoon of quilt at Remi's feet and yawned mightily before stalking down the cushions to stab Brick in the arm.

It was time for the furry hellion's breakfast apparently.

Carefully and with an uncomfortable amount of regret, Brick removed his hand from Remi's leg. He dragged himself to standing, wincing at the twinges from his back and hips. Thirty-eight was too fucking old to spend a night on the floor.

He adjusted the blanket over Remi, tucking it in around her. Then, because he was half-asleep, let his knuckles graze her cheek.

The cat clawed his leg through his pants and gave a plaintive meow.

"Don't be an asshole. It'll just make me feed you slower."

THE TIKI TAVERN was enjoying a bustling lunch hour thanks to sunny skies and temperatures that crept up to flirt with the low thirties.

Dressed and ready for his shift as part of Mackinac's finest, Brick had stopped in to confirm the bar's supply order and grab a sandwich. He'd left Remi and Spencer still sleeping in the living room.

He took a bite of smoky pulled pork and hit submit on the order. Considering his exercise in self-control complete, he called up a search engine and glanced around to make sure no one had a straight line of sight on his laptop screen before typing "Alessandra Ballard" into the online search.

The kaiser roll lodged uncomfortably in his throat when the first picture came up.

Remi—or rather Alessandra—stared back at him from eyes that looked bigger, more dangerous. She was wearing a low-cut evening gown the exact color of those eyes. Her hair was left long in loose russet curls and swept away from her face. As if the cut of the dress wasn't arresting enough, she wore a chunky pendant that dangled in her cleavage. She looked like she'd just stepped off the page of some fairy tale, a knowing kind of smile tugging at red, red lips.

Synesthetic artist Alessandra Ballard poses in front of her untitled piece inspired by Beethoven's "Moonlight Sonata."

It was stunning. *She* was stunning.

Ignoring the recent headlines predicting rehab and jail time for the "fallen art star," he clicked through more pictures and watched Remi's secret life unfold before him. Cocktail parties. Magazine interviews. Gallery openings. Secret smiles and smoky eyes. She was a beautiful person surrounded by other beautiful people.

He felt like he was staring at a stranger. The Remi he knew burst into a room with her hair a mess and a hundred words on the tip of her tongue. The woman before him was something...someone else.

He kept scrolling, headlines and pictures competing for attention.

Winthrope Gallery owner sings Ballard's praises

Impressive debut by synesthetic painter

Is Alessandra Ballard in rehab?

Alessandra Ballard sells out first show

Ballard's post-accident disappearance screams guilty

There she was on the arm of a dignified blonde woman, looking like she was on the prowl for trouble.

Artist Alessandra Ballard and socialite Camille Vorhees enjoy a night out at Chef Michael Matsui's new restaurant.

Camille. His attention snagged on the name, and he skimmed the short article.

Designer dresses? Photographers taking her picture outside restaurants? Was that who Remi wanted to be? Some goddess with mysterious eyes and scores of admirers.

She couldn't be that here.

The truth twisted in his gut like a knife. She had big dreams, the kind that he could never keep up with. The kind that could never be satisfied here, on their quiet little island. Even if she chose him. She'd end up resenting the roots he'd forced her to plant. And he'd never be happy in some city, surrounded by strangers. Not even if it meant having Remi.

This wasn't an opportunity to win her. This was simply a chance to patch her up and release her back into the world where big dreams flourished and new adventures awaited.

He would never be enough for her. It was time he remembered that.

"You look like you want to put a fist through that screen."

Ken Pacquiao was a man of contradictions. He had an affinity for sweater vests, but as the island's barber, his black hair was cut and styled into a faux hawk with indigo tips. He was a loud, proud vegetarian, but his favorite boots were made from ostrich leather. Where his boyfriend Darius was hard-bodied and outgoing, Ken was softer, quieter. But his deadpan observations usually had the power to surprise a laugh out of any audience.

Brick closed the laptop abruptly.

"Also, you're due for a haircut and a shave, my friend," Ken observed, sweeping him with a judgmental look. "What's with everyone on this island channeling the Sasquatch over the winter?"

"He's just jealous because he can't grow a beard," Darius said, leaning over the bar and squeezing Ken's baby-smooth cheeks.

"I'm not jealous. I'm dedicated to my craft," Ken sniffed.

"I'll make an appointment," Brick said grudgingly.

"Tomorrow. Eleven a.m." Ken announced.

Brick didn't see much reason to make the effort since the only woman he'd ever wanted would be leaving him here to go back to her glamorous and exciting life hundreds of miles away. But he was also very slightly afraid of Ken. So he'd keep the appointment. But he wasn't buying any more of that stupid beard balm, damn it.

"You're probably out of beard balm by now anyway," Ken said, reading his mind.

Before he could formulate a response, Brick's phone rang on the bar.

Remi.

"Hey," he said, sliding off the stool and trying to look casual as he stepped away from the bar.

"Before I say anything else. We're both totally fine. Mostly."

Brick gripped the phone so hard he worried it might crack.

"What happened? Where are you?"

"It's just a little scratch, but you know how head wounds are," she said. "But the real bad news is your snowmobile."

"Remi, where *the fuck* are you?"

SQUINTING against the sun and ice, he spotted the orange of Spence's snowsuit, prone on the ice. The red dot next to him that made Brick feel rage just looking at it had to be Remi. He gunned the department's Polaris and rocketed toward them.

The ice bridge was the strip of lake that froze solid—most years—connecting the island to the mainland in the winter. It was a relatively safe mode of travel as long as riders stayed between the dead Christmas trees that acted as pavement markings.

Apparently Spencer and Remi had not heeded the ice bridge rules. Seeing as how they were a few hundred feet out of bounds. His snowmobile, an ancient Yamaha that he'd bought third hand a decade ago, was nowhere to be seen.

As he got closer, he saw that Spencer was lying down, his head in Remi's lap. That put a tic in his jaw. His brother had lost that privilege years ago. Yet despite their breakup, somehow Spencer still remained close to her. They probably traded emails or texts. Probably aligned their summer visits and made plans to see each other on the island. His gloved grip on the handlebar tightened.

He let off the throttle as he approached, then cut the engine. Anger propelled him off the vehicle and across the ice.

"Hi!" Remi's chipper greeting echoed in his ears when he spotted the blood on her face and coat.

"Cavalry's here," his idiot brother said from his still prone position.

"What in the fuck—" He slid on his knees, reaching for her to find the injury, but Remi batted his hands away.

"Hold still," he snapped. "You're bleeding."

"Oh, that's not mine," she said breezily.

Spencer held up his hand. "It's mine."

Brick looked down and found the source of the blood. Remi had her scarf wrapped around his brother's head, her gloved hand pressed tight to his forehead.

"Head wounds, am I right?" Spencer snickered.

"He hit his head pretty good," Remi said.

"I totally would have beat your time if the ice hadn't opened up like that," Spencer complained.

Brick closed his eyes and took a breath. "Where's my snowmobile?"

"He's not gonna like it," Spencer predicted.

Brick opened his eyes and looked at Remi. She pointed to a snowmobile-sized hole in the ice a few yards away. His hands closed into fists on his thighs.

"How mad is he?" Spencer asked in a stage whisper.

"He's bundled up. I can't see the veins in his neck," Remi replied.

"What were you doing riding out here, and how aren't you dead?" Brick demanded when he'd regained the power of speech.

"Spence and I were just messing around with time trials. The bridge is a little bumpy in a couple of spots, so smarty-pants here thought he'd do his last run on fresh ice," Remi explained.

"So you weren't on board?" Brick clarified.

"I was at the finish line with the timer," she said cheerfully.

"Are you mad, B?" Spencer asked. "You look mad."

"Mad?" Brick was several steps past furious. "Why should I be mad that you two are out here pissing around being irresponsible? Why would I be mad that you destroyed my only mode of transportation—"

"You still have Cleetus," Spencer said helpfully.

Remi punched his brother in the shoulder.

"Ow!"

"Why would I be mad that I'm the one who has to ride to the rescue and play clean up?"

"Sorry, Brick," they said together.

Damn it. He *hated* when they said things in unison. Hated being reminded that he was somehow separate from the two of them. Hated that he was on the outside of their inside jokes.

"Un-fucking-believable," he muttered.

18

She wasn't squeamish by nature. Her mother had taught Remi and Kimber when they were young how to clean up scrapes and cuts common to growing up on a rugged island. Remi, of course, had required more first aid than Kimber. While Kimber had been reading books and hanging out with cool teenage friends, Remi had been climbing trees, pushing snowmobiles past their limits, and playing street hockey with the boys.

Blood didn't bother her.

At least it hadn't until it was Camille's all over her hands, dripping into the snow.

Now, it was Spencer's. Who was going to be just fine.

"Just fine," she repeated to herself.

She'd gone with the Callan men to Mackinac Island Medical to make sure there wasn't anything terrifying about Spence's head wound and to make sure Brick didn't decide to murder his little brother. She'd excused herself immediately upon hearing from the not very impressed Dr. Ferrin that his "thick head" just needed a handful of stitches.

Brick had looked at her like he was going to argue about

her leaving, but she hadn't given him the chance. She'd ducked out of the waiting room and, after doing her best to wash most of the blood off her hands, she'd hightailed it home.

Her hands were still red. Her gloves were unsalvageable, thanks to Spence's fountain-like geyser of O+. Her coat also looked a bit like she'd been an accomplice or a victim of a murder.

She'd burn the lot and order brand new from the general store, she decided.

That was a bonus to having actual money in the bank. She no longer had to run calculations down to the penny to see if she could afford to treat herself to a latte. Her first few years off-island had been tight. City living on gallery associate and undiscovered artist salaries was... impossible. She'd gone without groceries one week, without a prescription the next week. But she became pretty damn ingenious when it came to keeping her bills paid while still scrounging up enough cash for art supplies.

When she'd sold her first Alessandra Ballard painting for $3,000, she'd celebrated by catching herself up on all her bills and then buying a hefty gift card to her favorite coffee shop so she could continue to treat herself when times were tough again. Then, because she was flying high and wanted to share her fortune, she'd taken another $200 in cash and stopped for every homeless person in a three-block radius around her apartment.

Success was meant to be shared. Jackpots were meant to be spread around.

Now...Well, now that initial success had grown beyond her wildest dreams. She could order a fancy new coat without obsessively checking her bank statement. Hell, she could probably order a coat for every person on the island without missing her own rent in Chicago.

It was still novel, she thought, letting herself into the cottage and stripping off her gear. The fact that she was living her dream and being wildly compensated for it.

She'd yet to tell her family. She'd had grand plans of flying them to Chicago for a gallery showing so she could impress the hell out of them. Then the accident had happened, and that sparkly reputation she'd worked so hard for was tarnished. Now if she told them, they'd just shoot her pitying looks and swap worried whispers behind her back.

She'd made it. Finally. But she'd waited too long to share the good news. *Could a woman who couldn't even hold a paintbrush still call herself an artist?*

"Damn Spence and his excessive bleeding," she muttered under her breath. She turned on some music—something soft and easy with blues and purples—and headed into the bathroom to wash away the red.

Finally clean, she changed into leggings and a sweater and was just ready to start seriously thinking about online shopping for Brick's new snowmobile when there was a thunderous pounding at the door.

Only one man knocked like that. *Brick.*

He stood in her doorway, expression unreadable. But the vibe was loud and clear. The man was pissed off.

"Look, I'll replace your snowmobile," Remi said, before he could start a fight. "I'm sorry. It was irresponsible and it won't happen again. I didn't know Spence was going to go that far off course."

Brick closed his eyes in that annoyingly patient way of his when he was trying to get his temper under control. "It's fine," he said, eyes still closed. "I'm glad you weren't hurt."

He sounded like he was being strangled.

"How's Spence?" she asked.

"Whiny." He brushed past her and stepped inside.

"If you want, you can dump him here for the rest of the day so you don't have to deal with him," she offered.

"I think you two have spent enough time together," he announced, taking off his cowboy hat and throwing it on the table.

The man insisted on wearing the full uniform every shift, no matter how cold it got. She, and the rest of the female population on the island, did not mind how his uniform pants looked hugging his butt.

Butt bongos. Ugh. What was it about this man that made her so desperately stupid?

She sighed. "Can I get you something?" she asked, feeling suspicious.

"Coffee," he said. "Please."

"Coming right up." She ducked into the kitchen and fired up the coffee maker. Meanwhile, Brick prowled the sunny space like a big, pissed-off cat waiting to pounce on something and rip its head off. "So, how's your shift so far? Before your brother and I ruined it," she said, reaching into a cabinet and producing two mugs.

"Fine."

A man of few words and much annoyance.

"You got something to say?" she asked. "Because a conversation that goes both ways is usually more productive."

"You and Spence," he began.

She picked up the carafe and poured. "Cream? Sugar?" she asked, knowing full well he took it black.

He shook his head and stared at the mug when she set it on the counter and pointed to it.

"You two need to start thinking about growing up," he announced, looking just a little green around the gills.

Remi poured herself a cup of coffee and then offered him a flat smile. "Do we now?"

"I can't have you running around the island pulling pranks and getting into trouble. I get that you're bored—"

"I hear what you're saying," she said through clenched teeth. "And I appreciate your feedback."

He stilled. "What the hell kind of bullshit is that?"

"It's me not biting your head off for unsolicited advice. If you want to tell your little brother how to live, that's one thing. But you don't get a say in me and my decisions."

"I do when I'm the one who has to clean up your mess."

"I get that you're upset about your vehicle."

"It's not the fucking snowmobile."

"Then what is it?"

"Maybe it's time you head back," he said abruptly.

"Oh, for Pete's sake. I am so sick of the one step forward thirty-six steps back dance with you!"

"Is this still you not biting my head off?"

"Brick, you either say thank you and drink that coffee, or I'm going to throw it in your stupid, stubborn face."

He blew out a breath, obviously trying to rein in his temper. "Fine. I'm sorry," he began stiffly.

"Don't apologize to me. I'm the one who helped your brother sink your snowmobile."

"You don't want an apology, then what do you want?" he demanded.

"I don't know. Maybe pick a lane! Last night you're all, 'here's the studio space I made for you,' and today you're shoving me out the door for Chicago. You make a girl's head spin and not in the good way. More like in the 360-degree way!"

"Okay. Fine. I'm not sorry. You are. Let's leave it at that," he said.

"Why did you come here?" she asked as he picked up the mug.

"To make sure you were all right."

The man was infuriating. He was lucky she hadn't swamped him in the lake instead of his snowmobile.

"Thank you for showing up for him."

"I didn't do it for him." His tone was surly, gruff.

He looked like he wanted to say more. Like there were words he was fighting back. She was so damn tired of his silence, his mysteriousness.

"Oh, come on! What the hell's that supposed to mean?" she demanded. When they got like this, it was like two firecrackers that just kept reigniting the other. Someone always got hurt, and dammit, she was sick of losing fingers.

He lifted blazing blue eyes to hers. His hands were fisted at his sides, and his nostrils flared. She could very definitely see the veins in his neck now. But she wasn't about to back down.

"You wanna say something to me, then open your damn mouth and say the damn words," Remi said.

There was a long beat during which neither one of them moved. They'd never held eye contact this long. She felt undressed, cornered.

And then he started to move toward her. Slowly. Prowling. "I don't think that's what you really want, Remi."

The way his voice, all gravel and whiskey, caressed her name made her legs tremble. There was meaning there. But she didn't know what. She didn't have a Brick Callan Dictionary available for translation.

She took a step back, then another one. But he just kept prowling toward her. He set his mug down with a distinct snap. She stopped when her back met the cabinet. Any second now, he'd look away. He'd leave and walk away without giving her a second thought. Just like he'd always done.

But this time he didn't. He stopped when his boots touched her toes.

"Are you scared, baby?" his voice was a rasp. There was fire in his eyes.

She shook her head from side to side as her pulse rabbited at the base of her throat.

He placed one big hand on the cabinets behind her head and leaned in even closer.

Yep. She was just going to have a heart attack or infarction or whatever the hell it was called when a heart just gave up trying to work.

His beard was magnificent up close. She wondered if anyone had ever told him that before, then decided now wasn't the time.

"You should be," he said.

Beard. Heart attack. Sexy hand and lean-in. Oh, right. He'd asked her if she was scared, she remembered, walking it back in her head.

"Why should I be afraid of you, Brick?" she scoffed. Sure, her knees were literally shaking. But it wasn't from fear. It was so much worse.

"Because…" he said, leaning in closer and closer in slow motion.

She stopped breathing and realized she'd flattened herself against the kitchen wall like a cartoon character pancaked by an anvil. He was so damn tall. She had to tilt her head way back to look up at him. And what she saw in his eyes made her wish she would have looked south rather than north.

He stopped an inch from her. So close that she could feel the hum of awareness firing between their bodies. So close that if she took a deep enough breath her breasts would brush against his chest and her nipples would celebrate.

"Take a breath before you pass out, Remington."

She took one. A ragged, wheezy one. "Why should I be afraid of you?" she repeated.

He held up a hand like he was going to caress her cheek, but his palm stopped just short of touching her, and he withdrew it. It was his turn to take a jagged breath. "Because if you knew all the things I wanted to do to you, you'd leave town tonight and never look back."

All the things he wanted to do to her? Like tie her up, throw her in a trunk, and murder her in the woods things?

His lips quirked. It wasn't a smile per-say. But it was a sign of amusement. "Sometimes I can hear you clear as day in my own head. Sometimes—like when you're calling from the ice bridge because you're bloody and stranded—I'm thinking about murder. But most of the time..." His hand was back. And this time, he trailed his index finger down the side of her neck, over her clavicle, and under the neckline of her sweater.

She was on fire. He was *touching* her. On purpose. The trail his finger left behind was fire, lava, lightning.

"Most of the time?" she repeated.

"I showed up for the same reason I do everything."

"What's that?" she pressed. She was getting lightheaded and hoped she wouldn't do something undignified like pass out at his feet.

"For you, Remi."

Maybe she wasn't having a heart attack. Maybe it was one of those strokes that garbled language processing. Maybe he was looming over her, telling her he did what he did because the baby hippopotamus at the Cincinnati Zoo told him to.

She opened her mouth, and nothing came out. No sound. No air. Nothing.

Brick Callan had just pulled the rug out from under her.

"Are you fucking with me right now?" she asked.

Those lips quirked again and she thought for half a second

he was going to close the distance, cross that last inch that separated them and kiss the ever-loving hell out of her. She'd probably die from it, but she was okay with that.

But then his eyes were shuttering. The heat between them sputtered out.

He withdrew from her, and she felt the absence like an ache that was never going to be satisfied. Because for whatever reason Brick had, he didn't want her bad enough to make the move.

"I'm gonna go," he said without a hint of emotion.

"If you walk out that door without telling me exactly what you mean, you will no longer exist to me," she warned him.

He paused between her and the door. His back to her. He brought the hand that had touched her to his mouth, then dropped it.

"That's not how this works," he reminded her.

"That's how it works from now on. You either tell me why you keep showing up for me but refuse to tear off my clothes, or this is all over. No more fights as foreplay. No more riding to my rescue. No more family dinners together."

He turned to face her. Hands on his hips, staring at his boots. "You know the reasons."

"Tell me."

He raised his gaze to her, and she saw icy fire in those eyes. "You're too young. You dated my brother. I married your best friend. And your mom is my boss."

She shook her head slowly. "Those are *excuses*. Not reasons. I'm done being rejected. Maybe you're too thick-headed to understand how I feel about you. How we would be together. Or maybe you're just a big, muscly chickenshit. Either way, I deserve someone I don't have to beg into my bed. Someone I don't have to convince to love me. I'm done waiting on you, Brick."

A single, stupid tear slid down her cheek, burning her skin as it went.

His jaw clenched. Hard. But he remained stoically silent.

The weight of his gaze made it hard for her to breathe. It smoldered and suffocated with unsaid words. But she was done with the unsaid. One of them had to make things clear.

"That's what you're walking away from today. This is your *last* chance, Brick. Life is too short for me to wait for you. So be sure that walking away is what you really want."

He swiped a hand over his beard. But the mask never slipped.

He picked up his hat from the table. "I'll see you next time you call me for something."

She shook her head. "No, you won't. Because I won't call you next time. Or ever again."

His eyes blazed, boring into her. "Yeah, you will. And I'll be there."

19

Twelve years ago...

*E*ighteen years old with a diploma metaphorically in hand, Remi was free. Even the weather had cooperated, rewarding the early June date with a bright and shiny day warm enough for her to wear her new dress. A long, backless number in watercolor blues and greens. The breeze tugged at her skirts. The rest of her classmates, all six of them, had shown up to the post-graduation celebration in St. Ignace in shorts and t-shirts.

Just another way that she didn't quite fit in. But it finally didn't matter.

With high school officially behind her, she was a few short months from reinventing herself. The fragile asthmatic. The weirdo synesthete. The trouble-making little sister. They all disappeared with one last ferry ride to the mainland in August.

Then her life would officially begin at art school—thank you, scholarships and financial aid. Sure, Detroit was still in Michigan. But it might as well be a separate country from idyllic Mackinac. She'd be close enough to home in case she flamed out in the first week or two, but she wanted the fresh start bad enough that she wouldn't let that happen.

The art shop, her intended destination, beckoned the eye with windows full of color and order just begging to be messed up and rearranged. Brand new brushes pined for a swath of paint. Miles of blank canvas held its breath, waiting for someone to write their story across them.

Waiting for her to create a future.

"What are you doing, Remi?" He appeared in worn jeans and that gray t-shirt that fitted to his broad chest. Every time she got within a foot or two of the man, her skin buzzed with awareness. He wasn't that many years ahead of her and her classmates, but Brick Callan was all man.

"Daydreaming. What are you doing, Brick?" she asked with a flirtatious smile.

"Making sure you don't get into any trouble. Why don't you go back to the party?"

She threw her arms wide and spun in a little circle. "Haven't you heard? You can officially retire now."

A smile played on his firm lips. "Just like that?"

She shrugged, annoyed that he wasn't seeing the magic of her transformation. "I'm eighteen. An adult. A high school graduate. I'm leaving for college in August."

The hint of smile disappeared. "I am aware," he said.

She let the silence stretch on, testing him to see how long it would take for him to break it.

"I didn't get you a graduation present yet," he said finally.

"Did you get Spencer one?" she asked.

"Nope."

She wasn't quite grown-up enough to hide the triumphant flush.

"Are you still mad at him for the accident?"

He uncrossed his arms and pressed a palm into the stone above her head. His nearness disoriented her like one too many wine coolers. He made her feel small but safe. Treasured. Protected. And part of her craved it. But there was another piece that wanted to break free, to shed this life and its expectations.

Maybe then he'd see her for the woman she was instead of a collection of amusing anecdotes and memories.

"I am."

His voice held the rough edges of anger. She winced. "I'm sorry about your truck."

While other schools salivated over the chance to host their prom on the island, the senior class of Mackinac delighted in venturing to the mainland. Her platonic date Spencer, who'd been devastated when Audrey moved with her family, had been too busy rehashing his mother's invitation to visit her in Vegas for the summer to realize the traffic light had turned red.

"There's prostitutes out there, Remi! Lot's of them."

She'd been just about to remark that he was more likely to get into trouble with a loan shark than a prostitute when a Honda Fit had bounced right off the passenger door.

Brick had looked positively murderous at the ferry landing.

The look he leveled her with was stormy. He held her gaze for a tumultuous minute before he gave a rueful shake of his head. "It was never about the truck. He wasn't careful with you."

Her breath caught in her throat. They'd been dancing around the issue for an eternity. She was single. She was of age. And she was more than willing. *Was he finally admitting that he cared?*

"Breathe, Rem." His hand, big, warm, callused, closed over

her shoulder and covered part of her chest. It felt so *good*. So right. So inevitable. *Why the hell wasn't he kissing her yet?*

"Brick. I'm eighteen. I'm out of school. I'm not seeing Spencer anymore. I'm not a damn virgin. What the hell are you waiting for?" The words tumbled out of her mouth in a rush.

"Don't," he warned.

"Don't what? Damn it, Brick. Don't you want me?"

"Is that what you think?"

"I'm tired of thinking, of guessing. Spell it out for me. You're there every time I need you, sometimes even *before* I know I need you. You know all my deepest, darkest secrets. You are the only person who can tell when I'm lying. When you look at me after you've worn through all your willpower for the day, sometimes it looks like you can't decide if you want to devour me or destroy me."

She could see the clench of his jaw, how the cords of his neck stood out, and knew he was close to breaking.

"God damn it, Remi. Please stop talking." But he didn't back up. He didn't take his hand off her. It anchored her to the spot, to him. It gave her the focus and the strength to see it through.

"You need to say it," she insisted. "One way or another, you need to tell me where I stand with you."

"You're safe with me. That's all you need to know." His fingers curled into the flesh of her shoulder like they couldn't help themselves.

"Oh, for Pete's sake. I'm sick of being safe. Aren't you tired of protecting me?"

"Yes!" he bellowed. "I'm fucking exhausted! Are you happy? I'm tired of keeping you out of trouble and keeping my damn hands off you."

Her hands shot up triumphantly. "Finally!" The transformation was already beginning. He could see her as something more than his little brother's annoying friend. He would let her *be* more.

"Remi. You're leaving for school in a couple of weeks," he said.

"What's that got to do with anything?" To her, a summer fling was the epitome of adulthood. Being grown-up to enjoy a temporary relationship that they both could look back on fondly? Share secret winks across the Thanksgiving table. Maybe pick back up where they left off once she was done with college. Yes, please. Sign her up.

"You're leaving," he said stubbornly.

"And?"

His jaw clenched in that adorably annoyed way of his. "And I don't want to ruin you."

"Ruin me? Good lord, man, have you had your ears cleaned? I'm not a virgin."

"Jesus, Remi!" He threw a glance over his shoulder and towed her into the alleyway between buildings away from the spring foot traffic. He kicked the decorative gate shut behind them and deposited her against the cool stone of the building. "If I let myself touch you? If I let myself go? Neither of us would survive."

"Well, somebody ate a bowl of Humble Flakes for breakfast this morning. Your chivalry is *so* admirable," she snapped.

"You and your goddamn smart mouth."

"Go ahead. Teach me a lesson," she taunted.

He leaned in until their foreheads touched. She wished she could bottle the smell of him. She'd call it First Crush and make a billion dollars.

"Remi, baby, if you knew one-tenth of the things I've thought about doing, you'd run away and never look back."

Her heart was hammering in her chest as adrenaline and

lust released into her bloodstream. "I don't run, Brick." No one had ever made her feel like he did. And deep down in some secret part, she was worried no one ever would.

"You better fucking start now." His voice was barely a rasp.

"If I reached under that belt right now, what would I find?" To drive her point home, she curled her fingertips into the waistband of his jeans.

He squeezed his eyes shut and hissed. "Jesus."

"No use praying for help. Jesus isn't worried about your dick, Brick."

"I'm not touching you." He gritted out the words like a rusty mantra.

"What if I touch you?" she whispered. She'd lost the thread of the fight. Lost the point she was trying to make. She skated her fingers over the buckle and listened to the intake of his breath. "Do you want me to? If you do, you have to say it. You can't just hope it'll happen. You need to say the words."

She watched his face change as he looked down at her, something like pain in his eyes. Oh, God. He was going to walk away. He was going to stroll down the sidewalk and leave her with wet panties and a broken heart. And she was going to have to make it her life's mission to torture the man for the rest of his earthly years.

Cool, rough stone at her back. Hot, hard Brick at her front. It was her new favorite place to be.

His gaze dipped to her chest where the material gaped, and he clenched his jaw so hard his cheeks hollowed.

Very deliberately, he placed a hand on either side of her head. She could see the war waging behind his eyes. Want and need with right and wrong. He *wanted* her. The extra-large bulge behind that soft denim told her that. But he was fighting it like she was poison.

"Do you want me to touch you, Brick?" she asked again in a silky whisper.

He was crowding her with that big, wonderful body of his. Looming into her space and still not touching her. As much as it pissed her off, his willpower, his desire to do the right thing, was a goddamn work of art.

His eyes were squeezed shut. His entire body was rigid, like a trap set to spring.

And then he nodded.

She sucked in a breath, not daring to blink. "Say it," she said softly.

Life went on outside the little alley. Tourists window-shopped. Baristas brewed coffees. Birds dipped into the water, hunting silvery flashes of fish. But none of it mattered. None of it existed. The only thing she cared about was the hum of Brick's body mere inches from her own. The scent of him burrowing its way into her brain.

"Yes."

It was a broken rasp.

And it set them both free.

She didn't give him a chance to rethink, to change his mind or regroup. To rebuild the walls she'd managed to knock down.

Remi slid her palm over his belt buckle and lower. When she cupped his erection in her palm, he shuddered against her like a man destroyed. Again, he dropped his forehead to hers. His hands fisted on the wall on either side of her head.

She felt strong, powerful. And when she pressed her palm against his rigid shaft, when he trembled against her, she felt like a goddamn goddess.

"Fuck," he groaned, thrusting into her hand.

One tight fist struck the wall in slow motion.

It wasn't enough. She needed to feel him in her hand. Needed to grip him, hard.

But when she reached for his belt, he stopped her. "No."

"Huh?"

"Remi, baby. If you take my dick out, I'm going to fuck you in a dirty alley."

A fantasy. Not being seen as some fragile little thing in need of coddling. To be *taken*. To be *needed*. To push him so far he could no longer take care.

"I see no problem with that," she said. Her breath was coming in little, short heaves.

"I do. Breathe," he reminded her.

"*You* breathe."

"We're not doing this here," he said firmly.

"Then where?"

"Not here."

"But somewhere? Soon?"

He dipped his head until his mouth hovered just above hers. "Yes."

She was dizzy with it. One word, and he'd made her feel like she was exploding into a thousand pieces. "Will you kiss me?"

His lips parted, and she breathed in his exhale, wanting every piece of him she could have.

"Tomorrow," he said.

"Promise me?"

"I promise."

❧

SHE WOKE in a mood brighter than the morning sun. An hour before she usually dragged herself out of bed, Remi bopped into the kitchen.

"Ooh! Bear claws," she said, pouncing on the box of baked goods. "What's the occasion?"

It was only after her first bite of sugary goodness that she started to read the room. Her parents looked...sad.

"What? What's going on?"

"Brick left," her father said.

"Left what?" The house? He'd been here? Had he asked her parents for permission to date her? The old-fashioned notion was both adorable and appalling.

"The island," her mother announced. "He got a job at one of the horse farms on the mainland."

The pastry turned to dust in her mouth.

"But..." Mackinac was his home. He'd said so. His grandparents were here. His brother. *She* was here. "Why? Did he say why?"

"He just said it was time for a change," her dad said as he gave the morning paper a shake.

"What about Spencer? What about his grandparents? He can't just abandon them. They need him." Her voice sounded shrill. He couldn't abandon *her*. *She* needed him.

"He's hiring in-home health aides for the summer, and Spencer's spending the summer in Las Vegas with their mom," her mother said, clearly not understanding that the world had just tipped on its axis and started spinning backward.

"He left this for you. It's a graduation gift," her dad said, nudging a brown paper bag from the art store toward her.

"I'm going to miss that boy," Darlene mused. "He has such a big heart."

Remi's heart, on the other hand, had just splintered into a million tiny shards. He hadn't wanted her after all. He hadn't even thought enough of her to say good-bye.

She was never going to forgive him as long as they both lived.

20

Remi felt energetic as the music thrummed a sparkling silver around her. Her fight with Brick had been invigorating. A purging, she decided, as she swirled a lovely cerulean blue into the tiny puddle of water she'd made for it on the paper. Watercolor wasn't her medium of choice, but because of that, she'd found a backdoor into her creative brain.

Left-handed through a back door in a medium she wasn't used to wasn't exactly pretty, but at least she was putting paint on paper. It counted as progress.

She ignored the online instructor's suggestion to water down the blue and added it to the paper in all its vibrant glory.

She liked her colors bright, bold. Full of feeling. Which was usually why she didn't like watercolors. They were too subtle for her liking. But since oil paints were still too trauma-tizing, she'd circumvented the whole stupid creative block.

Speaking of circumventing, she'd also managed to ignore the infuriating Brick Callan for the better part of a week. No small feat considering she was using the studio space in his house. The door between them was more than just a physical barrier. It was a psychological reminder that she was no longer granting him access to her.

She was stronger, steadier now that she didn't have the looming promise of his next rejection hanging over her. Forget the friend zone—she'd picked up his 250-pound, hard body and dumped Brick on the "vague acquaintance" list. Metaphorically speaking, of course.

She'd seen him at Doud's earlier when she was grocery shopping, like a *responsible adult*, thank you very much. She'd merely raised her chin in an acknowledgment of his existence before turning away and launching into a conversation with Connie Mackleroy about her seven grandsons. The look he'd given her as he walked past was pure smolder. She was surprised that Connie's Aqua Net hadn't ignited.

Remi was diabolical enough to thoroughly ignore the man in his own house. She absolutely could have done the water-color at the cottage. But just because *she* was forgetting about *him* didn't mean he should enjoy the same luxury.

Which was also why she'd ordered the big jerk a new snowmobile. A fancy one with a heated seat and handlebars, balance control, and a crapload of other high tech features that his ancient, now deceased sled had lacked.

He'd think of her every time he rode it. Which would make him feel like crap, and *that* made her feel pretty damn good.

With a dramatic sweep of sap green that bled and swirled into the purple, she decided that she'd be okay with earning "the one that got away" status. Thinking about him moping around, regretting his callous rejections made her cheerful enough to nudge the volume higher on Macklemore, just in case he had managed to distract himself from the fact that she was under his roof.

Her phone vibrated on the table next to her. The name on the screen had her groaning and turning off the music. "What do you want?"

"Hello to you, too. Are you PMS-ing or something?" Rajesh asked. "Most of my clients love talking to me."

"I doubt that. What's up?" she asked, transferring fat drops of water to the center of the amorphous blobs of color on the paper. Video tutorial be damned.

"Got a rando who reached out and asked if your *Harvest Moon* is for sale."

She opened her mouth to say "hell no," then shut it again. Fresh out of art school, surviving on $1 cheeseburgers and cereal straight from the box, and desperately homesick, she'd been feeling particularly low after another gallery curator had said her work in landscapes and still life was "pedestrian" and "boardwalk quality."

She'd lugged her portfolio back to her tiny apartment, opened a cheap bottle of wine, and painted to the Neil Young tune. It was the song she'd managed to talk Brick into slow dancing to at Kimber's wedding. Every time she heard it, she was instantly transported back to that dance floor on the lush green lawn of the Grand Hotel. Back into Brick's strong arms encased in a dress shirt. His broad palms warming the skin on her back. The dizzying rush of champagne on an empty stomach. The sparkle of stars in the night sky high above them.

It was also the night he'd arrested her. But *that* was another story.

Her *Harvest Moon* piece was an elementary attempt on a tiny canvas. Her craft had grown by leaps and bounds since that painting. To anyone else, it was practically worthless. Professionally, the amateur attempt to capture music in color was embarrassing. But to her, the painting meant Brick. So she'd kept it close.

"How'd they even know about it?" she asked.

"I don't know. Something about seeing it in the background of some interview photoshoot you did a hundred years ago. It's just sitting there on your nightstand catching dust."

"Stop yardsaling my apartment, dick!"

"If you'd get off your broken-armed ass and start producing real paintings again while the attention is on like this, I wouldn't have to snoop through your place for Alessandra originals."

"I really regret giving you a spare key to my place."

"Hey, if you don't come back, can I have your apartment? It's bigger than mine, and the natural light highlights my glorious brown skin."

"I'm coming back," she insisted. She had unfinished business to take care of.

"Whatever. Can I sell the painting or what, bro?"

Remi bit back a groan and dug out her resolve. She didn't need to cling to something she'd kept only because it reminded her of Brick. Not anymore. "Yeah. It's fine."

"Awesome. Also, where do you get this fabric softener? I dig it."

"Are you doing your *laundry* at my place?"

"My washer broke. I needed somewhere to wash my delicates."

"I should fire you," she mused.

"I might fire *you* if you don't start producing again. How long does it take bones to heal anyway? And can you at least send me some pics of you pretending to work wherever the hell you are? This whole social media silence isn't looking good."

"Whatever. Don't leave your underwear hanging all over my place," she said before disconnecting.

Looking down at the watery mess she'd made on paper,

she decided she wasn't in the mood to paint anymore. Instead of a soft, full heart floating on puffy clouds, hers was a sharp, mottled one, split down the middle with colors bleeding under it as if the contents were swirling down a drain. After a quick clean-up, she let herself out the French doors into the bracing chill of the backyard before skirting the house to leave through the gate.

Squinting against the sun that bounced off the world of white, she stuffed her hands in her coat pockets and produced two brand-new, insulated gloves in hot pink that she definitely hadn't put there. *Brick.* She didn't know how or when, but the protective gesture had his annoying name all over them. On principle, she refused to put them on in case he was watching from a window. So it was with ice-cold fingers that she picked up the package leaning against the cottage gate.

She hurried inside to the coffeemaker. While it burbled to life, she used a steak knife to cut through the tape. Hoping for some of the art supplies she'd ordered, Remi's eyes narrowed when she lifted the lid to reveal a newspaper clipping sitting on top of some kind of shredded material.

Ballard sells most recent piece for 6 figures.

She glared at the paper. She hadn't done a damn thing. She hadn't made any calls, sent any emails. She hadn't tunneled into the hospital basement to break into Camille's room. She'd followed his fucking rules, but the bastard still wasn't happy. He wasn't in control of the entire narrative. Alessandra Ballard's reputation wasn't his to crush.

She stomped over to the door and jammed her hands into her new stupid gloves. If he'd been dumb enough to leave fingerprints, she'd use it against him.

Carefully, she lifted the clipping and set it aside to study the packing material. It was ragged scraps of sunny yellows and oranges with streaks of turquoise.

"You motherfucker," she hissed.

"Open it!"

"I used to love surprise presents," Camille had said, running elegant fingers under the tissue paper.

"This one isn't an I'm sorry," Remi had assured her. "This is a thank you for being my friend. And a promise for a brighter future."

"It's beautiful." Camille's soft gasp of surprise, the way she stroked her fingertips over the textures and colors Remi had committed to canvas made her feel like she'd done something right.

"It's 'Shake It Out' from Florence and the Machine," Remi had explained. "It's about moving on."

White-hot rage boiled in her veins as she stared down into desecrated remains of what once stood for a hopeful future.

With shaking hands that wanted to hurl the entire box into the lake, she parted the scraps and ribbons of canvas to dig to the bottom. It wouldn't be complete without a threat. He wouldn't just send her her own shredded painting. He was far too theatrical and full of himself to miss the opportunity. And there it was, scrawled in black on thick linen paper.

It's a shame what accidents can befall pretty things.

Remi seethed from the inside out. Her entire body shook with some poisonous mixture of fear and fury. Tears filled her eyes, blurring everything.

She wanted to douse it with lighter fluid, set it on fire, then go to Chicago and do it again.

But that wasn't how wars were won. Monsters beaten. Shadows vanquished. No, she needed a plan. And for that, she'd need to calm the hell down. She wouldn't be terrified into submission and silence. He'd fucked with the wrong woman.

Her phone buzzed on the counter, startling her. She ignored the new text messages and, as bile rose in her throat, she opened her camera app and snapped pictures of the box and its contents. When she was done, she carefully bagged the note, clipping, and the remains of her lovely little painting in food storage bags. It all went into what she'd dubbed the Blackmail Cabinet next to the refrigerator.

She was shaken. But he'd missed the mark with this. The unnecessary ruin, the insinuation that a woman was nothing more than a "pretty thing," was something Remi would make him regret.

Somehow.

She squeezed her eyes shut. *Damn it.* She needed to think. She needed a plan. She couldn't just sit here and wait for the end.

Blowing out a breath, she swiped her hand over her face.

She needed a distraction. Something to occupy her time while ideas simmered in the back of her head. Something to calm her down and steal her focus away from the nausea swirling in her belly. That's how she approached a new painting. She worked around it, until it took shape in her head.

Her phone buzzed again, and she snatched it off the counter.

It was a group text led shockingly enough by Brick.

Brick: Spoke to the chief. She's asking for a progress report on our initiative.

Kimber: And by progress report, I suppose she wants more than, "We talked about it and did nothing"?

Brick: That's my take. Are you two available to meet tomorrow night? We could grab dinner.

Brick was inviting the sisters Ford to dinner to talk. It was the least Brick-like thing he'd done in recent memory. She was getting to him. Not that it mattered, of course.

Kimber: Fine with me. How about the grille at 7?

Brick: That works.

Brick: Remi?

Instead of responding, Remi made a call.

"Hey, Dad. Do you think you can sneak me into the school? I've got a special project I need help with."

21

*H*e felt like an idiot. Not only had he gotten that haircut and shave—plus the hot towel facial Ken had strong-armed him into—he'd also applied beard balm *and* clipped the tags off a new flannel shirt he'd never gotten around to wearing. All this on the off chance that the woman who was freezing him out would show that night. The woman he was not going to pursue.

The woman who hadn't been out of his mind for the past fifteen days since she'd returned to ruin his quiet island life.

Her efforts in ignoring him made the temperature on the island feel twenty degrees colder than it already was. Such were the powers of Remington Ford.

In the grocery store, she'd given him a cool nod, looking through him rather than at him. She was treating him like a stranger. Like he was nothing to her. He made it all the way home before he realized he'd forgotten the damn beef broth for his damn stew and had to go back to the store.

They'd both shown up to watch that week's street hockey game, and when she spotted him, she'd crossed the damn street to watch from the front porch of a fudge shop rather than spectate near him. He ended up catching a ball to the chest because he was too busy glowering at her to watch the game.

Despite her complete and total avoidance of him, there were signs of her in his own house. Like the clean coffee pot resting upside down in the drying rack next to the sink. Or the dozen oatmeal chocolate chip cookies on his kitchen counter with a sticky note that said simply "Rent."

For the life of him, he couldn't figure out how doing the right thing had landed him in this situation.

But it didn't matter. Because he had something to discuss with her. Something she'd want to hear.

He arrived early at the grille, a restaurant that opened on the weekends in the winter for Mackinac's stalwart residents. It was a few decades overdue for a renovation with its nautical decor, but the food was good, and the heating system worked well.

He took a booth toward the back with a view of the front door. It was cozier. And she'd either have to decide to sit on his side where their bodies would definitely end up touching or Kimber's where she'd have to look at him.

He fiddled with the menus and his phone, looking up every time the bell on the door jangled.

It wasn't until his jaw started to ache that he realized he was scowling.

He had an ace up his sleeve that meant she'd have to talk to him. Kimber arrived a few minutes later, looking pink-cheeked and frazzled.

She spotted him and slid into the booth across from him. "You look good. What's the occasion?" she asked, snagging one of the menus.

He winced, self-conscious now that he'd overdone it on the whole appearance thing.

"No occasion. Ken dragged me into his chair for a hair cut."

"He's terrifying and talented," she noted, perusing the specials. "Hear anything from Remi?"

His jaw clenched reflexively, and he cleared his throat. "No."

"Me neither. She's probably blowing us off. Ooh! They brought back the beer cheese soup!"

Brick pretended to stare down at his menu until the door jangled at the front again.

He nearly stood when he spotted her. Red hair confined to a long braid over one shoulder. A navy wool hat that made those wide eyes look even greener. She shrugged out of her coat and took his fucking breath away. The mustard yellow henley and dark jeans cuffed above waterproof ankle boots hugged her curves hypnotically. Once again, she'd massacred the sleeve of her shirt to fit over the cast.

She looked edible. Fuckable.

It took him a full breath before he realized she wasn't alone.

The toothy, happy-go-lucky Corporal Carlos Turk was taking her coat and hanging it up like he was her goddamn date or something. Brick's fist closed on the specials page and crumpled it.

"Hi, guys," Remi said, looking at her sister and pointedly ignoring him. "I think we're going to need a bigger table. I brought reinforcements."

"Hi, Mom!" Ian poked his head out from behind Carlos and grinned.

"Did you kidnap my son from his grandparents?" Kimber asked.

"Tonight he's not your son," Remi said. "Everyone, meet our technology officer, Ian."

They moved to a bigger table, and Brick cursed his luck when Remi managed to end up at the opposite end as far away from him as possible. The grinning Carlos at her elbow as they debated sharing an appetizer.

The top button of her thermal shirt was undone, like an invitation to appreciate the swell of her breasts. He should not be thinking about her breasts. Not in front of her sister and impressionable nephew.

Orders placed, Kimber interlaced her fingers on the table. "Who wants to explain why my son isn't with Grandma and Grandpa finishing his homework?" she asked, a hint of brittleness in her tone.

"There's a good reason for it," Remi promised. "Why don't we start with how far you two got on the volunteer front, and then we'll get to Ian and Carlos?"

Kimber and Brick shared a glance. He shrugged at her. He was the one who called the meeting and assumed that was effort enough.

"I have it on my list to call Mira Rathbun and Mayor Early to talk to them about rounding up some volunteers," Kimber said grudgingly. "And that's as far as I got."

Remi nodded enthusiastically. "Great." She waited a beat, and when no one else added anything, she winked at Ian. "While Ian sets up his presentation, I'll add that I spoke to Dad, who was able to get ten volunteers to officially commit. Then I reached out to Carlos here since he's such a well-liked, friendly member of both the police department and the community."

That was definitely a dig at him, Brick decided. And she'd delivered it without looking at him.

Remi leaned forward and continued. "Carlos was able to provide the complete list of the people the department checks in on during the winter. I reached out to half of them so far and divided them into two lists. Ones with low-technology acumen who preferred to commit to a day of the week for their visit. And ones who are willing to help test the Visit Request functionality you're about to see."

"Oh," Kimber said, looking as surprised as Brick felt.

"All set, Aunt Remi—I mean Technology Coordinator Remington," Ian announced from the head of the table. He spun the iPad around on its stand. "Ladies and gentlemen, may I present the Mackinac Visits end user interface."

TWENTY MINUTES LATER, food forgotten in front of him, Brick listened with rapt attention.

"So the volunteer list receives an email every time a new visit request is made. They can decide if they want to accept the request and add it to their own calendar, which will also include the birthdates and anniversaries of visitees and volunteers," Remi explained as Ian's chubby little hands flew over the wireless keyboard. "We're also discussing additional capabilities like a forum for volunteers to share notes about their visits. And as my colleague Ian explained before, everyone's private information remains secure behind the login and firewall. Any questions?"

"How did you do all this?" Kimber asked, still looking stunned.

Remi winked at Ian. "I borrowed the school's Online Media Club yesterday and today. They were already working with the kind of modules this project needed. The Branding Club heard about it and got involved with writing the copy and finalizing the photos. They're also working on email automation for new people who fill out the volunteer form that includes a campaign advising what to do or talk about during visits."

Brick blew out a breath. "That's...impressive." He was fucking dazzled by her. She'd known he and Kimber would have expected nothing from her. So she'd delivered the entire project on a platter as a subtle but effective "fuck you." What she was able to accomplish when motivated by revenge was awe-inspiring. And terrifying.

There was no way he was going to survive this.

Remi looked at Ian instead of him and beamed. "You hear that, Chief Technology Officer? You're impressive."

"Hey, Mom. Does this mean I can have a brownie explosion for dessert?" Ian asked, looking hopeful.

"I can't come up with a good reason to say no," Kimber admitted.

Ian celebrated by pumping his fist and then digging back in to his dinner of pancakes.

"I think if we spend all of next week testing it, we could be ready to roll it out the week after," Remi announced.

"Chief's gonna love this," Carlos predicted, flashing a grin in Brick's direction that made him want to punch the man in the face.

"On that note," Remi said. "I'm heading out."

"I've gotta go, too. You want a ride home?" Carlos volunteered.

"That would be great. Thanks," she said, showering the jackass with unnecessary and excessive attention.

"I'll go warm up the sled," he said, pushing his chair back.

Remi high-fived her nephew. "See you guys around," she said. He was presumably included in the "you guys" even though she only looked at her sister when she said it.

Brick caught her at the door, where she was sliding her arms into her coat.

"Can we talk?"

"Maybe some other time," she said with a perfunctory smile that was a goddamn sucker punch to the gut.

Their tech officer was already heading out the door with his mother.

"It's about Camille."

That earned her attention. His entire body lit up when those green eyes finally landed on him.

"What about her?" she asked. There was a note in her voice that worried him. Something that hinted of fear. The front door opened, and a family of four wandered in, bringing an icy gust of wind with them.

He nudged her into the alcove near the restrooms so they were out of the cold and away from any prying eyes. People were used to them being close, being places together. But this time, Brick didn't trust himself to maintain that respectful distance that reassured everyone he wasn't interested in Remi Ford.

"I made some calls," he said.

"To who?"

She looked so stricken he took her by the shoulders. "To a cop friend I met at a LEO conference a few years ago. He works in a precinct in Chicago. He got me an update on your friend."

"What—what did he say?" she asked. Her muscles felt like concrete beneath his hands, and he gave her shoulders a gentle squeeze.

"He couldn't get me much. But she's okay. She had surgery for a collapsed lung and broken ribs. Things were touch and go for a while. But they're expecting her to go home soon."

"Home?" Remi repeated.

He nodded. "I'm sure you'll hear from her once she's recovering in her own bed."

"Did you mention my name to your friend?" she asked, bringing shaking fingers to her lips.

"No. He didn't get the information directly either. So there's no connection to you."

She blew out a breath, then nodded. "Okay," she said. "Thanks."

He nodded, feeling awkward now. He'd expected her to maybe collapse with relief in his arms or something along those lines. But she was practically vibrating with anxiety.

"What's going on, Remi?" he demanded.

He watched the mask slide back into place on her pretty face. "Nothing. Thanks for the information. I'll see you around."

And with that, she slipped out of his grasp and through the front door where Carlos "Dead Man" Turk was waiting astride his snowmobile.

"Fuck."

22

*B*etween looking over her shoulder, obsessively checking her phone for any messages from Camille, and ignoring a certain burly bartending police officer, Remi officially debuted Mackinac Visits with a motley crew of thirty-plus volunteers and a roster of residents looking forward to their first visit.

At this point in the long, bleak winter, most everyone was feeling a little stir-crazy, which had led to a bigger influx of both volunteers and visit requests than any of them had expected.

Remi signed up to take the Kleckners, an adorable elderly couple who lived in a little ranch house tucked away in the woods mid-island.

Lois was a retired school teacher who'd worked with Remi's father. Ben had worked as an engineer on the mainland for forty years before dementia complicated things. Remi hadn't seen either of them in well over a year, but she did vividly remember Ben's sweet tooth.

She opened the doll-sized oven and sniffed. Molasses

cookies were neatly taking shape on the baking tray. She'd had to get creative, baking only a dozen at a time.

Her baking skills radically improved as her creative talents withered and rotted on the vine.

She pulled the tray from the oven and set it on the cooling rack, then surveyed the kitchen mess. This was her fourth dozen. The first was going to the landlord across the street who would remain nameless. She'd avoided exchanging a single word with the man for an entire week now. A feat considering she spent so much time staring at blank canvases in his house and meeting up with old friends for drinks at his bar.

If Remi Ford had a superpower, it was nurturing a good grudge. And Brick was feeling it. The average person wouldn't know it just by looking at him, but she knew that beneath that stoic surface, her freeze-out was slowly killing him.

She was proud of the effort. At least she was doing something. And something, no matter how immature, was better than nothing.

Remi bagged up two dozen cookies and put on actual pants. However, thanks to her bulky sweater, rebelliously skipped a bra.

She ran a brush through her hair, slicked on some mascara and Chapstick, then realized she looked fourteen and spent another minute or two on real makeup. If she wanted the island to realize she was more than a teenage troublemaker, she had to look the part. But she still wasn't putting on a bra.

It was a damp, gray day. Snow was in the forecast because it was winter in Michigan. Still, she decided to walk instead of borrowing her parents' snowmobile. She needed to move and breathe. To do something with this pent-up energy. Even if it was only nineteen degrees outside.

She bundled up in her new parka that didn't have Spencer's head wound blood all over it. She'd gone with a bright yellow this time. Yellow like the sun. Yellow like the notes in the Caribbean steel drum album she'd been listening to as the world outside froze.

Hat, coat, gloves, keys, cookies. She took inventory of her pockets and body like a responsible adult. *Oh, yeah. Phone.* After a frantic search, she found it under a book she'd pretended to read on the couch. Her mind was too full of worry for Camille and what it meant to go home.

With a final glare at the Blackmail Cabinet in the kitchen, Remi stepped out into the winter not-so-wonderland.

She headed up Mahoney Avenue and hung a left on Cadotte. The Grand Hotel's historic charm came into view as she puffed up the hill. It sat on the rise, dignified and distinguished, overlooking the Straits of Mackinac like some grand dame presiding over the island and lake. In the winter, the place sat shuttered and empty except for a few property caretakers.

As a kid, Remi recalled fantasizing about sneaking into the hotel in the winter and hiding herself away in one of the luxurious suites. Pretending she was rich and famous. A butler to bring her hot chocolate. A collection of scrunchies in every color of the rainbow. An entire closet full of her favorite candy that never ran out. *Ahh, the dreams of an eight-year-old.*

Here she was, thirty, with enough money in the bank to make those little girl dreams come true. But the reality was, money didn't buy you the things you really wanted. Including safety.

To save herself an unnecessarily frost-bitten face, she cut across the road and hopped on a cart path that circled the snowy Jewel Golf Course. It was a shortcut that only existed in the winter without thousands of tourists birdieing holes or sunning themselves on emerald green lawns.

The Kleckner house was a one-story ranch with a wishing well in the front yard and a flock of fake flamingos in the flower beds. Given the fresh snow, the pink metal birds were up to their bellies and looked like they were swimming on a lake of white.

Smoke puffed cheerfully from the chimney, promising a toasty reception inside.

Remi knocked on the yellow door.

"Coming!"

A minute later, Mrs. Kleckner, in a Wolverines sweatshirt and jeans, opened the door. She was a weathered seventy-five with a short cap of silver hair. Her face was softly lined, something she attributed to raising three kids and a few decades of Mackinac winters.

"Remi Ford," she said. "It's good to see you, kiddo. Come on in. I was just making a pot of coffee."

"That'll go perfectly with fresh molasses cookies," Remi said, holding up the bag.

Lois slapped a hand to her chest. "A girl after my own heart. Come on in, and I'll check to see if Ben's up from his nap yet."

Remi shed her winter layers at the front door and followed her nose toward the coffee. The kitchen was outdated but spotless. The appliances were white, yet they looked as though they'd never been used. That was due to Lois's obsessive cleaning routine. The woman vacuumed the carpet in the living room and hallway every single day.

It was a miracle she and Ben had stayed married for fifty years considering the man trended more toward slob. Remi noted the coffee mugs already neatly set out on the counter, the little dessert plates, and the neatly cut pieces of coffee cake.

Lois rushed back into the room, her face ashen.

"Ben's not in bed," she said, bringing trembling fingers to her mouth.

It was a small house. If Lois hadn't passed him from living room to bedroom, Ben wasn't inside.

"Okay," Remi said, putting the cookies on the counter. "Where does he keep his coat?"

Lois pointed toward the door off the kitchen. "Mud room."

Together, they made a beeline through the door. There were two winter jackets, one bright blue and one orange, hanging on hooks. But there was only one pair of boots on the drying tray beneath them.

"Oh my God. If he went out there without a coat..."

She didn't have to finish the sentence. It was a warm day by Mackinac standards, but for a man without proper gear who might be wandering in confusion...Well, Remi didn't want to dwell on the possibilities.

She opened the back door and stared at the fresh tracks in the snow that led up the hill toward the woods in a meandering path.

Lois made a move for her coat. "I have to get out there and find him." Her voice shook.

The woman was unflappable. Permanently prepared for whatever chaos life had thrown at her. But Remi could only imagine the toll that watching her life partner slowly disappear behind the fog of disease had taken.

"How long was he napping, Lois?"

"I don't know. An hour, I guess?"

"Were you inside the whole time?"

She pushed a hand through her hair. "I went out to shovel

the walk. Maybe a half hour ago? I didn't want to start too early in case the snow started again."

"Do you still have your old snowmobile?" Remi asked.

"Yeah. It's next to the lean-to in the back," Lois said. "I need to get out there and start looking."

"You need to stay here and call the police," Remi insisted.

"I can't just leave him out there. We walk in the woods every morning together. What if he went there and wandered off the trail?"

Remi took both of Lois's hands in hers. "You're going to call the station and tell them everything you just told me. In the meantime, I'm going to go look for him." When Lois started to argue, she held up a hand. "You have to stay here in case he comes back. My mom will want to get all the details from you. You need to be here."

The woman let out a shaky breath. "I can't believe I let this happen."

"You didn't let anything happen. You are doing a damn good job given the shitty circumstances," Remi insisted. "This is not your fault. We're going to find him and bring him home and have coffee cake and cookies. Okay?"

Lois was wide-eyed but nodding. "Okay," she repeated. "Okay."

Remi ran for the front of the house and pulled on her gear. She spotted Lois's phone sitting on the counter and grabbed it. "Here," she said when she returned to the mud room. "Call dispatch. They'll be here in five minutes, and with any luck, I'll have already found him. I have my phone on me, and you have my number."

Lois nodded again, looking numb and terrified.

Remi grabbed the blue parka and a fleece blanket that had been folded neatly on top of the dryer. She snatched the keys that said Arctic Cat off the hook by the back door.

Lois's hands shook as she dialed her phone. "Thank you, Remi. Be safe, and you call me the second you find him."

Remi nodded grimly and bolted through the back door. Her adrenaline surged as she trudged through knee-deep snow, making the air seem warmer than it actually was. She pulled out her phone and, after a hesitation, dialed.

Voicemail.

Shit.

"Hey, Mom. It's Remi. I'm at the Kleckners. Ben wandered off about half an hour ago without a coat. Lois is calling dispatch. I'm taking their snowmobile and following his tracks. It looks like he might have headed toward the woods."

There. See? She didn't need to call Brick for every little thing. In fact, *she* was going to be the hero this time. Ben Kleckner was not going to stay missing. She'd find him and deliver him back to Lois before the cops had even assembled.

Remi found the ancient snowmobile under a tarp next to a garden shed.

She stuffed the coat and blanket into the bin on the back and climbed astride. Even the keys looked rusty.

It coughed to life on the third try. The vibrations from the engine shook her bones, but the gas tank was full.

She managed to shift the machine into drive and, after a few necessary seconds getting a feel for the accelerator and suspension, she gunned it.

She followed the tracks away from the house, away from the worried Lois. The wind, on one of the higher points of the island, was bitter and brisk, already erasing parts of Ben's trail. Her tracks would be easier for the search team to follow.

The woods loomed in front of her, beautiful and brutal. Snow clung to naked branches and sharp needles. The sky melted into the horizon of the hill. White on white. Thick clouds bringing the promise of more snow soon.

"Couldn't have picked a nice warm summer day to wander off," Remi said to herself over the whine of the engine. Glancing over her shoulder, she noted the cloud of blue smoke. She was definitely going to have to make sure Lois had this beast serviced when she got back.

When she got back with Ben.

The trail was wide and thankfully neatly groomed. She wished she would have asked Lois what her husband had been wearing. Hopefully it wasn't white or brown like every damn thing in front of her.

Trees speared toward the white sky above. Boulders and brush shot up out of the snow from below.

The trail crested the hill and opened into a small pasture. The airport was just to the north. But the forest thickened ahead. The tracks were getting fainter, and she urged the engine to go just a little faster. She couldn't afford to lose the tracks.

Wincing, she spotted an empty indentation in the snow. He'd fallen. Or sat down. Then got back up. In another spot, his tracks circled themselves before continuing on.

She had to be getting close. Another gust of wind hit her from the side, stealing the breath from her lungs.

She heard the faint wail of sirens in the distance. The island was small enough that residents always knew when there was an honest to goodness emergency.

"Thank god," she whispered. The trail dipped down and to the right around an outcropping of rock. She followed it another twenty feet before the tracks stopped.

"Damn it." She stood on the back of the snowmobile and scanned in all directions. Had he turned around? Had he followed his own footprints back and then veered off the trail?

"Ben!" she shouted into the icy wind. "Ben Kleckner!"

She paused but couldn't hear anything over the ticking of the engine. She shut it off and repeated the call.

"Ben!"

Silence.

"Ben Kleckner! I have cookies!"

Her body tensed before her ears even registered the sound. It was faint and far away. Carried by the wind. It sounded like "help."

"Ben!" she bellowed. "Where are you?"

There was no response that she could hear.

"Damn it," she muttered.

She zeroed in on the direction she thought the sound had come from and started the engine again. Down the trail, she went another fifty feet before turning the engine off and repeating her calls. The wind was picking up, and the flakes in the air looked suspiciously like new snowfall, not white stuff tumbling off branches.

Another fifty feet. "Ben!"

"Help!"

This time she heard the cry more clearly. Her heart pounded in her chest as her teeth started to chatter. "I'm coming! Where are you?"

"Help me." The plea was feeble, and Remi realized she hadn't thought about what condition she might find him in.

"I'm coming, Ben. If you can move, head toward the sound of the engine!" she shouted. Her throat was raw. The cold stripped the air from her lungs, burning them. She did *not* have time for an asthma attack right now.

Breathe. In. Out.

The engine coughed but wouldn't turn over. Finally, on the fourth try, it choked to life. She followed the direction of Ben's voice and veered off the path into the woods, heading downhill.

She wanted to fly through the trees and rocks to get to him, but running the man down with his own machine wouldn't exactly constitute a rescue. So she kept her momentum slow, even as her heart pounded in her chest. *Go. Go. Go.*

A few seconds later, she spotted an opening in the trees and an indentation in the snow. More footprints. She was on the right track.

"Halle-freaking-lujah," she whispered. When she coasted out of the tree line, she spotted something bright red against the snow across the clearing.

"Ben!" she shouted over the engine.

There, tucked between a boulder and the trunk of a huge pine, Ben Kleckner raised an arm in the air, and she gunned the accelerator and flew toward him. The machine zipped across the snow, rattling hard. And for a second, she thought everything was going to end just fine. But the rattling got worse, and just as she eased back on the accelerator, the suspension disengaged from the right ski.

"What the f—"

She didn't get to finish her thought before the ski wrenched off in the absolute worst position, tipping the snowmobile and Remi over. It threw her, sending her skidding across the snow a good ten feet over sharp, hidden rocks and very not soft tree roots before she finally came to rest on her back.

Surprise. Shock. Pain. They all coursed through her. Her breath came in short pants, and she realized it was too late to prevent the attack. She was already in it.

"Damn it," she wheezed. This is how people got hurt. Her luck with snowmobiles was 0 for 2 this winter.

She heard muffled applause and, after making sure she wasn't actually dead, lifted her head.

"Sure know how to make an entrance," Ben said through blue lips.

She really needed a cookie now. And that coffee.

Patting her pockets, she dug for her phone only to come up empty. *Damn it.* Her mom was going to murder her. And when Chief Ford was done murdering her, Brick was going to get in line.

23

*C*leetus trotted out of the stables, and Brick steered him toward the center of the island. A missing person report was never fun. In the summer, at least they had the weather on their side. Today, the snow was just beginning again, and the wind had a mean bite to it.

When the call had come in, he'd headed off to the stables to saddle up Cleetus. They'd attack the search coordinates on foot, snowmobile, and horseback to cover the most ground.

He nudged his mount into a lumbering trot up the road.

The department SUV and ambulance were parked in front of the Kleckner house when he got there as well as a half dozen snowmobiles.

There was a buzz on the scene. Emergencies always had a kind of frenetic energy to them. But it was worse when it was one of their own.

He urged Cleetus around the side of the house to the back-yard, where he found Chief Ford and the rest of the crew hunched over a table with a map of the island. Volunteers were arriving on foot and joining the planning session.

Lois Kleckner, cheeks and nose bright red, huddled to the

side in a parka. She spotted him and came running.

"Awful glad to have you here, Brick," she said, wringing her hands.

"We'll bring him back, Lois. We'll find him," he promised.

"Listen. Remi Ford was visiting when I realized Ben wasn't in the bedroom. She went after him."

His fingers tightened on the reins. "How long ago?" he demanded.

"Maybe ten minutes?"

The trouble that woman could get into in ten minutes was immeasurable.

"She took the snowmobile out before everyone else got here. I tried to get her to stay put until everyone else got here, but you know Remi."

"I know Remi," he agreed through the tightness in his throat. "What was she wearing?" He hoped to God the woman had at least remembered to put on fucking pants before charging out into a snowstorm.

"Bright yellow coat. Sweatpants. Fuzzy hat," Lois said, waving a hand around her own head. "One of the skis on the Cat is a little loose. I haven't had time to get it into the shop. I'm worried it might give her some trouble—"

"We'll find them both," he promised her.

"Brick."

He rode over to where Chief Ford was checking radios and cordoning off sectors on the map.

"Chief."

"I just checked my voicemails. Had one from Remi." Her tone was neutral as always. Darlene was a rock at all times. But he saw the flash of worry in her green eyes. "Said she was going out looking for Ben."

He nodded. "Mrs. Kleckner just told me."

"She's not answering her phone now," Darlene told him.

His fingers flexed on the reins. He needed to be out there now. Searching. Remi hadn't been through a winter on Mackinac in a long time. Long enough to forget how quickly weather conditions could change. How Mother Nature could take things from bad to worse on a whim.

"I'm gonna head out now. It looks like she followed his tracks onto the trail, so I'll see if I can come in from the other end, just in case Ben wandered into the neighborhood at the end of the switchback."

Darlene gave a brisk nod and handed him a portable radio. "Bring her back in one piece."

"Will do."

He didn't wait for the briefing or the assignments, simply nudged his mount into a trot as fat flakes of snow began to fall.

He was a cop. He'd dealt with missing people. With medical emergencies. With accidents. None of this was new. But the fact that it was Remi out there, not answering her fucking phone? Something worse than the cold was creeping into his gut. Fear.

Remi was out there somewhere. And she wasn't answering her phone. He dialed again and listened impatiently as it rang through to voicemail.

Brick gave Cleetus a kick behind the ribs and urged his horse faster. With no sign of any recent traffic, he headed up the hill and picked up Remi's trail from an offshoot.

Irresponsible.

Reckless.

Rash.

He was going to lecture her until he ran out of words and breath. Then he'd start all over the next day.

Cleetus picked his way carefully up the trailhead, and Brick found himself in a winter wonderland. The trees were covered in fresh powder. There were no tracks here. Either she'd veered off the trail or the wind had erased her tracks. He couldn't hear anything besides the creak of his saddle, the steady plod of Cleetus's hooves.

For once, he wished he was on a machine, flying over the snow to get to her. Of course, he no longer had a snowmobile, thanks to her and his irresponsible, reckless, rash brother... He'd yell at her about that, too, as soon as he found her.

His heart skipped a beat when he spotted them. Tracks here. Faint ones. Parallel lines. But no sign of Ben's prints. He radioed the find back to the chief and pressed on.

"Remi!" he called. His voice rang out harshly in the wild. "Ben!"

There was no answer. He tried her phone again with the same result.

He needed to hold on to his anger to keep the fear at bay.

She hadn't called him. Just like she said she wouldn't. Brick hadn't believed it. Not really. He was who she always called. He was the one who always fixed it.

The idea that he'd lost that place in her life was...crushing.

This was exactly what he'd thought he wanted. *Well, not the missing in the fucking woods in the dead of winter part.* But he'd assumed his life would be so much easier if Remington Ford didn't need him anymore. He just hadn't realized what not being needed would do to him.

"Remi!" he shouted again, the cold air biting at his throat.

Cold and exertion were bad for asthma. She better have at least thought to take her inhaler with her.

He urged Cleetus to pick up the pace as the trail opened up again. The tracks were still intact here. He noted an indentation on the side of the trail. Like someone had fallen or sat down. The tracks paused there, then started again.

"Come on, buddy," he said to the horse. "We're getting close, aren't we?"

The horse's ears perked up.

Brick listened for a minute, then called again.

There was nothing but silence, so he pressed on. Nothing but snow and trees and rocks spreading out before him. "Remington!" he bellowed.

He almost didn't hear it. Almost missed it. But it caught his ear, and Cleetus shuddered under him.

"Help!"

It was so faint, he couldn't tell if it was Ben or Remi.

"Fuck," he muttered under his breath.

"Remi? I'm coming!"

This time, the cry was a little louder. He kicked Cleetus into a jog and followed the tracks. He spotted her turn off the trail into the woods and urged his mount to follow.

"Ben! Remi!"

"Down here," came the reedy cry.

He maneuvered around an outcropping of rocks, and that's when he spotted the mangled snowmobile on its side. Half of one ski was embedded straight up in the snow. His heart nearly stopped then. That bright splash of yellow against the sea of white.

He didn't even realize he'd nudged Cleetus into a run until they were bolting into the clearing.

"Remi? Baby. Are you hurt?" He dismounted and strode toward her. The foot of snow barely slowed his progress.

"Ugh," she groaned from against a boulder. "Only my... pride." The wheeze in her voice scared the life out of him.

She climbed to her feet slowly as he approached. She had a scrape on her forehead that was bleeding. One on her chin, too. But she was *alive*.

"Why did it...have to be you?" she grumbled.

"Where's your inhaler? And where's your fucking phone?"

"Language, young man," Ben barked. The man was

bundled in a winter jacket and blanket, wearing Remi's hat and eating fucking cookies out of a Ziploc bag.

Remi, on the other hand, was wheezing like a deflating bagpipe.

He patted her pockets and found four hair ties, a phone charger, and a wad of tissues.

"Where's your fucking inhaler?" he demanded.

"Forgot it," she said. The strain it took her to force out the words caught him by the throat.

"Sit the hell down and stay there," he ordered, pushing her back to the ground. Keeping her in his line of sight in case the woman somehow managed to start an avalanche or spontaneously catch fire, he moved over to examine Ben and pulled out his radio.

"Both victims found safe," he reported.

"Thank fucking God," Chief Ford responded. "What's your location?"

Brick gave the coordinates while watching Remi's chest rise and fall through labored breaths.

He spent the next three minutes glaring at her while he waited for the EMTs to arrive.

"Here comes the parade," Ben said cheerfully as three snowmobiles broke through the trees and raced toward them.

Brick stomped over to meet them and grabbed the paramedic. "Got a bronchodilator on you?"

Edison McDonough, island native and twenty-year emergency medicine veteran, had red hair going gray that peeked out from under a thick ski cap. He glanced in Remi's direction and reached into one of the dozen pockets of his bag.

Brick fought the urge to snatch it from the man's hands and shove it into Remi's mouth himself to put an end to her torture...and his. There was a protocol to be observed. Rules that existed for a reason.

"You check out, Mr. Kleckner," Edison told Keisha, the other EMT. "I'll deal with Chief's kid."

"You got it," Keisha said, grabbing her bag off the back and heading for Ben. "You got any cookies for me, Mr. Kleckner?"

"Remi Ford. Still getting in trouble, I see," Edison teased, kneeling down in front of her.

Brick positioned himself at her back, standing guard.

She wheezed out a laugh. "You know me. Always...dying to be...the center...of attention."

"Can we hurry this along?" Brick snarled, ignoring the looks they both shot him.

"Well, since I'm here." Edison pulled his stethoscope out from under his coat.

"Is Mr. Kleckner...okay?" she asked, peering over the paramedic's shoulder to where Keisha was coaxing Ben onto a sled behind one of the snowmobiles.

"He looks good," Edison said. "It's a good thing you found him when you did. You kept him warm and awake. Could have been a lot worse."

Brick doubted that she was aware of doing it, but Remi had sagged back against his legs. It helped loosen the tightness in his chest.

"Is this any worse than previous attacks?"

"Ha. Walk...in the park," she joked. But her labored breathing was like razor blades in Brick's gut.

"Don't have your rescue inhaler on you?" the paramedic asked, as if it wasn't colossally irresponsible of her not to be carrying it. Brick's fingers curled into fists. There was a time for bedside manner and there was a time to lay down the law.

Her shoulders tensed, and she shook her head. "I didn't bring it. I'm...fine," she insisted. "I can wait...until I...get back."

Brick met Edison's eyes and shook his head.

"All the same to you, Remi," Edison said. "I'd sure feel

better if you'd let me treat you here. You don't want me having to face the wrath of your mom, now do you?"

"She is...terrifying," she agreed weakly.

"Then let's get some albuterol in you, and we'll go from there. It's too bad you don't have your rescue inhaler on you," he said, pulling a nebulizer out of his bag.

"Ah, shit," Remi croaked, pressing her hands into her knees.

"You know the drill," Edison said.

THE PARAMEDIC LEFT Brick to supervise Remi while he checked on Ben's condition. Brick stayed where he was, supporting her from behind as she took slow breaths that fogged the mask. He couldn't seem to stop his own fingers from toying with her hair. She'd pulled it back in a long tail at the base of her neck.

In less than five minutes, her breathing was easier, and she ripped off the mask.

"Remi, I swear to God if you don't—"

"How's my other favorite patient?" Edison interrupted. He took out his stethoscope again and listened to her chest. "You're going to need to get looked over by the doc. And it's a real small island, so I'm gonna know if you don't go straight there."

"She'll go," Brick promised.

She looked up at him and frowned. He gave her hair a tug.

With Ben swaddled in thermal blankets and strapped to a sled, Brick gave the signal, and the EMTs packed up.

"We're set to head out. Want a ride, Remi?" Edison offered, patting the back of his snowmobile. "I can take you straight to the med center."

"She's riding with me," Brick snapped.

The paramedic threw him a salute and started up his machine.

Remi hadn't argued with him, which added concern to his roiling temper. He boosted her onto Cleetus's back with a hand on her ass.

"You need a keeper," he said, climbing up behind her.

"We both know...you're not volunteering," she shot back through chattering teeth. She was holding herself stiffly away from him, shivering in the thermal blanket they'd given her since her coat was soaked through.

With quick, mean moves, he yanked her blanket away, opened his own parka, and yanked her back against his chest. He spread the blanket in front of her and clenched his jaw as she wriggled the soft curves of her ass against his already aching dick. The madder he got at her, the harder he got for her. Needing to discipline her was a sickness swimming in his blood.

She tried to pull away from him, and in the ensuing struggle, her sweater slid higher. He couldn't stop himself from splaying one hand over her now bare stomach.

"Hold the fuck still," he ordered as he spread the thermal blanket around her.

He tried not to think about his thumb's discovery that the infuriating woman against him was not wearing a bra. There was nothing between his thumb and the soft underside of her left breast. Just full, silky flesh begging to be squeezed, sucked. His pinky finger was wedged an inch into the waistband of her sweatpants.

He kicked the horse into motion and gritted his teeth. The slow roll of the saddle added a constant friction between Remi's sweet, round ass and his granite erection. Heaven and hell intertwined as he finally learned what she'd feel like under his hands.

They broke out of the trees minutes later into civilization.

"Where are we going?" she asked when he guided Cleetus away from downtown and the health center.

"We're going to your place to get your rescue inhaler and the rest of your prescriptions. Then I'm taking you to the med center and telling the doctor to lecture you until you actually listen."

"I don't need your...assistance," she sniped weakly. "I can do all that...myself."

"Yeah. Sounds like you could run a lap around the island right now, too. Would you rather I dropped you off at the Kleckners so your mom can give you that scary look of hers?"

"No," she said sullenly.

"Are you warm enough?" he asked in her ear.

"I'm fine."

They lapsed into silence. Her heart thumped steadily against his palm, and her skin gradually began to warm under his touch.

The snow fell harder now. Fat flakes floating from the sky, blotting out the horizon as Cleetus picked his way down the road.

"I swear to Christ, if you ever leave your house without your inhaler again, I'm going to lock you up."

"If my recollection serves, I *didn't* call you. This isn't your problem."

She sounded stronger at least, but of course it was because she was fighting him.

"You didn't call, but I came anyway. That's the way this works. You will *always* be my problem."

For some goddamn ridiculous female reason, his answer had her relaxing against him. He could spend a lifetime studying Remi and knew she still wouldn't make any damn sense to him. But he had bigger problems to deal with now. With her new relaxed position, his thumb wasn't just brushing her breast, it was pinned under it.

"You couldn't throw on a bra and put your inhaler in your coat, could you?" he muttered.

He winced when she shifted against him. She *had* to feel how fucking hard he was for her with his cock wedged up against her ass like that. Every rock of the saddle was a new level of hell for him.

"No one told you to put your damn hand up my shirt," she reminded him. She sounded better, brighter, perkier.

"I don't hear you asking me to remove it," he shot back.

"I didn't ask you to remove your hard-on from my ass either. I'm too polite."

"Jesus, Remi."

But when he made a move to drag his hand away, she held it in place. "Don't," she whispered.

"Why not?" he asked through gritted teeth.

"It makes me feel safe. Okay?"

They were literally the only words that could have kept his hand where it lay, and she goddamn knew it.

She gave his hand a little squeeze through her shirt before dropping it.

On an icy breath, he tested them both. Brick slipped his palm a little higher until his thumb and index finger cupped the underside of her breast.

When he began to rub tiny, gentle strokes into that soft, warm flesh, she melted against him and let out a little sigh.

"This doesn't change anything," she said suddenly.

"No. It doesn't," he agreed. But it *did* mean he was going to savor these minutes, these touches. Because this was as far as it would ever go.

24

The nerve of the man she hadn't called to come bail her out of a mess. Remi tried to ignore him. And his big, warm hand. And the feel of his hard thighs beneath her. No easy feat as the sway of the horse reminded her with every step.

She was hot and cold. Overwhelmed. Confused. Irritated. Irrationally turned on. And recovering from an attack. It was a festering stew of a mess.

He steered his hulking horse onto Lake View Drive, and Remi refused to dwell on how romantic this would be if they were anyone else but the two of them.

She'd given him his chance. Millions of them. And he'd turned his back on every single one of them. Just because it felt damn good to have that big, rough palm under her shirt was not a reason to thaw. He'd made his choice, and getting himself worked up worrying about her wasn't going to sway her.

Ugh. It still felt really good. Really, really good.

She shifted against him, unable to help it. And when she did, the hard-on pressed against her ass responded with a jerk.

The school appeared on their left. A small, cozy brick building where she'd spent her formative years. Learning that people were different. That not everyone thought the letter L was orange.

All these years later, she didn't feel that much different from the energetic little girl who dreamed of bigger things.

Red Gate came into view as they rounded the bend, and Remi sighed with relief. She didn't know how much longer she could stand being held by Brick without either slapping him in the face or ripping her own pants off and shouting, "Take me, you fool." Cleetus was a sturdy mount, but she doubted he'd be okay with them fucking on him.

When they got to the gate, Brick slid his hand out from under her shirt, his fingers blazing trails along her stomach. Like little tracks of fire.

Wordlessly, he dismounted and, before she could do the same, he plucked her off the horse and set her down.

Tired and mad, Remi opened the gate and let it slam behind her, hoping he'd just go away rather than see the whole doctor appointment thing through.

She unlocked the front door and let herself inside. The snow was falling onto the frozen crust of the lake beyond her wall of windows. Inside it was cozy and warm. She just wanted to curl up on the couch and sleep for a week.

Attacks always left her exhausted. But she couldn't let Brick see that.

She found her purse, a patchwork leather in shades of greens, next to the dining table. Rifling through turned up nothing resembling her inhaler.

"Where the hell is it?" she muttered to herself.

She moved on to her toiletry bag in the bathroom and was pawing through it when she heard the front door open and close, the boots on the hardwood.

"Damn it," she muttered.

No inhaler there.

Ignoring the looming, frowning cop in her living room who was staring at her with his arms crossed, she went into the bedroom and dragged her suitcases out of the closet and began going through the zippered pockets.

"Find it?"

Brick's voice came from the doorway behind her.

Remi ignored him and opened the nightstand drawer. Shit. Where the hell was it?

She put her hands on her head and paced in front of the tiny closet, trying to pinpoint the last time she remembered having it. She always carried it to yoga class after her instructor had told her she was a "boner head" for not keeping it with her. She'd gotten in the habit of stashing it in whatever purse she was carrying.

She paused, mid-step.

The headlights in the mirrors. The hard jerk forward and the snap back.

"Fuck," she whispered.

"What is it?" Brick asked grimly.

"I...I think I lost my inhaler in the accident."

"You haven't had one since you broke your arm?"

It was such a blur. The ride home. The pressure in her chest. The hospital afterward.

Remi swiped a hand over her face, trying to push the images away. Trying to focus on the present.

"I guess so," she admitted.

It was irresponsible. Especially given the fact that she'd ended up in the emergency department with an asthma attack while her friend fought for her life in the ICU. That's when the attending doctor had realized her arm was broken.

Her only thought after that was to get out of town. To go where no one could find her.

"That's unacceptable, Remington," Brick said. He'd stepped into the room, crowding her against the bed. She could feel the heat pumping off him at her back. His aura was probably a roiling mess of frustration and anger.

She couldn't exactly blame him.

"Do you at least have your daily meds?" he asked.

"I ran out two days ago," she said in a small voice. She crossed her arms over her chest and hunched her shoulders against the judgment she was sure he was going to deliver.

Instead, she heard him sigh. Felt the heat of his breath on her neck.

"Come on then. Change out of your wet clothes, and let's get it taken care of," he said.

She turned to look at him. "What? No lecture?"

"I think you've been through enough for one day. I'll lecture you tomorrow or the next day when I'm not so pissed off."

She wasn't going to say "thank you." Because she didn't want him to think he was forgiven for any of his other transgressions. Instead, she gave him a tight nod and skirted around him. "Fine," she said.

DR. SARA FERRIN WAS A TALL, competent Black woman with a no-nonsense bedside manner. But Remi wasn't fooled by her cool, professional demeanor. The woman was wearing Ferragamo pumps in the health center at the end of February. There was a human being with great taste beneath that white coat.

Unfortunately, right now, that human being was judging

her. Racing into a rescue situation with no training. Going without a rescue inhaler for weeks. There would be no lollipops for Remi from the inimitable Dr. Ferrin.

"It was the cold and probably a bit of the adrenaline," Remi said, wincing at the cold stethoscope on her back.

"Mmm," Dr. Ferrin said.

"Oh. And then there was the yelling," she added. "I did a lot of yelling. So that probably didn't help."

"You know what would help?" the doctor said mildly. "If you'd be quiet while I tried to listen to your lungs."

"Oh. Right. Sorry," Remi said. She felt compelled to further apologize but then decided the doctor would probably rather she shut her mouth.

So she sat still and breathed as she was told while Dr. Ferrin moved the stethoscope around her back.

"Okay," the doctor said, sitting down on the rolling stool. "I think you got the albuterol in time to beat a more serious attack. But since I have you here, I'm going to want to run a test or two. Now, let's talk."

Talk. This was when Remi would have batted her eyelashes at the former island doctor and told him a funny story, and he'd let her off without a lecture.

Assessing brown eyes unwilling to be charmed studied her. "How is your condition management?"

"I manage it fine...usually," Remi added.

"You were in here just days ago with your friend who was injured while messing around on the ice bridge. You've got a broken arm, and this is your second serious asthma attack in what? A month?"

"Yes, but—"

"That doesn't sound like management," Dr. Ferrin observed.

"There were extenuating circumstances."

"Seems like a lot of extenuating circumstances to me. I'm not saying that you're purposely making terrible decisions. I'm saying trouble is attracted to certain people, and you are most definitely one of them. However, you did rescue Mr. Kleckner, and I am awfully fond of him and his wife. So that weighs heavily in your favor."

"Did you see him? Is he okay?" Remi asked.

"Mr. Kleckner will be fine. Thanks to you and our fine emergency services. Let's talk about what you do when you're not in the midst of extenuating circumstances. Tell me about your prescriptions, your exercise, your diet."

"Don't you have other patients to see?" Remi asked weakly.

Dr. Ferrin's smile was sharp. "It's your lucky day. There isn't a ton of doctoring going on in February on an island of five hundred. Now, prescriptions, exercise, diet. Talk. And if there's enough time left over, maybe we can figure out when your cast can come off."

FORTY MINUTES LATER, Remi stepped into the waiting room with three fresh prescriptions and a host of medical advice about how she was living her life all wrong.

Worse yet, Brick was still there. Standing hip-shot, arms crossed, staring at her as if he'd been willing her to appear.

"Well?" he asked.

"Everything is fine," she said.

"Good. Come on."

"I don't need a babysitter, Brick."

"I'm not babysitting you. I'm feeding you lunch because you earned it and then taking you home."

"I earned it?"

He sighed and held the door open for her. "If you hadn't

gone to visit the Kleckners, it might have taken Lois a lot longer to check on Ben. He could have been out there for an hour or two before anyone realized he was missing. His tracks would have been gone."

"So I *wasn't* incredibly irresponsible?" she asked, fishing for a compliment.

"Maybe not in this case. Though not wrecking their snow-mobile would have been a better solution."

"That wasn't my fault."

He held up a big hand. "I know. That thing has needed an overhaul for fifteen years."

"Where are you taking me for lunch?" she asked, suddenly starving.

The Cherry Blossom Cafe was a little lakefront place with water views and really good pies. Remi settled into the cherry red booth and rested her head against the cushion for a moment before opening her eyes to study the man in uniform across from her.

He looked as exhausted as she felt.

They placed their orders without making any eye contact and when the server skedaddled, Brick stared down at the stainless steel tabletop.

"You didn't call me," he said finally.

"No. I didn't. I called my mother."

"I didn't like it."

"I'm not apologizing for that," she said.

"I'm not asking you to."

"Then why are you telling me."

His sigh moved those massive shoulders up, then down. "I don't really know."

The buzz of the heater above them filled the silence. The snow outside turned finer, like dust.

"You scared the hell out of me today," he said.

"Why?" she scoffed. She'd been born and raised on this island. She knew the trails, the woods. She understood the dangers of winter.

"You scare the hell out of me every day, Remi."

She shook her head. "Let's not. I don't want to do this."

"Do what?"

"I don't want you to let me in just a little. Give me just a glimpse of what goes on in your head. Because you're just going to shut me out again. You're just going to reject me and tell me I'm not good enough or not what you want or get pissed off about something I do. So let's not."

"Remi."

"Brick."

"I don't know how to be what you want."

She looked up at the ceiling and took a breath. "You can't be what I want, and I'm accepting that. This is what you wanted. Distance."

"It feels...wrong," he admitted.

"Just because something feels wrong doesn't mean it's not right," she said.

He combed a hand over his beard. "That's the least Remi-like thing I've heard you say."

"Maybe I'm trying to be less like myself. Maybe it would all be easier for everyone if I were someone else."

"The world needs a Remington Honeysuckle Ford."

"The world does, but not a lot of people do," she pointed out.

"That sounds like bullshit to me," Brick observed.

Fortunately, the conversation was cut short by the arrival of their food.

She dug in to her turkey breast with mashed potatoes and gravy and a side of lima beans. See Dr. Ferrin? She could be healthier. She could make the effort. She wasn't incapable of trying. Sure, she was definitely having a bowl of Marshmallow Munchies when she got back to the cottage, but the lima beans still counted.

His phone buzzed on the table. Idly, he flipped it over, and Remi saw his expression sharpen.

"What is it?" she asked.

He looked up at her. Those blue eyes focusing in on her face. "It's a news alert. Camille Vorhees was just released from the hospital."

She launched forward, snatching the phone out of his hand.

"Oh my God," she breathed as she stared at the photo on the screen. There was Camille, looking elegant and exhausted on crutches. She wore an ivory cashmere coat and black trousers. Her blond hair was pulled back in a sleek twist.

Relief coursed through Remi as she zoomed in. Camille's delicate face looked very pale and very thin. She looked fragile and glamorous and lovely and very much alive.

The screen blurred, and Remi swiped at a stray tear that escaped.

"Why do you have a news alert set for Camille?" she asked.

He looked at her long and hard. "Because she matters to you."

~

A KEYED-UP REMI locked the door of the cottage and leaned against it. Camille was out of the hospital. In any other situation, it would have been incredible news worth celebrating. But in this one, it meant she was in a whole other kind of danger.

She pulled off her coat and boots and paced the floor in mismatched socks, her head spinning.

On a whim, she picked up her phone and scrolled through her contacts.

"Need someone to post bail?" Her brother-in-law sounded haggard but amused.

"Hey, Kyle. I don't need bail, but I do need some hypothetical lawyerly advice," she said, wandering around the dining table.

"I've got five minutes before court reconvenes. Hit me."

"Say a bad guy did something bad, but no one knows he did it, and no one knows he's bad."

"Okay. Squeaky clean bad guy. Got it," he said over the din of voices.

"Say a good guy knows the bad guy committed the crime, but no one is listening to her. I mean him."

"Unreliable witness," Kyle filled in.

"Yeah. That. How does an unreliable witness protect herself and the victim of the original crime if no one believes her? Or him," she added.

"What kind of crime are we talking here?"

She tapped her fingernails to her teeth. "Let's say something along the lines of attempted murder."

There was a pause on her brother-in-law's end of the call. "Remi, what's going on?"

"Nothing," she insisted, forcing a laugh. "I'm just helping a writer friend work on her thriller."

"Are you sure?"

"Don't use your scary trial lawyer voice on me, Kyle Olson. I held your leg while you did keg stands at your law school graduation party."

The background noise on his end was getting louder. "You swear this is fictional?" he pressed.

"Cross my heart," she lied.

"Then the good guy would need to either find evidence

that the bad guy committed the crime, or he'd need to find evidence of another crime the bad guy committed."

Remi stopped pacing. "You're saying a bad guy doesn't usually just commit one crime."

"There's almost always a pattern," he said. "Shit. Listen, I gotta go. Call me later."

"Yeah. Yeah. Sure," she said and hung up.

25

*O*n a dissatisfied groan, Remi stared down at the half dozen sheets of watercolor projects she'd started and abandoned.

After an entire day of relentless internet searches, social media snooping, and meticulously documenting every insignificant find she'd marched over to Brick's house in the dark to clear her head and try her hand—ha—at some painting. But it wasn't what she craved. The colors were all wrong. The layering was impossible. She needed the texture and color she was used to.

Throwing down her brush, she rolled out her shoulders. Sitting and slumping over a work table wasn't exactly her speed either. Especially not after an eternity spent hunched over a laptop.

She got up and tossed her supplies in the sink, watching as the colors melded, turning into a dark, ugly purple before swirling down the drain.

A distraction. That's what she needed. Something to keep her from obsessively checking her phone for a message from

Camille. Something to get her mind off her friend trapped in a house with a monster.

She wasn't going to find that here. She could tell by the flicker of light on the door that the TV in the living room was on. Brick was on call tonight, so he was probably polishing his uniform boots or something equally anal.

Family, she decided. Family was fun.

Digging her phone out, she checked the time. 10 p.m.

Her niece and nephew would be in bed, but Kimber was a notorious night owl. Surely her sister would enjoy some company?

They still hadn't really talked since she'd come home. She'd been remiss in her sisterly duties. Kimber was obviously going through something, and maybe this was the opportunity Remi could get her to open up about it.

The best way to forget about her own problems was to immerse herself in the problems of others.

She left the brushes to dry on the bathroom vanity, shut off the lights, and bundled herself out the door into the backyard.

The night sky was crystal clear, lit by a half moon and millions of pinpoints of light. She already felt better about her idea. She'd pry it out of Kimber, and they could figure it out together. Reclaim the connection they seemed to have misplaced.

She tiptoed up the street past her parents' house. Old habits died hard. At least she didn't have to shimmy up the trellis this time.

Her sister's place, an adorable bungalow in daffodil yellow, was just one block down on the opposite side of the street.

It was the place her sister had dreamed of owning since she was a little girl. Remi was so proud the day Kimber and Kyle signed the papers she'd sent them a Welcome Home mat for the little front porch and demanded a picture of it as soon as it was in place.

Her dad had snapped a picture of Kyle carrying her sister over the threshold like a bride. One foot on the mat and one foot in the door.

She stepped up onto the porch and found the mat was still there.

Welcome Home.

It was worn now. Frayed around the edges. Some of the letters were fading under the abuse of sidewalk salt.

But it was still there.

She was about to knock when she heard a noise from around back. It sounded like the back door opening and closing.

Remi tiptoed off the porch and followed the walkway around to the fence.

She heard the flick of a lighter. Eyebrows raised, she knocked at the wooded gate. "Psst! Kimber?"

"Remi?" she heard her sister say.

"Yeah. Want some company?"

There was a hesitation that pained her. Not only had they lost their connection, her sister seemed like a stranger now.

She let out a breath when the handle on the gate jiggled, and it swung open.

"Holy shit. Are you—"

Kimber stood in plaid pajama pants and a black parka. "Smoking? Yes. I am. You can withdraw the judgment."

She blinked. "I've just never seen you do anything..." Bad. Wrong. Inappropriate. Unhealthy. "Like that."

"It's my own little rebellion," Kimber said flatly. "I thought you of all people would be proud."

It sounded and felt like a dig. "What are you rebelling against?"

Kimber blew out a stream of smoke into the night air. "Does it matter?"

"Of course it does. If it's a good cause, I'll join the rebellion."

Her sister's laugh was dry. "That's the *last* thing I need."

Remi took a breath and tried to focus on what lay behind her sister's words. "Are you and Kyle okay?" she asked.

"Define okay. Yes, we're still married. No, he didn't come home for Ian's Media Club Awards at the school tonight because it was easier to stay another night instead of seeing his kids and commuting in the morning."

Remi winced. "Does he do that often?"

She ignored the question. "You know what he did have time for? To ask me if everything was okay with you. Apparently you called him looking for some vague legal advice, and now he's worried you're in trouble."

"It's nothing," Remi said quickly.

"Nothing? Do you know what it would take for my husband to remember that I exist in any capacity beyond folder of laundry and raiser of children?" Kimber's voice rose shrilly.

Remi decided to stay quiet. She was no stranger to emotional volcanic activity. But this was her first time witnessing her big sister lose her cool.

"Since Kyle's concerned. And Mom and Dad are concerned. Why don't we talk about you? How's *your* life, Remi? How's your asthma?"

"I'd rather talk about you."

"Really? I thought you only thrived with all the attention in the room on you." A tiny tear tracked its way down her sister's cheek.

"Okay," Remi said, taking a step back. "You're obviously going through some tough things. I should go."

"What's it like being fascinating? No one's found me interesting, let alone fascinating, since before I had kids," Kimber mused. "Maybe never."

Remi started for the gate. "Call me later."

"You and your technicolor brain and your deficient lungs and your whole 'watch me get in trouble' without consequences. How do you do it, Rem?"

"Do what?" Remi asked, feeling tired and sad.

"Ever since we were kids, you just sucked all the attention out of the room."

Remi closed her eyes and absorbed the blow.

"I mean, I don't begrudge you your 'special sparkle,' but I get why Audrey married Brick." Kimber's laugh was humorless.

Remi's head was spinning at the unexpected attack. "What does one have to do with the other?"

"She took something you couldn't have. You could charm your way into getting anything. Except Brick. Who could blame Audrey for taking something that you wanted? At least she got to feel as if she was just as good as you."

Remi was stunned into silence.

"Haven't you ever noticed? Standing next to you makes everyone else invisible. You know what happens when someone like you lights up the room? It makes the rest of us dimmer. And I know it's not your fault. And I still love you because it's impossible not to love you, though frankly, that pisses me off, too."

"I'm going to go," Remi said again. She wasn't sure how many more direct hits she could absorb before she reacted.

"When we were growing up, everything in our lives organized itself around you. Your asthma. Your synesthesia. You getting grounded. There was no other option for me except to be the good one."

"You about finished?"

Kimber let out a breath. "Yeah. I think I am."

"Feel better?"

Kimber put down the cigarette and picked up her drink. "Yeah. I think I do. I should have a fucking meltdown more often."

"Listen up. I never asked to be protected. I left because I was suffocating here, surrounded by people who were never going to accept that I'd grown up. Who'd never stop seeing me as the flighty screw-up who needed saving. I never asked to have fucking asthma."

"But you also never gave managing it a second thought. Because someone was always going to be around to bring you an inhaler or carry your ass to the doctor."

"I was a *kid*, Kimber. Hell, I was still a kid at twenty-five. The only thing I felt as if I had control over was my own fucking body. So I made choices. Bad ones just because no one else could make them for me. And no one noticed when I fucking grew out of it."

"You *still* haven't grown out of it! Brick had to ride to your rescue yet again."

"Oh, fuck off. I didn't ask him to do that."

"Maybe not this time, but what about every other time? The man is your real-life guardian angel."

"I DON'T NEED GUARDING!"

"YES. YOU DO! And now that you're an adult, your decisions can hurt others."

It was a direct hit. The one that broke through her resolve to stay calm. "I know that. And that's my problem to deal with. You know what your problem is?"

"Gee, I can't wait to hear this," Kimber scoffed.

"Your problem is *you*. Your husband checked out on you?

Who let him? Who made that an option? Who didn't throw down an ultimatum? Either check back in or get the fuck out. It wasn't me. Whose fault is it that you don't have a job to give you back a piece of your identity? Whose fault is it that you're unsatisfied?"

"Fuck you, Remi!"

"Fuck you right back, Kimber. You don't get to lay the blame on me and my dumb ass for your current problems. I take full responsibility for the shit you had to deal with when we were growing up. I am aware that I sucked up all the attention, and not all of it was unintentional. I *know* that I'm hard to love, that I'm too fucking much. But in case you haven't noticed, I haven't lived here in years."

"What in the hell is going on here?" The flashlight blinded her, and she held up a hand to block the light.

"Gee. Look who shows up to save the day," Kimber scoffed as Brick kicked the gate shut behind him and stomped toward them in the snow.

"*I* didn't call him!" Remi insisted.

"No, but your sister's next-door neighbor did. Said it sounded as if there was some kind of fight."

"Oh, just fucking great!" Kimber was too far past the point of no return to stop. "Now the entire island is going to know my business."

"Why don't you blame that on me, too," Remi shot back. The adrenaline was making her chest feel tight. But it was the most alive she'd felt in a while.

"Remington," Brick threatened.

"If you reach for those zip ties on your belt, I will not be held accountable for my actions," she warned him.

"Don't make me use them."

"Goddamn you! How am I supposed to pretend you don't exist if you keep showing up?" Remi demanded, shrilly.

Between the cold, the yelling, and her generalized fury, she could feel her throat tightening.

"Because you always need him. You always need someone to bail you out," Kimber shot back.

Remi's gasp was more of a wheeze.

"You know better than to get her riled like this," Brick snapped at Kimber. "Where's your inhaler?"

"Fuck you, Brick," the sisters shouted together.

"If you two don't knock it the hell off right now, I swear to God I will take you both down to the station and call your mother."

It was the wrong move for him to make. Sisters divided were still sisters. And he'd just united them against a common enemy.

Remi picked up a fistful of snow.

"Don't even think about it," he growled as she formed it into a ball.

~

"I AM NOT HAPPY," Chief Darlene Ford announced through the bars of the holding cell. She was wearing pink bunny fleece pajama pants and a Mackinac Police parka.

"Hi, Mom," Remi and Kimber said innocently.

"Zip ties, Sergeant?" Darlene observed.

"I hit him with a snowball and tried to kick him in the balls," Remi said cheerfully.

"I kicked him in the shin," Kimber announced.

Darlene blinked, then sighed. "Let 'em out, Brick."

"Only if you promise not to murder them," he said. "I don't want to deal with the paperwork."

Remi watched her mom accept the keys from Brick. "You two are grounded."

Kimber snorted. "I don't think you can do that."

"Yeah. We're adults," Remi agreed.

"Well, one of us is," her sister said snidely.

"You wanna go again, Kimber?"

"That answers the zip-tie question," their mother observed. "Cut 'em loose."

Minutes later, they were bundled up and booted out onto the street to face the wrath of their bunny pajamaed mother.

"I'm not going to ask what this was about," Darlene began. "Because frankly, I don't give a shit. You're both obviously going through something bad enough to get zip-tied and dragged downtown. By the way, Kimber, the kids are fine. Mrs. Croix let them have ice cream and watch an episode of *Schitt's Creek* before putting them back to bed."

"Great. I'll never hear the end of this," Kimber muttered under her breath.

"Enough." Darlene's voice cracked like a whip in the stillness. "If you have problems in your marriage, they sure as hell aren't your sister's fault. And you," she said, pointing at Remi. "I don't know what the hell is going on with you. But you'd better get your head out of your ass and figure it out. We're your parents. We love you both. But you two are fucking adults and you need to start solving your own problems. Not blaming them on someone else or running away from them."

With that, she turned on heel and stalked off to the snowmobile parked on the street.

IT WAS A LONG, cold, lonely walk back to Red Gate. Glumly, Remi glanced around the living space. There was no one here to talk to. Not that she needed to talk. Not that she needed the attention. She winced and dragged her hat off.

Was that it? Did she require so much attention just to exist that she eclipsed other people? People she cared about? Was that why Audrey had seemingly floated out of her life only to marry the one man Remi loved?

She needed a drink.

Her phone vibrated in her hand, and she glanced at the screen.

Brick: *Need to talk to you.*

There was no way in hell she was having a conversation with him right now. That would only reinforce every accusation Kimber had thrown in her face.

Another text came through.

Brick: *Answer your phone or I'm coming over.*

Ha! The *gall* of the man.

When the phone rang a second later, she ignored it. The same with the second call, too. To ensure she didn't cave, she silenced the phone and headed into the bathroom.

"I'll just drown myself in a nice hot shower," she decided, turning the faucet to scalding. She cued up a playlist and blasted Queen's "Someone to Love" through the speaker on the vanity counter. Stripping out of her clothes, she piled her hair on top of her head and slipped beneath the water.

The steam rose toward the ceiling as hues of red and orange shifted like clouds with the beat of the music. She closed her eyes and pretended not to hear the distant pounding on her front door. He'd give up and go away. Brick wasn't the kind of man to cross any lines or disrespect a boundary. At least not where she was concerned. The rules mattered more to him than the reward for breaking them.

She held her face under the stream of hot water and pretended she was under the surface where everything was quiet, where she could scream and no one would hear.

The music cut off abruptly. "Damn it!" She drew back the curtain and froze. The opening note of a shriek climbed her throat, ending in a squeak.

For one split second, she thought it was *him*. The shadow that haunted her. The slicked-up charm that was only a veneer. And it froze her to the spot.

"Remi."

Legs braced, arms crossed over his monumental chest, Brick Callan took up all the space in the room. He was still in uniform, still looking as if he wanted to throttle her.

"Did you *break down my door*?" she demanded, yanking the curtain closed. A flimsy barrier between them. She closed her eyes and willed her pulse to slow. He was so quiet on the other side of his many walls.

Finally, she heard a jingle and looked up. He was holding a keyring over the curtain rod.

Oh, right. He was so trustworthy and dependable. Of course he had a key.

"Go away, Brick. I'm too tired for a one-sided conversation with someone who doesn't exist."

Her jaw dropped when the fabric separating them was ripped open. There were three veins visible in his neck. Which meant he was seconds away from going nuclear. But an angry Brick was still safer than a smiling villain.

"Excuse me! I'm naked here," she snarled, putting her hands on her hips and wishing she had a better shot at his balls.

The white, fluffy bath towel hit her in the face. "Cover up."

"Cover up? You break into my bathroom while I'm in the

shower and tell me to cover up? What the hell is wrong with you?"

"You," he said. A tremor of rage shook that one syllable, giving it too much meaning.

Of course she was his problem, she fumed, tucking the towel between her breasts. She'd ruined Kimber's life. She'd turned a childhood friend into an enemy. And she'd put a good friend in a situation so dangerous there was no way out.

"You know what? I'm getting really tired of being everyone else's problem. If you all hate being around me so much, leave me the fuck alone!"

She was so tired, she just wanted to sink down to the bottom of the tub and stay there. As if reading her mind, Brick reached in, shut off the water, and plucked her out of the tub.

Her wet legs left a damp trail over his crotch as he lowered her to the floor. Either he was hard or he'd found a new place to stow a nightstick. But it didn't matter anymore. None of it did.

She needed to sleep. To curl up in a ball and sleep until the world was ready for her.

"You're shaking," he observed.

"You will be, too, if you don't get the hell out of my bathroom."

He ignored her threat and pulled her into the living room. She stood there and watched as he found the control for the fireplace and nudged the gas higher. When he started to pace in front of the fireplace, Remi gave up on standing and flopped down on the couch.

"What did you mean tonight?" he demanded, pausing mid-stride to stare at her with a strange intensity crackling in those blue eyes.

"You'll have to be more specific," she said, lolling her head on the back of the sofa. "I talk a lot."

"When you were talking to Kimber."

"I said a lot of things to my sister. And none of them are your business," she said, pulling a soft throw off the back of the couch and spreading it over her legs.

He was pacing again.

"Wait, you're mad at me about something I said to my sister in a private conversation?"

He stopped again and took a step toward her, then shoved a hand through his hair. "Mad doesn't begin to describe how I feel."

She'd never heard that tone from him before. It was brittle, jagged. He swallowed hard like the words were lodging themselves in his throat. But she squashed the desire to fix it, to make him more comfortable.

"You told her that you were hard to love. That you thought you were too much."

The man had fought her off, zip-tied her, then hauled her ass to a holding cell, and *he* was upset that she'd announced a universal truth to her sister.

She tucked her feet under her. "I'm tired. What's your point? What do you want me to say?"

He was moving again. Stepping into her space, he put his hands on the cushion on either side of her head. The fire flickered behind him as he loomed over her.

"Do you believe that?" His voice was a rasp, his eyes almost silver in the low light. A long beat of silence stretched on, broken only by their breaths.

Finally, she nodded. It was the truth. One she'd known as long as she'd known her own name.

"Remington, anyone who *ever* makes you feel as if you're hard to love is a damn fool and doesn't deserve to be in your world."

She blinked. His nearness was taking the chill out of her bones, lighting up the shadows.

"Why do you care?" she whispered.

In slow motion, he removed one hand from the back of the couch and gently cupped her cheek. On instinct, she nuzzled against his palm and was rewarded with his hiss of breath.

"Because you're the best person I know."

His words were like a caress. A balm on some raw spot that had never healed. His thumb brushed over her lips. Once. Twice.

And then he was pulling back, straightening away from her. "Go to bed, Remi." The order was gruff yet gentle.

Mouth open in stunned silence, she didn't move from the spot as Sergeant Brick Callan put his hat back on and walked out, locking the door between them.

26

It had been a long, shitty day.

She spent the morning in her parents' basement when Darlene and Gilbert forced their daughters to prime and seal the cinderblock walls. Apparently adult children could indeed be punished by their parents.

Kimber had barely spoken a word to her for four straight hours.

After that, Remi had gone straight to the island's medical center, where Dr. Sara Ferrin had asked about how many vegetables she'd eaten that week and then cut off her cast. It should have been a celebration, the end of healing, the return to normal. But normal still eluded her.

She'd gone straight to Brick's house, and the brush she'd held in her good hand had pulled a Brick Callan and done not a damn thing.

It was depressing. Her past had caught up to her. Her present was a dismal tightrope routine with nowhere to go but down. And at this point, her future was non-existent.

It was as if she'd just walked into a giant pit of quicksand

and then let it swallow her whole. She was creatively, physically, mentally stuck. And she hated it.

Sweaty and dejected, she turned off Radiohead's "No Surprises" and switched over to a relaxing instrumental playlist. She forced herself to put brush to paper, finally managing to swirl a few oils around in what looked more like brush technique exercises than any real exercise of creativity.

"This is bullshit," she bitched at the canvas.

"Know what else is bullshit?"

"Mary J. Blige! Spence, what the fuck are you doing here besides giving me a heart attack?" Spencer Callan was sitting on one of her work tables, eating ice cream out of the carton.

"It's March 1."

"You're kidding. Right?"

He shook his head and shoveled in another mouthful of ice cream. "It's March 1, and we're both here."

"No. I'm not good company right now," she warned him.

"Good company or not. You're coming with me."

"I'm not speaking to your brother."

"He's gonna be so busy he won't even notice you're there," Spencer said, sliding off the table. He peeked at her canvas and frowned. "What the hell is that?"

"It's garbage just like the rest of my life," she grumbled, swiping the painting off the easel like a bad-tempered cat.

"Self-pity is a new look on you," he observed. "Want to see something that will cheer you up?"

He pulled out his phone.

"Unless it's that pit bull in the bathtub wearing a shower cap, no."

"Here's Brick when I hand-delivered his new machine today." Spence swiped through his photos. "That's his surprised face. I only point that out because it looks a lot like his pissed-off face."

Remi's lips quirked. It was very, very difficult to stay self-pitying and mad around Spencer.

He swiped again. "This is when he realized the giant bow on it meant it was for him. And then here's his face when I told him you bought it for him."

Remi snorted. In the picture, Brick looked as if he was about to punch a hole through Spencer's phone.

"You chipped in," she reminded him.

"Yeah, but it was funnier to tell him this way."

She had to agree. "What was his reaction?"

"Claimed he wasn't going to accept it. I called bullshit and moved it into the yard, and I caught him doing this right before he left for his shift." He showed her the last picture of Brick sitting astride the shiny red and white snowmobile, hands gripping the handlebars, a fierce frown on his handsome face.

"I think we can consider our debt paid," she said.

"Which is why you're coming out with me," Spencer insisted.

"Ugh. Fine. But if your brother picks a fight with me, I'm not backing down."

"I'd be disappointed if you did. You might want to shower first."

WHILE NOT A NATIONAL HOLIDAY, March 1 had special significance on Mackinac. It meant only another month of long, dreary winter before the seasonal workers and tourists began to return to the island in April. The Tiki Tavern made a tradition of celebrating the first with a boozy country Caribbean mash-up party that ran from opening until close.

By the time Remi arrived on Spencer's arm, the place was

packed with people. It was wall-to-wall Hawaiian shirts and flannels. Despite the chaos, Brick *still* looked up from the bar when she walked in, his gaze locking on hers like a heat-seeking missile. Like he'd been waiting for her to walk in.

It hit her like a shockwave. The realization that no matter what they decided, or how they acted toward each other, there was something branded in their DNA that would always recognize the other. She would always feel that shiver of awareness when he was in the room.

"Well, if it isn't Little Remi Ford," someone beckoned her from across the room.

"I'll go get us drinks," Spencer said in her ear and made his way toward the bar.

Remi pretended to throw herself into socializing, catching up with two classmates, her old history teacher, and Kimber's next-door neighbor, who apologized for calling the cops on their argument. She wondered how long she could stay before disappointing Spencer and heading home to mope.

Spencer returned with two bright yellow drinks and a beer, and they made themselves at home in the corner using the windowsill as a table. "Brick said not to let you drink too much," Spencer reported.

That fucking guy.

"Did he tell you about Mom?" Spencer asked.

Remi shook her head. Brick rarely mentioned either parent. "What about her?"

"Says she wants to come for a visit this summer. Stay at the hotel, get the whole island experience."

"She's never been here before, has she?" Remi asked.

Spencer shook his head and waved across the bar at someone. "Never. I catch up with her once a year or so. We meet up in a city for a long weekend or whatever. But Brick hasn't seen her in years. I don't think he ever forgave her for leaving. Or maybe he never forgave himself for being so hurt when she left."

Remi winced, not wanting to think about Brick or Brick being a human under his disciplined, grumpy, hard-bodied exterior.

"How old were you guys when she left?" she asked as Spencer tugged at the label on his bottle.

"I was ten. Brick was almost eighteen. He was gonna do the military thing after high school but changed his mind when she left. He didn't trust Dad to take care of me."

Remi reached out and gripped his shoulder. "It's a good thing he stuck with you. Otherwise you two might not have ended up here, and we wouldn't have had the opportunity to sink your brother's snowmobile."

He smirked. "It's funny how things work out."

"How's your dad these days?" she asked.

"Good. Real good. Started his own business. Seems to be keeping out of trouble with the law. We talk a lot. I think he's trying to make up for all the Before years."

Remi's gaze slid to the bar where Brick and Darius were working the taps in tandem. "Does Brick talk to him?"

"Nah. He wrote Dad off before the prison door slammed shut on him. In Brick's mind, both our parents up and left us. I was always glad he had your family. Your mom was the one who talked him into applying for the force."

Remi nodded. "I remember. Good crowd tonight," she said, changing the subject.

"I thought maybe Audrey would come back for the first," Spencer said, his eyes flicking to the door.

"Hey, how come you two never got together?"

"Me and Audrey?" His shock was 100 percent fake.

"You had a crush on her in high school," she pointed out.

"That was just kid stuff," he insisted, taking a giant

swallow of his drink. "Is that Travis Mailer over there? I'll be right back."

Remi watched him run away from her question. She was just reaching for her drink when her phone buzzed in her back pocket.

It was a text from Brick. She thought about ignoring it, then decided she was wasting too much energy and opened it.

It was a link to a news article, and she nearly spit her drink out when she read the headline.

Senator's wife holds 'no ill-will' toward artist that caused accident.

With shaking hands, she opened the article and skimmed it.

"Camille Vorhees...recently released from the hospital..."

"I hold no ill-will toward Alessandra Ballard for causing the accident. The tragic events have made me even more grateful for my husband and the life we're blessed to lead. We are both happy she is getting the help she needs and hope everyone will respect her privacy at this time."

There was a photo of Camille in front of the fireplace in the library of her Chicago home, looking hauntingly fragile in an ivory sheath. Somehow she made being on crutches look elegant.

Dizzy and sick. Oddly relieved. Her body started to shake, her teeth chattered.

The press of the crowd was too much. The music too loud. She needed a moment to breathe. Weaving her way through tables and warm bodies, she veered off down the hallway toward the restrooms.

She'd sneak up to the second floor and have her meltdown in private. The office door opened just as she was walking past it. Brick filled the doorway, and her feet rooted to the floor. He looked furious. But she didn't want to deal with this. With him.

She shook her head and forced her feet into motion. But she didn't make it a second step past him. His hand closed around her wrist with a stinging grip, and she found herself being yanked back into the office. He used her own body to force the door shut before pinning her to the wood with his hips.

"What the fuck is going on?" he demanded.

"Now is not a good time," she hissed.

"You're shaking like a fucking leaf. Why is your friend saying that bullshit about you?" He crowded her against the door, using his body to absorb her tremors. "Talk to me."

He believed her. He believed her over Camille, over what everyone else would be saying, the rumors that would be flying. *He* believed *her.* For some reason, that faith made her want to cry.

"I can't."

"Can't or won't?"

"Both. She has her reasons. You need to leave me alone, Brick. We've done this dance before." She hated that the weight of his body against hers instantly made her feel calmer, safer.

"Why? So you can date my brother?" Now he didn't look furious. He looked miserable as pain bloomed in those sharp blue eyes.

"For Pete's sake, Brick. Spence is like a brother to me. And *not* in the way you keep pretending to think of me as a sister. But you don't get to tell me you don't want to be with me and then throw a fit when I end up with someone else."

He bared his teeth at her, and she half expected him to take a bite out of her. Instead he shifted gears. "Are you just going to let everyone believe you were the one driving that night?"

She shrugged. "Maybe."

He shook his head slowly. "The Remi I know would have that woman by the lady balls and crying for a teddy bear for lying. So I repeat. What the fuck is going on? Why aren't you burning down her world right now?"

The laugh she tried to force came out as a half sob. "This doesn't concern you. Leave it the fuck alone."

He muttered something under his breath about murder, and Remi looked at him. Really looked at him.

"You really do believe me, don't you?"

He looked annoyed. "I know when you're lying."

"Yeah. When I was eighteen. But I could have gotten better at it. I could be a different person. One you don't know," she pushed.

"I know that if you fucked up like that, you'd move heaven and earth to make it right. You'd have confessed on the scene, demanded a breathalyzer, and put yourself in the back of a squad car if you thought you put your friend in the hospital."

She slumped against him, anger mixing with something more primal. "I did put her in the hospital," she hissed. "Just because I wasn't behind the wheel doesn't mean I wasn't responsible."

"Your so-called friend is trying to ruin you, and you're still worried about protecting her. What would happen if I talked to her?"

Remi felt the color drain from her face. She grabbed him by the front of his shirt and held on. He went hard against her, his erection swelling behind his jeans. "Don't you dare try to get involved in any way. Do you hear me?"

"You expect me to just stand by and ignore the fact that you're in some kind of fucking trouble?"

"Yes! That is *exactly* what I expect you to do! Because you can't have it both ways. You can't be my keeper *and* keep me at arm's length. You can't protect me from the big, bad world while protecting yourself from me!"

She'd never known *want* like this. Never been able to put a label on the desire she'd always had where Brick was concerned. But being pinned to the door by the pissed off, barely restrained giant, she finally had the word for it. She wanted to be dominated, wanted him to trust her enough to take everything he needed to give. She wanted to push him past those stalwart limits so he would finally take what he wanted.

She needed those vibrations shuddering through his body to ruin his walls, release that white-knuckled control, and set him free. His erection swelled, rigid and straining behind the fly of his jeans. She *ached* for him. And hoped like hell he was in the same pain.

"Now unless you plan to use that dick for what it was intended, back the fuck off," she said, her voice low and shaking.

"I'm not good for you, baby," he said. "I wouldn't be gentle or sweet. I'd be mean, rough. And you deserve—"

"If you say that I deserve better than to be fucked exactly the way I want to be fucked, then clearly you're not the man for the job."

His eyes narrowed to slits, and Remi wondered if this was the time that he'd make good on all those threats to murder her. His entire body was bunched and trembling as if ready to spring.

One thing was clear. Brick wasn't keeping his distance now.

As if reading her mind, he thrust his hips against her, pressing that hard, denim-covered cock against her, making her whimper. The tendons in his neck stood out beneath his beard as he gritted his teeth and growled.

It wasn't enough for either of them. When he dipped his knees to press against her center, when he rammed himself between her legs, her head fell back against the door. Again. Again. Again. Desire choked her as her inner walls fluttered, desperate to be part of the brutality of his thrusts.

He stopped just as abruptly as he'd begun, but this time with his hips wedged between her thighs. His cock pulsing between them, his breath ragged.

Her pulse was racing, and she was hot, light-headed.

How had he never kissed her? How had they touched so intimately, shared so much vulnerability, yet his mouth had never taken hers? What would it be like to breathe his air? To feel the stroke of his tongue? To taste his words?

Footsteps sounded on the other side of the door. Their eyes locked, but neither of them moved. They were trapped just a few steps outside the real world. Here in this cramped, dark office, they didn't have the rules that existed on the other side of the door.

"What would I find if I slid my fingers into your panties right now?"

Her mouth went dry, and the insistent throb between her legs became a frantic drumbeat.

"Why don't you find out?"

He fisted a hand in her hair, dragging her head back. He leaned in closer until their lips were a breath apart. "That fucking mouth, Remi."

She let out a tiny, ridiculous whimper.

Oh, God. This wasn't happening. This was one of those fantasies. One of those dreams she'd wake up from and realize Brick Callan was never going to touch her the way she wanted him to.

"Would you be wet?" His whisper was harsh, making her nipples tighten. "And if you were, would it be for me? Or someone else?"

Her eyelids were too heavy to stay open. She felt drugged and dreamlike, being held like this by him.

"These are the questions I ask myself every fucking day. I can't concentrate when you're around. When I know you're just across the street. Just across the dinner table. Just across the bar."

Her entire body was trembling against his. She *needed* him. Needed more than what he was willing to give her.

"Every day, you lure me a little closer. And one day, I'm not going to be strong enough to step back."

"Then stop stepping back."

One of his fingers toyed with the zipper of her jeans. Brushing lightly over it.

"There are rules, Remi."

"I'm not a teenager. I'm not dating your little brother. You're not married."

"Your mother is my boss."

"You want my mom's okay before you'll stick your dick in me? We're both adults, Brick. We don't need a permission slip!"

His hand abandoned her zipper and coasted up her sweater to rest just under her breast. Her nipple strained against the confines of her bra, needing his touch. She was shaking again. But this time, it wasn't from fear.

"I don't want to know what you feel like from the inside if you're just going to pack up and leave. I don't want to watch you walk away knowing what you taste like between those fucking thighs. I don't want to say good-bye to you knowing what my come looks like spread over your perfect goddamn tits."

Her knees gave out on her right then and there. But she didn't fall. Because once again, Brick Callan caught her.

"How the hell should I know if or when I'm leaving? And why does that give you the right to torture me?"

"You aren't hearing me, Remi. If I got anywhere near that sweet pussy of yours, I would punish you for making me wait so damn long. I'd discipline you for wanting to leave me. You're safer if I never touch you. And so am I."

As he said the words, his cock flexed between them.

She was shaking now. He'd put voice to it. Her deepest, darkest desire. He wanted to dominate her. The thought of it, the thought of that big, hard man bending her over and...

"Show me."

He flinched, and she saw his jaw tighten as his throat worked. "You don't know what you're saying."

"Test me. Show me how you'd punish me. How you'd make me apologize for all those lonely hard-ons I've left you with. All those times you had to get yourself off because you just couldn't help it. *Show me*."

She wanted, craved, *needed* to know what it felt like to have him powering into her, making her come.

"Never." His whisper was jagged, broken. And it sliced her into ribbons.

"Then I guess you're never gonna know what you'd find if you forgot about your dumbass rules long enough to slide that hand between my legs."

His growl was a warning that she was pushing him too far. There was nothing she wanted more than to push him even harder.

"If you wanted me like that, nothing would stand in your way. Nothing would stop you from taking me and giving me what I want. So don't stand there and act so conflicted when you're more concerned with what other people would think if you got off your high horse and fucked me."

She shoved at his big, broad chest. Soft flannel over hard muscle. He didn't move an inch. Dear God, that turned her on. She was well on the road to humiliating herself and needed to take a hard detour before she threw herself at his feet and begged him to take her hard and mean. *Just this once.*

"Back the fuck up, Brick. You've said your piece. I've said mine. I'll just go back to pretending you don't exist. And you can go back to wondering just how wet I get. Just how hard you'd have to work to get all the way inside me. How tight I'd squeeze you when I come."

He pulled her hair hard and snarled something unintelligible, but she wasn't about to be intimidated.

"For the rest of your life, you can comfort yourself that you'll never know. Congratulations on your sky-high morals, Brick Callan."

"Fuck."

In one swift move, he swung her around and bent her over the desk. One hand gripped the back of her neck. The other rested on the curve of her ass, fingers flexing into her flesh.

Her thighs quaked with anticipation.

She wanted this. Wanted what he was fighting his instincts to do. She wanted to be the one to push him too far and to take everything he had to give.

The hand on her bottom vanished, and in her mind's eye, she could see him hauling back, ready to strike. But the slap didn't come. Tears, hot and suffocating, blurred her vision. If Brick couldn't give this to her, she'd never have it.

What was so wrong with her that he couldn't give her what they both wanted?

He was breathing like a stallion behind her. She wished for his chest at her back, belt buckle digging into her skin above the waistband of her jeans. But he made no move to touch her. To take her.

"Sorry, Brick. The only man who gets to slap this ass is the one who's going to fuck me."

Both hands tightened on her for a second. Just long enough to give her hope that he was finally going to let her win. That he was going to shove down her jeans and ride her right here until they both came.

She was so wet she was sure he could see it through her jeans. The denim was going to freeze to her crotch on the long, lonely walk home.

Carefully, as if she were made of glass, he removed his hands. He stepped around her, putting the desk between them. His thick, swollen cock strained behind his fly, hands clenched at his side.

At least this time, it was his breath that was ragged. It was a small, pointless victory.

Remi straightened away from the desk. She didn't look at him as she tugged the hem of her sweater down. "That was your last chance, Brick. I hope you don't regret it."

He didn't say a fucking word as she marched out of the office without a backward glance.

27

He was too lightheaded to take orders or make change. Small talk was impossible when his thoughts were filled with how close he'd come to losing his mind. He'd bent her over his desk. The threads of control that had once been so tightly wound were frayed to the breaking point.

"So. You and Remi, huh?"

At the mention of her name from his brother's mouth, Brick flinched. "What?"

"You two just about committed arson with that little bonfire on her way out," Spencer said, toying with the coaster.

"Fuck," Brick muttered. The last thing he needed was word to get back to the chief that one of her sergeants practically dry-humped her daughter in public then yelled at her when she tried to leave. And then almost climbed over a dozen bodies to get to her when she flipped him off and stormed right on out the front door.

Remi Ford was bad for a man's sanity.

"There are rules," he pointed out to his brother.

Spencer smirked. "What good is having your own rules if they just keep you from doing what you want?"

"That's exactly what rules are for," Brick said dryly. The pulsing in his blood was still there. Adrenaline making him sweat. He was like a junkie who needed a hit.

"What rules specifically apply to this situation?" Spencer asked. "You're both single adults living on an island within feet of each other. What's the problem?"

"For one, she's your ex-girlfriend," Brick reminded him.

"That was a million years ago. That's not a rule. That's a fucking excuse, man."

"It was not a million years ago. It was barely ten years ago. You don't date your brother's exes," Brick insisted.

"Really? Would you care if I dated Audrey?"

"Audrey?"

"Your ex-wife," Spencer said. "Would you have a problem with me dating her?"

Brick frowned, recalling a seventeen-year-old Remi predicting exactly that. "Do you *want* to date her?"

Spencer rolled his eyes. "Come on, man. We're focusing on that rule-abiding stick you've got shoved up your ass."

But it was there. That glimmer of interest in his little brother's eyes.

How had he missed it? And had it been there for long? Had Spencer had feelings for Audrey when he'd... Fuck.

Brick turned his back on his brother, pretending to rearrange the bottles on the shelf behind him while trying to decide if he'd already committed the crime he'd been trying to avoid by marrying Audrey.

"You can't avoid the question," Spencer said behind him. "I'm coming home with you tonight, so you might as well just get it off your chest now."

Brick turned back to him, a bottle of his favorite bourbon

in hand. He poured them each two fingers. "No. I wouldn't mind if you asked Audrey out."

"Then I have no problem with you having sex or whatever you'd like to do with Remi," Spencer said, as if it were the easiest decision in the world. "What's the next rule?"

"I married her best friend. I can't date my ex-wife's best friend." He'd stick with "date." It was a tame word for all of the many, many things he longed to do to Remington Ford.

"From what I hear, they haven't talked in years. Maybe since you married Audrey," Spencer mused.

Brick wasn't mentally ready to try to draw any parallels to that observation.

He'd fucked up marrying Audrey. He'd known that, but he was only now becoming aware of just how big of a fuck-up it had been.

"Still. It should be a conversation I have with Audrey first."

These were his rules. The things he clung to when his sanity was threatened.

"Uh-huh. So does Audrey run her dates past you?" Spencer asked.

Brick shrugged and stared at the amber liquid in his glass. "I don't know. But she's not seeing anyone from here. And that's the point."

"What about two summers ago? She and Billy Pellingham had that hot and heavy fling for a week or two over the summer." Spencer raised his glass to his smirking lips.

"She did?" Brick frowned, trying to remember. The summer two years ago, Remi had been in town for three long-ass weeks. He'd actually made up a fake fishing trip to get out of town for a weekend just to put some distance between them.

"Did she ask your permission?" Spencer pressed.

"No."

"So why do you have to get a permission slip from her if you want to strip Remi naked and—"

"Shut. Up. Spence," Brick growled.

His brother held up his hands. "I'm just pointing out the obvious here. You're holding yourself to some impossible standard that no one else would."

"You don't know that. Besides, I saved the best for last. She's my boss's daughter." *Go ahead and tear that one apart*, Brick thought smugly.

"You think Chief Ford is going to fire your ass for banging her consenting, adult daughter?"

"Spence, I swear to God, if you keep talking like that, I'm throwing your ass out of here."

Spencer grinned. "You're into her," he said.

"No. I'm not." Brick helped himself to a surly sip then fought the urge to knock back the rest of the contents.

"Holy shit. You don't want to just have some naked fun with her. You want more, don't you?" Spencer said, slapping the bar.

Heads turned in their direction.

"Keep your voice down," Brick warned.

"Are you in love with her?"

He winced and didn't cover quickly enough. Because his brother's eyes widened. All joking disappeared. "Holy shit, man. Why didn't you say something? Hell, why didn't you *do* something? How long has this been going on?"

Brick shot back the contents of his glass in one gulp that burned all the way down his throat to his stomach. He reached for the bottle again, poured. "Shut up, Spencer. You don't know what you're talking about."

His brother leaned back on his stool. "I thought you two could barely stand each other. I mean, you got along great when we were kids..."

Brick's stupid face must have betrayed him again because Spencer leaned over the bar. "Even back then?"

"She was underage," Brick warned.

"Please. She was sixteen and a half when we moved here."

"Which makes it wrong and illegal."

"But not *that* wrong or that illegal. Dad met Mom when she was sixteen. They got married when she was seventeen."

"Yeah. And look how that turned out," Brick pointed out.

Spencer eyed him but said nothing for once. Brick closed out a few checks and went out on the floor to clean up a table.

When he returned, Spencer was sitting there looking morose. "You let me date her when you had feelings for her."

"You were an age-appropriate option," Brick said. Plus, it had kept her close.

"So when you punched me over the prom truck thing—"

Brick hung his head. "Spence. Please. Can we not talk about this?"

"I think it's about damn time that we started talking about it, don't you?" his brother countered. "I put her in danger. You knocked me on my ass and told me to find my own way home and you took Remi back to the ferry."

"Spence." The memory of it still made his throat burn. Watching his brother walk away with the girl he wanted. Watching Spencer be careless with her.

"You must have been so pissed. Not only did your favorite little brother fuck up like that, I got your girl hurt, too. I can't believe I never saw it."

Brick's chest hurt. "We're done talking about this."

"Yeah, we are," Spencer said, getting off his stool and ducking under the service bar. "Go get your girl. I'll keep your tips."

28

"**W**hat the hell part of back off don't you understand?"

Remington opened the fucking door in just a sweater and white cotton briefs.

He pushed his way inside and collided with her like a freight train. He picked her up without missing a stride and kicked the door shut behind him.

This time, when he pinned her to the door with his hips, his mouth slammed into hers, sealing any protests, any smartass comments, any dirty talk between them.

That mouth. It had spent years tormenting him with smart comments and red lipstick. With fucking popsicles in the summer and chaste greetings where she pressed those lips to his and danced away again, daring him to grab hold and keep her there.

She didn't melt against him. There was nothing soft and surrendering about her reaction. No, Remington Ford counterattacked. And when he forced his tongue into her mouth, and she let out a sexy little moan, he knew he was going to find out finally just how wet she got for him.

Tonight. Now. Finally.

He hadn't earned her. He didn't deserve her. But for once in his life, that wasn't going to stop him from taking what he wanted. What he *needed*.

"Tell me what you want," she whispered, squeezing those thighs around his waist like he was a mount she was urging faster. "Show me what I can give you."

Eyes closed as he reveled in the feel of her against him, he shook his head. "It's what I need, and if I told you everything I need to do to you, you'd run."

"Try me."

His shaft, nestled up against those fucking white panties, throbbed as pictures raced through his mind.

"I need to suck your nipples so long and so hard they get hard every time you see me." The words came from a throat full of shards of glass. "I need to own your sweet pussy with my mouth and my dick. I need to know what it feels like to have you come on my hand, my tongue, my fucking cock. I need to come so deep inside you, you never stop feeling it."

She trembled against him, shaking like she was cold. But everywhere he touched, her skin was hot.

"I need to bend you over and peel down those wet panties so I can turn your cheeks red with my hand."

This was where she would laugh or cry. This was the part she would tell him he was sick. Even as he waited, holding his breath for the rejection, there was a powerful relief in finally putting the words out there. Finally releasing his secret.

She cut him off with her mouth. Pulling him down to her and kissing him like she was drowning and only he could save her. She trembled again, a full-body shiver that made him want to apologize for the confession even while he did every filthy thing he'd ever fantasized about to her.

Pulling back, she looked up at him, starry-eyed and stunned. "Yep. Let's do that. All of it."

He groaned.

"You don't mean that, Remi." She *couldn't* mean that. She couldn't understand what years of yearning would amount to if she gave him access to her body.

She lunged forward, her teeth caught at his bottom lip, and he tasted blood.

"This is where you tell me to walk away, Trouble," he whispered.

Those heavy lids lifted, and beneath thick lashes, those green eyes looked into his fucking soul. Her hair was a tangle of rich, red fire in his fist. "You never listen to me when I tell you to leave me alone. Besides. This time it's different. This time I'm saying yes to everything."

He thrust his hips against her. She let out a silvery little gasp. Music to his fucking ears. "You aren't hearing me. I want to use you, ruin you."

"Then you better get started." She wasn't taunting him. The woman meant it.

"I'm fucking serious, Remington. If I start, I don't know if I can pull myself back." *If he couldn't control himself, he was no better than his father.*

"I don't want you to pull back. I want you to trust me to take it all."

Fuck. Fuck. Fuck. The word echoed in his head as his blood pulsed painfully in his shaft.

Her lips parted as if she could feel him growing harder at just the thought.

As if the temptation of her pressed up against a wall panting wasn't enough, her fingers closed around the low neck of her sweater and pulled down.

He was already a goner. He knew it. But that full, round

breast with its perky nipple was the last kick in the balls he could take. He used one more short, hard thrust to hitch her higher. He was breathing like a horse after a long run as he leaned down. He ran his tongue over that pink peak in one long lick. Just that little taste sent electricity coursing through his body.

She felt it, too. Her gasp had his erection swelling impossibly bigger.

Desperation. It sunk its claws into him, drawing blood. He needed more. With one quick tug of her sweater, he bared both breasts.

She was perfection. Round and full and firm. Pretty pink nipples begging for his mouth. He treated them to what they craved, and when he'd bathed them both with the rough of his tongue, he sucked one point deep into his mouth. He suckled, drawing that tip deeper and lashing it with his tongue.

"Brick," she hissed out his name as her fingers gripped his hair.

"Keep fucking breathing, baby doll."

"Don't fucking stop, please," she begged, bucking against him.

He peeled her off the door and carried her toward the light. He wanted to see her. He wanted to memorize every moment of this night so he could carry it with him for the rest of his life.

She held his face in her hands as she kissed and bit his lips.

"Where's your cast?" he asked between assaults.

"Gone today," she murmured against his mouth. He regained control of the kiss, thrusting his tongue into her mouth just like he planned to do to that wet, tight pussy she had for him.

God. There were so many things he wanted to do. Needed to do.

As if reading his mind, Remi pulled back and squeezed his cheeks in one hand. "This is the first time. Not the only time. Got it?"

He nodded, not trusting his own voice.

"Focus on what you need to do this time, then we'll work our way around to all the want tos."

"Promise me." His voice was hoarse.

She looked surprised. "Promise you what?"

"That this is just the first time." He needed that guarantee. Needed to know he could have her again.

Looking him in the eye, she tightened her legs around his waist. "I promise you, Brick. Don't go slow. Don't waste time trying to be romantic. I want you to take me like you can't help yourself."

She had no fucking idea.

"Do you understand the permission you're giving me here?" he rasped. Half hoping she'd come to her senses. If she let him do this, how would he ever go back to the way it was?

"I do and I want it, too," she whispered.

His balls fucking ached. Brick wasn't sure he'd survive round one, let alone be physically capable of participating in round two. But damn it, he was going to try.

"Trust me. Show me what you like, Brick. Please."

The whimpered please got him.

Their entire relationship played out on fast forward in his head. He thought of all the trouble. All the yearning. All the smart-mouthed comments and the teasing. So much fucking teasing.

He knew what he wanted to do first.

The dining table was empty. He put her down, and just as she started to pout, he spun her around and pressed a hand between her shoulder blades. He increased the pressure until she folded over the table, her breasts and face resting on the cool wood. She was up on her tiptoes, thighs spread for him.

Just having her in this position in front of him was doing terrible things to his blood pressure.

He kept one hand on her back and stared at those white panties as he loosened his belt.

She dragged in a shaky breath when the buckle jingled.

"Breathe, baby," he ordered, yanking the belt through the loops with one quick pull. The end of the leather caught her on the back of the thigh as it shot free, and Remi let out a little gasp.

Dear God in heaven. She was pushing that sweet, round ass back against him as if she'd liked it. He couldn't be that lucky. Brick Callan was not that lucky.

Carefully, he nudged one knee between her thighs and lowered his zipper. His cock, now only confined by his underwear, sprang free in relief. But he couldn't afford to take it out yet. To grip his shaft and drag the tip of it over each ivory cheek. Not yet.

Giving in to the hypnotic taunting of her hips, he let himself grind against her. Once. Twice. Three times.

She was whimpering now, begging him for something she didn't seem to know the words for.

Reverently, he traced his hand up the back of her knee, coasting up her thigh and over the curve of her behind.

"Remi," he said, as he curled his fingers in the waistband of those virginal white briefs.

"Yes," she said. "Yes, please."

He dragged her underwear down, baring her tight little ass.

He'd dreamed of this. Fantasized about it. Jerked off to it so many times it almost felt real. But the reality of Remi submitting to him, bent over a table, waiting for him to touch her was incomparable.

"Breathe, baby," he said again. They both took a minute to catch their breath. The oxygen he sucked into his lungs was hot as his fingers gently trailed patterns over both her precious cheeks.

She was shaking hard.

"Are you scared? Should I stop?" he whispered, hinging over her to press a kiss to her neck.

"Don't you dare fucking stop," she said, her voice as shaky as her legs.

"Tell me if it's...too much."

He rested his palm on one smooth cheek and waited until she'd taken a breath. Then he pulled his hand back and let it fly. The slap rang out in the silence of the room, chased by Remi's sharp gasp. His palm stung pleasantly, and his cock jerked as her flesh jiggled from the blow. Her skin was pinking up like a pretty little blush.

Fuck. How would he ever go back now?

"Tell me what that one was for," she whispered.

"What it was for?"

"Tell me what the punishment is for."

Oh, God. He was a dead man. A fucking dead man.

"That was for smiling at my brother like you should have been smiling at me."

She pressed her hips back, begging for more.

Slap.

It was harder, louder. And this time, she cried out.

"Brick!"

He'd landed the slap on the opposite cheek and watched in twisted pride as a handprint slowly bloomed into being.

He was so fucked.

"That was for making me wait years before letting me do

this," he growled, fisting his cock through his underwear and rubbing it over the spot he'd assaulted.

She bucked against him.

Slap.

"Yes!" she breathed against the table.

"For those goddamn shorts when you were seventeen and I couldn't touch you."

Again, he soothed the spot by grinding his erection against her pink skin.

Slap.

Slap.

Slap.

"Brick!"

His palm burned now. His ears rang with the siren song of his hand connecting with her flesh. And his blood was thundering through his veins.

"Are you sorry you said yes?" he whispered, sliding his stinging palm over her pink ass. Hoping, praying for the right answer.

"Never," she whispered defiantly.

"Let's find out," he said.

Swiftly, he pulled her underwear back into place, hiding those sinful handprints. He shouldn't feel good about putting marks on a woman. Yet seeing his own handprints visible on Remi's flesh made his dick throb. Witnessing his brand on her awakened something raw, possessive, that had him by the throat.

She made a little whimper of disappointment and frustration when he stood her up and placed her on the table. Her face was flushed, lips swollen from his kisses. There were teeth marks in her lower lip. Her hair was a tangled mess of fire. And those tits. They had a siren's song of their own, begging for his hands, his mouth.

"Is that all you've got?" she taunted.

His erection rose to the challenge. "Not by a long shot, baby."

"Then why did you stop?"

He forced her thighs wide and stared down between her legs. "To make sure you liked it."

"I could have told you—"

Her annoyance cut off when his thumb slid over the inch-long wet spot he found on the front of her underwear. He felt like a goddamn caveman.

"Oh," she breathed.

"Is that for me?"

"It's always for you."

"Always?" He didn't trust himself to look her in the eyes.

"Every guy I've been with was you when I closed my eyes," she whispered. Jealousy and pride ripped through him, laying waste to any remaining chivalry. He wanted to be the only one.

"God damn it, Remi. You can't like it," he swore, even as he shoved his hand into her panties. "You can't fucking let me do that to you." He thrust one finger into her and growled when she sobbed out his name.

Not just damp. Wet. Soaking. Drenched.

Not just tight. Clenched. A slick vice, closing around his middle finger.

She spread for him, leaning back on her hands. "But I do," she whispered. Even as she said the words, her walls rippled around his digit, and he went a little insane.

He added a second finger and fucked her as he thrust his cock against the soft flesh of her thigh. Her breasts were too much of a temptation. He couldn't ignore them, so he dipped his head to taste each pink bud. To draw each one into his mouth and suck and lick and tease.

"Oh, fuck," she breathed. And just when he was sure he

had the upper hand, she reached for the waistband of his underwear and freed his dick.

"Remi," he gritted out her name when those small fingers finally closed around his shaft. He was pulsing in her grip, and if she moved that goddamn hand, he was going to come. To prevent that travesty, Brick closed a hand over hers and held her still while he sucked her nipples into diamond-tipped points.

She moaned when her thumb swept over the sensitive slit in his tip. He was leaking like a fucking colander, and she was spreading the moisture over the rest of his crown.

He only had one course of action here. One way to distract her from making him come.

Keeping his hand over hers, he pumped his fingers into her tight channel and used his thumb to find that delicate bundle of nerves between the lips of her sex.

"Ride my hand now, Remi," he ordered.

She did as she was told. A miracle in itself. Just like the one unfolding inside her. "Brick! I need..." She didn't finish her sentence. Remi was too busy shaking against him, whimpering as earthquake tremors wracked her beautiful body. The picture she made when she let go and flew into her release was stunning. Unforgettable.

What happened inside her was magic. Her walls closed around his fingers so hard he was ravenous to feel the same on his dick. Closing and releasing. Rippling around him as her orgasm rolled on. She shook with pleasure while he watched, witnessing every wave that crashed over her. It was a privilege making Remington Ford come.

She clung to him with her free hand as she writhed against him, around him. It went on and on, and when those bottle green eyes finally opened again, they were glassy and unseeing.

He snatched her off the table and carried her, warm and pliant in his arms, to the bedroom.

There were so many ways he wanted to take her. He wanted to turn her ass pink and then sink between her legs as she came up on her tiptoes to take him. He wanted to fuck her against a wall so she had no escape from his hard thrusts. He wanted her to ride him on the couch, legs spread wide over his lap, his mouth on her breasts.

But this first time, he wanted to see everything.

"How conventional," she teased as he lay her on the bed. "I took you for a bend a girl over the arm of a couch kind of man."

"Give me time."

All humor disappeared when he slid his thumbs in the waistband of his underwear and shucked them off. Remi looked dazed as his erection stood tall and proud like a warrior.

"Fuck," she whispered.

"That's exactly what we're going to do," he said grimly as he climbed onto the mattress between her legs, encircling her delicate ankles with his palms.

29

*N*aked Brick Callan, kneeling between her feet with hooded eyes and the longest, thickest, *angriest* hard-on she'd ever seen, was enough to take a girl's breath away.

She'd known he'd be big. Hell, the rest of him was super-sized. But this was...impressive. And maybe just a little bit terrifying.

That first orgasm that had blazed through her, the one that rendered her weak-kneed and silent? The one that had hollowed her out?

She wanted another one from *that*.

She wanted him bending her over every flat surface in the cottage just so he could slap her ass until she begged for his cock. She wanted his mouth on her nipples, pulling, tugging, drinking her in, while his beard scraped her skin pink.

She wanted to be the place he found and lost himself.

"You're doing a hell of a lot of not touching me right now," she observed, keeping her tone light. If he had any inkling how much she wanted him to force that thick shaft inside her, he'd find a way to say no. To decide she couldn't handle it.

"I'm hanging on by my fucking fingernails, Remi. I can't not be inside you for much longer." His confession reignited the fire between her legs. Her core pulsed greedily around the empty space inside her.

"Then put us both out of our misery," she begged.

"First, you're gonna show me how wet you still are for me. Then I'm going to taste you because I've been dying to know your flavor for as long as I can remember."

She swallowed hard. "And then?" she squeaked.

"And then I'm going to sink my cock into you and make you mine."

With that, he sat back on his knees, naked and fucking glorious.

"If you get up from this mattress without what we're both dying for, I will chop your big, beautiful body up into pieces and feed you to the goddamn fish," she threatened.

He gripped her jaw in one hand. "Baby, I'm the only one who gets to make threats in bed."

She was perfectly fine with that. She bit his thumb and nearly came when she saw his cock jerk between the stone monuments of his massive thighs.

"The only reason one of us is getting off this mattress is to rehydrate," he promised. "And if you don't behave yourself, I'll roll you over and make sure you think of me every time you sit down tomorrow."

She was also good with that. Very, very good.

"Now, show me how wide you can spread for me."

For once in her life, Remi wanted to obey. She let her knees fall open and reveled in the rumble in his chest when he stared down at her.

"So fucking wet. Do you like being my plaything?"

Brick Callan was dirty-talking her. She was light-headed with the fantasy come to life.

"Yes," she confessed, her voice shaking.

"Good girl."

It made her feel treasured and tortured. But there wasn't time to worry about which one was more important, because Brick was sliding her underwear down her thighs again. Only this time, he took them all the way off.

He swore under his breath, eyes looking possessed, and then he was slipping his palms under her behind and lifting her up.

The first swipe of his tongue elicited a near scream from her and a pained groan from him. This was happening. The object of her fantasies was...God...fucking her with his tongue. She was raw and sensitive already, and the stiff thrusts of his tongue into her opening followed by long licks against her seam had her fingernails digging into his biceps.

"You taste so fucking good," he said, pausing his assault to bite her inner thigh. "I need more time. I need more time with you," he demanded.

"Yes. Okay," she whispered back as her core turned to lava.

"Look at me, Remi," he ordered.

With heroic effort, she managed to pry her eyelids open. He looked like a debauched devil between her legs. His beard rubbing at her inner thighs as his tongue darted out to tease her greedy clitoris.

"Fuck," she dropped her head back against the pillow.

"Look at me," he said again.

She lifted her head in frustration.

"Give me more time."

"Ugh. Yes. Fine. Whatever."

"For as long as you're on this island, you're mine." His hands tightened on her hips and ass. "Say it, Remi. Promise me."

She bit her lip. She didn't want to make this promise. He'd

hold her to it. And that would put him in danger. Unless she left.

One of his hands found her breast, fingers tugging restlessly on her nipple. "Promise me," he demanded, his delicious, talented finger probing her entrance.

Desperate, needy, and maybe in her deepest recesses, there was a part of her that wanted to make this promise to him. She cracked. "Yes. Fine. As long as I'm on this island."

"Finish it," he said, sliding only the first inch of two fingers into her.

"I'm yours," she breathed.

He sank his fingers into her and crawled up her body while they pumped in and out of her. "Good girl," he whispered against her ear before nipping it.

What did it say about her that she fucking loved it when he said those words to her? She'd worry about that later. After another orgasm.

"Are you on birth control?" he asked harshly.

She nodded.

"I'm asking because I've got a condom in my wallet wherever my pants are, but there's nothing that I want more than to feel you from the inside with nothing between us. I haven't been with anyone since...in a long time. If you have any sense, you should say no."

She felt the weight of his body on hers, felt it anchoring her onto the mattress. Like it was the rightest thing in the world to have his weight on her.

"Good thing I've got no sense," she whispered.

He closed his eyes and dipped his forehead to hers. "Baby," he breathed. "Don't give that to me just because I asked. Just because I've got my fingers in you."

"Then take your fingers out," Remi ordered.

On a groan, he slid them out. She watched in wide-eyed

fascination as he fed them between his own lips to taste her again like she was some kind of expensive dessert.

"I want that, Brick. I've never done that with anyone. I want it to be you. I want to *feel* you. Please give me this."

"You are a fucking dream," he whispered fervently.

"Just one thing," she said as he took his shaft in his hand and lined the thick tip up against her entrance like a kiss, a promise. It was enough to make her lose her train of thought.

"What one thing?" he asked gruffly. His chest hair tickled her breasts as he inhaled.

"If you try to hold back on me, I will knee you in the balls and then get myself off while I make you watch," she warned him.

He grinned. An honest-to-god evil smile. "You're going to be the death of me."

God, she hoped not.

He pressed against her a little harder, and she shuddered as he eased the first two inches into her. Bare. Raw. No barriers between them.

"You remember the art shop alley?" he whispered against her jaw.

"Uh-huh," she said on a shuddery breath.

"That was less than two years of blue balls."

"So?"

"This is a decade and a half. So hang the fuck on."

"God, I hope you mean that."

There was no warning. He simply thrust home in one brutal motion, burying himself in her flesh.

"Brick!"

"God damn it, Remi!" His shout echoed in her ears.

Somehow she still hadn't been prepared for just how much he needed her to take. Stretched to capacity. Maybe even just beyond. There was pain. A jagged edge of it, but there was something much, much stronger. The fullness, the *feel* of that thick member breaching her with nothing between them. It was so *intimate*. So *raw*.

Her muscles rippled around the head of his dick, and he groaned through his teeth.

"That's not all of it, baby. I need you to relax."

Her laugh was brittle. "Make me."

He pulled out and rammed himself back in two more times before he was finally fully sheathed in her. Every inch buried in her welcoming pussy. Joined.

Neither of them moved as they both struggled to get used to the new sensations. Remi felt as if she was being split in half. Yet the pleasure, the joy, the rightness of Brick's body joining hers was unimaginable.

It was so perfect it hurt her heart. All those years of wanting this exact moment, and now that it was here, now that it was more beautiful than even she could have imagined, it was too much.

Her breath was coming in short pants as she struggled to relax around him.

"Baby, I swear to fuck if you have an attack right now," he groaned into her neck.

He was sweating from the effort to hold back. She needed him to let loose inside her. Needed to be the place all of him was welcomed. And for that to happen, she had to relax.

She forced a breath and then another one. On the third, he gave a strangled kind of moan and slowly pulled nearly all the way out.

The relief from the pressure she expected never came. She only felt empty again. "Brick. Please."

"You're crying," he whispered softly. He sounded pained.

"Because it's so beautiful," she sobbed. "Because I *need*

you. I need all of you holding me down here, making me feel safe and beautiful and wanted."

"Remington." Her name was a broken prayer.

Urging him on with her body, she pulled her knees higher. "Please."

When he sank back into her, it was again too much and not enough. But this time, he pulled out faster, thrust in harder. *This. This. This.* As his body rocked into hers, he set a rhythm she couldn't keep up with.

This was what she needed, where she belonged. Taking each punishing drive. Relaxing her body to accommodate him. Giving Brick what he needed somehow gave her what she needed. She hung on to him, nails digging perfect little crescents into his shoulders as he buried his face in her hair and fucked her.

Every thrust, every time he hit bottom, every slap of his sack between her thighs, every pained grunt swirled into an intoxicating recipe for her senses. She felt closer to him than any other human being on the planet. She wondered if their souls were touching. If they were becoming one.

The pace he set was brutal. Sweat slicked his skin and hers as he forced her to accept him. Every inch. Every dark secret and need.

She was ecstatic. The build, the climb was so steep, she'd never been to these heights before. The trembling started in her inner walls and spread everywhere from the roots of her hair to her fingertips. Something her body had never experienced was about to happen.

"I feel you getting tighter and tighter around me. Do you feel how it makes my dick swell inside you?" he demanded as he pummeled into her body.

She bowed back, lifting her hips to meet his thrusts.

"Baby. My baby doll," he breathed. "You're gonna come on

my cock. And when you do, you're gonna squeeze me so tight you milk every fucking drop out of me."

She couldn't see anything but the picture he was painting. Her heels dug into his thick, bare behind, urging him to go faster, harder. She could take it. She would take anything if it gave her the privilege of feeling him let loose inside her.

"Yes, Brick," she whispered, knowing it would drive him wild.

"That's right, baby. Take me."

There were so many pulses of light sparking to life in her body. So many nerves frayed open to the sensation of being dominated. She hadn't known it would be like this. Hadn't known how fucking beautiful it would feel.

His hands were under her again, lifting her hips, spreading her ass cheeks as he speared into her over and over again.

The climb was over. She'd reached the top, the peak. There was a serious concern that she wouldn't survive the fall. But Brick wouldn't allow her to step back.

"Now, baby doll. Now," he grunted as he slammed into her tight sheath again. This time, he held at the bottom. Her muscles clamped down on every inch of his swollen arousal. It had to hurt him, didn't it? There wasn't enough room.

There was a split second when she worried that her muscles would never relax again. That she'd spend the rest of her life clamped around Brick's perfect dick even long after he was gone from her.

But then he went rigid against her, in her. Holding in deeper than anyone had ever ventured, he let go on a shout of triumph. She felt it hot and thick, painting her insides as the first rope of his release let loose.

Her body exploded as if on command. Her muscles loosened just as he pulled out, only to clamp back down as he slammed into her again. She bucked against him.

She held on tight to her anchor. Her Brick as the world spun around them.

Every time she contracted around him, he ejaculated deeper into her. In sync, their bodies rode out their world-ending orgasms together, using each other to maximize the absolute pleasure.

Soul-changing. There would be a definitive before and after in her life. Before she'd felt Brick come inside her and after. It was warm and welcoming and messy and perfect. And she wanted *more*.

"My girl. My Remi," he whispered brokenly as his hips bucked against her, drawing out the last quakes of their orgasms together.

30

*B*rick woke in the dark, awareness slowly creeping in through his senses. His body felt loose-limbed and well-used. The tension that had coiled within him for years was gone, replaced by something else. Something... warm. Almost glowing. Something that spread through him, waking him up and making him feel alive.

The air and sheets smelled like them. Their unique scent.

She was unsurvivable. A man didn't just get up and walk away from Remi Ford. He stared up at the sky and wondered what the hell had just brought him to his knees.

Had he known it would be like this? Is that why he fought so hard to stay away?

There was a clear demarcation in his life. Before he'd made her his. And after. Now.

He reached for her in the dark, intending to pull her warm little body into his arms and feel the beat of her heart. To remind himself it hadn't been a dream.

But she wasn't there.

He sat upright and tried to peer through the darkness. The

warm, glowing thing inside him gave way to fear. Sharp and claw-like. Where was she? Had she left?

An irrational panic sliced through his post-orgasmic bliss. Kicking off the tangle of sheets, he found the bedside lamp and slapped it on. Her side of the bed was rumpled. She'd been there. It hadn't been a dream. He realized she'd slept in the dark with him and wondered if he'd made her feel safe enough.

Maybe that's why she'd left.

He found his underwear halfway under the bed and dragged them on.

When he burst out of the bedroom door, he found her immediately, and his body reacted with a mixture of relief and longing.

She was curled up in one of the chairs in front of the dark windows over the water. Her hair was a curtain of fire that he longed to run his fingers through. Those slim fingers were wrapped around a mug. She had music playing softly from a speaker on the table. Some kind of instrumental jazz. He wondered what it looked like to her.

She studied him with an unreadable expression.

"What's wrong?" he rasped, his voice still thick with sleep.

She smiled then. A soft kind of opening that had him by the fucking heart.

"You look awfully cute when you wake up," she said quietly. "I always wondered."

Self-consciously, he combed a hand through his hair. He wanted to go to her. He wanted to wrap her into his arms and never let go. She belonged to him now. And he was fucking terrified that she didn't understand that yet.

Instead, he walked into the kitchen and helped himself to a sturdy mug of coffee. To feel closer to her, he opened the fridge and added her creamer.

"I thought you liked it black?" she said when he took the chair next to her.

"I thought you slept at four a.m."

She took a sip of her coffee and used a bare foot to toe the chair around to face him. "I can't sleep."

He had about a thousand questions on the tip of his tongue. But none of them came out. Did she have regrets? It would annihilate him if she regretted what they'd done. What'd he'd done.

She was wearing the same oversized Mackinac PD sweatshirt he'd seen on her just a few weeks ago.

"I've been looking for that shirt," he said mildly.

Her smile was coy, and it went straight to his gut.

"I borrowed it a few years ago."

"Remi, are you okay?" he asked finally. "With what we did?"

Her face softened again, and she reached out with one pale hand. She gripped his arm with a strength that surprised him.

"I don't have any regrets besides the fact that we didn't start doing that years ago."

Those green eyes were so earnest he could have fallen in and drowned.

"Are you sure?" His voice sounded shaky to his own ears. He hated the gnawing need he had for her. Hated the knowledge that it wasn't enough just to share his body with her. He'd served up his fucking heart to her.

Remi rose and put her mug down on the small table between the chairs. With one step, she was standing in front of him and then climbing into his lap.

He nearly hurled his coffee to the floor to get his hands on her as she straddled him.

When her arms came around his neck, when her body

settled against his chest, he let out a breath and wrapped her into his arms. Content to sit here in this chair with her and rock for the rest of his life.

"I have to tell you something," she whispered against his neck.

He squeezed her tighter. Something was about to change.

When she said whatever she had to say, they wouldn't be able to go back to before. To now. He wasn't prepared for that. Hell, he wasn't prepared for what had happened between them mere hours ago. Their lives had changed. At least his had. His course altered. And there was no going back.

"Go ahead, baby," he said, sinking his fingers into her hair and holding her face against him.

She took a shuddery breath.

"I have to work my way up to it."

Fuck.

"Okay."

She pulled back to look at him. That sad smile was still there, and he wanted to kiss it away.

"Do you want to talk about what we did tonight?" she asked.

His cock stirred against her as the memories etched permanently into his brain flickered through his thoughts. She'd let him do so many things to her.

"Do you?" he hedged.

This time her lips spread into a grin as a flush tinged her cheeks pink. "I liked it. A lot. Wait, that's not true."

He stiffened again. Fearful that this was the moment it all came crashing down.

"I loved it." She framed his face in her hands and pressed a kiss to his mouth. Chaste and sweet. A reward. A gold fucking star for treating her like a plaything.

"You can't be real," he whispered.

"I kept wondering if I was born like this. Or if it was for you. Did I sense it in you, and I wanted to be what you wanted?"

"Remi." He closed his eyes as his erection began to throb. It was *not* the time for an encore. She had things to tell him. He needed reassurances. Neither of them would get what they needed if he slid his dick into her.

She shifted against him and bit her lower lip. *Fuck.*

He gripped her hips and held her still. "No distractions."

"You have to admit, doing more of that would be more fun than talking," she said, rocking against him again.

He growled, fingers finding their way under the hem of her sweatshirt to grip her ass. She was wearing some kind of silky underwear that made his fingers feel even rougher by comparison. Unable to stop himself, he gave her a quick, hard upward thrust. Then another.

"Brick." She leaned into him, drawing her lips to his and stealing the oxygen from his lungs.

"Baby," he breathed. Fingers digging into the soft curves of her ass. "Stop."

"I'd rather do this than talk," she said, raising up on her knees only to grind down against his aching arousal.

He fisted one hand in the hem of her sweatshirt, holding it against her back and gave her ass a stinging slap with his other. Her intake of breath was sharp. Seeing her eyes go wide and glassy with arousal didn't help his predicament. He wanted more. Wanted to do more. Taste more. Wanted to memorize the sound his hand made when it connected with her.

"Talk," he ordered gruffly.

She pouted prettily, and his dick reacted accordingly.

"How can you want to talk when your erection is trying to tunnel its way into me right now?"

On a groan, he stood and dropped her in the chair she'd originally occupied. "Stay. Talk," he said, sitting back down.

"Geez. Someone might lose an eye around that thing," she said, admiring how his stupid dick strained against its confines.

He sat down again and picked up his forgotten coffee to take a sip.

"Well, that little slap on my ass goes pretty far in reassuring me," she said.

He choked as he tried to swallow and inhale at the same time. "Reassuring you about what?" he asked, mopping coffee out of his beard. It was sweet with the creamer and reminded him of her.

"I thought you'd go into a Brick spiral and take thirty steps back after tonight," she said.

"A Brick spiral?"

"When you let yourself get a little too close to what you want and then you...I don't know, leave the island for an entire summer to make sure you don't get it."

He closed his eyes and leaned his head against the back of the chair. "Remi," he sighed. "I'm sorry about that."

Thinking about her eager hands cupping him through his jeans as he pinned her against a wall in an alley wasn't helping him focus on what she needed to talk to him about.

How could he want her so much when what they'd just done had gutted him, emptied him, then refilled him? How could he want to do so many other things to her?

"Tell me why you left that way," she said. "Tell me that, and then I can tell you my thing."

He heaved a sigh and swiped a hand over his face. "Fine. When we were in that alley. When you..."

"Grabbed your cock?" she offered smugly.

"Touched me," he corrected, shooting her a warning look.

"I knew there was nothing that would keep me from touching you back. I knew that I wouldn't be able to keep my hands off you. I knew I'd spend the rest of that summer worshipping your body."

"No wonder you hightailed it," she said with sarcasm.

"You were always going to leave at the end of summer. No matter what, you were going to pack up and move on, and I'd be left here. Without you. I wouldn't survive that if I knew what it felt like to make you mine. If I knew what it was like to have you on your knees in front of me like a good girl or bent over like a bad girl. I wouldn't be able to function without you."

"So *you* left," she prompted softly.

He pinned her with his gaze. "It was better if I didn't have you. Because then I could pretend."

"Pretend what?"

"I could pretend that what I felt for you wasn't real."

She let out a breath. She was back to looking small and forlorn. But if he went to her now, he'd just end up fucking her against the glass as the sun came up.

He knew her. Inside out. So he dug into his Remington Ford survival pack. "Did you really think I'd have regrets about being with you after tonight?" he asked.

She shot him her "no shit, Sherlock" look. "The thought may have crossed my mind." She watched him over the rim of her mug, and he tried not to focus on the fact that he could see a little triangle of purple satin between her legs when she pulled her knees up to her chin. "You let yourself off your leash. You let me in."

That he had.

"If I did anything that upset or hurt you, Remi—"

"You're still trying to find something wrong with it," she

scoffed. "Can't you just sit with the fact that we did something amazing and wild and wonderful together?"

"I'm not sure if I'm capable of that." The purple satin had a streak of wet in the very center. He wanted to go to sleep with his face pressed against it.

"I just need you to understand a few things. First, whatever we do together is exactly right. I can hear your distressed inner monologue about striking a woman and leaving a mark—"

"Did I mark you?" He was appalled. Mostly. There was also a small, ugly part of him that wanted to see it. Wanted to be proud of it.

"Focus, Brick," she said, snapping her fingers to get his attention. "I'm saying what we did together was consensual and really fucking great."

"So you didn't mind..." What was he supposed to say? *Hey, Remi, you didn't mind being bent over a table and taught a lesson? How about when I pinned you to a bed and fucked you so hard I saw goddamn stars?*

She dropped her knees open and leaned forward. The damn sweatshirt obscured his view of her pretty purple underwear.

"I loved it. I want more. But you have to know all the facts before you decide you're up for more."

His dick was ready to agree to anything. It didn't care about the facts.

"Jesus, you're not married, are you?" The very thought of it filled him with a possessive rage. He'd hunt down the man who'd tried to lay claim to her and destroy him.

She rolled her eyes. "No!"

He relaxed.

"It's worse than that," she said.

"Fuck. Remi. Just tell me. Put me out of my misery so I can

get on my knees and bury my tongue in you before I make you ride me while the sun comes up."

She opened her mouth, then closed it again. "Uhh."

It was his turn to snap his fingers. "Focus. Talk."

She looked up at the ceiling and took a breath. "Okay. But maybe we could cover up your chest acreage so I could focus?"

On a weary sigh, Brick grabbed the knitted throw off the back of the chair and covered up.

"Better?"

"It'll have to do. There's more to the story about the accident," she began.

31

January 30
A few weeks earlier

She'd chosen the floor-length emerald green dress and gold filigree earrings because they made her feel as far away as possible from the rough-housing teenager her hometown knew her as.

But as she'd wandered the concrete floors of the gallery, admiring her own paintings, she realized that inside, she still felt like the same girl. The same giddy, wild girl in search of her next adventure. That next adventure was now.

While her smarmy yet somehow charming agent, Rajesh, schmoozed long-distance buyers—or ordered prostitutes—on his phone, Remi gave herself a few quiet moments alone with her paintings.

Starving artist hadn't been a stereotype, it had been a long, necessary reality. But it was officially in the past now. Just like the girl who'd pined for a man who could never love her. There was a new, wonderful reality to grow into.

The week before, she'd sold a piece for more than what it

had cost her to go to art school. She didn't recognize her bank account with more than three digits in it.

She turned in a circle, watching her paintings drift past. Around and around, a merry-go-round of color and music. Of light and life. She was officially a big fucking deal in the art world. Well, Alessandra Ballard was.

Just a few months ago, she'd sold a piece to some charming British guy in Florida just so he could stick it to an asshole. Remi liked him so much when Mr. Charm came back to negotiate the purchase of another piece his fiancée had fallen for, she gave him a discount that made Rajesh cry.

"Happy?" Rajesh asked, tucking his phone in his suit jacket and adjusting his cuffs. "Because if you're not, you're a big enough deal that you can throw a temper tantrum and make them rearrange the whole thing."

Remi snorted. The gallery had gone above and beyond to make sure the entire collection was beautifully and respectfully displayed. Each painting had a nameplate that included the name of the piece as well as the song it had been inspired by. Throughout the evening, the playlist would run through each song, and the lighting would change to match the colors that synesthesia produced in her head.

It was a sensory experience that would give visitors and patrons an idea of what it was like to be in her world. She approved.

"I still say it would be even better if they could watch you paint something. Have one of the money bag buyers pick a song, and everyone could watch you paint it. They'd drop six figures easy for a piece you create on the spot in front of them."

Remi rolled her eyes at him. "Nope." No one watched her paint. That was a rule.

"There you go being difficult again."

"I'm an artist. I'm temperamental. You don't like it, go sell car insurance," she said, snatching a glass of champagne off a tray.

"I'm just pointing out how you could raise your profile and your profits."

"Yeah, by putting my process up for sale," she complained. "Not happening. What happens between me and the paint and the music is personal. And I'm not letting your mercenary little heart commercialize it." She booped him on the nose, just to annoy him.

"You're missing a huge opportunity."

"No one watches me paint."

"Why?"

"I only paint naked," she said. "Now, if you'll excuse me. I'm going to go eat half a tray of appetizers before they open the doors."

She was mid-conversation with the gallery curator and a couple on the board of the Chicago Arts Coalition when heads turned toward the door.

Camille Vorhees had been bred to turn heads. She was classically beautiful with honey blond hair always chicly styled. Her wide gray eyes had a beguiling innocence to them. And she'd been blessed with a bottom-heavy mouth and the sharp cheekbones that came from generations of aristocratic breeding.

She was elegant, lovely, and apparently she had lost her damn mind.

"Alessandra," Camille said, reaching out to take Remi's hands.

"Camille." They leaned in for an embrace. "What are you doing here?" Remi whispered in her ear.

"I couldn't stay at home another second knowing I was

missing out on this," her friend said, pulling back and giving her a wavering smile.

"You didn't have to be here."

"Ladies, would you mind a picture?" a blogger asked, his camera already raised.

They paused and smiled while Remi ran through the questions in her head. She thanked the photographer and turned back to her friend.

"He's going to find out," Remi said, a tickle of panic climbing her throat.

She'd grown up fearing nothing. Never having to fear anything. She'd had her parents, her big sister, her community, Brick. All ready to have her back whenever necessary. But here. Now. She didn't have their protection and neither did Camille.

"We'll talk about it after," her friend insisted. "For now, this is your show, and we're both going to enjoy it. Now lead the way so I can tell you how brilliant you are."

Remi linked her arm through Camille's and plastered on her brightest smile. If anyone could put on an act, it was Remington Fucking Ford, even if she was starring as Alessandra Ballard.

They admired her art. Drank champagne. Talked to art lovers and critics. Camille stood by her side while she answered the same questions over and over about synesthesia.

Yes. She actually saw the colors.

No. It wasn't like being on LSD.

No. She didn't have brain damage.

Remi didn't let Camille out of her sight the entire evening. Every time the door opened and a man in a suit stepped inside, a shiver skated up her spine.

Warren wouldn't let this pass. Not without a reminder of who was in charge.

Remi had never hated before. Sure, she'd temporarily despised. She'd even attempted a few voodoo curses in her early twenties. But she'd never hated anyone until Warren Vorhees.

At the end of the night, instead of elation at how many subtle sold stickers appeared next to her work, she felt a grim kind of fear.

"Want to come back to my place with me?" Camille asked, digging through her clutch for her keys.

"Sure," Remi said.

"We can celebrate your huge success by packing."

Remi choked on the last gulp of champagne she'd been about to drain from the glass.

She sputtered it down her chin and into her cleavage.

"I beg your pardon?" she said, eyes watering.

Camille handed her a cocktail napkin with a smile. "I'm ready."

"Really?" Remi squeaked. She grabbed her friend by the shoulders and looked into her eyes.

Her friend nodded, eyes shining with unshed tears. "It's time."

"Yo, Alessandra!" Rajesh called out as she headed for the door.

"Not now, Raj."

"Don't you want to know how you did?"

"I'm sure you'll tell me all about it when you take your percentage," Remi called over her shoulder.

Camille's car was glossy yet understated, just like her. The Mercedes purred to life when she pushed the start button.

"Well, that was quite a night. I think the entire art world is going to be saying your name," she said, waiting for Remi to fasten her seatbelt before pulling out of the parking space.

"Let's go back to the packing thing," Remi suggested. Her

commercial success was nothing compared to her friend being ready to leave.

"Warren is in Washington for the next four days. Something terribly important about next year's campaign," Camille said, pointing them toward the expressway, leaving Chicago's cold but sparkly downtown behind them.

"Where are you going to go?" Remi asked.

"My parents' first," Camille said. "I already called my mother. She thinks it's a spontaneous visit, so she'll be very disappointed when I tell her the real reason."

"But they'll support you, won't they?" Remi pushed.

"They'll have to," Camille said. "I have a lawyer friend in town and I have an appointment with her on Tuesday. She already has a copy of the prenup."

"You didn't send it from your phone, did you?" Remi asked. Camille seemed awfully calm for a woman who'd just decided to leave her husband. A man who'd mentioned on more than one occasion that if she did leave, he'd end her life.

Remi believed him. She'd noticed something, a twinge, really, when she'd met him. But he'd been so smooth, so charming. He seemed like such a doting husband. And she'd never met a real monster before.

Now she knew.

"Are you okay? How much are we packing? When do you leave?" Remi asked, unable to hold back the onslaught of questions. Camille guided the Mercedes down the exit ramp and headed toward luxury suburbia and the senator's ultra-modern mansion. It made Remi's semi-renovated loft look like a garage where people got murdered. Well, to be fair, red paint looked an awful lot like blood.

"I'm okay," Camille assured her with a genuine smile. "I'm terrified, of course. But it's now or never."

"Did he hurt you?" Remi asked, trying to keep any of the seventy-five emotions she was feeling out of her voice.

"He always does."

Camille turned on the radio. Radiohead's "No Surprises" filled the interior of the car. Its colors and their textures calmed Remi. This was a good thing. This was what she'd fought for. This is what she'd put their friendship on the line for.

"I'll come with you," Remi said suddenly.

"Where? To my parents'?"

"Yeah. They can't misunderstand you or downplay it if I'm there telling them to their faces it's all true. They can't try to make you go back to him if I'm there to kick them in the balls into supporting you."

"You're a good friend, Remi," Camille said as the car began to climb into the hills. It was a moonless night, and the sky was thick with clouds. The snow was deeper here, and tree boughs bending under the weight flashed by in the headlights.

"After your parents and the lawyer, you should come home with me," Remi said suddenly.

"To Mackinac?" Camille asked. "I have to admit, it sounds idyllic from your description."

"Oh, not in the dead of winter. But you'll be safe there. It's this beautiful, quiet snow globe. You could really get away. No one in their right mind would follow you there," Remi promised.

"Hmm. Will I meet Brick?"

"Brick?" Remi repeated innocently.

"You've never said as much, but I put a few things together. Brick is the guy who broke your heart, isn't he?"

"Can anyone break your heart when you're young and dumb?" Remi asked airily.

"You've still got a heart even when you're young and dumb."

"Ugh. Brick and I may have had our differences. But I wouldn't say he broke my heart."

"Oh, so it was someone else then," Camille said slyly.

Remi snuck a look at her profile behind the wheel. Her friend was smiling.

"No. He was the one who temporarily dented my ego."

"Ah, dented your ego. That sounds much safer than broke your heart."

"Let's talk about what you're packing," Remi said, changing the subject.

A set of headlights appeared in the rearview mirror. High beams that looked as if they were approaching much too fast.

"Remi. It's him." Camille said, her hands tightening around the steering wheel.

"Maybe it's just a drunk—"

But the car didn't slow around the bend. They could hear the squeal of tires, the revving engine over the music.

"Call 911," Remi said a split second before the sound of metal crunching into metal rang out.

The Mercedes lurched forward and across the double yellow line. Camille gave a shrill yelp while Remi upended her own purse in her lap and grabbed her phone.

Camille was crying silent tears. The hope, the plans from moments ago seemed to vanish into the dark.

"911, what is your emergency?"

Before Remi could speak, Camille gave a heart-rending sob as the headlights got closer, blinding them in the mirrors.

"He's trying to kill us," Camille whispered.

"I won't let him," Remi said.

"What is your emergency?" the operator repeated.

But it was too late. The car rammed them from behind

again. The impact sent her body lurching against the seatbelt as the Mercedes smashed into the guardrail that separated them from a dark drop-off. Metal scraped and buckled. Sparks lit up tiny pockets of the night.

Shrill screams echoed over the music. Remi didn't recognize her own voice.

The high beams disappeared around the next bend in the road.

"Hello? Can you hear me?" Remi yelled, blindly feeling for her phone.

Camille was frozen in the driver's seat, hands gripping the wheel. Chest heaving in shallow breaths. Remi's own lungs burned.

The Mercedes was still running. But the acrid smell of smoke and rubber filled her nostrils.

"He's gone," Remi breathed. "He's gone."

Camille was shaking her head. "He's never gone." Tears glistened on her cheeks in the light of the dashboard.

"We have to get out of here," Remi said sharply. "We have to get out of the car."

"He'll find us. He won't stop."

Remi was reaching for her seatbelt when more lights cut through the windshield. High beams traveling much too fast. For one second, Camille's lovely profile was frozen in time, burned in the light of the approaching vehicle.

And then there was nothing.

SHE WASN'T sure if she'd been knocked out or if she'd blinked and the world had gone away. Her vision was obscured by the airbag that had deployed. Something felt unstable, wobbly. Almost as if the car wasn't on solid ground anymore.

Camille's head hung limply, face down.

Remi could smell something besides smoke now. The brackish tang of blood.

"Oh my God. Oh my God."

The music was still on, still loud. But the world tipped. Or was it just the car. Through the splintered, fractured windshield, Remi saw trees and twisted metal.

He'd pushed them through the guardrail. And they were balanced precariously on the edge. How long of a drop was it? Her brain scrambled to calculate how far from Camille's house they were, but her thoughts were sluggish.

Behind them, maybe above them, Remi thought she could hear the muffled purr of another engine. Another car. But turning her head hurt.

The world tipped. Or maybe it was the car. But this time, it went just a degree farther.

As the nose of the car dipped, Remi opened her mouth to scream, but no sounds came out. There was just the music loud in her ears and the first roller coaster hill drop in her stomach as she went weightless. As gravity pulled the car down, down, down.

There was a crunch, and the car's descent slammed to a brutal stop. Her seatbelt cut painfully into her chest.

The music cut off and was replaced by a hideous creaking sound. Trees. A pair of them sprouting out of the steep ravine and stretching toward the black heavens had stopped their descent. But how long could they hold back the mangled wreckage of the car against gravity?

"Camille?" Remi whispered. She reached out and touched her friend's limp arm. "Camille. We have to get out of here."

There was no response. She was sick and woozy and fucking terrified.

But in the eerie silence, she heard something else. A car door closed.

If she could hear that, they couldn't be that far from the road, she realized. Maybe they could climb back up and—

She realized whose car door it was. Whose footsteps she could hear through her broken window. Her breath was nothing more than ragged whimpers, and she clamped her free hand over her mouth, trying to muffle the sounds.

He was looking down at them, debating if his job was done. If he could go home and start practicing looking concerned, then shocked. That motherfucker. Hate fueled her, giving her a cold kind of calm she'd never before experienced. An icy rage took root in her soul. He wouldn't win this. He wouldn't end Camille's life because he found her humanity inconvenient. And he sure as fuck wouldn't end her life. She had paintings to paint. Men to kiss. Worlds to explore.

He wasn't going to take those things from them. He didn't deserve to wield that power.

She let it play on a loop in her head until her breathing slowed. Until she didn't have to fight the panicked screams in her throat.

She sat in silence, ears straining for the sound of his approach. If he climbed down here to finish the job, there was nothing she could do. They were too vulnerable. All he'd have to do was give the car a push, and they would plummet out of existence.

She sat and she waited, gripping Camille's limp hand in her own. Brick Callan's stern face flashed into her mind. He'd know how to fix it. He'd ride to the rescue and save the day. He always did.

She held on to that image of her hero as she waited for the villain to appear in the dark.

The tree in front of her gave an ominous creak, and there

was a cracking sound. Tears leaked from her eyes as she silently willed him to walk away.

That's when she heard it. That faraway, dismissive laugh.

That disgusting motherfucker was laughing at them.

The laughter carried down to her, sounding inhuman and evil. Just like the man himself. The sound of it branded her soul. When she heard the car door slam again, the engine rev and then grow fainter before finally disappearing, a keening wail built from aching lungs.

He'd left them there to die.

Remi blinked through the tears, peering into the black beyond the trees. The car gave another shudder as one of the tree trunks groaned. "Fuck," she whimpered, unbuckling her seatbelt. "Please don't let me step into nothingness."

A thick branch tumbled out of the dark and landed on what was left of the hood of the car.

"Okay. Fuck. Calm the hell down," Remi warned herself. The sound of her voice cut through the unbearable silence. "Just climb around and get Camille out. That's all I have to do."

Easy peasy. No big deal. She felt for the door handle, but it wouldn't budge. She tried muscling it open, but the motion rocked the car, terrifying her into stillness.

"Okay. No on the door. That's okay. I've got three others to try, Camille. We'll be fine."

Carefully, because her friend's life depended on it, Remi climbed into the back seat. Her lungs were on fire, and each breath became like an impossible task.

"How lucky am I that I didn't end up conked on the head or with a broken face," she wheezed conversationally. "This is good. This is fine."

The rear driver's side door was jammed shut, but the one on the passenger side eased open when she tried the handle.

"Oh, my God. Thank you, Sonny and Cher." Her cheeks were wet, and she realized that she was crying. "Thank you thank you thank you," she chanted as she eased herself out into the snow.

She sank in up to her ankles, immediately losing both her stilettos. It was fucking cold. But damn it, she'd been born on Mackinac Island. She could survive a barefoot stroll through the snow.

Her teeth chattered until they felt like they were going to pop out of her head, but fear and determination kept her warm as she slipped and slid her way around to the front of the car. Only one lonely headlight illuminated the dark. Smoke and snow glowed eerily in the beam. Beyond it was nothing but a dark void.

In order to get to Camille, she was going to have to crawl in front of the car. The car that was suspended by two skinny, splintered saplings.

Her breath coming in wheezes, Remi slid and scooted her way along the hood. She wrapped her hands around the first tree and scooted forward, her foot catching on a rock. Pain warred with the numbness. Air became a precious commodity.

Another foot forward. Another tree. This one was leaning hard toward the valley or ravine below. She was almost grateful for the dark. Almost relieved that she couldn't see what was waiting for her below.

The tree gave another groan, and the carcass of the car slid forward another inch.

"Fuck. Fuck. Fuck," she whispered. Picking her way carefully around the base of the tree, her heart pounded so loud it sounded like a drum beat.

This was fear. She'd never experienced anything like it

before. Never come face-to-face with her own potential demise.

It wasn't fun. She didn't recommend it. But everything that had mattered to her to this point stretched out in front of her in a glorious kind of clarity. Mackinac. Her parents and sister. Brick. The way she felt when her brush moved across the canvas, erasing the blank whiteness, fulfilling potential.

She thought of the things she loved. The people she loved. Of cold Vernor's on a hot day and red lipstick. She wanted more. More of all of it.

She wanted to be loved.

She wanted to live.

She let out a broken cry when she finally made it around the car, crawling her way up the steep grade to Camille's door.

"For the love of Ella Fitzgerald," she whispered and wrapped her frozen fingers around the handle.

Tears froze to her cheeks as the door creaked open. Then she realized it wasn't the door, it was the tree. There was a horrible splintering noise and then a groan.

It was going to give. And without that anchor, the car could fall.

Now or never. She reached inside, pushing the airbag down and fumbling for Camille's seatbelt. Her friend was still horrifically motionless.

Don't move an accident victim, she heard her mother's voice clear as day in her head.

But it was either move Camille now or watch the car plummet to the bottom of a goddamn ravine.

The car slid another few inches forward, dragging Remi's feet with it.

It took a long moment before she realized that the broken sobs she heard were coming from her.

"Come on, Camille. We're not letting him win. This is not the end!"

Her fingers finally found the buckle and released it. Trying to figure out the best way to pull her friend from the car, planning swiftly changed to action when the first tree gave up its fight and cut through the beam of the headlight in slow motion.

"Shit!" Remi grabbed Camille by the shoulders and heaved.

She fell over backward, awkwardly dragging her friend's unconscious body with her. She barely had time to get them both clear before the wreckage shifted and slid. Only this time, it didn't stop. The weight was too much for the broken tree to bear.

With a terrifying snap, the tree and car disappeared into the black.

They were sliding, too. Slipping into nothingness as the wreckage crashed and crumpled its way down the steep incline. With one arm looped around Camille's chest, Remi scrambled for a grip with her other.

Her arm struck something. Hard. She only imagined the sound of the snap, Remi told herself as pain lit up numb nerves.

Through the pain, she managed to curl her arm awkwardly around the thing, arresting their decent. She dug her heels in. And tried to breathe. Tried to think of what next.

The guardrail and road were above them. Somewhere. She didn't know if it was danger or safety that waited.

"Fuck," she whimpered through chattering teeth.

She closed her eyes and pictured her parents' kitchen. The place she was happiest. She'd missed Christmas with them. Why hadn't she gone home? Because she'd found out about Warren, she reminded herself. She found out her friend was married to a monster and didn't want her to be alone with him.

What if that had been her last chance at Christmas morning with her family and the monster still won?

"NO!" she sobbed out the denial.

He wasn't stealing anything else from her or Camille.

"Camille, we are going to climb up there, get some help, and we are going to put that motherfucker behind bars," Remi whispered. Her friend remained motionless in her grasp.

"I know I give you shit for being so thin. But it really worked out in your favor tonight," she said as she carefully set her heels in the snow and scooted a few inches up the incline. When she felt her footing was secure, she released her grip on the rock. Her arm sang when she tucked it under Camille's. But it was either feel pain and move or feel pain and freeze to fucking death on the side of a ravine.

Or pass out from an asthma attack and let them both tumble into the dark.

Gritting her teeth, she leaned back, pulling Camille with her. Again and again. Inch by inch. There was no time. Only distance. Darkness. Cold. The hitching sound of her own labored breathing.

And then there was a flicker. Blue. Then red. Again and again. It landed on the brush surrounding them, lighting up the fog, painting the snow and her breath. Blue. Red.

There were voices now. And more lights.

Her heart sang. She wanted to call out, but her lungs wouldn't allow her to suck in enough air. So she hung on to her friend's limp body and sent up a silent prayer.

When her eyes opened, a beam of bright light blinded her. *Was she dying? Was this officially it?*

"I've got two vics on the slope," a voice reported.

"Get me a rope and the sled," someone else barked.

Remi squinted up into the light, still clinging to Camille. They were safe.

She'd tell the police everything, and they would go break down Warren's door and arrest him. She'd go with them and kick him in his motherfucking balls.

That's when she noticed the tall shadow looming over the guardrail.

"Senator, we need you to step back."

32

"Remi." Her name fell from his mouth in two strangled syllables.

He was pacing in front of her without even remembering rising while she told him her story.

He wanted to pick her up in his arms, promise her that no one would ever get that close to hurting her again. He wanted to fly to Chicago and break every fucking bone in Warren Fucking Vorhees' body.

He wanted to carry her across the street, lock her in his house, and stand guard.

As a cop, he knew how dangerous domestic disputes could be. How quickly they could go sideways. The thought of Remi putting herself between a friend and a fucking monster took ten years off his life.

"Are you okay?" she asked, those jade green eyes searching his face.

Brick stopped mid-stride and pinched the bridge of his nose between his fingers. He would never be okay again.

"Do you want some water or something?"

"Just…give me a minute," he said, finally managing to

choke the words out. Visions of her, restrained by a seatbelt, holding her friend's hand as she tried not to cry out. As she waited for a madman to end her life.

She nodded and picked up her coffee. And waited for him to calm down enough to pretend she hadn't shattered his goddamn world for the second time in one night.

He would fucking fix this. He would make sure she was never alone in the dark again. Never faced an enemy alone. Never without a protector.

"So Vorhees was with the first responders on the scene?" Brick asked, trying to shift into cop mode. His hands fisted at his side, and he realized it was impossible. There was no way to be objective about the man who had tried to murder two innocent women. Especially not when one of them was his. There was no justice swift enough for that. Would he be satisfied with putting this animal in a cage for the rest of his life? Would the law give him the vengeance he needed to protect Remi? That gray area that lived between right and wrong suddenly began to make sense to him.

"Yes," she said, answering his question. "It's kind of a blur. But he was there with the cops. I think he spun some story about flying home to surprise her. When he realized she wasn't there, he got worried and tried to track her phone."

"So his story is he flew home, tracked her phone, and called the cops?" Brick summarized.

Remi nodded.

"What happened when they pulled you up?"

She wrinkled her nose. "Well, you won't be surprised to know I did something stupid," she confessed.

He wished he could sit with her and hold her. But he was afraid to touch her with this much rage flooding his system. "Just tell me what happened, baby."

So he could finish having this aneurysm, turn in his badge, and go beat a man to death.

"They pulled Camille up first on a sled—she was still unconscious—and then they helped pull me up. When I got to the top, I was understandably distraught."

Brick remained silent and waited for her to collect her thoughts.

"I kind of lunged at Warren and called him something like a tiny-pricked sociopath with no balls."

"Jesus, Remi."

"Oh, he played it cool. Pretended to be the devastated husband. Played the part. But I saw it in his eyes. That dead-eyed stare. There's nothing inside him. Nothing human, at least."

"What happened then?"

"It took an EMT and a cop to pull me off him. He told the officers I'd obviously been drinking. Then he asked me how fast I'd been going as if I had been the one driving."

Brick swore under his breath.

"I told them I wasn't driving. But I think it got drowned out in the midst of me trying to tell them what he'd done. That he hurt her. That he'd forced us off the road. That he'd stood there to make sure there were no survivors."

"They didn't take you seriously?" he demanded.

"I was half-frozen and most of the way hysterical. Plus I couldn't catch my breath. So I probably looked a little unhinged. But he went all buddy-guy with the cops. 'Obviously my wife's friend is distraught. She's been drinking. She has a substance abuse problem blah blah blah.'"

"Fuck," he murmured, rubbing the back of his neck.

"A trooper drove me home."

"You mean to the hospital," Brick prompted.

She shook her head. "No. He drove me home. Since I didn't seem to be hurt."

"You broke your fucking arm." His facade of calm was showing Grand Canyon-sized cracks.

"Well, I didn't know that at the time. I was more worried about Camille and terrified that he was going to off her in the ambulance or at the hospital. I tried to tell the cop—Trooper Martinez—the whole story again, but I sounded hysterical even to myself. I did get him to give me a breathalyzer though, which I passed."

"So a cop drives you home, and then what?"

"Raj, my agent, showed up at my condo with a bottle of champagne, wanting to celebrate."

His hands clenched to fists on the word "celebrate."

"Easy, big guy. Not like that," Remi assured him, then frowned. "At least I don't think so. He sure does call a lot though."

He shook his head, deciding to file away the agent issue for later. "He shows up at your place, and then what happened?" he prompted.

"I was trying to change my clothes so I could go to the hospital. I didn't want to leave Warren alone with her. I was hyperventilating a little." He pinned her with a stare. She rolled her eyes. "Fine. A lot. He overreacted, called an ambulance, and they took me to the emergency department."

"That's where they discovered your arm was broken."

"Yes. It's also where I was escorted out by security after causing a scene in the trauma bay where they were stabilizing Camille. Raj stopped me from kneeing Warren in the balls. I haven't forgiven him for that yet."

She was getting worked up—he could tell by the hitch in her voice.

"Someone called for security, and Warren pretended to

help Raj restrain me. He leaned in real close and he told me if I caused him any trouble at all, he'd take it out on Camille. He said her life depended on me."

That fucking piece of shit was going to wish he'd never been born. Brick was going to make sure of it. He was going to destroy the man.

There were more questions. But they could wait, he decided. Enough of the pieces had fit together to give him a clearer picture to decide what happened next. He already knew Remington wasn't going to like it.

"We were talking about you when it happened," she said, her smile a little dreamy as she rested her chin on her knees. "Camille and I. Now, here we are. It's ironic, isn't it?"

It wasn't ironic or coincidental. He and Remi had been drawn together since the day they met. She belonged to him.

That's why she'd walked into his arms her first day back. Why she'd chosen the house across the street. Why she'd shared her bed and her secrets with him.

Jesus. She wouldn't have told him, he realized.

"Would you have told me this if we hadn't slept together?" he demanded, stopping in front of her and putting his hands on the arms of her chair.

She looked way up at him, amused. "No."

Just the possibility of that what-if had his blood pressure spiking.

"Are you okay?" she asked again. "You're breathing kind of heavy."

He closed his eyes. "I'm fine," he lied.

"You really don't sound fine. How about I get you that water? Or maybe some cookies?"

He plucked her out of the chair and carried her over to the couch, where he sat with her in his lap and tried not to crush her against his chest.

"Do you believe me?" she asked, her fingers toying with the hair at the back of his neck.

"Of course I believe you."

She relaxed against him, seemingly oblivious to the fact that he was a ticking time bomb about to go off.

"What was your plan?" he asked, trying to keep his voice neutral. If he knew one thing about Remi, she would never allow the man to walk the earth consequence-free.

"My plan is to go back to Chicago and confront—"

"No." The word came out ice-cold, casting a chill over the room.

"No?" she repeated.

"That's never going to happen," he said firmly, consciously loosening his grip on her. "You aren't going near this man," he told her. "Not ever again."

"But—"

"No."

"Brick," she sighed.

He gave her a squeeze. "Remington. You shared your secret with me. Now we'll work on a solution that doesn't put you in harm's way."

"We?" she asked, looking at him with hope in her eyes.

"We," he sighed.

"You're not going to tell my mom are you?"

It was such a 16-year-old Remi thing to say that he lowered his forehead to hers. "I'm not making that promise."

She started to squirm in his lap. Intending to challenge him. To argue. It had the unintended consequence of making him go stone-hard.

She moved to stand, but he stopped her, pulling her over his thighs so she straddled him. He slammed her down against his erection and held her hips still.

"Stop it," he enunciated.

He saw the light of rebellion and lust in her eyes as her lids went heavy. Her lips parted.

There were so many things that he needed to do. So many things he needed to say. But in that moment, he had one priority. He needed to remind Remington just who she belonged to. Who she gave herself—problems, secrets, and all—to.

"Brick," she said, more breathlessly this time.

Using her hips like handles, he dragged her over his arousal and back down.

Her breath caught in her throat.

"Are you sore?" he asked gruffly.

She shook her head even as she whispered, "Yes."

"We should sleep," he said, repeating the motion but adding a thrust of his hips.

"We should?"

The motion was sliding the waistband of his underwear down enough to release the head of his penis. Her whimper had him throbbing, and he couldn't stand not being inside her a moment longer. He stripped the sweatshirt over her head and tugged those silky purple panties to the side.

When Remi's eager fingers wrapped around his thick shaft, guiding it between her legs, his head fell back against the cushion. The kiss of her core, wet and warm, around his tip sent a fire racing through his body. He was being invited back to heaven.

"Slow." His whisper was harsh as she tensed around him, lowering herself onto his aching dick.

So fucking tight. Remi's channel gripped his erection in a velvet fist and squeezed. Every nerve ending was fired up. There was so much to feel. Pleasure at finally being where he'd dreamed of for so long. Pain for not being deep enough. *Yet.*

"Baby, you're not ready to take all of me yet," he warned her, tightening his grip on her hips.

"You sure about that?" She gritted out the words as she sank lower to take more of him.

She was going to be the death of him. He should go slow, make this special for her.

Brick stilled, holding there, reveling in the possession. Her muscles quivered around him, electrifying his senses. Making him crazy with the need to rut. To forget everything but the way her body welcomed him.

Being this deep in her had his arousal swelling, stretching her even farther.

He'd finally found his way home.

She was chanting his name over and over again.

"Are you okay? Am I hurting you?" When she didn't answer him right away, he nipped her shoulder. Hard. "Answer me."

"I didn't know," she said on a broken whisper.

"Didn't know what?"

Those jade green eyes fluttered open and locked on to his face. "How *right* it would feel," she confessed.

His cock flexed inside her at the confession. It *was* right. This was everything he'd ever wanted and so much more than he'd known was possible.

And he'd almost lost her before he ever had her. The realization terrified him to his soul.

"Baby doll, I need to move."

"Move. Fast and hard," she ordered. "Make me yours."

"You *are* mine." There would be nothing else between them from now on. He gave a testing thrust that had her writhing against him, loosening his tenuous grip on sanity, chivalry.

"Spoiler alert: I'm gonna come real fast, Brick."

"That's just the first time."

"Thank God you're not all talk," she said through trembling lips.

He dug his fingers into her hips. "You asked for it. If it's too much, you tell me to stop."

"I want too much. I need you to give me too much. Don't let me think about anything else."

There was no holding back. Not with her permission snapping the leash he had on his control. Not with the sinful slide of her as he pulled out and the slick victory of slamming back into her. His hips worked into a wild rhythm that had nothing to do with finesse.

His balls slapped against her as he lunged into her. Unrelenting.

He couldn't get deep enough, couldn't go hard enough. He needed to erase the distance between them. She came immediately, choking his cock so hard with her inner walls he almost poured himself into her then and there. But he held on —barely—and rode out the ripples of her pussy.

"Fuck, you're good at this," she gasped, trying to catch her breath. "Would it be greedy if I asked for another one?"

He gripped her jaw and throat with one big hand. "You will ask me for anything you want. And I'll give it to you. Do you understand?"

She sank her teeth into her lower lip while he leisurely fucked her.

"Do you understand?" he repeated, tightening his hold on her just a fraction.

There was a glimmer of excitement in her eyes when she nodded. "Yes, Brick."

"Good girl. Now tell me what you want."

She looked triumphant, and he wondered if he'd walked into one of her little traps. "I want you to bend me over the arm of this couch and fuck me until you come so hard you can't stand up."

He went a little mad then. Because he didn't remember standing up or folding her over the rounded arm of the couch. But he did come back to himself to appreciate in exquisite detail peeling those underwear off her behind and down her legs. His eyes feasting on the subtle souvenirs his hands had left on her soft skin.

He trailed his fingertips over her back, her ass, her thighs, until goose bumps rose over every inch of her skin. Going slowly now, because once he was seated inside her, there would be no slow, no gentle, no savoring. He pushed her hips a little higher on the arm, bringing her to her tiptoes so he could line up with her entrance.

It was fucking hypnotic, watching the first two inches of his cock slide into her. "So fucking tight. Are you going to make me work for it?"

She moaned impatiently into the cushion and bucked against him. He gave her a light slap, then gripped her hips and slammed home.

"Brick!"

Her scream made his ears ring. His answering shout of triumph made his throat raw. The angle took him so impossibly deep.

Her breath was coming in gasps, each one tightening her hold on him.

"Calm down and breathe, baby. I need to move, and I can't do that until you relax."

"So deep," she cried.

"That's right," he said, stroking a hand down her back. "There's nothing between us. No secrets. No holding back. Just holding on."

He couldn't take it anymore. Need had him by the throat.

He pulled out, staring down in erotic fascination at how slick she'd made his hard-on with her arousal. He worked his way back into that inviting warmth, and when she moaned, something broke inside of him.

Brick leaned over her and wrapped a handful of her hair around his fist like reins. Worshipping her scent, he slammed himself home again and again, powering his hips into her until his balls slapped rhythmically against the back of her thighs.

She was completely at his mercy, folded over and bared to him. Yet she was still chanting "yes."

He'd offered her the world, and all she'd asked for was for him to fuck her so hard he couldn't stand up after he came. He didn't want to blink. Didn't want to miss a second of this tableau as he pistoned into that tight, welcoming pussy.

His balls were churning, desperate to release their load. He told her so through gritted teeth. He told her everything, all the dark and dirty things he wanted to do to her. Whispered lewd promises against the silk of her shoulder as he fucked her into oblivion.

When she quickened around him, when her muscles tensed, he thanked the gods for this woman, this fucking miracle.

He wanted to erase every memory of terror she had. Wanted to replace it with a new memory. Of what happened when she trusted him with her body, her heart, her soul. He'd take away the pain and the fear one kiss, one fuck at a time.

"Brick!" she whimpered. "You're making me—"

Her entire body seized around him. His cock was locked inside her as thousands of tiny muscles gripped and clutched. Biting his lip until he tasted blood, he held on as her pussy rippled up and down his shaft. She was shaking as her release rolled on. He couldn't see. Couldn't hear. Could only feel Remi's body accepting what he gave it.

And when she was done, trembling and loose, when his own release was scorching its way up his shaft, he pulled out. Gripping his dick, he gave it two savage pumps with his fist and came violently on her back, her ass, her thighs. His shout scorched his throat as his semen branded her on the outside. Over and over again, he fucked into his fist until every last drop was hers. Until his balls were empty, his heart full.

Until he'd given his woman what she needed and she'd rewarded him for it.

He cleaned them both up then carried her back to the living room. Not ready to be apart, he settled her in his lap and sat against the couch, legs stretching toward the fireplace.

"How are you still hard?" she whispered, shimmying over his unflagging erection.

"Fourteen years of not being inside you," he told her, pulling a blanket off the back of the couch and wrapping it around her.

"I don't feel close enough," she murmured, reaching between their bodies and guiding his cock between her legs.

"Baby, you've got to be sore," he cautioned, stroking a hand through her wild hair.

"We don't have to move," she said as she slowly lowered herself onto it. "I just feel empty without you."

He couldn't argue with that logic. Not when he could hold her and stay where he most wanted to be, buried deep inside her.

She sighed, pressing her face into his neck, and he let himself trail his fingers up and down her back.

"Are you cold?" he whispered, pressing a kiss to her temple when goose bumps erupted on her skin.

She shook her head. "Nope."

He smiled against her hair. Breathed in the scent of her shampoo. There was something happening in his chest. And it wasn't a heart attack. It was much, much worse.

He was in love with Remi Ford. He always had been. And someone wanted to take her away from him.

He stared into the fire and tried to focus on where their bodies were joined instead of the rising panic.

She sighed into his shoulder, and her tongue darted out to taste his skin there. His half-hard cock flexed inside her.

"Mmm," she murmured as it swelled thicker. "This feels so fucking good, Brick." She shifted forward just the tiniest bit, and the little gasp that left her mouth made him even harder.

She rocked back down and sighed. Gently, tenderly, she welcomed him into her body.

Slow. Measured. Torturous. Every undulation had him growing thicker, harder.

Remi sat up and put her hands on his shoulders. There was a glassy-eyed gleam in those beautiful green eyes as they peered at him from under thick lashes. Her lips were full and parted as if there were more secrets she had yet to reveal, and all he had to do was make her feel good enough, safe enough, to share.

He let her rock into him, thighs tightening around him as she changed angles.

Her breasts were at the perfect height for some much-needed attention. As she worked his cock lazily with her slick pussy, he pulled one tight tip into his mouth and latched on.

The moan that climbed its way out of her throat was downright sinful. He wanted to hear it again and again. He wanted his touch to be the only one that could elicit that pleasure. He sucked, taking long, leisurely pulls at her breast, and felt the answering quiver in her core.

His hands slid down from her waist to her hips, and then around to cup and spread her cheeks. She let out a long, luxurious sigh as he kneaded the muscle beneath that smooth, freckled skin.

She tweaked her hips, arching her back, and Brick read the invitation. As he moved his mouth to the other breast, he drew his middle finger along the cleft of her ass.

When he took his next long pull at her nipple, he nudged his fingertip against the tight ring of muscle he found there.

It wasn't a gasp of derision that escaped her lips. It was a breathy sigh of "yes."

This woman. This fucking woman. He sucked harder, reflexively tensing at this as yet unexplored fantasy. He wanted to know every inch of her. Needed to know it.

If she wanted or craved something, he would be the one to give it to her.

She tilted her hips again, taking his shaft all the way to the root and rocking against his finger at the same time.

He reached lower, to the place they were joined, and spread the wetness he found there higher. Again and again, he followed the path from where she was filled by him to where she was empty.

Each time, he pressed a little harder, a little deeper.

Finally, he slid his finger in deeper.

"Brick." She breathed out his name reverently as if she was saying a prayer, giving thanks. She began to move again, riding his cock and his finger.

He laved her nipple with his tongue.

His erection was fully hard and aching at the slow, gentle slides of her walls around it. He wanted to thrust. To lunge into her trembling, tender sex until they both forgot everything but the scent of each other.

But this, this was fucking beautiful. Remi riding him leisurely as he nuzzled at her breasts, teasing her toward another orgasm.

"It's so good," she whispered. His teeth grazed her nipple, and then he returned to the long, deep pulls.

His finger worked her tight little ass in time to her languid pace.

"Please don't stop," she whispered. Her eyes were squeezed shut, her lips parted in what looked like awe.

His chest felt as if it might burst with love, with pride, with the need to tell the world she was his.

"More," she begged.

She started to rock a little harder, a little faster. He could feel that slick, swollen bud against him when she hit the bottom of his shaft. The greedy little tilt of her hips gave him the easiest access to her ass and helped her drag her clit over him.

He went back to the first breast and started rhythmically sucking, hard and deep. Her fingers dug into his shoulders, and her breathing went ragged.

He wanted to stop. To tell her to fucking breathe. But she wanted him to trust her. Trust her to take everything he needed to give her. Trust her to be able to accept it.

"Oh, God," she whispered. "Oh. God."

His cock jerked in her, making her walls quake around him. Moving like fingers on piano keys. Making beautiful music.

He pushed harder with his finger and sank in all the way. There he could feel the trembling too. She was going to erupt around him, and when she did, she would milk another impossible climax out of him.

"Brick, I'm coming."

The most beautiful fucking sentence in the entire English language was Remi telling him he was making her come.

He was right there with her. Those delicate little muscles clamped down like a vise, making his cock shudder. When her muscles released, he thrust himself as deep as he could go and the first wrenching spurt of his orgasm exploded up his shaft.

He grunted against her soft breast, sucking harder, fucking harder with his finger, timing it to the waves of his own release. The waves of her pleasure surging and fading around his dick, his finger. Her greedy core demanding he surrender every last fucking drop of his seed to her.

She cried out as he filled her with everything he had to offer. He was rewarded with her shudders as she clung to him and whispered his name, loving him with her body.

No one was going to hurt her.

No one was going to get close enough to try.

33

*B*arely two hours later, Brick woke to the light of morning in a new world. A world where Remi Ford slept beside him.

The night before felt like a fever dream. The light those green eyes took on when she came. The way she clung to him like he was her rock. The feather-light caresses of her fingers on his back. Her body responding to his in a way that was so right he couldn't remember his reasons for fighting.

Remi's confession.

There was work to be done. Preparations to be made. Battle plans to be drawn. Because he wasn't going to let anything scare her, hurt her again. No matter what the cost.

She was sound asleep on her stomach, one hand tucked into his armpit as if she was afraid he'd disappear.

In turn, his palm was splayed over one firm ass cheek, anchoring her to his side.

Her hair spilled out over her bare back onto the ivory pillows like a river of fire.

The wave of possession that crested inside him nearly took him under. Everything was different now. He had work to do.

Work that required him to do the impossible—walk away from naked, sleeping Remi.

Which took superhuman effort. Telling himself her safety was more important than his need to hold her for the rest of his goddamn life, Brick quietly climbed out of bed and went in search of his clothes. His underwear were MIA, but he found his jeans and shirt.

After one hit of old, cold coffee and one of mouthwash, he crept back into the room.

"Remi? Baby?" he whispered, stroking his hand over her hair and down her back. Silk on silk.

"Mmm," she muttered into the pillow.

His lips curved. At least some things remained the same. This new Remi wasn't a morning person either. He had so many memories of her slinking down the stairs at her parents', hair disheveled, grunting good morning.

Unable to help himself, he pressed a kiss to her shoulder blade and, when she still didn't wake, he nipped at her skin.

"Mmm. Brick."

He'd go to any length to make sure his name was the only one she muttered in her sleep for the rest of her life.

"I have to run an errand," he said in her ear.

She grunted what sounded like a mournful whine.

"Be here when I get back," he ordered.

"Mmph," was her only response.

He indulged himself and brushed that long curtain of hair off her back so he could kiss her neck. "Go back to sleep, baby doll."

He fussed over the sheets and blanket for another minute before dragging himself out of the cottage and locking the door behind him.

He locked the gate, too, and hunched his shoulders against the wind that whipped off the lake. The low-hanging clouds, an off-gray color, melded with frozen waters. But in his gut, a coal burned bright and hot. Hate for a man he'd never met. Rage for the careless disregard of something so precious. The idea of living in a world without her was unthinkable.

IT WAS A DEHYDRATED, thoroughly wrung-out Brick who burst into his boss's office ten minutes later.

"Well, good morning to you," Chief Ford said, glancing up from a stack of reports and eyeing his rumpled appearance.

"Got a minute?" he asked.

"Isn't this your day off?"

"It is. But there's a problem."

"Sit," she said, gesturing toward the chair in front of her desk.

He closed the door behind him, removed his hat, and sat.

"This must be serious," she observed.

He crossed an ankle over his knee and tried not to look like a man who had just fucked the boss's daughter. "I've got reason to believe someone on the island is in trouble. Serious trouble."

The chief steepled her fingers and waited.

"This individual was threatened off-island. I believe it's credible, and I think there's a good chance trouble could come here."

Darlene slumped back in her chair and rubbed her temples. "What's Remi gotten herself into now?"

"I didn't say it was her."

Great. Remi was going to murder him. And then who was going to protect her?

"Brick, honey. You show up here in last night's crumpled

bartending get-up, missing buttons, glowing brighter than the sun with two love bites on your neck."

He slapped his hands to his neck as if he could feel his way to the hickeys.

"You and Remi finally got horizontal, and she told you why the hell she showed up here in the dead of winter pretending everything was fine," Darlene summarized.

"I— Uh. We—" He couldn't focus on the conversation and rebutton his shirt at the same time.

"It took you damn long enough. Do you realize how lucky you are that she held out for you this long? My daughter has the attention span of a gnat. If she didn't feel something powerful for you, she'd be working on divorce number two to some idiot she met at Burning Man or an organic cheese tasting by now."

Brick's tongue had double-knotted itself to his tonsils.

"Erm." It wasn't a word so much as a gulp.

"Anyway, what's my daughter gotten herself into?"

"I'm not at liberty to say," he said, thankful when his mouth formed actual words.

"Swore you to secrecy, huh?"

He looked at his boss, the woman who had given him a career, helped him carve out a place on this island, dead in the eyes and said nothing.

"But you came straight here anyway?"

Remi was going to kick his ass when she found out.

"It's serious enough to chance incurring someone's wrath," he said.

Darlene swore under her breath. She picked up a pencil and tapped it against the desk.

"It wasn't her fault," he said.

The chief's eyebrows rose. "For once. How serious we talking?"

"From what I've heard, very. But I'd like to do some digging before I formally brief you and get my ass kicked for it."

She blew out a breath, the pencil tapping double time now. "Okay. I am trusting you to get to the bottom of this. Figure out what we're up against. How credible this threat is. What's the likelihood of it coming here or—God forbid—her going to it. Then we'll talk specifics. Whether my daughter likes it or not."

He gave a curt nod and got to his feet, suddenly anxious to get back to her. To stand guard while she slept. To pump her for information until he knew exactly what he was up against.

"Oh, and Brick?"

He paused, hat halfway to his head. "Yeah?"

"I don't like to give my cops or my daughters relationship advice. But be good to each other. By my calculations, you two have been circling this for a long-ass time. I'd hate to see one of you fuck it up."

He swallowed hard. "Are you giving me your blessing to date Remi?"

She snorted. "I'm not an idiot, like someone *else* in this room. You've had my blessing since she was of age. Not that *I* was going to broach the subject. They don't come better than you."

She put down the pencil and picked up a half-eaten donut. "You two are what the other needs. But if you know my daughter at all, having my blessing is just as likely to push her out of your bed. So if you want my advice—which I'm giving you anyway—don't tell her anything about anybody blessing anyone and quit wasting your time. You two have been tangled up together for far too long without doing anything about it. Now get out of here and don't let anyone else see those hickeys, or you'll never hear the end of it."

Dismissed, Brick settled his hat on his head and he walked out with a distinct spring in his step.

REMI WASN'T in bed when he got back to her place. A lick of panic flamed to life in his gut as he checked the bedroom and bathroom. There were no signs of her. It wasn't until he returned to the main living space that he saw the note on the table next to his neatly folded underwear.

I'm at your place. Get your ass over here.

The words were encircled with a heart.

Carried by both temper and the driving desire to see her again, he hauled ass across the street.

"I see you took my advice," Spencer said, stepping out of the kitchen, a smug look on his face and a bowl of cereal in his hand.

Brick stared down at the toes of his boots and squashed the urge to toss his brother aside like he wanted. "What advice would that be?" he asked, trying to sound innocent.

Spencer punched him in the arm. "Remi's in the back. Weird coincidence about you both showing up with matching hickeys."

Brick slapped his hands to his neck to hide the evidence.

"Relax. I'm happy for you, man," his brother said with a genuine grin. "Seriously."

Brick reached out and squeezed Spence's shoulder. "Don't be happy for me yet," he said grimly. "I have to go lay down the law with her."

His brother snorted. "That'll go well. What kind of lining do you want for your casket?"

"Flannel," Brick said, shooting the smallest of grins over his shoulder as he stomped down the hall.

She was wearing one of his old t-shirts and singing at the top of her lungs behind the easel. Just seeing her swamped him with a wave of possessiveness. *Mine.*

Tears streaked her cheeks, and he wanted to go to her. To stand between her and whatever was upsetting her. But there was something triumphant in her stance, in the way she held brush and palette that held him back.

Shoulders back, head high. She jabbed the brush at the canvas. Her ability to not just feel emotions, but embrace them, always floored him. Where some sought to numb themselves, Remi welcomed them all.

He stepped into the room and stopped. She didn't let people watch. She'd always been fiercely protective of her art, her process. Magnus hopped off one of the work tables and came to wind around Brick's feet. He bent down and stroked a hand over the cat's long tail.

The song started over, and she swiped at fresh tears with the sleeve of her shirt. He wondered what it was about this particular song that captivated her. Or haunted her.

He wasn't sure how long he stood there watching, but when her eyes found his, when her mouth stretched into a victorious smile, time stopped.

She crooked her finger at him, and he wandered down the ramp in her direction. Her hair was pulled up in a high tail. There was a smudge of purple paint on her jaw and flecks of blue and red on her fingers.

He was still two feet away when she launched herself into his arms, locking her legs around his waist.

The lecture he was going to deliver, the questions he needed answers to, fell out of his head as she cupped his face in her hands and poured herself into a kiss.

Her mouth was jubilant against his. On instinct, he gripped the back of her head and coaxed her mouth open so he could taste her. The kiss spun out into something wild and free, like her. When she pulled back, he tried to follow her. But she stopped him.

"I painted," she whispered over his lips. Then she sank her teeth into his lower lip.

He growled his approval and gave her a nip of his own. "I can see that."

"Look," she said, turning his head in the direction of her easel.

It was hard to look at anything other than her lovely face. The shadows had been vanquished from her eyes. Selfishly he hoped he'd played a role there.

"It's kind of just a draft. Sometimes it takes me a couple of attempts to get it right. But this was more of an exorcism," she said, unaware that he was still looking at her instead of her painting.

He managed to drag his gaze away from her and focus on the canvas in front of him.

Dark purple bled into unrelenting black around two jagged, off-white splotches. Sharp, hard lines in orange and yellow divided the eerie night from the bottom of the canvas. She used the palette knife not so much to blend, but almost to rend. The bottom was a snowy white with scarlet red stains.

Brick's heart started to hammer in his chest with recognition. He knew what she'd painted.

Pain, trauma, terror. Lights cutting through the dark. And the unholy splatter of red on pristine white. It made him feel. Rage, bone-deep fear.

A few colors on a canvas, and she'd made him feel as if his heart was being carved out of his chest.

She turned back to him, tears and triumph on her face, rendering him breathless. "I won," she whispered.

She'd vanquished demons. She'd painted their likeness. She'd risen from the ashes in oils and color.

Remington Ford wasn't scared anymore. But he needed her to be.

34

"*A*gnes is going to kick your ass. Is this absolutely necessary?" Remi yawned while Brick glared at the general store's selection of security cameras.

"Only if your personal safety is a priority," he said grimly.

"You're cranky after you have a lot of sex," she observed.

He grabbed four cameras off the shelf and threw them in the basket she was holding. "I'm not cranky because we had sex. I'm fucking furious that there's some asshole out there who thinks he gets to decide whether you feel pain or not."

Remi shut her mouth.

"I'm full of rage thinking that this man—this fucking predator—believes he is in charge of whether you live or die. I'm livid knowing this motherfucker is out there walking around consequence-free while you're here with a broken arm afraid of the dark because of him."

"Brick—"

"He had no right to make you fear anything. He had no right to take that fearlessness of yours that drives me crazy on a good day. No right to put those shadows in your eyes. And he sure as fuck had no right to lay hands on his wife."

It was the longest speech she'd ever heard him make. The possessiveness, the unmitigated rage he felt because someone dared cause her pain burrowed itself into her chest and planted roots.

She laid a hand on his arm, noticing how rigid the muscle was. "It's going to be okay," she promised.

He turned to face her. "You're damn right it's going to be okay."

"We'll make him pay, right?"

He nodded solemnly. "He'll pay."

"And Camille will be safe?"

"You won't have anything to worry about," Brick promised, his voice fierce.

She knew it was silly. She knew it was impossible for him to make that promise and keep it. But just knowing that he was willing to share her burden gave her enough space to think more clearly. But his certainty, his over-the-top protective instincts, still made her believe.

She wanted to kiss him. To slip her hands under his coat and lose herself in a kiss that would make her forget everything except how much he wanted her.

"Oh, my. Well, isn't *this* cozy?" Mira Rathbun appeared at the end of the aisle, looking like she'd just stumbled upon the juicy story of the century.

Remi took a step back from Brick. The *last* thing she needed was the scrutiny of the entire island gossiping about them. "Brick was just helping me..."

Helping her what? Up her orgasm level?

The man slung a possessive arm around her shoulder and hauled her up against his side. Remi gave an awkward laugh and tried to extricate herself from his grasp. But the wall of man was stronger, more stubborn.

"Nice to see you, Mira," Brick said.

"What are you doing?" Remi hissed at him.

Mira looked positively delighted. "Are you two *together*?"

"No," Remi said.

"Yes," he said.

She glared up at him, wondering if he'd had so many orgasms he'd lost his damn mind. "You'll have to excuse Brick," she said through gritted teeth. "I think he hit his head or something. He's been saying crazy things all day."

"And all night," he said, giving her a wolfish smile. "Isn't that right, Remi Honey?"

Remi shot him her best "you are a dead man" look as her cheeks burned.

"You've got a little bruise here, Remi," Mira said with a smirk, pointing to her own neck.

Remi slapped a hand over the area. "I-I walked into a door."

"With teeth," Brick said wolfishly.

Mira fanned herself with her shopping list. "Oh, my. I am just so delighted for you two!"

"We're not together," Remi said, panic building in her chest. She renewed her struggles in his grip, but he merely tightened his hold on her.

"She's such a kidder," Brick said with affection. "We're really happy."

Then, as if he hadn't already done enough damage, he grabbed her by the front of the coat and hauled her to her tiptoes before kissing the ever-loving hell out of her. She put up a good fight for about two seconds before losing herself to his heat, to the assault of his tongue, the domination of his will over hers.

When he pulled back, she clung limply to him.

"Well, I'll leave you two love birds to your shopping," Mira said, already digging out her phone and practically sprinting from the store.

"What. Were. You. Thinking?" Remi said, emphasizing each word with a smack to Brick's concrete chest. "She's going to tell everyone we're together."

"We *are* together, and if you tell me we're not, I'm going to fuck that tight little pussy of yours until you agree."

Her mouth fell open as an entire movie reel of very appealing images played in her head. She gave herself a little shake. "You don't get to just decide that we're in a relationship and then tell the biggest gossip on the island." She threw up her hands. "Oh my God, what am I supposed to say to my mother?"

"She already knows," he said, guiding her up to the register with one hand on her neck.

"She *what*?"

Her screech had the clerk raising his eyebrows.

"What. Did. You. Do?"

It was a shame she'd have to murder Brick so soon after discovering his prowess in bed.

He handed the cameras over to the clerk, keeping a possessive arm around her. "How's it going, Randall?"

Randall had graduated two years ahead of Remi. He knew the signs of an impending implosion. She managed to keep a lid on her temper until they were outside again. It was a gray, icy day, which meant fewer witnesses on the streets.

"William Eugene Callan," Remi said, digging her heels in when he pulled her toward his snowmobile.

He came to a halt and rounded on her. "If you think for one second that I'm going to let you pretend that last night didn't happen or that it didn't mean what we both know it meant, you are sorely mistaken, Remington. I'll be happy to educate you the second we get back to my house."

She gave a gasp of indignation. "*Educate* me?"

He leaned down until his lips brushed her ear, his beard grazing her throat. "I will walk in the door, drag those pants to your knees, and bend you over the stairs to remind you."

Her legs turned to wet noodles, and she almost crumpled to the sidewalk.

"Are you wet just picturing it? I'll slap that sweet little ass of yours so hard, every man on this island will hear you scream my name and know you belong to me."

Wet didn't begin to describe what was happening between her legs. Her vagina was going to need a life preserver. Her nipples had turned to hard points, and she didn't know what was happening on her face, but Brick clearly liked it. He tossed the bag on the seat of the snowmobile, then dragged her down the side of the building. Before she could lay into him and remind him that she made her own life decisions, he shoved her up against the wall and closed his mouth over hers.

Hard, demanding. He was doing more than seducing her. He was possessing.

She could out-argue and out-stubborn the man any day. But out-kiss him? That was impossible.

Her body reacted on its own, going pliant and loose against him. Welcoming that invasion, with its heat and friction. When he ground his hips against her, she felt the swollen length of his arousal.

On a low growl, he pushed a hand up under her sweater and palmed her breast.

"Do you feel how much I need you?" he rasped, pressing his erection into her belly.

She nodded, unable to stifle her moan of desire.

"I need you safe even more than I need you naked. That's how important you are to me."

Her head was spinning. After fourteen years of rejections, she couldn't just accept that this was the way it was between them. If she opened herself up to a relationship with him, a real chance at one, he could just as easily change his mind like he had before. Where would that leave her when she'd only just begun putting her pieces together again?

She had a chance at surviving a monster. But Brick? It would be fatal.

"Tell me what you're thinking right now," he demanded. Those blue eyes were hard and flinty as they searched her face.

She shook her head.

He dipped at the knee, bringing his hard-on between her legs and pinning her with it. Then he found her mouth and made her surrender to him. When she was sure she'd never draw another breath again, he pulled back. "Tell me, Remi."

"Ugh," she moaned. "I-I love it when you box me in like this. When you don't give me an escape."

"You were made for me, Remington. Don't ever fucking doubt that."

"I've done nothing but doubt that for almost fifteen years, Brick. There's no guarantee that this about-face of yours is going to last. One good night's sleep, and you could change your mind. You could marry someone else or decide to leave Mackinac and me behind again."

His face turned to stone. But he didn't argue. He didn't promise her that this time was different. He didn't say any of the words she needed to hear.

"All that aside, you're safer if you're not connected to me. If Warren gets it into his twisted mind to hurt me, he'll start with you. He'll start by destroying something I care about. I need you to keep some distance."

"There is no more distance between us." His tone was steely. "Got that? Not after last night."

She buried her face in her hands until he brushed them aside.

"Look at me," he demanded, waiting until she complied. "This is the repercussion of letting me into your bed, Remington. We both knew it would be like this. Now we have to deal with the consequences."

She swallowed hard around the lump in her throat. "What if I run?"

"I'll chase you down and bring you back. As many times as it takes."

Ignoring the fluttering around her heart, she slapped her palms to his chest and pushed. But he didn't budge. "It's not safe, Brick. Don't you get that?"

He gripped her upper arms tight. "I need for him to understand that in order to get to you, he has to go through me. I need you to understand it, too."

She shook her head as her eyes went damp. "You don't know what you're saying. You don't know what he's capable of. He found me here less than twenty-four hours after I got here."

"What do you mean, he *found* you?"

35

_F_or once, the law wasn't on his side. The gap between black and white, right and wrong, had widened overnight into a foggy, murky swamp of gray.

No judge would issue an arrest warrant based on some news clippings and a shredded painting. Certainly not when the defendant was a United States senator.

But that didn't make the threat any less real. Senator Warren Vorhees was a fucking monster. And sooner or later, he'd escalate beyond vague threats. And Brick would be ready for him. It was with boiling blood he'd logged the evidence and opened a case file. An unofficial one.

He included Remi's thick stack of research. It made his stomach churn to think of her alone, scared, scrolling through internet searches for hours hoping to find the key to putting the man who'd hurt her behind bars.

Well, she wasn't alone now. And Brick would build a goddamn prison around Vorhees if that's what it took to keep him away from Remi.

His phone signaled an incoming text.

Remi: Do you really think I can't bust out of Brick Jail when you leave Spencer in charge?

He'd charged Spencer with keeping an eye on her while he went back into the station.

It made him anxious to be away from Remi. Especially after seeing how upset she was over her own desecrated painting. She'd covered it up. But he could still see the hurt. That alone made him want to break the asshole's jaw.

Brick: I know exactly what you're capable of. I'm just hoping you'll choose to behave yourself until I get home.

Remi: Me? Spence is the one who just challenged Phil Coolidge to a pull-up challenge.

Brick felt the ghost of a smile on his lips. Phil Coolidge was an 82-year-old, retired triathlete who'd called Mackinac home since the late '90s. His husband was in a rehab hospital on the mainland recovering from bypass surgery, and Phil was lonely without him.

Brick: Don't let either one of them break anything.

She responded with a short video of Spencer and Phil running wind sprints on the street.

His phone rang and he answered.

"Remi."

"You can't keep me under guard forever, you know," she warned.

He closed his eyes. "I realize that. This is a temporary solution until I can find a way to keep eyes on Vorhees."

She blew out a breath. "This doesn't need to be your fight, Brick."

"I thought I made myself clear this morning."

"Your testosterone was in the stratosphere after fucking my brains out. You weren't thinking clearly."

He glanced around, making sure none of the other officers were within earshot. "You need to accept that this is the way it is. I know you're scared. But you're not alone anymore, and if you think I'm going to let you face this alone, then I really must have fucked that brain right out of your beautiful head."

"Dirty dirty dirty," she purred.

His cock stirred in his pants, and he pressed the heel of his hand against it. "Behave yourself."

"Do you have plans tonight?" she asked, all innocence now.

"Yes."

"Oh." She sounded disappointed.

"They involve you. Naked. In my bed."

"What about Spence?" she asked, sounding a little breathless.

"He's not invited."

Remi laughed. Then sighed. "By the way, the show you put on for Mira this morning seems to be the equivalent of pissing in a circle around me. Phil congratulated me on our 'new romance' when I got here."

"Good."

"Brick," she groaned.

"*Remi.*"

"You can growl my name as sexy as you want, but we're still going to discuss this. There's no reason for you to sign up to be my friend with benefits *and* my bodyguard."

If she thought the two were mutually exclusive, he had a lot of educating to do tonight. But he had to walk that line with care. Too much pressure, too many rules, and she'd spook.

"Looking forward to it," he said as Carlos Turk strolled over and leaned against his desk.

"Oooh. Cop voice," she purred. "Are you trying not to say anything *personal*? Like how hard you had to work to get every inch of that huge—"

His dick was engorged and throbbing. "I'll see you soon." It was a threat, and she knew it.

"Looking forward to it, big guy. Gotta go. Spence just took a header into a trash can. Bye!"

He hung up. "What can I do for you, Turk?"

"Heard about you and Remi Ford."

Brick looked up, ready to meet the challenge. "Oh, yeah?"

Carlos broke out into a grin. "Good for you, man. She's just what you need." He rapped his knuckles on Brick's desk. "Congratulations."

"Thanks?"

With a frown, he watched the corporal walk away.

Congratulations? She was just what he needed?

Why was everyone so happy for him? For them?

He'd been prepared to fight the island over her. Prepared for their derision, not blessings. Whispered truths that he wasn't good enough for her. Hints that maybe this attraction got its start before it should have. Hell, at the very least, he'd been sure there'd be barbs about fucking the chief's daughter.

These congratulations baffled him. But he had bigger problems on his hands.

Namely Remi's immediate safety.

He took his reports and tucked the printouts into a folder. He'd done a standard run on both Mr. and Mrs. Vorhees. Both had come up clean. But where Camille Vorhees had a few typical brushes with traffic citations in her younger years, Warren was spotless.

Spotless didn't mean clean. It just meant they were better at hiding the dirt.

A man didn't go from zero to abusive asshole to attempted murder overnight. There would be a pattern. Other incidents. Other victims. He'd find them and build his case. Whatever it took to get him out of Remi's life permanently.

But money and power brought with it special privileges. The kind his own father thought could be stolen, rather than earned or born into.

While he dug into the man's past, Brick needed eyes on the man in the present. It wouldn't be too difficult to keep tabs on him in Washington with such public work. But Chicago wasn't that far from Mackinac.

He couldn't afford to let him anywhere near Remi.

He debated for a solid hour before picking up the phone.

There weren't exactly a lot of options for a part-time island cop when it came to unofficially investigating a bad guy a few hundred miles away.

But he had one.

"Dad," Brick said.

"Will! Is it really you?" William Eugene Callan II sounded delighted.

"Yeah," Brick said gruffly, chafing at the name. "Are you still doing the investigative thing?"

"I sure am. Got my license and everything," William announced proudly.

A few years back, his father had decided to make good use of all his underworld connections and hung up a shingle as an investigator. Brick hadn't paid much attention to his father's latest vocation, but Spencer insisted on keeping him up to date. And while Brick had expected it to turn into yet another scam, his father had stuck with it.

"Then I need a favor."

"Anything, son. You name it."

The excitement in his father's tone irked him. "I need eyes on a suspect."

"Oh. A job. Okay." William cleared his throat. "Sure."

"Is there something wrong?" Brick asked.

"No. No. I just thought maybe you wanted... Never mind. Tell me who I'm looking into."

"First this needs to stay between you and me. I can't have anyone on your end getting a whiff of this."

"Of course not," his father scoffed. "What do you think I am, an amateur?"

"I'm serious," Brick said. "Lives are on the line, and if this guy has any cause to believe he's being followed, he could retaliate."

"If it helps you out, I'm willing to do whatever. I have a lot to make up for." William let out an awkward laugh. "I know I wasn't much of a father but—"

"This is what I need you to do," Brick interrupted. He filled William in on the basics of the situation, leaving Remi's name out of it.

It left a bitter taste in his mouth, asking for help from the man who had only ever let him down. But he didn't have any other options. If he flew to Chicago himself to do the legwork, he'd have to drag Remi with him to make sure she didn't get into trouble on her own. And he wasn't putting her in the same state, let alone the same city, as a monster like Vorhees.

No. He didn't trust anyone else to watch Remi, certainly not his own father. But he could trust the man to watch the monster.

36

Brick's kitchen was militantly clean, Remi noted as she snooped. Spencer was busy on sales calls in the dining room, which left her unsupervised. Just because she was humoring Brick's attempt at holding her prisoner didn't mean she was going to behave herself.

There were no dirty dishes in the sink. No forgotten produce rotting on the counter. No old takeout containers in the fridge.

The bulletin board his grandmother kept inside the door that led to the porch still hung in the same spot. But now, instead of church programs and coupons, it had a grocery list, Brick's work schedule, and a few personal items tacked up in evenly spaced increments.

The man had always been three steps past tidy, a fascination to someone like her who embraced chaos. One night in bed being deliciously dominated by the man proved to her that the need for control extended far beyond home organization.

Without a hint of shame, Remi flipped over the New Orleans postcard.

Happy Belated Birthday, Will. New Orleans is great! Call me if you're ever in the neighborhood. Love, Mom.

She'd never met his mother, the woman who had gifted a teenage Brick the beloved cowboy hat he still wore. In all her sons' years on the island, she'd never once paid them a visit. Busy with a singing career, Spencer had told Remi. Brick didn't say much about her, but what he did share was painted with a lighter, more forgiving brush than the one he applied to his father.

Remi frowned at the post date. It was several weeks after his birthday, and his mother had only gotten around to dropping him a postcard? Her own parents called her every year at the exact time she'd been born. 5:58 a.m.

She peeked at the Christmas card next to it.

To my favorite ex-husband. Try not to be too bah-humbuggy.
   Love, Audrey

Unsure of how she felt about that, Remi let the card flip shut. One night together didn't give her any claim on Brick. He'd pursued, proposed to, and married Audrey. Meanwhile, his track record with *her*...well, if history repeated itself, he'd walk through the door any minute now and either withdraw from her completely or awkwardly explain that he'd changed his mind.

There was a tightening in her chest and she tried to ignore it. Audrey wasn't here now. She was. That had to mean something.

Blowing out a sigh, she eyed the cards again. Brick Callan had been abandoned by his mother, the one woman who never should have left him. Yet he inspired the loyalty of his ex-wife, someone who had every right to move on and leave him behind. Now the woman he'd spent a decade and a half rejecting was standing in his kitchen snooping on the other women in his life.

It was too weird even for her.

Deliberately, she turned her back on the board. She could either spiral into a cycle of confusion and helplessness or she could do something productive.

~

SHE WAS JUST PUTTING the finishing touches on three towering turkey sandwiches when her skin prickled with awareness, with anticipation, with dread.

Brick.

Once she looked at him, she'd know if it was the man who had taken her to bed or the one who hadn't wanted her.

"Remington."

She closed her eyes at the rough caress of her name.

He stepped into the kitchen, and she followed his progress toward her without turning around. Her heart kicked into overdrive as he closed the distance.

"Hungry?" she asked, keeping her tone light.

He stopped just behind her. Not touching her, but close enough that an intense longing unfurled inside her.

One night with this man and her body was on high alert.

Then his hands were on her shoulders, and he was forcing her around, nudging her chin up.

"Starving." He looked rumpled and tired and undeniably sexy. He looked *hungry*.

She wasn't used to seeing him up close like this, to having his hands on her. It took her breath away. "I made sandwich. *A* sandwich. I made *you a* sandwich," she enunciated carefully, willing her brain to start functioning again.

Those lips that had only the night before whispered dirty promises and doled out unbridled pleasure quirked. But the almost smile was gone just as quickly.

"I'm looking into Warren Vorhees."

Remi sighed, wishing she could live a life without that man's name in it. "I knew you would."

"Camille made that statement about the accident being your fault to appease him, didn't she?"

She blinked in surprise, then nodded. He'd always been intuitive. "I believe so. Her survival depends on proving to him that she's loyal."

"And in order to do that, she has to ruin you."

"She has to try." It was an important distinction.

"He keeps underestimating you," Brick said as his fingers slid into her hair with something like reverence.

"His mistake," she said softly, melting into his touch.

"At some point, he's going to realize that. And he's going to stop underestimating and start trying to eliminate the threat."

His soothing touch helped insulate her from his words.

"I know."

"Then I need you to know, he'll have to get through me first."

"I don't want that, Brick. I'm not going to ask people to put themselves in danger."

"You didn't ask. You just need to accept it. You're standing for Camille. I'm standing for you. This Vorhees asshole doesn't know it, but he's breathing his last few free breaths."

She looked at him, into eyes the same depthless blue as the ocean. "Do you really think we can put him away?"

He cupped her face so gently she felt like she was made of glass. "Yes. I need you to trust me."

She trusted Brick Callan with her life. But could she trust him with her heart?

Not trusting her voice, she nodded.

"I like finding you here," he said finally.

"That better not be some crack about a woman's place being in the kitchen," she said, eyes narrowing.

He distracted her by tracing his fingers down her neck to her clavicle. "This room always made me think of you."

"Me? Why?" she asked, feeling a little breathless.

"This is where you got my grandfather to eat mac and cheese and play tic-tac-toe," he said softly.

The memory made her smile. "You remember that? It feels like forever ago."

"I remember," he said, very, very seriously. "That was the same day you ruined Spence's favorite shorts. On purpose."

She raised an eyebrow. "How do you know it was on purpose?"

"I may have been outside that door a little longer than I let on," he confessed, tilting his head in the direction of the porch.

"You were eavesdropping? What could your grandfather and I have been talking about that young Brick Callan would have found interesting?" she teased.

"You were telling him to give me a chance. That I wasn't my father."

Remi glanced down. "Oh. *That* conversation."

"You used that Remington magic to make him see me in a different light. I never forgot it."

She tried to cross her arms, but there wasn't enough room between their bodies, so she settled for stuffing her hands into the pocket of her hoodie. "Pop was as stubborn as they come. Blaming you for something you had no control over when really it was his daughter he was disappointed in."

She thought of the postcard again. A backhanded gesture, a belated recognition, yet he still hung it in a place of honor. It made her heart hurt. He deserved more than that. He deserved someone who not only remembered his special moments but actively celebrated them.

Had Audrey been that someone?

"That was the day he started trying," Brick said. "You convinced him to give me a shot."

"He would have eventually. A person can only be around you for so long before discovering your ridiculously big heart and your Dudley Do-Right complex." Testing him, she poked him in that mile-wide chest. "Do you miss them?" she asked. "Your grandparents."

He nodded, toying with a strand of her hair, rubbing it between his fingers. "I do. I didn't have a lot of time with them, but I'll always be grateful for the space they made for Spence and me. They gave us a home when we needed it. Paid for Spencer's college when I couldn't."

She caught the note of shame and zeroed in on it.

"You were twenty-four, Brick. What twenty-four-year-old can afford to send their little brother to college? Hell. What twenty-four-year-old is capable of raising a teenager?"

"Spence was my responsibility."

She shook her head. "He was your parents' responsibility. And when they couldn't or wouldn't step up, you did. You two were meant to come here. Meant to build a relationship with your grandparents."

He studied her but said nothing.

"Pop gave you the money to start up the Tiki Tavern because he loved that you fell in love with this place. They left you their home because they knew it was *your* home. They were so proud of you. Remember the summer you named a sandwich after Pop and a drink after your grandma? They went in once a week just to order their namesakes and support you. Mackinac is where you belong.

Whatever brought you here was just showing you the way home."

"Come with me," he said, his voice hoarse.

"Where?"

He cupped her face in one hand, crowding her against the counter. "I need a shower."

"I already had one," she whispered, mesmerized by the way he looked at her. "Not—not that you were inviting me to join you. Unless you were?"

His head dipped lower, and he brushed his nose against her cheek. "I just need you close."

She didn't know what was more terrifying, the prospect that he'd changed his mind or the fact that he hadn't. Yet.

"Okay," she whispered. "What about the sandwiches?"

"Later." One word, and he had her tingling from head to toe.

He let her deliver one of the sandwiches to Spencer, who was still on a call in the dining room, before pulling her up the stairs behind him. Spence flashed her a thumbs-up, and she blushed to the roots of her hair.

Brick's bedroom was the largest of the six. It was at the back of the house on the second floor, with windows that overlooked the backyard and the house next door.

The bed was a massive four-poster with a headboard with sexy leather inserts and not nearly enough pillows in Remi's opinion. The windows were framed by thick curtains in a dark navy, probably chosen for function—blocking out early morning sun after a long bar shift—rather than fashion, but they still worked.

She stood in the doorway and imagined him there on the bed, naked, sprawled on his back with one hand tucked under his head. His cock thick and swollen, balls heavy while he thought about her.

"What?" he asked gruffly.

Color burned her cheeks. "I was just thinking you need more pillows."

He flashed her a look that said he wasn't buying it, then distracted her when he unbuttoned his shirt. She wet her lips and watched as more and more skin and muscle were revealed. He looked as though he'd been carved from granite. Big, powerful, virile.

Brick didn't just look at her, he *smoldered*. As if he was reliving what they'd shared the night before and anticipating what was yet to come.

"So, just to be clear. You haven't changed your mind?"

There it was. That subtle quirk of his lips. He opened the closet door and deposited his shirt in the laundry basket on the floor.

"What do you think?" he asked.

She would have told him had she not lost the power of speech and thought when his hands went to his belt buckle. The whisper of his belt slipping free of the loops sent a delicious shiver down her spine. He coiled the belt with deft fingers and placed it in the top drawer of the tall dresser next to the bathroom door.

Swallowing hard, she watched as he undid the fly of his jeans and shoved them down his muscular thighs. He was hard. The thick shaft that bobbed between those bitable thighs acted as a hypnotist's watch. The jeans went into the laundry basket, too. He closed the closet door, giving her an impeccable view of the eighth wonder of the world, Brick Callan's ass.

Butt bongos. The phrase floated to her from the deep recess of her mind. "Oh my God," she groaned, bringing her hands to her cheeks.

He raised an eyebrow in amusement. "Problem?"

"I just remembered butt bongos."

Every inch of her skin heated under his leisurely regard. The man was going to melt her clothes right off without even touching her.

"Make yourself at home," he said, gesturing toward the bed.

Oh, boy.

He disappeared into the bathroom, and she heard the shower turn on.

"Get it together, Ford," she murmured.

She'd had sex before. Lots of it. This wasn't her first time in a devastatingly handsome man's bedroom. He was going to come out of that shower and use that big, hard body of his to make her scream. Despite the fact that she'd not only survived it but reveled in it the night before, she was suddenly as awkward and anxious as a virgin.

Brick made everything feel like it was an unforgettable first.

She hopped up onto the bed, testing the mattress. The white bedding was simple but soft. No potentially embarrassing squeaks that would broadcast their activities to Spencer downstairs.

She didn't have a view of him in the shower and considered it a little too pervy to stand in the doorway and watch him wash all of that aroused acreage. Too keyed up to relax, she opened his nightstand drawer to snoop. There was an unopened box of condoms, a notepad and pen, a flashlight, and a neatly folded scrap of cotton. White with gold pineapples.

Snatching it out of the drawer, she stormed into the bathroom just as he stepped out of the shower.

"Brick Callan! What's this?" she demanded, waving the thong at him.

He took his time cinching a white towel around his waist. Droplets of water on his chest caught the light, temporarily dazzling her.

"It looks like a pair of underwear," he drawled.

She wasn't fooled. "These are *mine*! I thought I lost them!"

His hand darted out, almost fast enough to snatch them from her, but she was faster and clutched the prize to her chest. She spun around to run back into the bedroom, but he caught her and deftly wrestled the thong out of her grip.

"I took them the night you were hiding from me in the shower," he said, walking her forward to the bed with both arms banded around her. He used his weight to bend her toward the mattress.

Her blood was electrified by his damp skin against hers. "You just got busted and you're not giving them back?"

"They're mine now." He tugged her sweater off and bit her shoulder gently. She hissed out a breath. "I thought they were the only piece of you I'd ever get to keep."

Her knees trembled from the weight of his words as he slid her pants down her legs. "Last night you got more than a pair of underwear."

He nuzzled against her neck. "I want as many pieces of you as I can get."

Her stupid heart was about to burst. But she couldn't let it. It was dangerous enough that she'd opened her legs to the man. Handing him the keys to the heart he'd already broken was a terrible idea.

There was only one thing to do. One weapon she could deploy to protect herself.

"Stand up."

He stilled against her. "Are you okay?"

She pushed him back and turned to face him. He looked concerned, but that spectacular cock was already reacting to the chemical changes happening inside her. His nostrils flared, a primitive part of him sensing both danger and pleasure.

She sank all the way down to the floor in front of him. The foot of the bed was at her back, a hard, desperate man at her front. "*Baby*." There was so much tied up in that one word. Hope, brittle need, intoxicating desire.

"Lose the towel," she whispered.

His eyes glittered, but he complied, reaching one big hand down to release his erection. She was lightheaded with want. With need. With the desire to give him another piece, another memory of her.

She watched in fascination as he fisted his shaft and gave it a long, rough stroke inches from her mouth.

He reached down and, with one swift yank, bared her breasts above the neckline of her tank top.

She cupped his balls in her hand and squeezed. He hissed in a breath through clenched teeth.

"Now, take my panties out," she instructed.

He hesitated until she gave another harder squeeze. "I'm keeping them," he reminded her. His tone left no room for argument.

"They're yours," she promised. "So is this." She leaned forward and took the smooth, swollen crown into her mouth.

He swore violently, and a tremor ran through his entire body. Curling over her, he slapped one hand into the mattress behind her head. The other, still holding her thong, wrapped around the base of his shaft and squeezed.

She took him a little deeper, running her tongue over the underside all the way to the sensitive tip.

She couldn't take him as far as she wanted, but between the slide of her mouth and the stroke of his hand, it was more than enough.

He was straining to hold himself back. But she didn't want that. She wanted him as wild as he made her. She dug her nails into his ass cheeks, and when he gave a testing thrust into her mouth, Remi hummed her approval. He did it again and again. Swift, shallow pumps that had his crown swelling between her teeth.

"Need to get you off." He gritted out the words like he was in pain.

"This is just for you, Brick," she murmured before taking him in as deep as he could go.

He used her hair to pull her head back, releasing his dick from her mouth. "Ah," he groaned, giving himself several vicious strokes with his hand before guiding the tip back to her lips. Moisture gathered there, and she licked it off. "Scared I'll hurt you. I want you so fucking bad."

"Fuck my mouth, Brick. *Please.*"

He couldn't say no to her or the demand, and they both knew it.

When he loosened his grip on her hair, she slicked her mouth over him again, relishing the texture and taste of him. Thick veins on his shaft throbbed against her tongue, making her dizzy with his desire for her.

When he tried to pull out again, she sank her nails into his ass cheeks and held steady.

"Dirty fucking girl," he groaned and then thrust between her lips.

She sucked hard and deep. Teasing with teeth and tongue then soothing with long licks over the sensitive slit. Sucking and plumping him, she steadily drove him mad.

"Goddamn you, Remi." She looked up at him and was gratified at the picture he made. His lids were heavy, lips full and parted. A god chasing his pleasure. And she was the one to give it to him.

One hand stroked his shaft in time with her mouth, the other gripped her hair. "Need more."

"Take it," she said before sliding her lips back down.

On a groan, he released her hair and once again folded over, this time forcing her head back against the mattress. His fist, still wrapped in her panties, worked the base of his cock viciously as his hips set the pace. She heard his fingers digging into the mattress next to her head as he fucked her mouth and she embraced a euphoric sense of panic at having no escape.

His thick, round head hit the back of her throat over and over again. She could taste it now as his release gathered, ready to uncoil. She palmed his balls where they hung heavy between his legs. Gripping, squeezing. Working them in time with his erratic pumps. Those huge thighs bunched and shifted with every drive. His abs tightened as he took her mouth.

"Remi. *Remi.*" He chanted her name like a prayer. Like a curse.

She hummed again, a vibration deep in her throat, and opened her eyes to watch him let go. He was already staring at her as his entire body tensed. The eye contact, the lewdness of what she was letting him do to her, had him collapsing onto his forearm on the mattress.

"Fuck, baby. Suck me hard. Make it stop hurting."

She felt the tension in him. Muscle, bone, cells. Everything coiling, tightening in on itself in his body. And then he was coming. His roar filled her ears as he ejaculated in her mouth, down her throat. Hot, thick spurts of semen. His dick pulsed in her mouth as it released its load. His fist continued to work his shaft violently as she swallowed as much as she could. Those muscular thighs shook against her. She was choking, drowning, dying, *living.*

He was still coming as he yanked her off her knees and shoved her back onto the bed. Still going off as he forced her legs open and rammed into her. Her wet mixed with his orgasm had him fully sheathed in two demanding thrusts. Heaven. Or hell. He'd propelled her into some other world, she thought, as her inner walls fluttered around the thick shaft.

"*Fuck*," he groaned brokenly as he continued to pump into her.

Something rough and wet rubbed against her clit, and Remi realized her thong was wrapped around his arousal.

The piece of her he'd stolen. Kept. *Treasured.*

It scared her, thrilled her, electrified her. The need he displayed for her was staggering.

There was no warning. Just her own peak suddenly looming in front of her. Jagged and terrifying.

"Come," he growled in her ear as one of his hands found her breast and palmed it. "Now, Remington."

She had no choice. Her body was already spiraling into the abyss.

"God, yes," he groaned as she clamped around him. An erotic vise. "Never giving up that greedy little cunt of yours."

He was still hard, still rolling his hips, still delivering pleasure.

Knowing that once wasn't enough for him had her own arousal spiking again.

"You want to come again," he said. "You want me to keep working my cock in you until you go off. Say it."

"Yes," she whispered. "Yes, Brick. I want you to make me come again."

He pulled out of her, but before she could complain, he pushed her onto her hands and knees in front of him. She held her breath as he knelt between her legs and stroked a hand down her spine before those strong fingers closed around her hip, kneading the curve of her flesh.

"God. I can't look at you like this without wanting to put my hand on you."

Her sex clenched around nothing. Making her ache with a need only he could fulfill.

"Do it. *Please.*"

"Just once," he rasped. She didn't know if he was promising her or warning himself.

"Then you better make it count," she whispered.

He blew out his breath behind her, reminding Remi of a bull pawing the ground.

She shivered as he guided the blunt head of his penis between her legs, parting the lips of her sex and nestling against the soft, wet tissue that was ready to welcome him back.

For a second, maybe two, the tension between them built as he tensed against her, holding his breath. And then that heavy hand connected with her rear end, delivering a sharp, biting slap.

She didn't have time to cry out, to beg for another, because Brick was gripping her hips and yanking her back against him, impaling her on his unflagging hard-on.

The low moan that wrenched its way free from her throat was drowned out by his animalistic grunt as her body surrendered to his invasion. The angle. Holy Mariah Carey, the angle had him filling her so deep she could barely breathe.

"Remi. My sweet, beautiful, Remi," he whispered behind her. His hands worshipped her in long, soothing strokes as he began to ride her. Revering her and defiling her at the same time.

She was flying headlong into the dark, but without fear.

Because this time, she wasn't alone. This time, he was there with her.

"Baby, I can't get enough of you." He gritted out the words like a sinful confession as he fucked her harder, deeper. Using his hands to both spread her cheeks wide and to control the speed.

Her shaking arms collapsed beneath her, and when she landed on her forearms, the head of his penis nudged something deep inside her. Again and again, until it triggered a new, powerful orgasm. The spasms began to build in her core and then radiated outward.

"Yes," he hissed. "Milk my dick with those hungry squeezes, baby."

She sobbed as her body complied. The orgasm detonated, sending shock waves through her entire body, her entire *being*. The world ended as she could only tremble her way through the release.

"*Fuck*. What you do to me," Brick groaned, his sweat-soaked skin slapping against her with each thrust of his hips. "I'll never be the same."

Neither would she. He'd ruined her. And she'd ruined him. But all that mattered was this beautiful, brutal moment of surrender and domination.

She squeezed around him, unable to respond in any other way, and felt triumphant when he went rigid behind her, inside her.

"*Remi.*" Her name. Always her name.

The first burst exploded inside her, hot and thick. And then he was pulling out of her, grunting his way through the orgasm with violent strokes of his fist. Wrenching, scalding spurts coated her behind, her back, her thighs.

He'd branded her inside and out, and she felt possessed. Adored. Protected.

37

They spent the better part of a week having sex, showering off the sex they'd had, and then having shower sex.

Remi was in twin, perpetual states of full-body soreness and bliss.

They'd spent every night together and most of their waking moments as well. When Brick was working, she was painting.

With Spencer gone, they'd explored kitchen counter sex, bent over the dining room table sex, and lots and lots of oral sex in front of the fireplace. Brick's tongue was just as talented as the rest of his spectacular body.

Since they'd been naked for almost an entire week, they hadn't made any public appearances together. Remi hadn't seen her parents, which meant she also hadn't discussed the Brick or Warren situations with her mother. A plus in her mind.

But Kimber also hadn't called or texted. And since everyone on the damn island knew she and Brick had finally knocked boots, there were only two conclusions Remi could draw. Her sister was either still really pissed at her or she was embarrassed.

While it was a pleasant respite chock full o' orgasms, she knew she couldn't keep avoiding her family. Not on an island this small. And if she and Kimber were going to repair what was left of the bridge to their sisterhood, it was going to have to be Remi's doing.

With Brick working the lunch shift at the Tiki Tavern, Remi decided it was time to pay her sister another visit. Preferably on neutral ground.

Fortunately, thanks to Mackinac Visits online calendar, she knew exactly where Kimber would be.

REMI STRAIGHTENED HER SHOULDERS, pasted a bright smile on her face, and tried not to look like a woman who had spent most of the previous night being ravaged.

The door opened, and one brown eye peered out. "What're you selling?" a wheezy voice demanded.

"Makeup, food storage, and sex toys," Remi said, holding up the plate of fresh chocolate chip cheesecake bites.

The man harrumphed and threw open the door. Lars Hyne was only two inches taller than Remi. He'd lost an eye in a boating accident twenty years ago and had relished the pirate appeal the eye patch gave him.

"Lars, when are you gonna stop torturing our visitors?" A lithe Alaskan woman with an edgy pixie cut and purple highlights crossed her arms over her chest behind him.

"Hi, Kirima," Remi called back.

"Come on in," Lars beckoned, snatching the plate of goodies out of her grasp.

The Hyne home was an eclectic timeline of their life

together. World travelers in the spring and summer, the Hynes perversely called Mackinac home all winter long. The living room's large jade floor tiles were covered here and there with thick woven rugs that somehow both clashed and matched. The walls were painted a deep shade of peacock blue. Treasures from their travels crowded shelves, crammed in between books, photos, and plants.

The eat-in kitchen was just as colorful and chaotic. The cabinets were white, but they'd gone with a fiery orange and yellow backsplash of hand-painted tiles from Mexico.

At the turquoise and glass dining table was Kimber, a steaming mug of tea and a half-finished puzzle in front of her.

"You're officially allowed to join us if you're sharing that cheesecake," Kirima said.

"I just so happened to make extra," Remi said as Lars ripped the plastic wrap off the top.

Kimber was avoiding her gaze. Which was fine. Remi would wear her down. It was what she did.

"I saw my sister was visiting and thought I'd pop in and say hello. I haven't seen you two in a couple of winters," Remi said, accepting the teacup Kiri pushed on her.

"What goes with cheesecake?" Lars grumbled as he perused their wine rack.

"Anything that involves a cork," Remi predicted.

"Kimber, any objections to starting happy hour early?" Kiri asked as she dug out the wine glasses.

"No objections here," she answered, slipping a puzzle piece in place and still avoiding Remi's gaze.

Being in good health, the Hynes weren't on the original welfare checklist, but they'd liked the idea of a little extra company during the long winter and had signed up to be both visitors and visited.

Lars opened a bottle of red and poured, the cheery tinkle of wine glasses filling the room.

"Kimber was just telling us about Ian's idea for a phone app for playdates," Kiri said, catching Remi up to speed.

"And I just introduced Hadley to the Sweet Valley Twins series," Kimber said. "She read the first ten in a weekend."

"I can't believe how fast they're growing up," Remi admitted. "It seems like just yesterday they were crawling around in your living room, and Kyle was using his law books as blockades."

Kimber finally looked her in the eye. "That was both another lifetime ago and also yesterday."

"I remember when you girls were a few centuries younger," Kiri began. "Do you remember the trouble you two got into when you caught Remi cutting her hair before kindergarten picture day and you cut yours to match?"

Remi winced. "I forgot all about that," she confessed.

"Mom was not happy," Kimber reminisced with a faint smile.

"Speaking of, I heard you two are still in trouble," Lars teased.

"It's time the world faced it. The Ford sisters are never going to be good at coloring in the lines," Remi said, raising her glass.

"I'll drink to that," Lars chuckled.

"And how's that husband of yours?" Kiri asked. "Seems like he's off-island more than he is on this winter."

Kimber toyed with the stem of her glass. "He's fine. Busy with work. He caught a few cases that required a lot of extra time. But he's enjoying it."

There was a flat, resigned quality to her tone that had Remi's sisterly radar activating.

Kiri rested her elbows on the table and picked up a puzzle

piece. "Remi, how about you? What brought you back to town?"

"Think Brick will put a ring on it?" Lars asked, pulling up a chair.

She choked on a mouthful of a full-bodied merlot. Coughing and sputtering, she reached for a cheesecake bite to wash it down.

"I was missing my family," she said, stuffing a bite of cheesecake into her mouth. "Thought I'd take a few weeks of vacation and have a nice long visit."

"And put a smile on Brick's face," Kiri said, fitting the piece into place.

Heat flooded Remi's cheeks. "We're just enjoying spending time together. There will be no putting rings on anything."

Any day now, he was going to come to his senses and turn her loose again into the world, ruined forever by his invincible penis.

"I see a few new finds in here," Remi noted, changing the subject. "Where did you get that basket?"

THEY ATE and drank and chatted for another half an hour. And when Kimber said she needed to head home to get the kids from school, Remi volunteered to go with her.

"You look relaxed," Kimber observed as they walked, avoiding patches of ice and piles of still pristine snow.

"Me?" Remi asked innocently. "I must have gotten a good night's sleep."

"That's not the face of someone who slept well," Kimber said dryly. "That's the face of someone who had a half dozen orgasms in rapid succession."

"Let's talk about something other than my face and orgasms," Remi insisted.

Her sister let out a sigh, watching the cloud of breath appear and then vanish in the cold. "I'm sorry for going PMS 5000 on you. I was spiraling, and it really had nothing to do with you."

"I'm sorry for blowing back up at you."

"You held out admirably. Which only served to push me over the edge," Kimber admitted.

"You were overdue. I mean, what normal human doesn't lose her shit every once in a while?"

THIS TIME, in a vast improvement over the last visit, her sister invited Remi inside. The family's moderately overweight beagle thumped his tail from his blanket on the couch. Princess Megatron joined the Olson family after Kyle cracked under the pressure of endless pleading from the kids. He surprised a very unhappy Kimber with the puppy. The kids were given naming rights in return for promising to be entirely responsible for the dog's care.

That lasted all of about thirty minutes. Mega, as he was now known, quickly discovered who was in charge of food in the house and attached himself to Kimber.

"You painted," Remi said, unwinding the scarf from her neck as she appreciated the soft umber on the walls. Visitors would never guess that two active kids with a vast array of toys, hobbies, and books lived under the tidy roof.

"And redid the floors," Kimber said without enthusiasm. "And finally sanded down the paint on the molding around the transoms. And painted the god-awful beige brick on the fireplace."

"It looks like one of those houses on HGTV."

It did. It was clean but cozy. Colorful but calm. Her sister had a real eye.

"No, it doesn't," Kimber said, shucking her winter gear and stowing it on the neat hooks above the driftwood bench.

"I'm serious," Remi told her.

"Thanks. No one's really paid attention to any of the changes. I don't even know why I keep making them."

"I know you're into the parenting thing and all, but have you ever considered working part-time as a designer? I mean, think of all the summer rentals that are in desperate need of an overhaul. Wicker couches and pleather futons have lost their charm."

Kimber let out a strangled laugh. "Have I thought of..." She stopped herself and shook her head.

"What?" Remi asked.

"I've thought of nothing *but* doing something. Anything."

Treading lightly, Remi followed her sister into the tiny mudroom at the back of the house. On the wall, mounted between tidy cubbies and the laundry, was a giant whiteboard calendar. Colored sticky notes, patterned tape, and hand-lettered notes lay the groundwork for the family's entire existence.

Kyle trial in Detroit Michigan.

Hadley recital and sleepover.

Ian book club.

Turkey burgers and salad.

Video chat with dog trainer.

Laundry day.

Groceries.

It was hypnotic in its precise structure.

"What the hell is this?" Remi asked in awe.

"That is my life," Kimber said, crossing her arms. "Well, my family's life. I don't seem to have one of my own."

"I don't know what to say."

"Impressive, isn't it?"

"I was going to go with terrifying. Where's your stuff?"

"My stuff?" Kimber's laugh was humorless. "I don't have stuff. My stuff is making sure everyone else has their stuff. Kyle is never home. And I love my kids. You know I do. But kids are so fucking hard, Rem. Hadley is just tiptoeing into puberty, and I don't know if either one of us will survive it. I didn't sign up to be a single parent. Some days I just want to erase everything and see what happens."

"You have really great handwriting," Remi noted.

"Just what I wanted to be known for. 'Age thirty-four, mother of two. Had nice handwriting.'"

"Okay, that sounds like the world's worst obituary. Let's drink some alcohol and talk."

"You don't want to hear your middle-aged sister complain about getting the life she always thought she wanted," Kimber said, her gaze on the mason jar filled with a rainbow of dry erase markers.

"I want to talk to my sister about her life. I'm not here to judge you."

"That's what I've been doing to you."

"Uh, yeah. Caught that," Remi said. She stepped back into the kitchen and rummaged through cabinets until she found a bottle of vodka tucked behind two boxes of whole-grain organic pasta.

"Straight or what?" she asked, wiggling the bottle.

"Get the glasses," Kimber said, pointing at a cabinet. Remi skipped the tasteful rocks glasses and found two tumblers with cartoons and big, bendy straws.

Kimber snorted when she saw them.

"These hold more," Remi insisted.

Kimber mixed drinks and gave Mega his afternoon treat while Remi sat on the counter and listened.

"I remember thinking how much I liked Kyle's ambition when we were in college," her sister said.

"And now?"

She shrugged. "I don't think I realized that his ambition would only extend to his job. Not his family or his home or his wife. I thought that I wanted to stay home and raise our kids. And for a while I did. But somewhere along the way it started to feel like not enough. Kyle got more important in his job, and that meant more money for us, but also more travel for him. He stopped being around. He goes days without talking to his kids. There are days when we only exchange one or two text messages."

She blew out a breath and shook the ice cubes in her cup. "It's like the more important Kyle got at work, the less important I got in my life."

"Well, that's bullshit," Remi said.

"Excuse me. This is my existential crisis. Not yours."

"I'm just saying, what's more important—other people recognizing that you are more than just a label or a role or *you* recognizing it?" Remi asked, then blinked. She swore softly under her breath.

"What?" Kimber asked.

"Ever give great advice to someone else that you should be taking yourself?"

"I haven't eaten a salad in six weeks but I made Hadley and Ian try four different Brussels sprouts recipes last week. What do you think?"

"I think you know what I'm talking about."

Kimber raised her cup in the air in a mock toast, and Remi did the same.

"I don't even know if he's happy," Kimber said.

"Are *you* happy?"

"I'm fucking miserable. Haven't you been listening to me yell at you?" There was no heat to her sister's words. "I mean, I basically tried to pin years of dissatisfaction with my own life on you because you were handy and Kyle made time to be concerned about you."

"What would make you happy besides selling your children to the circus and dumping Kyle's body in the lake?" Remi asked.

"I haven't really thought much past Ian on a trapeze and Hadley barking for the bearded lady."

Remi felt the glimmer of recognition. A glimpse of the smart, snarky big sister she'd idolized. "Who could blame you? So what have you tried?"

"Tried?" Kimber asked, pausing to make a slurping noise at the bottom of her drink.

"With Kyle, with the kids. You want something more than home improvement projects and that creepy whiteboard. What have you talked to them about?"

"Well, nothing really. I mean, I yell at Kyle for skipping out on yet another family event. And then I yell at my kids for making demands like doing their laundry faster so Ian can have his lucky underwear for his math test. Or Hadley forgetting to tell me she signed up for the junior high bake sale and needs four dozen cupcakes tomorrow."

"Mm-hmm. So yelling," Remi said, hopping down off the counter and strolling into the laundry room. She picked up the hot pink eraser from the chalk tray.

"How long does it take you to update this every week?" she asked.

"About an hour and a half. But that's after I've worked out the meal plan, made the grocery list, and reviewed Kyle and the kids' schedules," Kimber said.

"Hmm. Interesting." Casually, Remi lifted the eraser and swiped it right through the column labeled Monday, erasing the day from existence.

Kimber's eyes went wide. "You erased my Monday."

"Yelling," Remi repeated, and wrote it on the board in red. "Did it work?"

Kimber shook her head, still staring at the damage to her weekly schedule. Then she went back into the kitchen, and Remi heard the telltale sound of vodka pouring into a sippy cup.

"What else?" Remi called.

"Guilt trips," Kimber said, reappearing. "The back of the hand to the forehead kind of martyrdom as I carry another laundry basket up the stairs like a peasant woman in pioneer days."

"Guilt trips," Remi wrote. "Good. Any results?"

"Yeah. They all got even better at ignoring my under the breath mutterings," Kimber said.

"If these are the only two approaches you've tried, I think there's a lot of fresh options. For instance, have you considered kicking Kyle in the balls instead of doing his laundry?"

Kimber laughed, choking on vodka and tonic. She hiccuped. "I'm saving that for a last resort."

"Now, feel free to ignore me because I don't have children and a house to run. But I'm seeing a whole lot of doing things for other people and nothing like 'take bath with waterproof vibrator and romance novel' on your list."

"You aren't actually selling sex toys are you?" Kimber asked.

"Ha. Ha. We're talking about you right now. It looks to me like you're filling your hours with responsibilities and tasks for other people. What's the worst that could happen if, instead of making turkey burgers on Wednesday, you just told the kids to make whatever they want."

"They would eat ice cream for dinner, make a huge mess in the kitchen, and I'd be forced to spend two hours cleaning chocolate syrup off the dog," Kimber said.

"So it's easier if you do it all yourself?" Remi pressed.

"Well, yeah. No one else is going to do it the way I want it done. So it's just easier for me to be the one to do it."

"In theory," Remi said, wielding the marker, "if your goal was to raise children incapable of making themselves a peanut butter and jelly or doing their own laundry, you would be correct."

Kimber pursed her lips. "Shit." She took another slurp from the straw. "You are making a point that I'm not sure I'm mentally ready to accept. I may need to linger longer in the martyr zone."

"Understandable and valid," Remi said, handing her sister the eraser.

Kimber hopped up on top of the washer and took another long pull on her straw. "I'm really sorry for being a raging asshole to you the other night. I hate people who take their existential misery out on others, and that's exactly what I did to you."

"Apology accepted," Remi said, stretching out on the spot-less bench perched above a neat row of snow boots.

"You shouldn't accept apologies so easily. That just gives assholes like me the opening to be assholes again."

"You're not a real asshole. At least not a permanent one."

On a sigh, Kimber dropped her head back and stared up at the ceiling. "I just never had the path like you did, you know?"

"What path?"

Her sister gestured with her Dora the Explorer sippy cup. "You know. Painting. You were destined for it. The only thing I knew for sure is that I wanted to have a family."

"There's nothing wrong with wanting to have a family, weirdo," Remi pointed out.

"Of course not. But what's it say about me that I got what I wanted and I can't stop complaining about it? We tried for a year and a half to get pregnant with Hadley. My entire life was ovulation charts and sperm counts and researching whether microwaving leftovers could destroy my eggs."

"Just because you wanted something and you worked really fucking hard to get it doesn't mean you don't get to acknowledge what a horrific pain in the ass it can be," Remi pointed out.

Kimber's eyebrows rose. "Jeez, Rem. When the hell did you get all wise?"

"Recent experience," Remi said, rattling the ice in her cup. "There's nothing wrong with wanting more. There's also nothing wrong with demanding help so you can pursue things you want to do. Is it more important that all of Ian's snow pants are dry on Friday or that he knows how to shoulder his share of the work in a home and a relationship?"

Her sister was silent.

"And what's a better example for Hadley? Seeing her mom

sacrifice everything, including her already questionable mental stability—"

"Hey!" Kimber threw a box of dryer sheets at her.

"—for her children?" Remi continued. "Or seeing a woman who knows how to take care of herself first as a whole, complete person with goals and interests and at least one goddamn slot on her own calendar?"

"You know, *I'm* the older sister," Kimber said. "I should be the one advising you."

"How many days do you have to catch up on the disaster I'm making of my life?"

"Well, apparently I have Mondays free now," her sister quipped.

"In that case, I'll come back Monday and tell you that I had a breakthrough year as an artist painting under another name. My bank account has actual commas. It was going great until I found out my best friend's husband was abusing her, and when I tried to help her get out of the relationship, he nearly killed us both in a car accident. So I ran here to lick my wounds and ended up licking Brick's spectacular body instead. Now I'm exhausted and sort of, maybe happy and very terrified and sore from having too many orgasms. My orgasm muscles are *sore*, Kimber. And there's a distinct possibility that Brick legitimately ruined my lady parts for all other men. I'm seriously entertaining the idea of dating only women when he runs away from me again just so I don't have to compare future sexual partners to the literal god of sex."

Her sister stared at her with an open mouth for several long beats. She looked down at her cup. "I think I'm going to need another drink."

They were on their third round of drinks and explanations when the front door burst open. "Mom! We're home," Hadley called.

"Mom!" Ian bellowed. "Did you remember Grandma and Grandpa's anniversary? Grandpa said in school today it's a big one and he thinks you and Aunt Remi forgot."

Remi and Kimber shared a glance.

"Well, shit."

38

"*I*f you open that oven one more time, I'm going to skewer and marinate you." Jenise Heffernan, supreme ruler of the Tiki Tavern kitchen, slapped Brick's hands away with a wooden spoon. She was 6'1", blonde, somewhere between the ages of forty-five and sixty, and did not tolerate people—including the boss—invading her space.

"I just wanted to check—"

"You're acting like you've got stage fright. This isn't Tiki Tavern's first private party, and this sure as hell isn't my first catering gig. Now get your ass out of my kitchen and go panic over something else. The food will be perfect," she promised.

He took her advice—and the parting slap on his ass with the wooden spoon—and headed for the stairs. An unseasonably warm March Saturday had worked in their favor barely a week after Remi and Kimber had come to him with big eyes and pouty lips.

Between his off-the-books investigation, getting Remi naked as often as physically possible, and actual work, he'd managed to pull together what he hoped would be an appropriate celebration of the Fords' thirty-five years together.

He jogged up the steps and pushed through the door into a Caribbean wonderland. So themed out of necessity rather than sentiment. Their decor choices were either country-western or island, and the girls had gone with tropical. He'd negotiated the use of a tent from the Grand Hotel, setting it and a dozen patio heaters up on the Tiki Tavern's rooftop bar.

Darius and Ken had gone all out on the decorations. The big fake palms they kept in storage until spring had been dragged out and dusted off. Strands of white Christmas lights hung from the tent rafters. The tables were decked with colorful linens and floral centerpieces. Every item downstairs that fit the festive theme had been hauled up to join the party.

The buffet table stretched out along one wall, ready for Jenise's tropically inspired eats.

The margarita maker at the bar had been filled with Darius's latest cocktail concoction, the pink and frothy 35-to-life.

Kimber waved from the DJ booth where she was making the last-minute changes to the slideshow she'd put together. Thirty-five years in one highlight reel. Darlene and Gil had been married almost as long as he'd been alive.

"Need anything?" he asked her, wiping his hands over the seat of his jeans.

She shook her head. "Nothing besides making sure my kids don't get at those signature drinks," she said with a harried smile.

"Got that covered. I made virgin strawberry daiquiris," Brick told her.

She shook her head. "You're a good man, Brick. Any woman who lands you permanently is going to be very lucky."

Permanently. His palms were sweaty.

After Audrey, he'd sworn off permanent. He'd tried and failed. And learned there was no way to guarantee the person he chose would stay the same. Would want the same things forever. He knew what he wanted. To be here, on this island, with his community. But now there was a wild card in play. Remi.

The last two weeks had been the best of his life. Walking in the door and finding Remington Ford in his kitchen, covered in flecks of paint and very little else. Waking up each morning to her star-fished facedown on the bed, one hand clamped possessively around whatever body part of his she could get to. Witnessing her surrender her body to his again and again. He was living out a fever dream and never wanted to wake up.

He wanted more of exactly that. A lifetime of it.

But what kind of a lifetime did Remi want? She wasn't one to plant roots. And he wasn't one to comfortably tumble from place to place. He disliked cities, the anonymous crush of busy strangers. He loved horses, open expanses of water, and the people he served.

But he couldn't ignore the gravitational pull of her. Just being in her orbit made his world bigger, brighter, more color-ful. And he was fucking terrified.

He wandered over to the buffet table and inspected the plates, the utensils, checked the flames on the burners.

"Holy Lady Gaga."

That familiar voice, the awe and excitement he heard in it, stuck him like one of Jenise's famous jerk chicken skewers.

Remi didn't look like Remi. She looked like Alessandra Ballard in a sequined dress that stopped several sexy inches above her knees. It shimmered like she did. Catching the light and the eye with its peachy gold sparkle and graceful long sleeves. Ken had done something goddess-like to her hair, pulling it back from her face in a high ponytail that rained down in thick red curls. Her eyes were smokier, lips bolder and redder.

His heart tripped in his chest, and for a second, he couldn't believe she was his. And then he remembered. She wasn't really. Not all the way. But that didn't stop him from wanting to slide his hand up between her thighs and discover what she wore underneath that dress. Or wrapping that fiery tail around his fist. Or kissing her so hard, so rough that red lipstick smeared.

"Brick, I can't believe you did this," she breathed.

Maybe she didn't look like his Remi, but she sounded like her. And it made him only want her more.

He crossed to her, drawn to her like a planet orbiting its sun. A masochist ready for his next punishment.

"You like it?" he asked gruffly. His fingers flexed at his sides, wanting to touch her, but he was afraid once he started, he wouldn't stop.

She nodded, and when she looked up at him again, he saw tears in her eyes.

He drew in a sharp breath. The desire to touch her, to taste her, was overwhelming. He wanted to give her this. He wanted to give her everything. To prove to her he was worth staying for.

A hand fluttered to her chest.

"Where's your inhaler," he asked.

She flashed him an aggravated eye-roll. "In my clutch in my coat, hanging up right inside the door," she promised. "I'm just overwhelmed by this."

He shrugged, pretending like it hadn't occupied nearly every waking hour for the last week. Pretending that he hadn't done it to put that exact look on her beautiful face. "It was no problem."

"Well, shit." Remi snatched a bright yellow napkin off one

of the tables and dabbed at the corners of her eyes. "This took work. A lot of that. I can see it. Thank you."

"You're welcome," he said, his voice strained.

Need had taken over. He couldn't stand not being able to touch her.

When she looked at him, he read it in her eyes.

"Can I see you for a second to talk about that thing?" She hooked her thumb toward the door and batted those big green eyes at him. When her teeth sank into that full, red lip, he barely managed not to pick her up and carry her out of there.

"Sure," he said, absolute shit at pretending.

His heart raced as he held the door open for her. When she made a move for the stairs, he grabbed her arm and hauled her inside the storage room instead.

He hadn't even managed to shut the door or find the light switch when her arms looped around his neck and dragged him down for a kiss.

It was pitch black in the room, but his senses were full of her. That electric scent. The breathy little moan she made when he forced her mouth open so his tongue could thrust inside. All the soft, willing warmth of her body under his rough palms.

It was insanity. An obsession. This need that grew bigger in him, threatening to overwhelm him. The desire to claim her choked him.

"How much time do we have?" she whispered.

"Thirty minutes," he said, dragging his teeth down the column of her neck.

"More than enough time to reapply my lipstick," she said cheerfully. Her gasp was music to his fucking ears when his hands coasted down over those generous breasts.

"You are so fucking beautiful, Remi."

She laughed lightly. "It's pitch black in here," she teased.

"You looked beautiful in the light and you feel beautiful in the dark."

Her breath hitched and then her fingers began to work their magic in the waistband of his pants.

"Remington," he growled.

"I forgot how hot you are in a tie. The beard, the tie, your sleeves rolled up. God, the way you look at me. It makes me stop thinking about anything but you."

Fuck. His dick swelled behind his zipper. He hated that suddenly the words weren't enough for the rest of him. He wanted more than Remi wanting his hands on her. He wanted her to need him, to love him.

"Let me thank you, Brick. Let me show you how much this means to me," she insisted, her hands working his belt open.

His stomach muscles tensed as she undid the button and lowered his zipper.

"What are you doing?" he groaned as her hands slid down his thighs when she dropped to her knees.

"Thanking you," she said. Her breath was hot against his aching cock.

His next words were forgotten as her velvet mouth closed over the tip of his cock.

Blindly, he slapped his hands against the door to hold himself upright as Remington Ford performed miracles on her knees. That mouth. That fucking glorious, wicked mouth was doing things to him in the dark that he couldn't comprehend. The rough of her tongue, the drag of her teeth. And when she gripped him at the root, when she closed those eager fingers around him tight, he knew he'd never be the same.

"I want to make you feel good," he said, the words coming out rough and tumble.

"You will. Later. This is just for you," she said, her lips

feathering over the tip. Tongue darting out to dance over the slit where even now moisture gathered. Getting sucked off by Remi in a dark closet. It had probably been a fantasy. Probably been something to keep him up at night after another family gathering. Another dinner across the table from her.

He couldn't go back now. He couldn't go back to before he knew what she felt like writhing under him, begging him for everything he could give her. Couldn't go back to a time when he didn't know what it felt like to fuck her sweet mouth. There would be no more Thanksgivings or Christmases together if she left. He wouldn't be able to look at her and not remember *this*. She was going to ruin him.

And he couldn't stop himself from letting her.

Her lips coasted down over his shaft, taking him to the back of her throat, working him in wet strokes. He could imagine her on her knees in front of him. Picture those green eyes looking up at him in wonder as he swelled in her mouth. As his balls drew up against his body, fire burning inside them.

She gave him so much with her body. But he wanted more. He wanted forever with her.

But right now. *Right now.* She was taking him to heaven.

His fingers dug into the metal of the door. He couldn't help himself, he had to thrust. Fisting one hand in that glorious hair. He used his grip to guide her pace. Soft grunts clawed their way out of his throat as a pleasure so intense burned him from the inside out. It was building at the base of his spine. In his balls. The pulsing throb was almost painful.

Remi moaned, the hum of it like a match to turpentine. It lit him up.

"Remington," he hissed.

She gripped his shaft tighter with both hands and took him deep.

Again and again, he thrust into her mouth until he was mindless, until nothing else existed to him but the razor's edge of pleasure.

"Baby," he rasped. "I'm going to come. Don't try to—Oh, God."

She wouldn't let him pull out. It only made her suck him harder. And when she released one hand from the root of his erection to palm his balls, he lost it.

The release caught him by the throat as it lanced through him. It scalded him from the inside out, that first fiery rope of come as it exploded forth. Into her mouth. In a panic, he found the light switch and slapped it on just so he could watch.

She was worshipping him, a goddess on her knees.

His breath caught, every fiber of muscle in his body tensed as pleasure sharp as pain stabbed him. Again and again, he rocked into her mouth, bucking his hips in erratic thrusts as she took everything he had to give. As she milked every drop from him, allowing nothing to be held back.

That's what she did. She'd never settle for anything less than all. And for once, he wanted to demand the same.

Even after he was done, even after she'd sucked him dry, he kept up with the shallow, greedy thrusts.

He was dizzy. His thighs quaked with the effort it took to hold himself upright. Remi had been made for a lot of things. One of those things was giving him pleasure. He was sure of it.

Drawing in a shaky breath, he couldn't do anything but lean his forehead against the door and try not to collapse on top of her. Try not to tell her that he loved her. That he'd always loved her. That he'd never be the same without her.

Her hands were stroking up and down his thighs. Soothing the beast after she'd riled it.

"Are you okay?" he asked gruffly after a long minute. "Did I hurt you?"

"Okay?" There was laughter in her voice. "I feel like a million bucks making big Brick Callan's knees shake like that."

She'd been making his knees quake for years.

"Baby, you are going to be the death of me," he whispered.

Her lips skimmed the sensitive head of his still half-hard penis. A kiss. Christ. How in the fuck was he supposed to survive this? Realizing he still had her hair wrapped around his fingers, he loosened his grip.

Unable to do anything else with his body, he stroked his hand over her hair as she tucked him back into his pants.

He finally managed to reach down and pull her to her feet.

"That was... You are... I'm..."

She framed his face with her hands. "Thank you for doing this for my parents," she said. "For Kimber. For me. Thank you for always being there. Thank you for always taking care of me. It means the world to me."

"Uh-huh." It was all he could manage.

She kissed him on both cheeks and then once on the mouth. "I'll see you out there, big guy."

"Uh-huh."

She was reaching for the doorknob when he caught her and pulled her back against him. "Wait."

She tilted her hips against him, teasing his half-hard dick with that sweet ass. "I don't think we have time for another round," she teased.

"Can I touch you? Out there I mean. Can I hold your hand? Dance with you?"

Remi turned in his arms to face him. She looked stunned. "Of course."

"We haven't been out in public together. We haven't been together in front of your parents." He needed to be able to touch her. To remind them both that while she was on this island, she belonged to him.

"Everyone knows we're...you know. It's not a big deal," she said, patting his arm as if trying to reassure him.

Not a big deal. The words echoed in his head. *We're...you know.* It was a big deal, and no, he didn't fucking know. She was trying to shoehorn distance between them after she'd gotten on her knees for him. After he'd barely slept for a week trying to do this for her.

"Just don't try to find out what kind of underwear I've got on under the table, or I might embarrass us both," she said lightly.

It seemed there was only one language Remi understood. He caught her by the hair and dragged her over to the folding table that until about an hour ago had been buried under catering supplies.

"Brick! We don't have time," she said, her voice husky.

"Don't make a sound," he warned her as he forced her to fold over it.

The dress rode up indecently high, sending him into possessive overdrive. She was already pressing her thighs together, trying to relieve some of the pressure. He'd relieve it for her. And in the process, he'd remind her that what they were to each other was a very big fucking deal.

Impatiently, he nudged her feet apart and shoved the skirt of her dress up. He loved the bite of the sequins against his skin, but it was the view he was obsessed with. She wore a skimpy black thong with straps that crisscrossed above and around her shapely cheeks.

"Hold on to the table," he growled.

She obeyed, her entire body vibrating, anxiously anticipating what he was going to do to her. He wanted to punish her for making light of what they had. To parade her around the dance floor with his handprint hidden under that dress.

But more, he wanted her absolute submission. Wanted her helpless and needy.

For that, he sank to his knees behind her. He hooked his fingers into the delicate straps and dragged the material down to her thighs. She was shaking now as he admired how wet her folds were. There was no time for reverence though. Just enough time to dominate.

He leaned forward and brought the flat of his tongue to the slick flesh between her legs. She let out a choked sob, which he rewarded by grabbing both of her cheeks and spreading them wide. He continued to tongue her, stroking through the folds, licking her from clit to anus and back again. Back and forth, until he could feel her clenching hollowly around the tip of his tongue.

"Brick! *Brick*!" It was half whisper, half moan, and went straight to his dick.

He pulled back and let his hand fly hard and fast. The sharp slap and her soft, breathy gasp rang out in the small room, making his balls ache. He returned his attention to her sex. Stroking over that tight bundle of nerves with his tongue before dipping into her entrance. He wanted to devour her. Wanted to bathe in her. He wanted to break her. Again and again, until she was strung so tight he thought she might snap.

She bucked against his mouth, begging without words for more. And when he knew she was close, when he knew it was time, he sank two fingers into her tight channel. She was biting her lip, trying not to make a sound as he fucked her.

"Good girl," he rasped as he pressed his thumb against the tight ring of muscle in her cleft.

She rocketed up from the table on a gasp as he slid inside.

"Do I need to put my hand over your mouth or can I get

you off with it?" Brick demanded in her ear as he pumped his fingers in and out.

She nodded quietly.

"Then put your hands on the table, Remington, and spread your legs for me."

He felt like a fucking hero when she complied. When she submitted, hinging forward and pressing that tight little ass against him.

He could come again. He could fuck his way into that tight pussy and go off on her hungry squeezes, but he needed to hold back something. Needed to keep a part of himself safe from the devastation.

She was riding his hand now, bucking against him as he thrust into her. He slid his free hand around to her front.

"You're so fucking wet, baby. Did sucking me off do that to you? Did making me come in your mouth make you hot?"

She nodded, a small sob clawing its way out of her throat.

"Don't forget who makes you wet." He brought his hand between her legs to possessively cup her sex. "Don't forget who you belong to. Who makes you come."

Using the pads of his fingers, he circled her swollen clit. The shuddery moan that escaped her drove him to the edge of sanity. He couldn't stop himself from grinding his erection against her ass while he fucked her with his fingers.

"Say it, Remi. Who do you belong to? Who's making you fucking come?"

She was writhing against him, lipstick smeared, eyes shut tight, as she waited for *him* to deliver her pleasure. It was an arresting, filthy picture that was only complete when she tightened around his fingers.

"Y-you," she whispered.

"That's right, baby. Push back against me. Come all over my fingers."

Her lips parted, and her body went rigid against his. He kept on thrusting with his fingers, with his cock against the soft curve of her ass. Kept on rubbing dirty little circles over her clit as she went off. Clenching, clamping, releasing, relaxing. She collapsed to her elbows, covering her mouth with her own hand as she sobbed through a devastating release.

She trusted him to give her this. To take it so forcefully. She trusted him to protect her. But it wasn't enough. He wanted it all.

He waited until she was done, weak and shaking, before pulling back. Before he gently tugged her thong back into place.

His fingers traced the outline of the handprint he'd left on her, making goose bumps appear.

She made no move to stand after he smoothed her dress back down, thrilling him with a perverse triumph.

They'd both gotten off and they'd both lost something.

"Next time you want to tell me this isn't a big deal, or you don't want to say that we're in this together, I want you to remember this," he said darkly and then he walked out the door.

39

*R*emi brought her hands to her flushed cheeks and watched in delight as her parents whirled past her to a Zac Brown Band tune. At some point in their thirty-five years together, they must have taken dance lessons because they practically sailed across the dance floor in perfect unison.

Darlene and Gilbert Ford got each other. They were wildly different yet still managed to stay in sync.

Kimber and Kyle were at a table, avoiding eye contact.

And Brick, in that fucking sexy tie, was everywhere at once. Keeping an eye on the food, restocking plates, and generally wielding control over the chaos. And shooting her looks that made her knees go weak. It was clear that he was mad. It wasn't clear what he was mad at. Especially since he'd seemed fine between their orgasms.

But even pissed at her, he was still there making sure her parents had the best last-minute surprise anniversary party possible.

He was so good, so solid and sturdy.

Like her father, Brick Callan would always be there.

But he was holding himself back. And so was she. Worse, Remi didn't know if either of them had it in them to go all in.

She went with the flow. Stayed open to opportunity. She didn't tie herself down as a rule. That's what a relationship with Brick would be. At least a real one. He wouldn't exactly collar her and keep her tied to a bed. But wouldn't she feel the obligation to be more of what he wanted, less of what she wanted?

And what about all those past rejections? Just because they'd gone farther in the past few weeks than they ever had didn't mean there wasn't still progress to be made. Didn't mean he would want to take her on. She was too loud, too emotional, too chaotic. It's what had kept him at a distance for fourteen years.

Sex couldn't magically make things easier.

Her parents were the unicorns, she decided, watching as Darlene spun around in a short black dress that showed off her long legs. In the only impractical pair of shoes she owned, she was the same height as her husband.

They looked happy. They practically glowed with it.

And then there was Kimber and Kyle. Barely twelve years into their marriage, they'd gone from hot and heavy high school sweethearts to roommates who couldn't communicate their most basic needs.

This was the reality of most of the relationships Remi saw. People didn't stay happy. Hell, most times they didn't even stay together.

What would happen when things ended with Brick? Would Mackinac still feel like home? Or would she avoid the island even more than she had after his marriage?

His marriage to her best friend. They still hadn't talked about it. It wasn't a topic of conversation for acquaintances or casual lovers. And she wasn't sure she would like the answers she got.

The Audrey Remi remembered from high school was pretty, book smart, and easygoing. She'd never witnessed sparks flying between her best friend and her crush. The sparks had been reserved for Remi and Brick. Yet he'd pursued Audrey, married Audrey. The reliable one. The comfortable one. The easy to love one.

She remembered the hurt, the utter devastation. She'd been invited to their wedding, had actually come back to Mackinac with the intention of going. Of showing Brick that he didn't have her heart anymore. But when it came time, she couldn't do it. She couldn't bear watching him pledge himself to another woman.

So she'd feigned the flu and then told herself that it was just the remnants of a silly teenage crush. She pretended that she was more hurt by Audrey not telling her they were even dating. Their friendship had fizzled somewhere after high school and college. Somewhere along the line, Audrey and Brick had become strangers to her with their own lives apart from hers.

She watched Brick, sleeves rolled up as he traded an empty chafing dish for one full of pulled pork, her father's favorite.

He was a caretaker, a protector by nature. He wasn't open to the wild tumble of life, the flow of picking up and moving on. He was a monument. Cast in stone and planted in permanence. And sooner or later, he was going to break her heart again.

Only this time, it would be worse.

How would she survive? How would she look at him across the table in her parents' dining room and not remember the filthy promises he'd whispered in her ear as his body had taken hers to new heights?

This couldn't work out. It was destined to end horribly. Maybe that's why he'd fought the attraction so valiantly. Maybe Brick always understood the potential damage while she was only beginning to realize the truth.

Kyle was staring at his phone, thumbs flying across the screen, as his wife danced with Ken. Hadley and Ian were working their way through their parents' abandoned slices of cake.

A soul could wither up and die in that kind of life, Remi realized. Even if he wanted her to stay. Even if she gave it her all, there was no guarantee they wouldn't find themselves in a similar position. And when it ended, everything would be different.

"You look like you could use this," Darius said, appearing at her side with a frothy orange drink.

"Me?"

"Yes, Ms. Paler Than a Snowman. What's wrong? Is it your asthma?"

"It's not my asthma." It was her stupid freaking heart trying to break itself to pieces over the same man for a third time. "When are people going to stop treating me like an invalid?"

"Maybe when you stop looking so Disney princess-eyed and fragile?"

"Eww. Shut up."

He nudged her shoulder. "What are we wasting our time bickering for when there's a dance floor begging for us to wow it?"

Remi drained her drink and did what she did best, blocked out everything but the present moment. "Let's show 'em what we've got."

After a few energetic laps around the dance floor, Darius deposited her in her brother-in-law's arms and headed back to the bar.

"Hey," Remi said.

"Hey yourself." Kyle Olson's nickname when Kimber met him was Pretty Boy. It still fit. He had neatly coiffed blond hair, wore dark suits with skinny ties, and flashed a charming smile that disarmed juries and—at one time—her own sister.

Brick walked past them and leveled her with a heated glare that made her feel like her dress was on fire.

"How's your friend's novel going?"

Remi missed a beat and stepped on Kyle's foot.

"My what? Oh! It's good. Good."

"You had me worried that you were in some kind of trouble." Kyle was a trial lawyer. He had a bullshit meter that was more sensitive than most.

"Speaking of worried," she said, dodging his unasked question, "what is going on with you and my sister?"

His jaw tightened. "I wish I knew."

"You're going to work this out," she said firmly. They had been so in love once. The idea that it could all just disappear was heartbreaking.

"I would if I knew what the problem was. Every time I ask her, she shuts down."

"Do you ask her like her super cute husband who cares about her and wants her to be happy, or do you ask her like she's a hostile witness under cross-examination?"

His smile didn't quite reach his eyes. "There's a difference?"

"Ha. But seriously."

"Ladies and gentlemen," Kimber said into a microphone borrowed from the DJ booth. "It's time for a walk down memory lane."

Darlene perched on Gil's lap, each with a glass of champagne, and gestured for Remi to sit next to them.

"Get over here, Brick," Darlene said, waving him over. "Join the family."

Remi's body tingled as he took the chair behind her.

When the lights dimmed, Brick tugged her chair backward until she was caged in between his long legs. His warm, rough palm cupped the back of her neck possessively, and she relaxed. His touch was a drug that could soothe and arouse.

Prince's song "Kiss" blared from the speakers, producing a fine mist of yellows and oranges before Remi's eyes. The colors of happiness.

The crowd "awed" over the earliest pictures of Darlene and Gil's relationship. '80s hair. Ripped denim. Hair spray. They were so young and full of hope.

Young Darlene looked at the skinny, gawky Gilbert like he'd hung the stars in the night sky.

The photos tracked a timeline of love and laughter. An entire lifetime of happiness, Remi realized. Sure, it was a highlight reel. There had been fights and frustrations. There had been late nights with vomiting children and long talks about discipline. There had been bills to pay and parents to mourn. There had been rough patches and uncertainty. But they'd made a commitment to each other to grow and change together.

Tears filled her eyes as the happy couple stared down at fresh-to-the-world baby Kimber, sleeping peacefully as her parents gazed at her with awe. A family now.

There was Darlene, pregnant, working the dispatch desk at the station. Gilbert with his bushy mustache and plaid corduroys. Brick's hold on her tightened almost imperceptibly at the next picture. A tiny, red-faced, red-haired baby frozen mid-scream.

They'd made room for her. Loving her as fiercely as she'd loved them. Even though she'd been different. Even though she'd been too much and not enough.

Was a life like this possible? Could she build one?

She reached behind her and put a hand on Brick's rock hard thigh, reassuring herself that he was still there.

The song changed to Kool and the Gang's "Cherish," and the colors she saw shifted accordingly to purples and blues.

With care, Brick laced his fingers through hers and squeezed her hand, connecting them despite his unexplained anger, despite her confusion and fears. It was real and binding.

What he hadn't shared with her created a valley between them. But what they'd shared together, the intimacy, the vulnerability, bridged it.

She was electrified sitting there with him in the dark. As if her entire being was plugged into his. As if those broad shoulders and wide chest were the home she'd sought. As if he was a beacon in the dark, a lighthouse.

The craving to have his hands on her, even now, even among family and friends, was overpowering. Handholding had never been erotic before. It had never signified anything more than a flirtation. But in this moment it took on the weight of this secret between them, the weight of the secrets he carried. She felt the steady strength in his grip and knew that her body belonged to him even if her heart and mind couldn't trust it.

They needed to talk. Needed to set things straight. Needed to remember where they'd come from and where they were heading.

His thumb skimmed over hers as the screen followed the now teenage sisters and their parents. And there was Brick. It had to have been one of his first days on the island. He was standing in the Ford kitchen, cowboy hat on, quietly observing. He was so young. And there was hurt in the set of his shoulders. Sixteen-year-old Remi was standing in front of him, head tilted way back. She was smiling smugly up at him as if to say, "You're already mine. I've already won."

She'd loved him.

The truth of it struck true like an arrow. From day one, she had loved Brick Callan, and he'd broken her heart twice. What kind of a masochist kept coming back, kept asking for more?

She wanted to run. Wanted to get out of the tent, away from everyone. Wanted to turn up her music and pick up a brush and lose herself in the feelings. She wanted to exorcise the feelings onto canvas to make sense of them. How could she love a man she didn't trust with her heart?

How could she trust him not to hurt her again? He would protect her. She had no doubt of that. Brick would lay down his life for her. But would he share it?

Dizzy, she started to pull away, but Brick held her there, anchored to him with a solid grip that made her feel like running and staying at the same time.

His thumb brushed hers rhythmically, insistently.

The pictures flashed forward on the screen. Christmases, birthdays, Fourth of Julys. They all got older. The house changed. The town changed.

Remi tried to focus on the slideshow and the colors the music produced as they floated up to the peaks of the tent and wove their way around the people gathered to celebrate with them.

"What colors do you see?" Brick's voice was low and rough in her ear. His lip grazed her lobe, and she shivered involuntarily at the contact.

"I see greens and blues billowing like smoke," she whispered back. The desire to slide into his arms even after her revelation was intense.

She glanced back at him, but his gaze was on the screen. The strong jaw under the neatly trimmed beard, the crinkles around his eyes. The firm set of his mouth.

His grip tightened without warning, and she sensed him tensing next to her. Scanning the room for the threat, she spotted the photo on the screen.

Brick looking dapper and stalwart on his wedding day. Audrey, stunning in white lace, beaming at him. Darlene and Gil posed next to them like family at the altar.

She remembered then. The why this wouldn't work. He'd made his choice, and it hadn't been her.

40

*S*he gave serious thought to ignoring the knock on her door but recalled the shower incident and changed her mind.

"You ran away," Brick said, pushing past her, not waiting for an invitation. While she had changed into her oversized hoodie and knee socks, he was still dressed for the party in dark slacks and a tie.

"I did not. I walked home at a leisurely pace," she lied. As soon as the party wrapped, as soon as she'd done enough to help with the clean-up, she'd ducked out and run like hell before slipping on a patch of ice and almost taking a header through a tidy picket fence.

"You ran away. And that was after you shut me out."

"I would hardly call giving you a blow job shutting you—"

"Don't," he snapped. The icy fire of his temper was evident in his gaze, his stance. He was coiled and ready.

"Don't what?" she challenged.

"Don't try to reduce what's going on between us to that."

"Sorry," she said, heavy on the sarcasm. "I didn't realize sucking your dick—"

She found herself backed against the wall with a hard, angry man in front of her. His hands were gentle on her, but the rest of him vibrated with anger. For some reason, she found his restraint fucking hot.

"No. We're talking about this. No deflecting or distracting. We're having it out."

When he looked at her like this, it made her feel like she was the center of his universe. Like nothing else mattered but what was happening between them. But that wasn't the truth.

"*You* want to talk?"

He nodded slowly, his teeth bared.

"You never want to talk." Her voice shook as he leaned in and took a deep, carnal breath at her neck.

"I talk all the fucking time," he insisted.

"Fine. Then talk," she said, trying to duck under his arm but finding herself going nowhere as he cupped her jaw, holding her lightly by the throat.

"Do you know what it does to me to be that close to you and not be able to touch you like I want to?" he asked, his voice soft and jagged.

Wordlessly she shook her head.

"It's fucking torture. It's a new ring of hell to know what your skin feels like, to know what you taste like, but I still can't touch you unless we're alone."

The hand at her throat coasted down over her shoulder and chest to her breast.

She drew in a breath. Her body melted against him, succumbing, surrendering.

But then his touch was gone, and with a growl, he slapped his palm against the wall above her head.

"I can't keep doing this, Remi," he said.

Panic bloomed in her chest. He was doing exactly what she'd feared he'd do. *She* should be the one who was supposed to put an end to things. *She* should save herself the agony of...this. *She* should be the one to withdraw. But he was beating her to the punch. Again.

"Then don't," she snapped. Anger and fear joined forces inside her, making the world come into sharp focus. The flare of his nostrils. The parting of his lips. The fire in his eyes that threatened to burn her to ashes.

"I can't help myself," he confessed. "I know how this is going to end and I can't stop myself from wanting more anyway."

"What kind of more?"

His breathing was heavy and hot on her face.

"I saw what your parents have tonight. Decades of it. A life together. A partnership."

What was he saying? She was having trouble catching her breath. It came out in a shallow whistle.

Brick swore and pushed away from her. She sagged against the wall. Spotting her clutch on the table, he opened it and fished out her inhaler.

"I don't need it," Remi insisted as he returned it to her.

"Then take a fucking breath and prove it."

"God, you piss me off."

"Right back at you, baby. You piss me off, wind me up, and leave me wanting more of something I never should have had in the first place."

"Why did you marry Audrey?" Her question slashed through the air like a whip. Silence rang in her ears after.

His mouth closed in that firm line. His answers locked in the vault.

"What? You wanted to talk. So let's talk. Why did you marry Audrey? Why did you pick her? Why not me?"

He was so stubbornly silent.

She shoved at his chest, not moving him an inch. Somewhere in the back of her mind, it registered how much they both seemed to like it.

"Because I couldn't have you," he said hoarsely.

"Why the fuck not, Brick? You *knew* I loved you."

Again, she was met with silence. But this time it wasn't so indomitable. Brick was vibrating with an energy that demanded to be let out. With words that wanted to ring their truth.

"You *loved* me?" he repeated.

"Of course I did. I loved you, and you chose my best friend over me. Why?"

"Because I couldn't fucking have you!"

"What does that even mean? Why not? Audrey was my age. So it wasn't that I was too young. My parents have adored you since they met you. I wanted to be yours *so much,* and you just kept rejecting me." Her voice broke along with the dam of emotions she'd held back for too long.

He was trembling against her, and she knew something was about to happen.

"You rejected me over and over again," she whispered. "You made up reasons that we both know were just excuses. Then you chose someone else. And when you finally let us start to explore this thing between us, you give me a couple of orgasms and say you can't do it anymore. What do you want from me, Brick? Am I here just because Audrey isn't?"

"I married Audrey to ruin any chance I had with you."

She felt sick, dizzy, devastated. And in some mean, dark corner of her mind, a little voice said *I told you so.*

"Why?" She barely managed to get the word out.

"God damn it. I can't live with you looking at me like that," he snapped.

"Like what?" A tear slipped out of the corner of her eye and burned a path down her cheek.

"Like I just destroyed you."

Her laugh was humorless. "Many men have tried," she quipped, wiping her cheek with the sleeve of her sweatshirt.

"Don't fucking joke about that," he said, whirling her around to face the wall. She braced herself against the drywall and cursed her body for begging for what she wanted. She tilted her behind back, offering herself to him.

His hand coasted down to cup her rear end.

"Do you see what's happening here? I can't control myself around you. I never could." As if to emphasize his point, he tracked his fingers up the valley between her cheeks, finding the thin band of her thong.

"You've done nothing but control yourself!"

"I've been hanging on by my goddamn finger nails for years, Remi. I've got nothing left. Every time you make me chase you, I lose a little bit more willpower. Standing here now, saying the things I should have said years ago, and all I can think of is how much I want to pull this shirt up. How much I want to put my hands on you. How much I want to hear the sound of my hand connecting with your skin. How much I want to see that cheek turn pink with my mark. How much I want to hear you say you're sorry for making me chase you in that breathy little voice you have when you know you're about to get fucked."

Her entire body was shaking now, quaking between the wall and the man.

And when he sank behind her, when those hot finger tips under her sweatshirt skated higher, bringing the material with them, she let out a shaky moan. He held the hem against her back and stroked the skin exposed by her thong with the other.

"You haunt my every waking moment, Remington. The

best thing about this world is that you're in it. But I can't have what I want." She could hear the agony in his voice.

"You aren't making any fucking sense! What is so horrible about the idea of being with me?"

"Because I won't survive you! Because if I did get lucky enough to lock you down, eventually you'd find out."

"Find out what?"

"That I don't deserve you. That I'm not good enough for you. That all I have to offer you is protection and sex."

She gasped as he took a handful of flesh and squeezed.

"Those are the only reasons you come to me," he whispered. "The only reason you're standing here taking this is because you want it almost as much as I want to give it to you."

"What's wrong with that?"

"Nothing," he breathed, running his fingertips over her curves, "if there's more."

"What more do you want from me?" Again, she arched her back, tilting her rear end up in invitation.

"You're my dream come true wrapped in a nightmare. The only thing you're willing to give me is your body, and that's not enough."

"Are you saying I'm using you?"

"I'm saying I feel used. And I hate myself for still wanting you. For wanting that to be enough." He yanked her back against his thighs, and with a dip of his knees, he lined his arousal up between her legs and pumped viciously against her as if they weren't separated by their clothing. "I hate myself for wanting to fuck you like this now when I know it doesn't mean the same to you."

"You don't know that," she cried. "You don't get to take your mommy-daddy baggage out on me. Your parents sucked. That wasn't your fault. But what you choose to do now is just that. Your choice. You don't get to paint me with the same brush you painted them. You could have had me! I could have loved you. I could have been the best thing that ever happened to you!"

"Yes. Until it was over for you. Until you were ready for your next adventure. Your next city." He wrapped her ponytail around his hand and tugged. "Look at you. When you walked in tonight, my heart fucking stopped. It still hasn't restarted. You don't look like you. You don't look like the girl who sank my goddamn snowmobile or the one who cries every time she watches *Father of the Bride*. You look like Alessandra Ballard."

"I am Alessandra Ballard. And Remi Ford. They're the same damn girl. They're both me."

"You want things I can't give you. I'm never going to be happy living in a city surrounded by strangers. I don't want to get dressed up every night and go out for the attention."

He was hard. So fucking hard against her. It made her needy sex throb.

"So I tried to find my own happiness. I picked a nice girl who didn't scare the hell out of me. Who wouldn't ask me for too much. Who would make sure that I never had a shot with you again."

The truth fucking hurt.

"Why?" she asked, as his fingers kneaded her hair, as his hips ground against her.

"Because I love you. I've always loved you." His voice shook. "Because I won't survive it when you leave."

She froze.

"But you were always going to leave," he whispered against her ear. "You're *still* going to leave. Even after what we found together. You're going to get on a plane or a ferry or a goddamn snowmobile and you're going to leave. Me. You want a big life. You want adventure, novelty. You want to be great. How are you going to do that from here?"

Just like his mother.

It struck like the diamond point of lightning right into her heart.

"I don't fault you for that," he said, moving his lips over her neck. His beard abrading her skin. "I want people to look at what you've created and be dazzled by it, just like I'm dazzled by you. But this place is my home. The only place I've ever belonged. You gave that to me and you're the only one with the power to take it away. Because I'd follow you if you let me. I'd go with you. But you're not even going to ask. You're going to stay here long enough for me to put Vorhees behind bars and then you're going to leave."

Tears rolled silently down her cheeks as it all sank in.

Brick Callan loved her. And he was terrified of her.

"You wanted to know why I married Audrey? You should be asking why we divorced. Because of you. Your name is the last word I breathe every night. Your face is the one I see when I close my eyes. I couldn't hide that from her."

She let out a broken sob and sucked in a breath. "Oh, fuck that. And fuck you, Brick. You let me think I wasn't good enough for years. You purposely *hurt me* just so you could keep yourself safe."

"So much for safe! I'm going to go to bed every night for the rest of my life thinking about you, and where will you be, Remington? Will you even remember me? Every fucking time I make you come, I feel you getting farther away from me. But I still can't stop myself."

"Because I don't want you to hurt me again! I can't take another rejection from you. Not after..."

"What? Not after what? Sex? Not after we fucked a few times? That's the only reason I'm here, isn't it? Because I make you feel good. That's why you're pushing that tight little ass against my dick, isn't it?"

She spun around and let her closed fist fly. Darlene Ford's daughters didn't slap. They cold-cocked. Brick dodged the blow easily and pulled her in tight so she couldn't put a knee in his balls. They struggled, wrestling each other to the hard floor. When they landed, his hand manacled hers over her head as she squirmed under him.

She knew they were fighting. Knew she was furious with him. But being restrained like this, being pinned by his heavy body, muddied things. She needed more, and so did he. Remi bucked her hips against him, an invitation as much as a challenge.

He gritted his teeth before kissing his way down her neck. "I hate myself for wanting one last time with you. One last chance to make you need me. Because that's all I'm good for. That's all I have to offer you. A place to feel safe. A way to feel good. It's not enough," he said, even as he loosened his belt.

Her chest heaved as she dragged in a breath.

"Open your legs," he ordered.

She reared up and bit his lower lip. "Make me."

She saw it in his eyes. The glimmer of excitement. The thrill of the line she was asking him to cross.

"You're proving my point, and I *still* can't help myself," he said, levering up to free his swollen erection from his pants. "I still can't say no to you."

His weight was on her wrists, making them ache, but watching him work that thick shaft with brutal strokes blocked out any pain except for the empty trembling of her inner walls.

"Open your fucking legs, Remington."

Biting her lip, she shook her head against the floor.

He let out a low growl as if he were in pain. "You tell me to stop if this goes too far."

A nod was all she'd give him.

With permission granted, Brick inserted a knee between her thighs. She fought it, squeezing against him and loving the illicit thrill of being restrained.

She was no match for his brute strength.

"This is the last time," he promised, gritting out the words as he used his hips to pin hers down.

She wanted to argue with him. Wanted to stop him and be the one to walk away. She wanted to prove him wrong. But all of those things fell a distant second to the need inside her. The need to be dominated by him. Taken by him. Marked by him. That took precedence.

She bucked against him, half-heartedly trying to twist away. But he simply spread her thighs wide and yanked her thong to the side.

Digging her heels into the floor, she tried once more to dislodge him and was thrilled when he didn't budge. His hand connected with the back of her thigh, delivering a stinging slap.

Their gazes locked a split second before he lunged into her. Claiming her.

"Brick!"

He didn't answer her cry of ecstasy. Just drove into her tight sex again and again, forcing her to take more of him each time, until finally every inch of him was sheathed inside her. Their bodies slid and scraped across the floor.

Even then, he didn't stop.

Quivering around him, she was primed to come, and each masterful thrust, each aggressive entry, pushed her closer to the edge.

This solved nothing. This only served to further complicate things. But even knowing that, even knowing she was reinforcing Brick's fear, Remi couldn't stop herself from crying his name as they fought like two storm systems clashing for dominance.

He powered into her, setting a wild pace that was nothing like the measured man he was outside the bedroom. He was lost in her, and she had two choices—to either fight it or to give in and lose herself, too.

"My beautiful girl." He punctuated each word with a thrust. "My Remi. I love you."

A sob broke free from her chest. There was something so beautiful, so final about the way he touched her.

His eyes went glassy as he drove into her core. Again and again. A man on a mission, punishing them both for their need.

Even angry with her, even wanting to end things, he *still* couldn't help himself. There was a delicious thrill in that. It made her feel powerful, desired, craved. With impatience, he yanked her legs higher on his hips, changing the angle of his entry.

He was still fully dressed. Together they writhed on the floor in a race to find the promised fulfillment.

He shoved her shirt up, baring her breasts, and groaned as he dipped his head to suck one nipple into his mouth. She saw stars and fireworks and explosions behind her eyes as he worked her body toward the finish line.

"You will come. Now," he said through gritted teeth. Beads of sweat dotted his forehead. "Give it up to me, Remi. Give me what I need. One last time."

One breath she was suspended somewhere between pleasure and pain, the next she was hurtling into the darkness as she erupted around him in the disorienting annihilation of her orgasm. He was her center, her anchor, tethering her to the pleasure that threatened to wreck her.

He grunted his pleasure, burying his face in her neck.

"Good girl. I love you so fucking much."

She couldn't answer, couldn't respond. So she did the only thing she could, closed around his shaft. He tensed against her, breath frozen in his lungs, energy stalling in his muscles. She felt his release in her very depths. The hot shock as he let it loose inside her, spurting in agonized ecstasy. It was a miracle. An art form. A joining that could never be undone no matter how far she ran away. No matter how much he denied it. They were forever linked by this act.

"Remington!" he shouted.

Every muscle in her body participated in the detonation even as he continued to plunder, to curse her, to both treasure and torture her.

As he poured himself into her, he continued to fuck her through her own never-ending release. He whispered the words over and over again. "I love you. I love you."

She held on to him tight, wrapping her arms around him and holding on. He'd gone and done it again. Broken her fucking heart, but this time it was different. This time she had the truth. She just didn't know what to do with it.

He thought she'd used him. Thought she'd drift out of his life like his mother had. It devastated her. And pissed her off. Long minutes later, she was still in a puddle of confusion and physical satisfaction on the floor when Brick got to his feet. He was still half-hard, a feat that defied biology.

"Lock the door behind me," he said as he tucked himself back into his pants.

"Are you serious? You're leaving?"

"I told you. This was the last time. Lock the fucking door, Remington."

She managed to maneuver herself into a sitting position just in time to watch him walk out her door without a backward glance.

41

───────

Two nights later, after much soul searching and a near nervous breakdown, Remi juggled bags and her pride as she climbed the porch steps to Brick's house. The porch light cast a welcoming glow she was certain wouldn't be reflected by the owner.

Heart heavy, belly nervous, she pressed the doorbell and waited.

She heard his heavy tread as he approached the door and blew out a breath. Had they broken up? Had they ever been together?

The door swung open, and she found herself staring up at an unhappy man mountain.

He looked miserable, exhausted like he hadn't slept since their fight Saturday.

She had that effect on people, she supposed.

His hair stood up like he'd been running his hands through it. He was wearing gray sweatpants and a black hoodie. For some reason, that made her nipples harden. But she wasn't here for her nipples. She was here for her heart.

"Are you here to get fucked, Remi?" he rasped.

The way he said it, the heated look delivered with those words, told her it wouldn't take any convincing on her part to make him reconsider his stance.

There was a razor's edge to his voice, and she could smell the bourbon on him. He was stone-cold sober because he never drank too much. Never let himself get too out of control, except in bed with her. And now he was suffering because of it.

"No. I'm here to make you dinner," she announced, pushing past him and ignoring the way her blood zinged through her veins when her arm brushed against his. He didn't stand back to give her room, merely towered over her as she dropped her bags and shed her boots and coat.

"What..." He cleared his throat and tried again. "What are you wearing?"

"Pajamas," she said, picking up her haul and heading toward the kitchen. "I marinated a couple of the chicken breasts you gave me. I hope you like the recipe."

He followed her into the kitchen and watched as she began to unload the bags. "What are you doing, Remi?" he asked.

She turned and looked him in the eyes. "I'm dating you."

"Dating me?"

She nodded. "I'm making you dinner, and we're gonna watch a movie."

He stood there and watched as she slid the casserole dish into the oven and turned it on. Magnus appeared and wound his way between her feet.

Remi picked him up and gave the cat a loud kiss on the head. "Hey, buddy. I brought you something, too," she said, producing a toy from one of the bags.

Magnus's yellow eyes went wild and he pounced on the patchwork mouse.

She couldn't look directly at Brick or she'd break into a million pieces, lose her nerve, and run screaming for the door. "I'll be a couple of minutes," she said, flashing a smile in his direction. "Why don't you get Netflix ready to go? We can eat on the couch as long as your grandma doesn't find out."

He ran a hand over his beard, considering.

She pretended to ignore him while she cued up the Date Night Playlist she'd made for tonight. She was committed to whole-assing this relationship thing no matter what. If it failed, it sure as hell wouldn't be because she didn't try.

He came up behind her, stopping short of touching her, but she felt him all the same.

"Remi," he said quietly.

Crap. It sounded like a "You need to leave" Remi. Or maybe an "I don't want to be around you anymore" Remi.

She turned around and smiled brightly, hoping to confuse him. "Yes?"

"What do you mean you're 'dating me'?"

"You thought I was using you for sex."

He winced and rubbed a hand through his beard. "I didn't actually mean—"

She held up a hand. "It's what you were feeling. You don't talk much, and when you do, it's what's actually happening inside behind that big brick wall. I heard you. Now I'm showing you I can do better. That I want more from you than just your supernatural ability to make me orgasm."

"Why do you want to date me?" he asked, looking adorably stunned.

A chunk of her romantic heart broke off, pieces splintering into dust. "Because I care about you, Brick. Not just your dick or how many ways you can make me come. You've been a big, important part of my life for so long. I'm sorry I let you forget how much you mean to me," she said in a rush.

"So we're dating?" He looked so damn serious.

She nodded. He didn't get to decide to break up with her before she'd decided they were dating in the first place. If he was going to give her the size fourteen boot, he could do so after she showed him just how great a girlfriend she could be. She was going to woo his damn face off.

"We're dating," she affirmed. "You're important to me, and I'm sorry I ever let you doubt that for a second. And *you're* sorry for ever believing that I'd use you."

He nodded slowly, a smile tugging at his lips.

"I am sorry," he agreed, reaching for her.

She held up her hands, stopping him before he touched her. "One more thing."

He braced himself with a deep breath. "What?"

"We're not having sex until I've proven to you that I'm serious. About us."

His eyebrows rose. "We're platonically dating?"

"Think of it as friends without the benefits. Sex was confusing things." Hell, it had overtaken everything. "We're starting over and giving this a real shot. So that means no orgasms until you know I'm interested in more than just certain body parts."

"Why do I feel like I'm being punished?"

"You're not," she insisted, pressing a hand to his chest and reveling in the feel of his heart pounding beneath it. He was so calm on the surface, but underneath was a different story. "You said things..."

"Things like I love you?" Brick tucked a loose strand of hair behind her ear, and she shivered at the contact.

"Things that made me stop and think," she said. "Things that scared the hell out of me. And part of me is still waiting for you to change your mind and back away again. But regardless, I'm in this until the bitter end."

"Then we use this time for you to convince me you want more than just sex and for me to convince you that I'm not going anywhere this time."

Him saying the words had her heart tripping in her chest.

"Without sex," she reminded him.

"Without sex," he agreed with an arch of his eyebrow.

She gave him a little shove. "Why don't you go find us a bottle of wine? I'll get dinner ready."

She waited until he left the kitchen before sagging against the counter.

She'd seduced and enjoyed. She'd fascinated and dazzled. She could freaking woo Brick. Couldn't she? As long as she didn't take the man's pants off, she could stay focused on the goal: Making Brick Callan realize he was more than good enough for her.

How hard could it be to not have sex with a man she'd spent fourteen years not having sex with?

The sexy son of a bitch returned with a bottle of wine and a smirk. He flashed the label at her, and she recognized it as one of her favorites. Of course the man who stocked Kraft Mac and Cheese for her would also have her favorite wine.

The urge to climb him like a tree flared to life between her thighs.

But it was the look in those blue eyes that stopped her. *Hope.* He was hopeful.

Remi turned away and swallowed hard. He made her feel so raw it made her hands shake.

Brick watched her silently as he found a corkscrew and went to work opening the bottle. While she fussed over the salad, he poured two glasses and slid one to her.

Their fingers tangled on the stem, and her pulse spiked. Everything about the man drew her in. But she wasn't going to jump this time. She was going to take it slow. Magnus sprinted into the room, the mouse in his mouth giving her the needed distraction to extricate her fingers and glass.

"What are we watching?" he asked, looking down at her. A flicker of a smile curving those brutal lips. He could tell she was nervous, and she knew he liked it.

"*The Quiet Man*," she announced.

He frowned. "I'm not familiar."

She gasped theatrically, side-stepping Magnus as he wriggled into one of her shopping bags. "*The Quiet Man*," she repeated.

"It doesn't matter how many times you say it."

"John Wayne is a quiet ex-boxer who moves to Ireland and falls in love with Maureen O'Hara, a wildcat with a wicked tongue and red hair."

He gave her a sexy half smile that had her cheeks going pink and nipples tightening to points. She took a gulp of wine.

"Sounds familiar. At least the part about the red-haired wild cat with a wicked tongue."

They both needed to stop talking about tongues. It wasn't helping her heightened arousal situation. "It's a classic. Besides you have no choice. Sacrifices must be made when you're dating," she said airily.

"I can help you with dinner," he said. They both watched as his index finger hooked itself in the neckline of her pajama top.

Her heart rate spiked when his finger grazed her sternum.

Yes. Wait. No.

This was a dangerous game. She grabbed his hand. "No sex. Remember? What's so funny?" she demanded when he gave her the full wattage of the rare Brick Callan grin.

She felt a little light-headed. And also like she'd won the lottery.

"Me touching you with a fingertip makes you think we're about to have sex."

"After the past few weeks, can you blame me?"

"Hmm." His hum was like a caress over her skin.

This was going to be harder than she thought. *Dammit! Harder.*

She shook her head until her brain sloshed around inside. "Focus. No sex. Not until you feel appreciated."

"I feel appreciated when you scream my name and lock down around my cock."

Holy Johnny Cash. Her body unanimously voted for boosting itself up on the counter and spreading her legs as wide as they could go for the man who looked like he wanted to devour her.

But her heart managed a veto.

"You felt used. That's on me," she said. "Ergo, it's up to me to prove to you how much I want the whole shebang. Hebang?"

He raised an eyebrow.

She grimaced. "Forget the banging. My point is, I know there's more to us than just sex, and I'm going to prove it to you."

"By not having sex with me."

She nodded. "No orgasms for me...or you. I don't think I could control myself if I was making you come," she admitted.

He closed his eyes like he was in pain. "Jesus, Remi."

"Just go with it, okay? I want to make this right."

42

*a*s John Wayne plowed his fist into another man's face, Brick wondered how the hell he'd gotten so fucking lucky. He'd spent the last forty-eight hours hating himself for what he'd said. What he'd done.

What kind of an asshole says "I love you," delivers a rough good-bye fuck, then walks out while his girl was still on the floor?

The Brick Callan kind of asshole.

He'd been handed the woman of his dreams naked on a platter, and what had he done? He'd immediately looked for reasons why they wouldn't work instead of ways they could work.

Remi giggled next to him on the couch. The lights were on low. The fire burning off the chill of the cold night. Snow falling silently outside. Their empty plates were stacked on the coffee table. Magnus was curled up on Remi's feet under the blanket, exhausted from his catnip high.

It was like a fantasy. Not all of his fantasies had involved Remi naked. Some had been staged just like this. A quiet, snowy night with the woman he loved curled against him, borrowing his heat.

He stroked his hand through her hair, and she let out a sigh that sounded almost like a purr. It was perfect. This moment.

The fight on-screen moved from the pub into the street. Apparently, public brawls were a sport in Ireland. One he understood. He'd fight for Remington. He'd fight any enemy to keep her safe, to defend her honor. He'd fight to show her what was in his heart.

He let his fingers whisper up and down her arm. Slowly, rhythmically. Reassuring himself that she was there.

She wanted to spend time with him. To date without the distraction of sex. Of course, he'd been rail-hard since the second she'd walked in wearing her ridiculous plaid pajamas with her hair a mess and her face scrubbed clean. She was more beautiful to him like this. Because this felt like the real Remi.

Dipping his head, he indulged himself and dropped a kiss to her fiery hair. She looked up at him. Those wide green eyes spearing right through him.

He loved her. He always had. There had never been another choice.

Slowly he lowered his mouth to hers. The connection they shared was undeniable. His blood heated as her lips moved gently under his. As she sighed into his mouth and he breathed her in. *"Remington."*

He took the kiss deeper, fighting to stay easy and sweet. But when he tasted her tongue, when she let out that tiny whimper that went straight to his cock, he was ravenous for her. He teased with tongue and teeth, stroking into her mouth as he pulled her into his lap.

He was so goddamn hard for her. *Only her.*

Then she was pulling back and taking a ragged breath. Her cheeks were red, and those lips were swollen and parted.

It looked like an invitation for more. But when he moved to take her mouth again, she stopped him. "I'm going to head back," she whispered.

"What?" His arms banded around her, his body tensing at the thought of her leaving. He'd gone two nights without her in his bed. He wouldn't make it a third. "Don't people who date spend the night together?"

She gave him a wide-eyed, dazed look. "Brick. Honey. I can't trust myself to get between the sheets with you and not do all the things we're not going to do."

"I think I can fend you off," he scoffed, tracing a thumb over her lower lip. It quivered at his touch.

She slid around so she was straddling him. But she stayed high on her knees, preventing the friction he craved. "No," she kissed him. "You can't."

Gripping her hips, he yanked her down against his rigid arousal and watched as her eyes went glassy. Her gasp filled him with the kind of filthy desires one night could never quench. He needed more time with her. More from her.

He wasn't sure if he was testing her or himself. Did she really understand that there was more between them than sex? Did he believe he deserved more from her?

When she put her hands on his shoulders and leaned forward, it was a soft, chaste kiss that she pressed to his mouth.

"Thank you for a really nice night," she whispered, brushing another kiss over his cheek.

She took his fucking breath away.

"You can't be serious," he said as she got off his lap and started to gather their dishes. He rose, taking the plates from her and putting them back down.

"I'm serious. I hurt you. Now I'm making up for it."

The throbbing erection in his fucking sweatpants was

hurting him. He needed to be inside her. Needed to remind her how much she wanted him.

"You made your point," he said. "I shouldn't have said anything. We're good. Come upstairs, Remington."

"No." She said it simply, finally, then left the room. He followed her feeling flummoxed and panicky. As if one word from her could stop him from tossing her over his shoulder and carrying her upstairs, making her scream his name as he drowned in her body.

"You know how I feel about you saying no to me," he said, envisioning how satisfying it would be to tug down those pajama pants and lay a pink handprint on her ass. His pants weren't even trying to contain his hard-on at this point.

"I'm not making a point or playing games or doing some grand seduction, Brick," she said as she tugged on her boots.

God damn it. He could see right down her pajama top, and she wasn't wearing a bra.

She really was leaving.

"I don't want you to go," he admitted, his voice whisper-soft.

She straightened and put her arms around his waist, hugging him. "I swear I'm not leaving to punish you or hurt you. I'm committed to doing this right, Brick. You mean a lot to me. More than...more than I think I even realized. I want to show you how important you are."

"Then stay. Stay with me."

Her smile was so sad and so sweet it went into his heart like a knife through soft butter. "If I stay, we both know what will happen, and that's not what either one of us needs."

He needed it. He needed it desperately.

Fuck. He reached for his coat. "I'll walk you home."

"No," she said firmly. "You can stand here on the porch and watch me cross the street."

"I want you," he said, stunned that his voice actually shook.

"I want you, too. But I want to give you more than just a couple of orgasms. Okay?"

He didn't answer her. Couldn't answer her. His throat was too tight. Fear lodged in him. He'd pushed her too far. Been too honest. And now he was paying for it. She was leaving him. All under the guise of giving him what he'd stupidly said he wanted.

He wanted to pick her up, carry her upstairs, and reacquaint her with how desperate his need for her was.

But that wouldn't solve anything.

Magnus wandered up next to him and yawned out a meow.

Brick blew out a breath. He had to let her go. Had to trust that she'd come back.

"Okay," he said finally.

Her entire face lit up, and giving her what she wanted made him feel powerful in a way that conquering her body didn't.

"I'm going to be the best damn girlfriend you've ever had," she said brightly.

"Girlfriend?" She'd said the word. She'd labeled them.

"It's official, big guy. Better get used to it. Thanks for the date."

She rose on tiptoe and pressed another kiss to his cheek. "Good night, Brick."

"Good night, Remington." He stood there on the porch and watched her walk away from him. Watched her skip across the street and let herself in the cottage gate. She turned and waved under the streetlight, and he raised a hand.

"I can't tell if I really fucked up or if she's giving me everything I want," he said to the cat when Remi disappeared.

Magnus blinked and wandered back in the house. The lights in the cottage blazed to life, and Brick winced. She needed the lights when he wasn't there with her.

Because he made her feel safe.

He stood there for another long minute. Waiting, hoping she'd reappear and jump into his arms.

But there was nothing.

His cell phone rang inside, and with a sigh, he closed the front door and went in search of it.

Remi Ford.

"What's wrong?" he demanded, already turning for the front door.

"Nothing, you big goof. I haven't had enough time to get into trouble. I just wanted to talk to you while I get ready for bed."

"Seriously?"

"You're the one who wanted a relationship," she teased. "That means we have to have long, meaningful conversations over the phone. Let's start with what did you want to be when you grew up?"

"A pissed-off, turned-on man waiting for a redhead to come to her senses and climb into his bed."

"Congratulations on that oddly specific dream coming true."

"*Remi.*"

"Brick. Come on. Play along. You might have fun."

"Not as much fun as if you were naked in my bed."

"William Eugene Callan the Third. You are not helping my resolve," Remi said.

She didn't bust his real name out often, but when she did, she meant business. He cleared his throat. "Fine. I wanted to be a cowboy, a bodyguard, and a game show contestant."

"What game show?"

"I wanted to win both showcases on *The Price is Right*. I used to watch it with my mom. What did you want to be?" he asked, carrying their dishes into the kitchen. No room was the same without her in it. She took the light and color with her.

"You know, I don't think I ever really thought of a job or a label and thought 'that's who I want to be,'" she mused.

"I do recall you giving your guidance counselor some migraines."

"I knew what I wanted to feel instead of what I wanted to do," she said on an adorable yawn.

"What did you want to feel?" he asked.

"Happy. Respected. Loved. I wanted to feel like I was important to someone beyond my parents and sister. I wanted to matter and not just in the 'this is my weird little sister who sees music' way."

"That's not how anyone sees you," Brick said, climbing the stairs to his empty bed.

She sighed. "None of us see ourselves the way others do. Aren't you the one who just recently confessed to not feeling like he was good enough for a certain someone?"

"*This* is what you talked to your boyfriends about?"

"I'm talking to *you*. We're talking from a safe distance where no one's clothes will fall off and distract us from the issue at hand."

He sprawled out on his bed, one hand behind his head, and wished she was next to him. Wished he could turn his head and see that cascade of red hair spilling over his pillows.

"I'd rather talk face-to-face," he grumbled.

"You'd rather be face-to-face so you can get distracted from talking," she countered. "Now, tell me why on Miles Davis's green earth you would ever feel like you're not good enough."

His Remi had never looked at him through the lens of reality. Maybe that was one of the reasons why he couldn't leave her alone. He was addicted to the way she saw him.

"Come on, Brick," she cajoled. "I really want to know where you got the stupidest idea in the history of stupid ideas."

He sighed. "You know what my parents were like," he said finally.

"And?"

"And what? When we met, my father was in prison for fraud."

"I know that. And now he's out and running a business according to your brother."

"Remi, my mom walked away from us like we were nothing."

"Honey, that doesn't mean you were nothing. That doesn't mean anything about anyone but her. Same with your dad."

"It's easy for you to say growing up with Darlene and Gilbert Ford, Mackinac's answer to *Leave It to Beaver*."

"I am no more my parents than you are yours."

"Your parents loved you and each other enough to stay and work and fight for each other." His gave up, took the easy way out, walked away. Part of him had believed that if he would have been better, his parents would have, too.

She sighed, and he wished she were here in his bed. "It devastates me to know that you don't realize what a good, honorable man you are."

His throat tightened. "I love you, Remi." He knew she wouldn't say it back. Knew she wasn't ready. He had his own proving to do there. But he needed her to know. "So fucking much that it hurts."

"I don't know what to say," she confessed.

He recognized the note of panic in her voice and wished he could hold her.

"You don't need to say anything back. You just need to hear me. Do you?"

"Yes. I do." She sounded breathless.

His cock swelled against his stomach at the tremble in her voice. The never-ending need for her was a constant hum reverberating in his blood.

"It makes me feel dizzy, like I'm on a carousel trying to get my bearings," she said.

"That's how it feels for me, too."

"Do you really mean it, Brick?"

"Baby, I love you so fucking much I can't breathe unless you're in the same room. So much I wish I were saying it to your beautiful face and not just your goddamn ear."

His doorbell rang, and he swore.

"What's wrong?"

"Someone's at the door."

"Did you replace me already? Did you get yourself a new girlfriend before I even decided to be yours?"

"You were always mine," he growled as he headed back down the stairs. "Always. The reason I asked Audrey out? Your dad told me about the guy you were dating in school. He sounded like he was perfect for you. A French hipster sculptor with long hair, and I was just a dirty-talking cowboy waiting for you to come home."

"Jean-Claude? You gave up on me because of *Jean-Claude*? The guy smelled like mothballs and soup and he brought his fiancée along on *our* second date just so he could show off the pronunciation for *ménage à trois*. There was no third date."

Brick yanked the door open and found Remi standing there. She tossed her phone over her shoulder and jumped into his arms. "I love you. I'm *in* love with you. I've never *not* loved you," she said, raining kisses over his cheeks.

He wrapped her legs around his waist and held her tight

as he kicked her phone back into the house, then slammed and locked the door.

"Say it again," he commanded. His heart was going to explode out of his chest.

She cupped his face in her icy hands.

"I didn't want to say it over the phone. I wanted to say it in person. I love you, Brick William Eugene Callan the Third. I want this to work. I want us to be together here. I want to live near family and paint in your house and wake up next to you."

His arms banded around her possessively, and his mouth sought hers.

"You're making my fucking life, Remi," he groaned.

"Take me upstairs," she demanded.

There was so much more to discuss. So much more at stake. But for now, the only thing that mattered was in his arms.

He took the stairs two at a time, making her laugh against his lips. Kicking the bedroom door open, he fell on the bed, catching his weight in one hand so as not to crush her.

"Say it again," he demanded, his voice harsh.

Her green eyes lit up with something that looked a hell of a lot like love. "I love you. So much—Holy shit. Is that *mine*?"

Remi pushed against him, trying to free herself, but he was never letting go.

She pinched him hard right on the ass. "You bought my painting."

He lifted his gaze from her face to the small painting he'd hung above his nightstand. "Yeah. Also, I officially hate that Raj guy. He's a huge pain in the ass."

"You bought my first piece," she said, still staring at it.

He ducked his head to press a kiss to her throat. "I saw it in one of the photographs of you in your loft when I was cyber-stalking Alessandra Ballard. It made me think of us."

Her eyes were watery, and she blinked back tears. "Imagine that," she said softly.

Remi nudged his chin up so he was looking at her.

"What?"

She wet her lips. "Stop settling for pieces, Brick. Take all of me."

43

"I got everything," Remi scoffed as Brick methodically checked each kitchen cabinet.

With a smirk, he reached into the cabinet above the refrigerator and produced a two-inch flat brush and an unopened box of Marshmallow Munchies.

"Shit."

His mouth curved in wry amusement, making her heart trip over itself. Was there anything sexier in this world than a smirking Brick Callan in uniform? She still couldn't believe that the burly, bearded, bartending cop was all hers.

Since the official exchange of the "I love yous" something had shifted inside her. She was still terrified for Camille, still concerned about what Warren had planned for them both. But she felt...lighter. More hopeful.

They both had been careful not to talk about "the future," what would happen after "things" were resolved. No long-term plans beyond what they would bring to Darius and Ken's place for dinner.

There was too much standing between them and a cleared field to consider options that weren't real yet. Remi didn't know whether she wanted to stay in Chicago or on Mackinac. She didn't know if she'd have a career to rebuild.

And she didn't want to talk about options with a man who'd been abandoned before. A man who'd finally found a home here.

She appreciated the view when Brick bent to look under the sink, his uniform pants doing wonders for that spectacular ass of his.

He straightened and winked when he caught her admiring glance. "Cleaners will be here in a few. We should probably get out of their way."

She glanced around at the tidy living space, the tall windows looking out over miles of water. It was April, and Agnes's first reservation was arriving next week, effectively ending Remi's tenure at the cottage.

"I'm going to miss this place," she mused.

Brick slid the handle of the paintbrush into the back pocket of her jeans. "You're not going far," he reminded her.

There were a handful of semi-permanent lodging options for her to choose from. Topping the list were snagging a room at the Grand Hotel or moving back into her parents' house. Kimber's guest room had been considered and discarded after spending an entire pancake breakfast watching Kyle and Kimber take turns pulling each other into the laundry room to continue an argument that sounded older than either of their children.

"Thanks for letting me crash at your place for a few days until I decide," Remi said, toying with a button on his shirt.

"About that," he said, crossing his arms. There was a cocky confidence in his stance that she'd noticed more often recently.

"Having second thoughts?" she asked. She was already in the studio all the time, relearning her way around a canvas.

Any time not spent painting or with Brick working, they were cooking, lounging, banging, or sleeping. Mostly at his place. Despite that, moving in together—no matter how temporarily —was still a big deal.

"I am," he said briskly.

Ouch.

"Uh. Oh. I totally get it. I can stay at my parents' place," she said. She hadn't realized how much she'd been looking forward to sharing a roof with the man. Not until it was taken off the table.

He fisted a hand in her hoodie and pulled her to her toes. "I don't want you *crashing* with me. I want you *living* with me."

Her mouth fell open, and she couldn't quite remember how jaw muscles worked to close it. "Uhhh."

He shot her a bemused look. "You okay?"

"Uhhh."

His grin incinerated her panties. "Baby, I want you with me. Every night, every day. I want to come home and find you covered in paint in the studio or naked in the tub, or crying over John Wayne movies."

"Live with as in...not get a hotel room?" Clarification felt essential at the moment.

He rolled his eyes. "Yes."

"Is this because of the articles?"

A series of news articles and blog posts had popped up earlier that week with unnamed sources hinting that Alessandra Ballard had attacked the good senator in the hospital after the accident. So far, neither Camille nor Warren had commented on the speculation.

"Vorhees is a factor," Brick admitted. "But not the only one. Not even the most important one."

"What's the most important one?" A lot was riding on his answer.

"I can't stand to be any farther from you than I have been. So unless you want to rent a room from a next-door neighbor, I want you home with me. Every night."

She couldn't process this fast enough. He had shifted gears on her. He'd gone from slow and steady and punched it into overdrive without any warning.

"Your studio is there. I'm there. Magnus loves you. I love you. What the hell are we waiting for?"

Remi rubbed a hand over her chest. "This feels kind of sudden."

On a chuckle, he dropped his forehead to hers. "Baby, it's been almost fifteen years."

"Are you *sure*?" she pressed. Too often, the man chose "the right thing" over the thing he wanted.

"Say, yes, Remi," he growled.

She could see it. Planting roots, for the next few weeks at least. They could test the waters. Together.

"Okay. Yes."

"Good girl." He looked smug in his victory, and it made her happy to know she'd made him happy. "Now, let's get the rest of your stuff moved."

She squealed with delight when he tossed her over his shoulder and carried her into the sunshine and across the street.

Fifteen minutes later, Brick's cell phone rang, provoking a frustrated growl. He pulled back from Remi's mouth, leaving her breathless, perched on the kitchen counter. His expression hardened when he glanced at the screen.

"It's my dad. I need to take this."

"Your dad?" She blinked. As far as she had known, Brick's relationship with his father was non-existent.

"He's been keeping an eye on Vorhees for me when he's in Chicago."

The man had repaired a relationship with his estranged father to help keep her friend safe. Overwhelmed and stupidly in love, she grabbed Brick by the shirt and kissed him hard. "I love you."

He groaned and took a step back. "Finish this when I get back from my shift?"

They'd never be finished exploring each other, tasting each other. Devouring each other.

She nodded and blew him another kiss.

He winked, mouthed "behave," and walked out, leaving her swooning after him.

She was still in mid-swoon when her own phone rang a few minutes later.

"Raj," she said, answering the video call. "What can I do for my favorite agent?"

"Are you drunk?" He looked both over-the-top and dapper in a crushed velvet sport coat in amethyst.

"Nope. Just happy," she said, hopping off the counter.

"You know what would make me happy?" He pulled off his glasses and polished them.

"I shudder at the possibilities." She headed into the studio, knowing exactly why he'd called.

"I'd be happy if my client was painting something I could sell."

"Excuse me. I hope you're more understanding about personal crises with your other clients who haven't yet fired you."

"And she's back to mean," Rajesh said with satisfaction. "Tell me you've at least picked up a freaking brush."

She'd done more than that. Slowly but surely, she'd begun to forge a path back to her art. In Chicago, she'd painted nearly every day. Here, with a large, manly distraction constantly in her periphery, she'd started to settle into a new routine. One that could accommodate her aggressive sex-having schedule.

"I've got two pieces for you to look at," she told her agent.

"About fucking time, dude."

"Bite me." The man was a pain in the ass, but he "got" her. And her art. He had an eye for what was great and what was an imitation of great. She turned the camera around so he could see the painting.

"Burn it," he announced.

She rolled her eyes. "Ass!"

He was right, of course. It was sloppy. The colors were off, and she'd overdone it, not trusting her instincts that told her when the piece was finished.

"Hey, if you want your hand held, go get a different agent. If you want a motherfucking avalanche of dolla bills, stick with me. I'll tell you when a piece says 'badass baller.' *Next.*"

Early on in their relationship, she'd once broken a canvas over his head. He'd worn the wood frame like a laurel around his neck while he told her the next piece made her a goddamn genius.

"Fine. Here's the other piece," she said, moving the camera. This one was a bigger painting. Pastels in yellow and pink mixed with navy blue on a milky background. She's painted it to violinist Tim Fain's "Freedom" in a weekend while Brick had back-to-back shifts at the bar and station.

"Now *that's* baller, dude. I can sell the shit out of that."

"Really?" Remi couldn't quite hide the swift rush of pride.

"Shut up. You know it's good. Gimmie. Send it A-SAP."

"You realize that packages are delivered by horses here, right?"

"Dude, I don't care if you send it to me by orphaned carrier pigeons. Get it here fast before everyone forgets who the hell you are." He kicked back and draped his arm over the back of a sofa. *Her* sofa.

"Are you at my place again?"

"Your casa is my casa," he said affably.

"No. My casa is *my* casa."

"Eh. My Wi-Fi went out at home today. I'm borrowing yours on my way to some happy hour thing for the Arts Council. When did you say you were coming back again?"

She hadn't, and he knew it. "I still have some things to work out first."

"Be tee dubs. I'm sending you two hundred prints."

"Why?"

"Because we sold out of signed prints. Warm up that wrist, man."

"I thought people were forgetting who I am? Don't these people know I'm toxic?" She'd hidden her reaction as best she could from Brick. But the last round of bad press had stung. Like a thousand pissed-off hornets.

"Britney Spears still sold records after she shaved her head. But she also kept *working*."

"I am."

"Good. Show me what's on the easel," he demanded.

"Not happening." Her gaze flicked to the painting in question. She was dabbling with "No Surprises" again. Revisiting the accident in oils between other projects. She still cried when she listened to the song. But it was a cleaner kind of purging. A purification almost.

The doorbell echoed from the front of the house. "I gotta go, Raj. Someone's here."

"Put the painting on the Pony Express. I'll send you the prints."

"Deal. Bye."

She stashed her phone in her pocket and jogged to the front door, where she found Kimber pacing on the porch.

"I told Kyle I want a divorce," she announced. Her shoulders were ramrod straight, jaw set. One lonely tear slid down her cheek.

Wordlessly, Remi opened her arms, and her big sister walked into them.

"Do you remember way back when you asked me to move in?" Remi said into her phone as she pulled the bedroom door closed behind her, shutting out the happy chatter of Hadley and Ian, whose hearts were about to be crushed.

"It sounds vaguely familiar," Brick said dryly.

"How would you feel about having a few more house guests?"

She quickly filled him in on the situation.

"Remington, you know they're welcome to stay as long as they want," he said.

"You're being awfully amicable. You didn't even try to get any sexual favors out of me in return."

When he didn't laugh or growl as she'd expected, she knew something was wrong.

"What's going on, Brick? Was it something with your dad?"

He cleared his throat, making her even more anxious. "Dad saw Camille leave the house today and followed her. He noticed she was limping—"

"That fucking monster," Remi snarled. If Warren had

started up again, there was no telling how far it would go this time.

"He got some pictures of her. It's hard to tell, but it looked like she had some bruising on her neck."

"Brick." Her voice broke. "We need to get her out of there."

"I know, baby. I know. We'll figure this out. Dad couldn't get near her. She had a security goon with her. So he followed them from a distance. She's at some event for an art organization."

Her grip tightened on the phone until her knuckles ached. "The Arts Council?"

"Yeah. Are you familiar with it?"

"She's on the board." Her mind was already a million miles away.

"Listen, we're getting ready to take the MMR out to shake the dust off her," Brick said. The Mackinac Marine Rescue was a thirty-one-foot rescue boat operated by the island and crewed by a team of volunteers. "How about we swing by, and the kids can wave from the boardwalk?"

"That's sweet of you. They'd love that," she said. "I'll talk to you later."

"*Remi.*"

"I'm okay. I'm fine. We'll talk when you come home...to a full house."

He sighed, and she knew he hated leaving her upset.

"Brick. I'm okay. I'm just worried."

"I know."

"Thanks for letting my sister stay. I love you."

"I love you, too," he said, his voice low. "We should be out on the water in about half an hour, okay?"

"We'll be looking for you."

She disconnected and thumbed to her call log.

"Raj? I need a favor."

"Alessandra, how's the new piece?" he bellowed.

"Stop trying to get attention and start paying attention. I have an emergency, and you're the only one who can help."

"Tell me more," he said around what she assumed was a mouthful of party appetizers.

"Camille Vorhees is there. I need you to get past her security and give her your phone."

"No way, man. I just got it last week."

"Not to *keep*. To talk to me."

"That's a stupid idea. I don't know what went down with you two *because you won't tell me*, but there's no way this is going to do anything good for your rep."

"I don't care about my rep or how many cocktail shrimp you can fit in your mouth at once—"

"Actually, it's sushi."

"I need you to do this for me."

"Fine. But if I get punched out by Mount Saint Helens in a suit for my troubles, you're subletting your place to me."

"Yeah. Fine. Whatever. Just do it. And be cool. Try *not* to get punched for once in your life."

"Whatever."

Remi gnawed on her thumbnail and waited as she listened to the background noises of a typical fundraising event. Just like one of the dozens she'd attended with Camille.

"Camille!" she heard Raj say. Her heart started to pound. This was the closest she'd been since the hospital. The sound was muffled, and she couldn't make out anything that was being said.

Nearly a minute went by. Long enough for Remi to feel like she was going to barf.

"Hello?"

Relief crashed over her like a tidal wave. "Camille?"

"Remi? What are you doing? This isn't safe."

"I know. I just. Are you okay? Do you need help getting out?"

"I'm flattered," Camille said brightly. "I'll be happy to make an introduction between you and the designer."

"Is your security there?" Remi asked.

"Yes, of course," Camille said.

"I don't know how to reach you. I'm on Mackinac. Warren said if I didn't stay away—"

"My husband certainly appreciates your support."

"How do I get you out?" Remi hissed.

"I need a moment," Camille said to someone else, and Remi could imagine her friend pulling the Ice Queen routine with her security. "Remi, you can't do this. You can't make any kind of contact. It's not safe."

"You need to get out. Come to Mackinac. We can keep you safe. We can figure out a way to nail him for the accident. I know he's hurting you again."

"Hurting me doesn't earn him a lifetime behind bars," Camille whispered.

"Then what would? There's got to be something. Give me something to look into and get the hell out of there."

"Warren and I appreciate your generosity," she said a little louder. "He's looking forward to re-election. I'll give you back to Rajesh now."

And with that, her friend was gone.

Twenty minutes later, Remi stood behind her niece and nephew on the boardwalk that overlooked the lake as Brick and his crew maneuvered the Marine Rescue closer to shore. The kids, still a little unsteady from Kimber's announcement that they'd be staying with Uncle Brick and Aunt Remi for a bit while their mom and dad figured some things out, waved.

A glum-looking Mega plopped his butt on the boardwalk and leaned against Remi's legs.

The feeling that she'd just made a very dangerous mistake clung to her like a fog.

When Brick lumbered through the front door at midnight, she was waiting for him.

"What's wrong?" he demanded, not bothering to shed his coat. "What happened? Are the kids okay?"

Remi swallowed. "I think I fucked up."

He gripped her shoulders, ice in his eyes. "Talk."

To his credit, Brick restrained himself—barely—from murdering her while she explained.

He had his back to her, his hands on hips. She watched his shoulders rise and fall with the breaths he took to calm down. And for some reason, it made her feel safer.

"Remington, what you did was..." His voice was deceptively calm.

"Stupid and irresponsible. Believe me, I know. But I *talked* to her, Brick."

He turned to face her when her voice broke, his jaw tightening when he saw her face.

When he traced a thumb over her cheek, she nuzzled into the touch. He hissed out a breath. "I hate how you can make me feel like strangling you and holding you at the same time."

"I'm sorry. I'm scared, Brick. She sounded...I don't know. Resigned? Like there wasn't any fight left in her." She broke away from him, but he caught her wrists and pulled her back into his heat, into his hard body.

"Tell me again what she said. Exactly what she said," he ordered.

44

$\mathcal{T}$he first ferry of tourists at the end of April usually brought a sense of jubilance. However, this year, it had Brick staring grimly at each passenger as they disembarked. He'd kept vigilant watch as the ferry lines began their regular runs again, bringing freight, supplies, and seasonal workers back to the tiny island.

Warren Vorhees's face, one he'd never seen in person, was emblazoned in his brain. Trouble was coming. He could feel it in his gut. Knew Chief Ford sensed it, too. She stood next to him, her face impassive as always as she watched a family of four disembark for a chilly day of fun.

Brick envied them. Wished he could be escorting Remi out to her pick of restaurants that were now opened.

But circumstances being what they were with danger lurking nebulously just off the radar, he could only keep her close and wait.

Less than a week after Remi's ill-conceived call to Camille, security footage of her attacking Warren in the hospital was leaked to the press.

The entire story had blown up again, the flames fed this time with quotes from the Vorhees.

She'd pretended it didn't bother her. But Brick knew better. Every time she came in from the studio, green eyes rimmed red, Brick vowed to destroy the man. Take him apart piece by piece for every moment of pain he'd caused her.

So he'd begun in the most natural place. By alerting Vorhees that there was an obstacle. *Him.*

"What the fuck did you do?" Remi's reaction had been loud and emotional. *"Are you* trying *to make yourself a target?"*

It was exactly why he'd sent the pictures to Rajesh. One Kimber had taken of them locked in an embrace in Remi's studio as they flirted with an argument about dinner. Another, a selfie Remi had taken of the two of them in bed. She was beaming at the camera while Brick watched her with an undeniable hunger, his hand clamped over her shoulder and neck. It reflected only a tenth of the possessiveness he felt over her. But it served a purpose. It sent a message.

It had taken her agent less than two hours to have the pictures appearing on dozens of blogs and news sites.

Then he'd gone to the chief. Once the screaming match between mother and daughter was over, they'd prepared. They'd kept the circle small, including a few key members of the department, sticking with residents and year-rounders they knew they could trust. Chief Ford had also read in a few of the more trustworthy, eagle-eyed residents on the general situation. It was a small town. Someone would see him. Someone would report him.

"Maybe he'll send someone to do his dirty work. Someone we won't see coming?" Darlene mused beside him, steam rising from her coffee.

He shook his head. "He'll want to end this himself. He's hands-on that way." The words tasted bitter in his mouth.

Brick's father may have been cavalier when it came to things like the law and the gray areas between right and wrong, but the man had never raised a hand to a woman. It was a line that real men never crossed. "You'd better hope that we catch him first then," Darlene said, her cool green gaze finding some far off point on the water to fixate on. "Some of our fine folks are itching for a good fight after that winter."

"He's mine," Brick said coldly.

"I get that you want to be the one slapping the cuffs on him."

He wondered what the chief would think if she knew exactly what he felt compelled to do to the man who'd almost ended Remi's life. He should have wrestled with it himself. He was a man of the law. Of strong morals and a belief in rules and the reasons to follow them. But Vorhees wasn't human and therefore didn't deserve to have that same moral code applied to him.

He wanted to end him. To extinguish the threat so that the woman he loved would be safe. Would stay safe.

The last of the passengers exited the boat, a woman with a knapsack and suitcase. She beamed at both of them as she hustled toward the road.

People came to Mackinac for adventure, for the community.

But sooner or later, a monster would come to destroy.

"Don't let it cloud you," Darlene said, turning away from the ferry.

He followed her down the concrete pier toward the ticket booth and Lake Shore Drive, where fresh tourists eagerly clustered around maps.

"I won't," he said.

This time those green eyes assessed him. "Don't let a monster turn you into one," she said. "I've known you a long time, Will. Long enough to know that you've got an extra large heart beating under all that muscle. I know you'd do anything to keep the ones you care about safe. That you'd go the extra mile to protect them. I also know that Remi can inspire strong feelings. Don't let those feelings push you across a line you don't really want to cross."

There wasn't a line he wouldn't cross for Remington Ford. "I'll do whatever it takes to keep her safe, chief."

"I have no doubt. Just make sure you don't get yourself hurt in the process."

He nodded. "Any updates on the shopkeeper in North Carolina?" In Remi's research, she'd stumbled across the name of an old girlfriend of the senator's. A woman who had moved across the country, deleting her social media and starting fresh in a small town. Darlene had volunteered to talk to her woman to woman.

"She won't talk. Scared to death, the poor thing. I managed to get out of her that there was an NDA. Beyond that, she doesn't want to be involved."

He blew out a breath through his nose. "I've got a half-assed affidavit from the Vorhees's former housekeeper. She saw bruises, evidence of struggles, but never witnessed anything."

"In other words, we've still got bupkis," the chief said.

"When Remi talked to Camille, she mentioned re-election," Brick said, his gaze studying each face on the street, comparing it to the one he was searching for.

Darlene pursed her lips. "Maybe there's something there. Guy tries to murder his wife, why wouldn't he play it fast and loose with his campaign finances? He's above the law. The rules don't apply to him. I'll make a few calls to see if I can find out if there's an active investigation."

Brick nodded. In a perfect world, he'd keep Vorhees occupied with law enforcement in Chicago or D.C., keeping him far away from Remi.

His phone buzzed on his belt.

"Dad?" he answered briskly. Darlene gave him a salute and strolled off.

"How's the weather up north?"

"Do you have something for me?" Brick asked, not in the mood for small talk.

William cleared his throat. "Uh, I might. Maybe a source. I might be able to convince him to go on the record."

Brick's grip tightened on the phone. "You were only supposed to be keeping tabs on Vorhees," he reminded him. He could trust his father to follow a trail, but not jump into the middle of a mess like this. Not with Remi at stake.

"That's exactly what I've been doing," William assured him. "But in doing that, I may have struck up an acquaintance-ship of sorts."

"What did you do, Dad?" he asked, starting to feel panicky.

"I merely helped one of Vorhees's staffers out of a jam in a scuffle at a bar. Got him out the door just before the cops came. He's feeling appreciative."

"What does he do for Vorhees?"

"Security. I read the room and mentioned how I wouldn't mind getting some information on his boss's questionable activities."

Brick wanted to crawl through the phone and wring his father's neck.

"Did he give you anything, or did you just put a target on Remi's back?"

"Son, this ain't my first rodeo. I told my new friend that I wouldn't mind making a few bucks off his boss and I'd be inclined to share the proceeds if he was helpful. This was after I saw the senator spit in the man's face when he tried to help Mrs. Vorhees into a car. The senator didn't seem to like that."

Fucker.

"You told the personal security of a United States Senator that you intended to blackmail his boss?"

"Well, if you want it in a nutshell, then yeah."

Brick closed his eyes. "That was not a smart move. If word gets back to Vorhees—"

"It won't," William assured him. "He's the source you've been looking for. Insider. Been kicked around by the rich boss. Not feeling too loyal. Best of all, he knows a lot of dirt. "

"What kind of dirt?" Brick asked.

"Seems that the boss called him to pick him up at the airport a few months back. He wasn't due back in Chicago for another three days. When he got there, Vorhees took his car and told him to catch a ride home. Never saw his car again. It was a Chevy Tahoe."

Brick's mind ran through the timing.

"Fuck," he swore.

"Senator Vorhees was so appreciative he gave the guy a brand new Escalade."

"That still doesn't prove anything," Brick pointed out, frustration rising.

"I'd be inclined to agree if I didn't have pictures on my phone of the wreck. Tracked it down to a junkyard in the 'burbs. Looks like it hit something head-on. I also have the Lyft receipt of our friend getting picked up from the airport that night."

This was something. Something he could work with.

"Will he talk?" Brick demanded.

"I'm working on that. If there's money in it for him, he has no problem singing like a goddamn canary. But it's going to take some time to make him comfortable with the idea of the cops."

"Make him."

"This takes finesse, son. I'll do my best."

Great. Brick's best shot at ending this before Vorhees came hunting was to trust his unreliable father to deliver results without leading a madman straight to Mackinac.

"He also mentioned he's seen the senator get a little rough with his wife," William added. "Didn't go so far as to say he beats her. But he and some other team members have noticed it."

Without Camille's corroboration, they still had a whole lot of unsubstantiated rumors. It wasn't enough, but it was something.

"Okay," he breathed into the phone. "Okay. Let's see where this lead goes. I'll see about wiring some money if that's what it's going to take to get him to talk."

"This girl must really mean something to you," William observed. The smile Brick heard in his father's voice annoyed him.

"My feelings for Remi have nothing to do with bringing a man to justice."

"Of course not," William replied, sounding smug. "But you have to know that paying a witness for testimony would shoot more holes in your case than a slice of swiss cheese."

"Fine. Then I'll make him talk."

"Let me handle it. I'll see what I can do."

Brick blew out a breath. "Keep me posted," he said.

"Will do."

He disconnected before his father could switch back to small talk mode.

Looking around him at the storefronts, glass gleaming,

products positioned just so, restaurants with their specials boards, he felt a rising sense of helplessness.

He needed to see her. Needed to touch her and remind himself that she was safe, for now. She was safe and she was here. For now.

Brick unhitched Cleetus from the post on the street and pointed him in the direction of home.

He was just jogging up the porch steps when his front door opened and a miserable-looking Kyle Olson stepped outside.

"Olson," Brick said.

"Callan." Kyle was dressed down in jeans and a hooded sweatshirt. An odd outfit for a trial lawyer on a Wednesday. He looked like he wanted to say something. Brick hoped he wouldn't because he still felt pissed off enough to punch someone.

"I just don't know what she wants from me, man," Kyle said, shoving a hand through his thick blond hair, making it stand up on end.

Brick stifled a groan.

"When we were engaged, she wanted to be a mom and stay home and raise a family. She wanted to live here on this fucking expensive-ass island. So that's what we did. Now, it's not good enough. I became a trial lawyer because I needed the salary to pay off student loans and make everything else on Kimber's wishlist happen. And now it's not good enough."

All he wanted to do was go inside and grab his girl.

"People change," Brick observed.

"I get that. But how about a heads-up? How about giving me a shot to play catch up?"

Brick knocked his head back against one of the porch supports. "I don't want to get involved."

"My wife and kids and dog are living in your house. You're involved."

"I don't want to get involved, *but* from the outside, she's been giving you nothing but heads-ups for the past few years," he said stonily. "You're the one who ignored them. You're the one who decided to be a lawyer first and everything else second. No woman wants to come in second place with her husband. No mother wants her kids to come in second with their father."

"So what the fuck do I do?"

"Fix it," Brick said and stomped past him into the house.

"Remi?" he bellowed from the foyer. Mega raced toward him, barking. When the dog reached him, he stopped, licked Brick's hand, and then trotted into the dining room to collapse in a sunbeam.

"She's in the studio," Kimber called back from the bowels of the house.

He stuck his head in the living room. Kimber had taken over the round pedestal table next to the bookcases. She was frowning at her laptop, printouts and folders covering the tabletop.

"What's all this?" he asked.

"A little project I'm working on," she said, looking up from the screen. Her eyes narrowed. "What's wrong?"

"Nothing."

"You look like something's wrong."

"I just ran into your husband on the porch."

She shrugged. "Who knew all I needed to do to get him to take a day off was ask for a divorce?" she said grimly.

"Are you sure Remi's in the studio?"

On cue, the music changed, and they heard Remi belt out a few Missy Elliott verses.

"Yeah. Pretty sure," Kimber said. "What did she do now?"

"Nothing. Everything is fine. Why do you ask?"

"Usually it's only my sister that can put that half pissed-off, half panicked look on your face."

"Everything is fine," he repeated.

She raised an eyebrow. "You know, you can trust us to worry with you. You don't have to carry it alone. She's my sister."

He still itched to see her, to poke his head in the doorway of the studio and make sure she was there. Safe. His.

"I know," he said finally. "It's under control."

She pinned him with a *mom* look. "Are you forgetting who my mother is? My sister and I don't need to be protected from the truth."

In the past, he'd found that giving Remi the least amount of information possible had helped keep her in line. It's when she knew what dangers lay ahead that she made some of her worst choices.

But Kimber was another story.

"The plan is to stop him before he ever comes near Mackinac, let alone this house," he told her.

"Judging from the look on your face, it's not going well," she guessed.

The song in the studio changed to something with a thrumming beat. It tugged at him, pulling him toward Remi.

"It's a slower process than I'd like it to be." It was as much as he was willing to give her.

"Keep me posted," she told him. "You might be used to dealing with Remi, but unlike her, I only use information for good. I want to know when I need to start worrying."

He nodded.

It felt wrong to have to keep the people he cared about updated on a threat he hadn't yet mitigated for them. Like he was failing them. When the stakes were this high, he couldn't afford not to do things exactly right.

"That's all I ask," Kimber said. She picked up her reading glasses and, with a wink, turned her attention back to her laptop.

Dismissed, Brick headed in the direction of the music and Remi.

He wanted to see her in his house, covered in flecks of paint, grinning or glaring at whatever world she was bringing to life.

The doorbell halted him in his tracks.

"Are you expecting someone?" Kimber asked, popping out of the living room.

It was the world they were suddenly thrust into when doorbells signified surprises, and surprises could be deadly.

"No," he said, striding for the front of the house. "Maybe you should go wait in the studio?"

"I'll stay with you," Kimber decided.

There was more Remi in her than Kimber realized.

Casually, Brick reached down and released the snap on his holster.

But through the beveled glass, he spotted a familiar form. One that scared him almost as much as a murderous monster.

For a split second, he thought about not answering the door. But it was the coward's way out.

"Audrey," he said, opening the door.

His ex-wife looked good. Great actually. She'd cut her hair again, buzzing down the sides and leaving the top longer with tight curls. She had a stud in her nose—that was new. Her lips were painted a dark purple. She was tall and cool. Relaxed. Her black jeans and over-sized sweater were comfortable.

"Brick," she said with a wide smile. She stepped across the threshold, pulling a suitcase behind her, and gave him a smacking kiss on the mouth.

"Audrey," Kimber said, sounding as surprised as Brick felt.

He could all but hear the accusation in her tone. He was sleeping with Remington, yet here his ex-wife was with a goddamn suitcase and a kiss.

"Kimber?" Audrey paused and looked back and forth between him and his guest. "Okay, I gotta admit I didn't see this one coming." She waggled her finger at them both.

"Huh?" He couldn't come up with any other words.

"Me and Brick?" Kimber laughed. "Ah, no. The kids and I are staying here while Kyle and I decide whether to divorce each other or turn into completely different people to make things work."

"Girl," Audrey said. "I hear you."

Brick felt like the floor under his feet was shifting, cracking, crumbling.

Audrey and Remi under the same roof. Someone was going to get hurt. Multiple someones. He was definitely one of them.

"This isn't a great time..." he began. But trailed off when Audrey raised an eyebrow.

"It's really good to see you again," Kimber said.

He was so fucked. Beyond fucked.

"It's good to be back on the island. Heard things are getting pretty serious between my brother and Ken, so I thought I'd come out for a week."

"And you're staying here?" Kimber said. "Brick is so generous with his house, isn't he?"

"To a fault," Audrey said, patting him on his arm.

"Did I know you were coming?" he asked, finally finding his voice.

"You did. Well, sort of. The plan was for me to come in May. But I got a break between projects at work and thought I'd move up the trip. So what's new?"

Kimber and Brick exchanged a look.

"Uh. Well."

"Did you come home to take me to lunch, big guy?"

Remi's cheerful question had him whirling around in the foyer. His body the only barrier between the woman he loved and the one he'd married. Remi looked like a walking disaster. Her hair was piled wildly on top of her head. She had a slash of turquoise under one eye. Flecks of red dotted her hand. Every color of the rainbow lived on her green t-shirt.

Magnus threaded his way through her feet before wandering around Brick to greet Audrey. Mega, sensing trouble, tip-tapped into the foyer and cocked his head.

Brick's brain froze. He'd been trained to handle a wide variety of threats, but this was new.

Remi's eyes went wide in surprise.

Audrey's face was unreadable.

Uh-oh.

"Hey. Remi, I was hoping to run into you while I was in town," she said. "I have some things I need to say to you."

Mayday. Mayday. SOS. Officer needs assistance.

"Why don't we all take a minute—" Brick began.

"Sure. You want some coffee?" Remi offered.

"Love some," Audrey said. She turned and handed Brick her suitcase. "Mind putting that upstairs for me?"

He stood there holding the bag as he watched the two women disappear into his kitchen.

"I can't decide how fucked you are," Kimber whispered.

"I... They... Uh..."

"I think I'm going to take myself out to lunch before I witness any crimes. If you need any back-up, text me," she said, slipping into her coat and fluffing her hair.

"Um..."

"Good luck. Don't make any sudden moves," she advised.

45

"*S*o, you and Brick," Audrey said, wrapping her hands around the *Michigan: The one that looks like a mitten, you moron* mug.

Remi glanced her way as she poured her own cup. "Yeah. Me and Brick. After you and Brick." She fished out the creamer he'd stocked for her and poured generously.

There was a long silence.

"This is weird," Audrey confessed. "And I feel like he's just lurking in the hall, waiting to see if he needs to call for back-up."

"Poor guy. Want to go into the studio? We can crank the music and scare him even more."

"Good plan."

Remi led the way, waving to Brick, who was indeed standing in the hallway looking a little nauseated and a lot scared.

"He should have told you," Remi said, closing the door. "I should have told you."

Audrey shook her head, making her tiny earrings jingle. "Neither of you owes me anything," she insisted, perching on a tall stool. "In fact, if there's any apologizing to be done, it should be me."

"You? Why?" Remi asked.

Audrey adjusted her glasses, a gesture that brought Remi right back to high school. "I wanted what you had. And when Brick started paying attention to me, I felt like it was my chance to finally be the special one."

"I don't know what to say," Remi said, hopping up on a paint-splattered work table, letting her feet dangle.

"You were always the bright light. The one everyone was interested in."

"I was a walking disaster. To this day, people still expect me to shoplift candy bars or jump off the roof of the fudge shop."

"You were interesting," Audrey pressed.

Remi was getting real sick and tired of other women telling her how "interesting" she was.

"I just did what I wanted to do. Without thinking about consequences. It's not exactly admirable," she pointed out. Consequences, it turned out, were a vital part of the equation when it came to decision-making.

"You might not think so, but to those of us who are a little less brave, it is. You didn't bend to meet anyone else's expectations. You were you, and that was enough. Maybe the rest of us wanted to be like you. I knew how you felt about Brick, and when I had the chance, I took it."

"That's between you two," Remi said, shifting uncomfortably. "Your relationship has nothing to do with me."

Audrey sighed heavily. "It had everything to do with you. From beginning to end. I thought what you thought, that he didn't see you. That he didn't feel that way about you. So when he started paying attention to me..." She shrugged. "It was almost intoxicating. I was fresh out of college and had no idea what I wanted to do yet and he was just so..."

"Brick," Remi said, understanding completely.

Audrey nodded. "Exactly. I felt special. I felt like I'd won the prize. Like I'd been named Homecoming Queen."

"Uh, you were named Homecoming Queen," Remi pointed out.

"Yeah, because you refused to accept the nomination. That's not a real win."

Remi took a swallow of hot coffee and sat with what Audrey was saying.

"When you were off-island, it was different. Brick saw me, and I saw him," Audrey continued.

"You don't have to explain," Remi reminded her. "You don't owe me anything. And who wouldn't fall in love with the man who just walked past the door twice trying to figure out what we're talking about?"

"I spent so much time in my teenage years wanting to be you that when the chance arose, when Brick asked me out that first time, I didn't think. I didn't hesitate. I jumped at it. And I did that without wondering if my feelings for him were real or if I just wanted him because you wanted him."

"You loved him. You still love him," Remi pointed out.

"He's a hard man not to love. But it was never right between us. *We* were never right. Neither was cutting you out of my life. You came home after art school with all your big dreams and a job offer for a gallery in a city I've never been to. And I had no plans. I'd gotten my accounting degree that my parents insisted on and was no closer to figuring out what I wanted than when I was sixteen."

"I never meant to make you feel like you weren't enough or didn't have enough," Remi said.

"I know you didn't. You loved me for who I was. The

woman *I* couldn't see because I was too busy comparing myself to you and everyone else."

"You invited me to the wedding, and I didn't go."

"I didn't even tell you we were dating until we'd gotten engaged," Audrey countered. "That's when it started to gel for me. I realized I wasn't in this for the right reasons. I wasn't putting on that white poufy dress for Brick and me. I was doing it to prove I was the special one. That I'd earned something you hadn't."

Remi said nothing.

"Then I realized something even worse."

Remi wrinkled her nose. "What?"

Audrey's smile was sad. "He loved you. He'd always loved you. He'd already given his heart to you. I never had a chance. And to be honest, he never had a fair chance with me either."

"Maybe this is a conversation you should be having with him," Remi suggested.

"We've had it. At least parts of it. I left out the petty parts that made me look bad. But you deserve to know. He was a great husband. He was attentive. He did my laundry. He never complained about my taste in movies."

"You do have horrible taste," Remi agreed.

Audrey grinned. "He'd take me out on date nights and buy me flowers. But it was your name he whispered in his sleep."

Remi looked down at the freckles of paint, the mess she'd made. "I'm so sorry."

"I put myself in that position. And I'll be honest. I doubled down. I tried for a while to be better than you. To make him forget about you. But it was never going to happen. Especially not with me pretending to be someone I wasn't."

"So you felt like you had to leave Mackinac?"

Audrey shook her head. "I set us free. I started interviewing for jobs on the mainland, and when I got one at a design firm, I took it without even talking to him. Sure, we went through the motions of discussing whether I'd commute or he'd move with me. But we both knew it was the end."

Remi blew out a breath. "How are you now?"

Audrey shrugged, then grinned. "I'm happy. I love my job. I work with interesting people. I date men who have never met you."

Remi winced. "Mean."

Audrey flashed her a wink. "The thing I need you to know is I was a jealous, petty, shitty friend, Rem. You never did anything that deserved that, and I still made it my mission to beat you instead of love you. That kind of jealousy made me a worse person, and I'm sorry it's taken me this long to apologize."

"I'm sorry I made your life difficult," Remi said.

"*I* made my life difficult," Audrey corrected. "You didn't put me in your shadow. The sun was shining just as brightly on me. I just didn't notice it. It took all that for me to find the right path, my own path, to realize I was already standing in the sun."

Remi blew out a breath. "You know, I never felt special. I felt different."

"Girl, that's what special *is*."

"Well, I ran away from it. I ran away from who I was and tried to be someone else."

"It looks like you found your way back," Audrey observed.

"I guess I did."

"Now, as the lovable ex-wife, I need you to hear this. Don't play with him, Rem. He's been waiting so long for you. If you're not all the way in, if you're just going to pick up and move on when the wind blows, do him a favor and walk now."

"Things are...complicated right now," Remi admitted. "We haven't talked about the future."

"Well, you should at least be thinking about it. Don't hurt him if you can help it. He's one of a kind, and I really don't want to dislike you for something real."

"Message received," Remi said, feeling just a little unsteady. She caught a glimpse of Brick's face at the window again and fell just a little harder in love. "So what are *you* doing here?"

"My brother told me you and Brick finally hooked up. I figured it was time for me to do some apologizing."

"And scare the hell out of Brick? I've never seen him that pale before."

Audrey's grin was sharp. "His face when he opened the door looked like he'd just stepped on a trapdoor. He's probably out there wearing tracks in the hardwood as we speak."

46

$\mathcal{R}$emi sat front and center at Tiki Tavern's bar while Brick, Darius, and her very excited father on his first bar shift handled drink orders. She was determined to enjoy the night, to forget about everything weighing her down, and focus only on having a little fun.

The music was loud, bathing the packed bar in golds and shimmers of rose. The crowd still leaned heavily in favor of the residents, but there were enough seasonal workers and early tourists to shift the balance. As she sipped her drink, straight bourbon tonight, and kept up with the conversations around her, Remi thought about what she'd be doing if this were a normal night in her normal life.

In Alessandra's life.

She would have been painting, alone into the night. Or she might have been dressed up, made up, for an event to sell herself, her talent to buyers with the right kind of deep pockets.

Instead, she was crammed in between Audrey and Kimber and lusting after her bartending boyfriend. Kimber was doing her best to ignore Kyle, who had not only shown up but bought the last two rounds and was trying to coax her sister into a dance. Spencer—having shown up on the afternoon ferry the day before—was sandwiched in between Audrey and Darius's boyfriend, Ken.

Brick hadn't even blinked at the extra guest. With two kids, a separated sister, an ex-wife, and a dog, what was one more?

Remi, on the other hand, had blinked an eye on her way to bed, when she'd spotted Spencer sneaking into Audrey's room after midnight. Audrey's arm snaking out and dragging him inside.

Brick hadn't come home from his patrol until two, when she'd already been sound asleep, curled up with Magnus in his big bed. Their morning quickie had been interrupted before it started with a call from dispatch.

Between the full house and the beginning of the tourist season, they hadn't had any alone time, and she was desperate for him.

The feeling appeared to be mutual. Every time he turned back to her, his gaze dipped to the lace-up front of her sweater dress. It was a long-sleeved mini dress in hunter green that hugged her curves. She'd paired it with gray suede boots that stopped at mid-thigh.

All with the express purpose of driving Brick Callan crazy.

She knew the signals of his arousal. The tightening of his jaw, the flare of his nostrils like he could catch her scent. The narrowing of those blue eyes that burned with an intensity that took her breath away. The way his fingers lingered on the glass he served her.

He *smoldered*. And she ate it up.

When AC/DC's "Shoot to Thrill" came on in a storm of reds and oranges, Remi dragged Audrey and Kimber out on the crowded dance floor with her. They danced like they had in high school, shimmying and grinding for the pure enjoyment of it.

When a friendly red-headed guy in a button-down put his hands on her hips, she felt the weight of Brick's gaze on her. Heating her skin and making her nipples ache for his mouth, for that rough scratch of his beard. She tossed her hair over her shoulder and raised her arms as the song came to a climax, letting the colors, the beat of the music, flow over her.

The crowd whooped when the song ended, and Remi fanned herself. With a wave at her dance partner, she headed down the hallway toward the restrooms. A hand gripped her upper arm hard, and she found herself being propelled out the emergency exit.

Her pulse sky-rocketed as a pissed-off looking Brick whirled her around to face the facade of the building. He kicked a crate over on its side then lifted her to stand her on top of it.

"Hands on the wall," he ordered, lips tickling her ear as those big, broad hands of his traveled the front of her body.

Light and laughter poured from the window next to them as their friends and neighbors went about their Friday night business, none the wiser to the debauchery happening on the other side of the wall.

"Here?" she whispered, eagerly slapping her palms against the clapboard siding. He kicked her feet out, widening her stance, making Remi instantly wet and aching. She'd fantasized about this for so many years. Pushing him past his limits so he had to drag her away, had to take her, and remind her who she belonged to.

The sound of his belt loosening had her breath catch in her throat.

"You keep breathing for me, baby. Nice and deep."

She nodded vigorously. God, she hoped her breath wasn't the only thing going nice and deep.

The sound his zipper made as he lowered it was music to her ears. And when his hands slid under the hem of her dress, pushing it up over her hips, she whimpered.

Her fingers bit into the rough surface of the wall as she tilted her hips in invitation, offering herself to him.

He growled his approval and traced one finger over her underwear, dipping it into the seam between her cheeks. On instinct, she pressed her hips back against his touch. Wanting.

"You're *my* bad girl tonight," he rasped possessively.

"Yes," she hissed when she felt him fist his erection at the root and guide it along the same path his finger had just taken.

"You want my touch everywhere." To emphasize his point, he thrust the crown of his cock against her, the thin cotton barrier preventing him from penetrating her.

She didn't trust her voice to answer. To tell him how much she wanted him to take her and make her his plaything. So she nodded instead, trembling with anticipation.

He dragged her underwear down to mid-thigh. Adrenaline dumped into her bloodstream, mixing with the wild need she felt for him. Even here in the narrow walkway between buildings where they could easily be discovered, she trusted him implicitly to take care of her, to keep her safe, to take her the way she needed to be taken.

His breath was hot against her neck, his body hard and ready at her back.

She felt the current of air a split second before his palm connected with her ass in a stinging slap. The sound of it echoing off the wall of the building.

"That's for teasing me in public," he growled in her ear as

he held the hem of her dress at her back. There was a low rumble of triumph in his chest, and she could picture him fisting his cock with one big hand as he watched her skin turn pink.

Remi tried to squeeze her thighs together to relieve some of the pressure that had built to astronomical heights. But he didn't allow it.

"No, baby. You don't get to feel better yet," he said. She could hear the rhythmic stroking of his palm wrapped around his arousal.

"I'm sorry," she whispered.

He groaned again.

The next slap caught her by surprise, and she yelped. It was even harder, and the sting of it drove her crazy. Never in her wildest dreams did she think she could push Brick this far. That he'd have to drag her outside to discipline her while being so turned on he had to pleasure himself while he did it.

She felt the crown of his penis dragging across her abused flesh, leaving a slick trail.

His pleasure made hers even fiercer.

"That's for liking your punishment."

"I'm sorry," she said, nearly giddy with need.

"You know what I should do?" he pressed himself against her, and she gasped as the thick head of his erection slid between her legs, parting her folds.

"W-what?" she whispered.

"I should just use you to get myself off. Bad girls don't get to come."

She could feel his knuckles where he gripped his shaft against her. Guiding it through her folds. She tilted her hips, hinging forward so his head grazed her clitoris. Her legs shook, her core clenching greedily.

But Brick wasn't done torturing her. He dragged the head

of his cock back through her wetness and up the valley of her behind. Back and forth with violent strokes of his hand. He could make her come like this. When she was strung this tight, he could make her come doing anything.

"But then it's just as much a punishment for me if I don't get to feel you choking the life out of my dick."

Dirty-talking Brick Callan was irresistible.

He reached around her, shoving his hand into her dress to close around her breast. Her nipple instantly pebbled against his palm. His fingers tugged, rolled the sensitive bud until she whimpered.

She bowed her back hard and stepped her feet as wide as the box would allow, wondering if she would come or break into a thousand pieces from the pressure building inside her.

"I've got a bar full of people waiting for drinks. And you make me drag you out here to remind you who the fuck you belong to." He was panting now, jacking his cock hard against her. Every time he nudged her clitoris, she saw stars, and her body quaked.

He was going to come jerking himself off against her because he wanted her *that* much.

She felt vulnerable and powerful at the same time.

With one soft grunt, he started coming against her. His fingers spasming hard over her tender nipple. The slick head of his arousal nudged that needy bundle of nerves again, spurting hotly at the same time, and Remi went off. Exploding like fireworks, her inner walls rolled through the orgasm.

She whimpered as he aimed his next spurt against the tight hole between her cheeks. And then he was feeding his still-coming cock into her still clenching core.

"Take it. Take me, Remington," he said on an animalistic groan. He bucked into her, forcing her to take more and more.

With the hand that had been pumping his cock, he

covered her mouth a second before a scream ripped from her throat.

He powered into her on an abrupt thrust, bringing her up onto her toes. Her cry was muffled by his hand.

"Fuck," he gritted out against her ear. "Fuck."

The thick penetration, the lubrication from his never-ending orgasm, it was so fucking good. So magical.

As he spurted hotly inside her, Brick slid an arm around her hips, lifting until her feet were no longer in contact with the box, and then he started fucking her. Short, hard drives as she hung over his arm like a rag doll coming on his shaft.

The desperation of his possession rolled her orgasm into another.

"I'm still coming," she whimpered. He found her clitoris with his fingers and worked the swollen bud with tight circles as his semen slowly leaked out of her, slipping down her thighs.

They were both trembling through the aftershocks when he set her on her feet again. Her knees nearly buckled, then did when he slapped her on the ass hard.

"That's for making me do this to you. For making me drag you out here instead of waiting to lay you down, instead of worshipping your sweet fucking tits with my mouth. Instead of fucking you in front of the fireplace with my hand in your hair. For making me wish I could be inside you always. For making me obsessed with the sound my hand makes on your ass. How am I supposed to ever be without this? How, Remi?"

Jesus. He was done coming. But he wasn't done fucking her. Wasn't done branding her from the inside. He just kept thrusting into her, as if he were trying to find a depth that made them feel like one instead of two.

"Then don't," she wheezed between thrusts.

He stopped, his cock buried to the hilt. "Don't what?" His voice was steely.

"Don't be without this. Don't be without me."

His hands closed around her hips hard enough to bruise. "What are you saying?"

"I'm saying ask me to stay. Ask me to be yours."

"You *are* mine." His grip tightened, painful on her hips.

"It's really hard to have a conversation like this," she groaned.

"Fuck," he muttered.

Suddenly, he was no longer inside her. She whimpered at the loss.

"Hold on, baby," Brick said grimly, setting her back on the ground and tugging her underwear into place. They immediately soaked through with his orgasm.

"Brick!"

He dragged her dress down. When she spun around on shaky legs, she found him tucking himself, still fully hard, into his pants.

"Did I say something—"

But he clamped a hand on her wrist. "Let's go."

"Go? Where?"

But he was yanking the door open and pushing her inside.

"Are you seriously making me go back inside with a quart of your semen collecting in my underwear?" she hissed.

He shoved her into the office, shutting and locking the door behind him.

"Now. Say it again." He prowled toward her.

The gleam in his eyes made Remi very nervous.

"I-I forget. We can talk about this some other time," she decided.

But when she tried to slip past him, he merely picked her up and put her on his desk. He pulled the chair out and sat.

Her legs hung outside his own and forced her knees wider. His hands slid up her thighs, rubbing the tight muscles they found.

When his thumbs skimmed over the edges of her underwear, she began to tremble. Back and forth, up and down her thighs. Until she was almost relaxed. Until he reached into his jeans and pulled his cock out again. It lay there, thick and hard curving up against his stomach.

"Say it again," Brick ordered.

He looked so powerful sitting there, with his long legs spreading her own wider. His thick, veined arousal waiting for attention. His eyes on her. The boss. The dominant.

Both his strength and need bottomless.

"I said you could ask me to stay," she said, her voice was barely above a whisper.

"Do you want to stay here with me?" The intensity of his stare made her skin burn.

She took a shaky breath. "I have to fix things for Camille first. But after...if everything is okay..." *If she survived...* "I know we haven't really talked about after. But I want to be here. With you."

His face was unreadable, almost as if it had turned to stone.

"Unless that's not something you want," she faltered.

He shook his head slowly and then lowered his face to her lap. "You're a fucking dream come true."

"Dream or nightmare?" Remi asked.

"Both." He hooked his finger through the crotch of her saturated underwear and tugged.

"Don't you have anything to say?"

"Yeah. I do. Hold the fuck on to me."

She only had enough time to put her hands on his shoulders as he yanked her off the edge of the desk, down onto his shaft.

He filled her so deeply, stretched her so far with her legs spread wide over the thin metal arms of the chair, she almost came apart right then and there. The angle had him going so deep she couldn't catch her breath.

Her head spun as he held her there, impaled and immobile, legs dangling. She could feel the blood pulsing in his shaft.

"Breathe, baby. Deep, slow breaths. Let me in."

"I-I can barely take you like this," she whispered. Something was happening inside her. Like storm clouds gathering. There was pain with the fullness. Little lightning slivers of it. But there was also something else roiling to the surface. Something unsurvivable. Something beautiful.

She watched in fascination as the last inch of him eased into her body.

He groaned and yanked the top of her dress down, leaning forward to lap at her breast. "You're such a good girl. So fucking tight."

She squeaked out a breath and another one. Every time she inhaled, she felt like she was coming apart at the seams. Every swollen inch, every vein, every throb of his cock felt like it belonged to her.

"When you're ready, you're going to rock for me, and we're both going to come again," he told her, shifting his attention to her other breast. Her nipple felt cool and wet from his mouth.

"Okay," she whispered. She gave a testing squeeze of her inner muscles, and he moaned against her breast like a man starved for release.

"So fucking tight, Remi."

"It's starting to feel good," she confessed. Really good.

"I know. I can feel all those greedy little muscles in your

pretty cunt shaking with how much they want this, how much they need me to move. Are you ready to move, baby doll?"

"God, yes," she hissed.

He brought his thumb to that needy bundle of nerves and brushed over it once, twice, while drawing deeply at her breast.

"Move," he ordered.

She did as she was told, bucking against him with a roll of her hips.

He growled, the vibration of it tingling her nipple. Again she rocked her hips, barely moving on his shaft, but it was enough. He was so deep, so thick, and that thumb was working its magic.

"Brick," she whispered, her voice shaking.

"I've got you, baby. Let me make you feel good."

She levered her thighs down against the metal of the chair, shifting the angle until the head of his throbbing penis rubbed exactly the right spot. She wanted to close her eyes and focus on the sensation, but the view of him holding her like this, impaling her, was too much to look away from.

"Good girl."

He was panting, she realized. And so was she. She rocked against him, keeping him as deep as he'd ever been. Fire. It was inside her veins, racing through her body. It was scorching her skin everywhere he touched her. He was going to burn her alive. And she was going to let him.

The pressure built inside her, an exquisite torture.

He was so thick, so hard, so damn deep it didn't matter. His arm banded around her back, holding her impaled on him, and then he began to thrust.

"Mine," he growled, claiming her breast with his mouth. The long, hard pulls of his mouth echoing in the needy muscles that trembled around his shaft.

"Yours," she whispered as she rode him. His thumb pressed harder, and it was like a trigger had been pulled.

On a broken sob, she came apart on him. He went rigid under her, grunting against her breast as he came again, the picture of agonized ecstasy.

47

Brick was sound asleep, his body wrapped around Remi's in a tangle of limbs and sheets, when his phone chimed three times in rapid succession on the nightstand.

Remi grumbled into her pillow.

Whatever the notification was, it could wait until he'd gotten at least two more hours of sleep. He buried his face in Remi's neck. She smelled like *him*. It made him half-hard. But it was too early, and she'd be sore after their fun and games last night in the alley and the office. And then again in an actual bed when they got home.

Home. She was staying. She'd chosen him and this place he loved. She was committing to building a life with him here. And he was going to do whatever it took to finalize his claim on her. Starting with locking up Vorhees. The next order of business was a fucking ring. He'd force it on her finger with his cock inside her if it was necessary.

That's where she surrendered to him, trusting him completely to take care of her body. After so many years of chasing after her, the rush of possessing her physically was indescribable. And it already wasn't enough. He wanted the commitment. The papers. The fuss and celebration. The acknowledgment of the world that she was his.

His phone rang obnoxiously on the nightstand.

Remi growled. Smiling into her hair, he squeezed her sweet little ass before rolling over and reaching blindly for the phone.

"Hello?" he rasped.

"Brick, it's Juanita Houston from the coffee shop. Sorry for calling this early after you had such a late night at the bar."

Juanita ran the cafe across the street from the ferry landing and knew everything about everybody.

"What can I do for you, Juanita?" he said, trying to muffle a yawn.

Remi rolled over to snuggle up against his back, and he looked down at her, feeling his chest flood with warmth. She didn't look angelic in the early morning light. She looked more like a nymph, recharging her energy just to cause more trouble.

The wave of love, of possession, that crashed over him threatened to level him.

"I know you asked a few of us to keep an eye out for that Vorhees fellow."

His muscles tensed, and he jackknifed up.

"Yes," he said, his voice terse.

"Well, you know how I don't mind a little digging—"

Naked, Brick launched himself off the bed and headed for the closet, snatching his gun off the dresser. "Did you see him? Here?"

Remi stirred on the bed behind him.

"Oh. No, no. Not anything like that." Juanita chuckled.

He blew out a breath and closed his eyes.

"But I think I saw his wife get off the first ferry."

He glanced at his watch. The ferry would have landed less than ten minutes ago.

Swearing under his breath, he reached for his sweatpants.

"Was she with anyone? Did you see which way she went?"

"I got swamped with the morning rush," she said. "But I figured I should let you know."

"Thanks, Juanita," he said, dragging on the pants and sweatshirt.

"Oh, sure. I'll keep an eye out and let you know if I see her again or that Vorhees guy."

"Appreciate it," Brick said. He hung up and jammed his feet into sneakers, leaving them untied.

"What's going on?" Remi asked groggily.

"Nothing, baby. Go back to sleep," he said, pausing only long enough to press a kiss to her forehead.

"Nothing doesn't require a gun," she rasped after him. But he was already on the stairs.

The doorbell rang just as he hit the first floor. Keeping his gun at the ready, he reached for the deadbolt and threw open the door.

"Dad?" Brick was dumbstruck on his own doorstep.

"Camille?" Remi, dressed only in one of his t-shirts, pushed past him and carefully wrapped her arms around the woman standing next to his father.

She reminded him of one of his grandmother's prized swan figurines. Delicate and lovely. Spencer had broken it accidentally, in the midst of gangly puberty when he'd had no more control over his own body than a marionette.

The swan had shattered, its long graceful neck snapped. But instead of careless accidents, Camille's porcelain skin bore the evidence of grisly, purposeful violence.

"Oh, my God," Kimber, pink-cheeked and hair tousled, appeared on the porch behind his father.

"Where were you?" Brick asked.

"Uh. Out for a run."

She was a shit liar, but he had much bigger fish to fry.

"What's going on?" Ian demanded.

"Nothing, sweetheart, go upstairs," Kimber said, stepping past Brick and urging her son toward the staircase. "If you go back to bed for half an hour, I'll make you chocolate chip pancakes for breakfast."

"With gluten *and* syrup?" Hadley asked, peering over the railing from the second floor.

"Get inside," Brick snapped at William. A rage so fierce bubbled in his blood he was afraid he wouldn't be able to control it.

His own father baited the trap. Warren Vorhees would track his wife right to Brick's door. Right to Remington.

"Come on," Remi said softly, coaxing Camille across the threshold.

Brick watched, helpless, as she walked stiffly, carefully, like a woman decades older. There was a pained weariness in her gaze as it landed on his face.

"I'm so sorry to drop by unannounced like this," she said. Even through a split lip and bruised jaw, she had polish and breeding written all over her.

"Kimber, can you take my friend Camille back to the kitchen and make her some tea while I get her room ready?" Remi asked.

"Tea with bourbon. And my sister and kids made cookies yesterday," Kimber told Camille as she guided the woman away.

Brick's throat was closing in on itself, fury choking him. He couldn't even look his father in the eyes.

Before he could force out any of the words that clogged his throat, Remi had walked into his father's arms and wrapped him in a hug. "Thank you, Mr. Callan," she whispered. "Thank you for bringing my friend to me. You saved her life."

It was the tears bright in Remi's eyes that had Brick putting a stopper in his anger.

His father hugged her back awkwardly, a myriad of emotions flickering over his face. Awe. Embarrassment. Gratitude.

His Remi didn't see a criminal, a con man. She saw a man who brought her friend home.

"I know it's not ideal," William said. "But he went after her, and I couldn't walk away. Couldn't leave her there."

"You did exactly the right thing, and I'll be grateful to you for the rest of my life. You knew she'd be safe here. You knew Brick would keep her safe."

His father bobbed his head before looking to gauge Brick's reaction.

Remi pressed a kiss on his whiskered cheek, then did the same to Brick. "Be kind," she whispered to him before running up the stairs.

William Callan II looked much older than the last time Brick had seen him. His hair had gone gray, and it was shaggy and thinning on top. He'd put on some weight. A little paunch around the middle. He looked how a doting grandfather should. Not a felon.

"What the hell happened?" Brick demanded harshly.

"I've been keeping an eye on Vorhees like you asked. He comes and goes, flies to D.C. a lot. But this is the first time she's been out of the house on her own. No husband, no security. She just went shopping. When she got back to the parking garage, he was waiting behind her car. He grabbed her. There wasn't anyone else around, and he just lost his damn mind. He hit her in the face, and she went down."

"What did you do, Dad?"

"I did what I had to do. I called 911 and then hit the son of a bitch over the head with the bat I keep in the car. I picked her up, helped her into my car, and we took off."

"You drove straight here?" Brick ran the calculations.

"Straight through. Six hours. Police scanner picked up a mugging victim in the parking garage about forty minutes after we left."

"Fuck."

"He's a goddamn monster, son. I witnessed it firsthand. I'll say it in any court of law."

"You better hope you get the opportunity. Do you know who you're messing with? Do you know who you just brought to my island? To my doorstep?" To his woman. His future.

"I do know." William's tone was serious. "But what else was I supposed to do, Will?"

"It's Brick," he corrected automatically.

His father blinked. "Brick? As in brick wall?"

"Pretty much." He rubbed a hand over his forehead. He had too many things he needed to be doing right now. Too many preparations to make to have this conversation. "Look, make yourself at home. Or whatever. I need to make some calls."

"Sure," William said. "If you don't mind, I'll go check in on Cami. We bonded a little bit on our drive."

"Fine. Whatever," Brick said, already lost in preparations.

His father hurried off in the direction of the kitchen.

"Uncle Brick?" Hadley appeared on the bottom step, hand wrapped around the newel post.

"Yeah, Had?" he said wearily. He had a houseful of women that needed protecting. A houseful of women who would deny that until the bitter end. And his own father had goaded a madman.

"Are you mad at that man for bringing Aunt Remi's friend here?"

Yes. "No. I'm...concerned."

"Is she in trouble?"

He was big on protecting kids from ugly truths whenever he could. But in this instance, innocence needed to take a backseat to vigilance.

"She is. And that trouble could come here, Hadley. So I need you to keep an eye out. You're a good observer. If you see anyone paying too much attention to this house, or to your aunt Remi, I need to know. Got it?"

She nodded solemnly. "I'll keep watching."

Going on instinct, he gave the girl a one-armed hug and pressed a kiss to the top of her head. "We'll all be okay," he promised.

She gave him a small smile. "I know we will. You're here."

"Go check on your brother, okay? Make sure he isn't brushing Mega's teeth with my toothbrush."

She shot him a smile and disappeared up the stairs.

He gave himself a beat to think and then fished his phone out of his pants pocket.

Brick: Emergency. My place. How soon can you be here?

Chief Ford: Is there blood or do I have time for coffee?

Brick: No blood. But get it to go.

Chief Ford: Be there in 5.

Brick locked the deadbolt on the front door and bounded up the stairs two at a time. He found Remi in the guest bedroom next to theirs. She'd laid out some of her own clothes on the bed and was karate chopping the bed pillows with more violence than style.

He watched her as she moved around the room. Tension in her jaw and shoulders. Every few moments, she'd stop and take a deep breath. Over and over again, the tension built and rose until she breathed it out.

"Fuck," she muttered under her breath. She hurled a useless pillow against the wall and brought her hands to her face.

He went to her, banding his arms around her and holding on tight.

"None of this would be happening if I had gotten her out earlier," she whispered against his chest. "If I had talked her into it. Hell, if I had kidnapped her and thrown her in my trunk and driven to Rhode Island."

"None of this is your fault."

"It's not your father's either," she shot back.

He clenched his jaw. "He's going to bring Vorhees right to you."

She pulled back and looked up at him. "We both know he was always going to come for me. I never should have led him here." Her voice broke, and it took a jagged piece of his heart with it.

He hugged her hard, wishing he could keep her right there, against his chest, locked in his arms where she was safe.

"Listen to me, Remington. *None* of this is your fault. This is how it's playing out. There's no point in wishing away how it started. What matters is how we're ending it."

"I hope it ends with my foot in his balls," she whispered fiercely.

He vowed the man would never make it that close to her. Because if he did, a pair of handcuffs and a jail cell weren't going to be enough.

"I need you to focus on Camille. She's going to have to talk."

Remi's hands fisted in his sweatshirt like she couldn't bear any space between them. He knew the feeling.

"He's going to come for you, Brick."

He hoped to fucking God that was the way it went down. He wanted his shot at the man who haunted Remi's dreams.

"Don't think like that," he told her, stroking his hand over her hair. It settled him to slide his fingers through all that red gold.

"He's going to come for Camille. And me. And you because it will hurt me."

"I'm not going to let that happen." He would walk through the fires of hell first.

"I know you won't."

There was something else happening in those beautiful green eyes. Another worry that had surfaced.

"Tell me what else is wrong," he said gruffly.

She pulled in a shaky breath. "Is there something wrong with me that I want to be treated like...like I do when Camille was being hurt at home?"

His heart rolled over in his chest. Brick closed his eyes and took a breath. "*Remington.*"

A single tear rolled down her cheek and broke his fucking heart.

"You *know* it's different."

She sniffled. "I know *you're* different. But does it mean there's something wrong with me that I like it when my best friend..."

"Baby, come here." He couldn't stand watching her worry her way through this alone. He sat on the bed and pulled her into his lap. "What we do together, we agree on."

"Technically don't Camille and Warren have an agreement? She stays or he'll kill her."

Brick tucked her head under his chin. "This is different. You're the one who told me that nothing we do together is wrong."

She nodded. "And I believe that. I really do. It's just it feels muddled in my head right now. Like maybe I shouldn't want it. Or it shouldn't make me feel so...safe? So I don't know, treasured?"

He pressed a kiss to the top of her head. "Baby, what we have is different. This isn't me controlling you with physical force. You know that, right?"

She nodded. "It is about control, but you don't want to control me. You like it when I surrender to you."

He fucking lived for it. A wild creature like Remi giving up control to him, trusting him to take care of her, was a potent turn-on. It filled a void in him that he hadn't known existed.

"I do," he agreed. "And you like submitting to me and letting me take that control. We both get something out of it. It's a mutual agreement. A mutual satisfaction. Do you know that I would never hurt you in that way?"

"Don't be a dumbass just because I'm being one," Remi said.

"Then you also need to realize that if someone tried to hurt you the way Vorhees hurts Camille, I'd end him."

She stiffened in his arms and didn't relax until he began to rub little circles in her neck with his fingers.

"I'm not trying to humiliate you or control you, Remi. I'm trying to give you what you need. In return, you give me the same."

"What do you need?" she asked softly, melting against him.

"I get off on having the uncontrollable Remington Ford do

what I say. But, baby, when we have our clothes on and we're out in public, if you started playing submissive with me, I'd lose my damn mind. I love your wild side. I love your fearlessness. I love your independence even when it drives me fucking crazy. When you let me take you, when you give yourself to me? There's nothing more intoxicating in the world than you thinking I'm good enough to surrender to."

She was like one of the wild stallions that the ranch he'd worked on would round up every winter. They called it breaking, and some men went into it with the intent to break the horse's spirit. But in its truest form, it was about earning the respect of a wild thing. The grudging regard didn't make the horse any less wild. It didn't make it much easier for someone else to seat. But earning that respect made Brick feel like more of a man than if he'd taken it, broken it. Fear was no replacement for respect.

And that was something Vorhees didn't understand.

She let out the breath that she'd been holding. "Now, see, when you say it like that, I feel like an idiot for getting it confused. I mean, I'm not going to say, 'Hey, Camille, I get really excited when Brick pins me down and bangs me sixty ways to Sunday after spanking me.'"

He groaned as his cock stirred against her. She snuggled closer. "But I also don't have to feel so guilty about it now."

"It's that easy?" he asked.

She looped her arms around his neck. "It's that easy. You do what you do to please me, not hurt me. And pleasing you amps up my pleasure into the stratosphere. We're like two missing puzzle pieces that finally fit together."

He needed a ring on her finger. Needed that piece of paper binding her to him.

He held her quietly and waited for her to get to the next

thing that was bothering her. He could feel it simmering under the surface.

"While we're on the subject," she began.

He smiled and pressed a kiss to the top of her head.

"Have you ever...done this with...anyone else?" Her fingers were tugging at the hair on his neck.

He nudged her chin up to look at him. "You're the only one." She always had been. Somehow all those years ago, he'd known and he'd waited.

After a decade and a half of missteps, they'd found their way back to each other.

"So not even with Audrey?" she asked in a tiny voice.

"No," he said, stroking a hand over her hair and admiring the way it gleamed under the light. A thought occurred to him that had him tensing. "Have you?"

"With Audrey? No," she said, feigning seriousness.

"Remi," he warned.

She shook her head. "I wouldn't have even known how to ask for it," she admitted.

He relaxed slowly. "I hate thinking about you being with anyone else," he admitted.

"Think how I felt," she said.

"About what?"

"When you married Audrey. On your wedding night. On your first anniversary. Just imagine if it had been me and Spence," she said.

The slice of pain was instantaneous, as if she'd jammed a knife between his ribs. How would he have survived that? How would he have looked across the breakfast table when they'd come to visit him? Would the four of them have been friends? While he pined for the girl his brother had?

"Jesus. Remi," he said. His heart felt like it was in a vice.

"I remember your wedding day," she continued, oblivious

to the fact that he was one second away from groveling on the floor for her forgiveness. "I was here. In my parents' house. In my room. I told them I had the flu so they'd go without me. I couldn't go near that church. I couldn't be here anymore. Not when I knew I'd see you two looking so happy together. Not when I wanted it to be me. I emptied my savings and I bought a ticket to Chicago while you were saying your vows."

Vows that had made him sweat. He'd loved Audrey. In his own way. And she'd been in love with at least the idea of him. But it had never been right.

"Baby."

"It's selfish, but I'm glad you saved this for me," she said.

"Only you," he said fiercely.

She exhaled slowly. "Speaking of Audrey and Spencer. Would you be upset if they got together?"

Brick shrugged. "Why would I care?"

She wrapped her arms around his neck and squeezed. "Good answer, because I think they're banging."

"Speaking of, I just busted your sister doing the walk of shame up our porch steps."

Remi squirmed against him. "Are you serious?"

"Said she was out for a run."

"My sister doesn't run," she scoffed.

"She was wearing Kyle's law school sweatshirt."

"What a weird day," she said, grinning up at him.

"I love you, Remington." He felt like he was being swept away by a current stronger than he was. It was both terrifying and exhilarating.

"I love you, Brick. Now, let's go downstairs, solve everyone's problems, and go back to bed so I can show you with my mouth just how much I love you."

48

Brick sat at his own dining table and tried not to acknowledge the rage that blazed inside him. Camille Vorhees sat across from him, carefully sipping water through split lips as Remi clutched her free hand.

"I appreciate you doing this here," Camille said, automatically assuming the role of hostess as if the instinct had been bred into her.

"I'm sorry this is necessary at all, Mrs. Vorhees," Chief Ford said from the head of the table. "But I appreciate you trusting us. Where would you like to start?"

"I spoke to my attorney. He'll be filing for an order of protection and divorce tomorrow," Camille said. "He felt it prudent that I discuss the situation with law enforcement."

Darlene nodded. "We'll take down the information and pass it on to the Illinois authorities since that's where the alleged abuse occurred."

"Alleged?" Remi snapped. "He drove us off a fucking cliff. There's nothing alleged about it."

"Remington," her mother said crisply, then pointed to the tape recorder. Remi flipped the recorder the middle finger.

Brick wanted to reach out, to touch her, to reassure her with his body.

"Why don't you two go get us some tea or coffee or ice cream," Darlene suggested, looking between Brick and her daughter.

Camille gave Remi an encouraging smile. "Go ahead. I'll be fine."

Remi and her mother shared a meaningful look as she rose.

Brick followed her out of the room.

"I can't tell if she's giving us busy work so she can make Camille feel more comfortable or if she knows it was fucking torture for me just to listen to some of the things he's done," Remi complained.

He couldn't hold himself back anymore and pounced. Grabbing her mid-stride, Brick hauled her into his arms and carried her past the kitchen where the rest of their house guests were pouring coffee and eating pancakes.

He stepped into the living room but couldn't put her down yet.

"I want him dead, Brick. And I know that's uncharitable and bad karma and all of that. But he's a fucking monster, and I want his life over. He'll never stop otherwise," she whispered.

He held on tighter, unable to speak.

"Some protection order isn't going to keep her safe. If anything, it's just going to make it worse. I get it now. It was safer to stay. Even though it was going to always end with him trying to kill her. She's actually safer living in that fiend's house."

Brick felt like he couldn't breathe. "*Remi*," he finally managed to rasp.

She pulled back and looked up at him. Her expression softened. "Hey, it's okay, big guy. I'm not going anywhere.

Certainly not to prison for murder. I'll make it look like an accident."

"Remi," he said again. "He's going to come here. He's going to follow the trail and find you and Camille here."

She cupped her hands to his face, rubbing her palms over his beard. "And you're going to stop him. You aren't going to let him anywhere near Camille, and you're only going to let me close enough so I can relocate his balls to his throat."

"I can't—" He paused and cleared his throat. "I can't lose you."

She tried to squirm out of his arms, but he only held on tighter until she went still in his arms.

"Look at me," she ordered, her voice steady. "Look at me. I'm not going to do anything that puts me or Camille or anyone else in danger. Okay?"

"I can't handle the thought of him anywhere near you." His voice shook. She was so fucking precious to him. He wouldn't survive it if something happened to her. Wouldn't be responsible for his actions if someone tried to take her from him.

She gave him a hard hug, pressing her face to his chest. He cupped the back of her head and held her there.

"Come watch me paint."

He released her, frowning. "You're going to let me watch you?"

"They're going to be in there a while. Camille has a lot of incidents to report. I'll give you a behind-the-scenes peek at the creative process."

He let her lead him into the studio and suppressed a smile when she locked the door and drew the blind. Even when she hadn't been speaking to him, the door had remained unlocked, the blind open.

"Come on," she coaxed, tugging him down the ramp into her chaos.

He hesitated, feeling the pressure of the preparations he needed to make. But he'd always wanted this. He'd always wanted to see how the magic came to be.

"I'll even let you pick the song," she said, positioning him on a paint-splattered stool off to the side of the easel. She handed over her phone and pointed him in the direction of her music app.

He watched her as she pushed the canvas she'd been working on out of the way, replacing it with a fresh canvas.

The drop cloth on the floor wrinkled under her bare feet as she worked her hair into a high knot.

"Did you pick a song yet?" she asked.

He shook his head. "You choose."

"Gentleman's choice," she insisted. "What song makes you think of summers here?"

Inspiration struck. He typed it in with a quirk of his lips and hit play.

"Nice choice," she said with a sly smile as Neil Young began to sing about harvest moons.

"We danced to this at your sister's wedding," he said.

"I know. Crank it loud."

He did as he was told and watched as she began to sway to the beat. "Good song," she said again, her body seeming to loosen with every note.

She didn't reach for a brush immediately. Instead, he watched as she started organizing colors. Pinks, reds, oranges. Cocking her head at the ceiling, she added blue and purple.

He watched in fascination, wishing he could see what she saw. Wished he could be inside her head. Maybe then he'd finally feel close enough to her.

She danced and hummed and swayed to the song as she

organized her tools. Brushes, palette knives, jars of cleaner. Her palette was a thin slice of acrylic stained from all the other music, all the other paintings. A rainbow-colored echo of creativity.

Brick watched as Remi dribbled the colors one by one onto the palette and then dragged a long thin brush through the orange and white, swirling until the color got lighter and lighter.

He held his breath as she stretched her arm toward the snowy white canvas. The clean, blank space. With a deft flick of her healed wrist, she swooped a four-inch swatch of tangerine across the white. Just like she'd done with his life, his blank canvas, she added color, layering it, texturing it, turning the void into something more beautiful than he could have imagined.

It was like witnessing a miracle unfold.

His hands fisted on his knees. He wanted to be part of the miracle. Needed to touch her. He rose without making the decision to and closed the distance between them.

It hit him when he saw the painting straight on.

She put the palette down and cocked her head, studying what she'd created so far.

"It's like the one upstairs." His voice was hoarse.

She stood there in his t-shirt, looking smug. "Of course it is. It's the same song. I'm just a lot more talented now."

She'd painted their song before. She'd remembered dancing with him. Had wanted to commemorate that moment. She'd loved him then and now.

Brick sank to his knees and pulled her to him.

"What are you doing?" she whispered as he pushed the hem of her t-shirt high. He groaned when he realized she hadn't even bothered putting on underwear.

"Let me love you."

497

Swiftly, he hooked her leg over his shoulder and pressed his mouth to her smooth, soft folds.

Her gasp went straight to his dick, which was suddenly as hard as steel. She was already wet.

"You're ready for me," he said in wonder, letting his tongue flick out to taste her. "Does painting turn you on?"

Above him, Remi sucked in a breath and shook her head. "You watching me turns me on. It makes me feel...possessed."

He growled against her sex, and her legs began to shake.

There was nothing in this world that felt more like home to him than Remington Ford's tight, wet pussy. He slid two fingers into her wet opening and hummed out a prayer of gratitude as he began to tongue her slick folds.

Her flavor was intoxicating. And it belonged only to him. She'd made him a fucking king.

A jagged moan ripped free from her throat, and his cock swelled. He freed himself from his sweatpants with one hand while he worked her hot little cunt with his other. Precome flowed from his crown, dripping onto the drop cloth as he fucked her with his fingers, worked her with his tongue.

"Oh my God."

Her broken, breathy sob had him fisting his shaft in an iron grip.

She was bucking into his face now, the silky leg over his shoulder angled to open her wider for him. He rewarded her with a third finger, stretching her tight.

He danced his tongue over her clit with exactly the right pressure.

"Brick," she whispered. "You're gonna make me come."

He couldn't help himself. He ached for her. His hand jerked up from root to tip, releasing another thick bead of moisture, this one pooling on his fist. He groaned, the vibration taking her pleasure to another level as her legs quaked.

Stiffening his tongue, he went to work on her clit as his fingers pumped into her hard and fast. He jacked himself at the same speed with a vise-like grip.

He felt her needy muscles quiver on his fingers and nearly came himself.

There were so many things he should be doing, so many preparations to make, details to take care of, but in the moment, nothing but Remi's orgasm mattered.

She shattered around him, her cunt clamping down hard on his fingers as she came. He was right there with her, the first spurt of his release burning its way up his shaft, erupting like a geyser.

He licked and fucked her through her orgasm and wrung himself dry in the process.

Reminding them both exactly what was at stake.

"Got a minute, Sergeant?" Chief Ford asked.

Brick glanced up from the plate of pancakes he was sharing with a sated, loose-limbed Remi. "Sure."

She jerked her head toward the side porch, and he followed her outside.

"We've got a strong case," she said. "She's got six months of photographic evidence documenting injuries. A diary of each incident."

"Smart."

"I'm going to lean as hard as I can on the Illinois boys to move fast for an arrest."

"But?" he asked, reading between the lines.

"I think you and I both know how that will go."

He nodded. A man like Vorhees had power and money. Which meant he also had people. The justice system didn't exactly move swiftly, even without those added complications. And professional courtesy only extended so far when it came to a police chief on some tiny island in another state. Even if they could get him arrested, he'd be walking on bail in less than an hour.

"There's something else," Darlene said, turning around to study him. "Our vic hasn't just been recuperating at home since the accident. She's been doing a little digging on her own. Seems she got the idea from my daughter."

Brick closed his eyes. "What are we dealing with?"

"She's got some information the Federal Election Commission might be interested in."

"Campaign finance violations?" he asked.

She nodded. "And some election fraud."

"Evidence?"

"Enough for an investigation. Hell, there might already be a Matter Under Review happening. The FEC doesn't exactly broadcast their cases."

He crossed his arms over his chest as a little flame of hope began to burn inside him.

"Does it ever piss you off that a person gets a stricter sentence for financial crimes than abuse?" Darlene mused. "If she gets that protection order and he violates it, it's a slap on the wrist. Not even a year behind bars. But buy yourself an election, and suddenly the legal system cares."

"What do we do next?" Brick asked.

"I'm gonna head back and type up the report. I'll make some calls before I send it on its way and then brief the mayor. If shit's going down on Mackinac, we need to be ready."

"It can't come to that. We have to get him at home," he said.

"I know. Tell you what, you write the report while I see if I can get someone in Chicago and in the FEC to answer the phone."

His hands bunched to fists at his sides. Real danger lurked.

"Just remember, Brick," Darlene said, eyeing him. "We're the good guys."

He couldn't say he'd stay on that side of the law. Not if Remi's life was hanging in the balance. The rules no longer applied, and for the first time in his life, he felt the siren's call of the gray area between right and wrong.

49

*R*emi waited until the occupants of the house were occupied in a spirited argument about the best way to prepare and enjoy eggs before slipping out the front door. It was April, and while yesterday had impressed with a balmy forty-nine degrees, it was spitting a little freezing rain that morning.

Brick hadn't come home last night. She'd spent the night alone in his big bed after staying up late talking to Camille. They'd glossed over what was happening today and pretended to ignore the next steps that needed to be discussed.

Instead, they'd painted their toenails and talked about movies, men, and art.

But in the light of day, Remi couldn't ignore the tension that was building in her chest. She knew as well as anyone that Warren would see a gauntlet when Camille's attorney filed for divorce and asked for a protection order. Brick had already antagonized him with the photos of the two of them together. It would only drive Warren's need to save face by any means possible. And that meant danger to everyone she cared about.

The only upside was that with the reports made public, with an active police investigation, the whole world would be watching. And when he came after Camille, they'd be ready.

It wasn't good enough, she thought, pulling up her hood and hurrying toward downtown.

There were a few fudgies out today, braving the weather, buying their souvenirs, and downing hot chocolate on the run.

But overall, it was quiet. Strangers on the street made her look twice, each man looking more and more like Warren as the cold rain blurred her vision. She needed to talk to Brick. Needed to know what came next and how she could help.

Hell, she needed to see him. To touch him. To reassure herself that he was real and solid and there for her.

"WILLIAM EUGENE CALLAN THE THIRD."

Remi hid her smile when Brick's size fourteen boots unceremoniously hit the station floor a split second after what looked like the dredges of cold coffee.

He'd been kicked back in his chair, feet on his desk. It would have been the picture of relaxed if it hadn't been for the fact that the man had the heels of his hands jammed into both eyes.

Those blue eyes were more red this morning. His hair stood up in funny tufts as if his hands had spent the night wrestling with it. His uniform shirt was wrinkled.

"Remi," he rasped.

She loved him so fiercely in that moment it took her breath away. "You forgot something last night."

"I did?" he looked dazed, exhausted. She wanted to wrap her arms around him and hang on tight.

"You forgot to come home."

He reached for her, and she walked into his strong arms and buried her face against his chest. He rested his cheek on the top of her head, and for a moment, the whole world felt right again.

"Remington, when this is over, I'm going to have a sizable question to ask you," he rumbled.

Her heart tapped out an emergency SOS.

She pulled back to look up at his handsome face. "What kind of question?"

He rubbed his thumb over the pads of her palms. "A big one."

Her heart skittered and then restarted. Visions of rings and Brick down on one knee danced in her head. For some reason, she didn't feel terrified. "You could always ask it now," she suggested innocently. "Distract us from the mess we've got going on here."

"You make it damn hard to say no to," he said, rising to his full height before dropping a kiss on the top of her head.

"I like that about me," she whispered.

"So do I, baby. But the answer's still no. When this is over. When you and Camille are safe."

She looked up at him. Into those fierce blue eyes. The set of his jaw.

"Thank you," she said.

"For what?"

"For keeping not just me but also my friend safe. For opening your home to my sister and her kids. For not biting your dad's head off when he delivered my friend to me. For being happy for your brother and your ex-wife. Brick Callan, you sure know how to make a girl feel safe and special."

He was a protector by nature. A big, burly, broody man whose only goal was to keep his loved ones safe and happy.

And Remi was going to spend the rest of her life loving the ever-loving hell out of him.

"This is Chief Ford," Darlene said, her cop voice carrying through the open office door. She waved at both of them, summoning them. Brick dragged Remi along behind him, positioning himself in the door with her at his back.

Remi peeked around the massive man mountain, wondering what threat lay within that had his hackles raised.

"I see," Darlene said, her voice clipped. Remi recognized that tone. It was the *I'm very disappointed and very, very angry voice*. Someone somewhere was ass-deep in trouble.

"And how in the hell did that happen?" her mother asked, tapping out a staccato beat with a pen against her desk.

Brick swore under his breath.

She slammed the receiver back into its cradle and, in a moment of uncharacteristic rage, hurled her stapler at the wall of filing cabinets in front of her. "Son of a bitch!"

"What happened?" Remi demanded to Brick's back.

"How did it go down?" he asked.

"The PD had intel that he was in his office this morning. The uniforms showed up and found his office cleared out. His computer gone. Half his files shredded. He was nowhere to be found."

"Someone tipped him off." Brick's tone was colder than the sleet coating the station windows.

"Looks that way. I warned them. I told them to keep it under their fucking vests. But he still made them look like kids playing Nancy Drew," Darlene said, standing up to pace.

"What happens next?" Remi asked, pressing her face between Brick's hulking bicep and the door frame.

"Next, those bozos try to save face and search the greater Chicago area for him. They're checking on his plane right now. Knocking on the doors of some of his associates."

"They're not going to find him," Remi said, feeling an icy dread settle in her chest.

Her mother's desk phone rang again. "What?" she snapped as a greeting. "Mexico? Can't you turn it around?"

Remi slunk away from her mother's office and wandered back to Brick's desk.

She felt his calming presence behind her a moment later. "This isn't something for you to be concerned about, Remi."

"I know," she said.

"I'll protect you. I won't let that son of a bitch anywhere near you or Camille. Or anyone else on this island."

"I know," she said again.

He was silent for a long beat, and she felt the weight of his gaze on her. "However," he began.

She closed her eyes.

"This means you can't go anywhere alone. Neither can Camille. You two need to stay in the house until we find him."

"She said Mexico," she said, nodding in her mother's direction.

"That was his family's plane. The flight plan they filed this morning. The Chicago PD isn't too concerned about tracking down someone for domestic assault in Cancun."

"You don't think he's on that plane?" she guessed.

He shook his head. "Remi, it's already hit the news. The divorce, the abuse allegations, and now a botched arrest. He's got nothing left to lose."

She closed her eyes again and let out a shaky breath. The one thing, the tiny veneer of protection Camille had against the monster, had been stripped away. Warren Vorhees no longer had a face worth saving. He was already ruined. And there was only one thing worth living for now.

Revenge.

"He's coming here," she said.

"He won't get near you as long as you do what I say."

She felt utterly helpless and disgusted by it. Brick and her mother could strap on guns and march off to face danger. But she had to lock herself away inside and wait for someone else to finish the fight. It felt wrong. Because this was as much her fight as anyone else's.

If Warren was out for blood, so was she. She wanted to be the one to turn the key in the lock. To watch the embers of his power snuff out and die. She wanted him to be revealed for exactly what he was. An inhuman monster with nothing to live for.

"Remington," Brick said, the warning clear in his growl.

"What?" she asked, stubbornly.

"I know that look. This isn't some illegal party on Round Island that you're missing out on. This is life or death. This is a battle I'm trained to fight. One that I'm not going to lose. But you have to do your part."

"Yeah. My part is to play the damsel in distress in my stupid ivory tower because once again, I'm incapable of taking care of myself." She crossed her arms over her chest.

"This isn't me going off to fight your war. We're partners in this. And we've got to play to our strengths. Which means I go break the bad guy's face while you keep Camille in one piece. She needs you right now. She's minutes from falling to pieces. That's why she came to you. Because you're the strong one. So let me fight the enemy while you protect your friend."

She glared at him, then rolled her eyes. "Damn it. You're really good at that."

He pulled her into his chest, ignoring the hustle and bustle of the busy bullpen around them. "Yeah? Just wait till I ask my big question."

"Brick, I swear to God, if you turn it into something like 'Remington Honeysuckle Ford, will you get tacos with me

507

tonight?' I will be ordering an extra large body bag and digging a real big hole in the Grand Hotel's rose garden."

He ran a hand gently over her face. A sweet, soft, soothing touch. "Are you telling me you'd turn me down for tacos?"

She felt a smile tugging at her lips. "Of course not. I'm not an idiot. I'd eat the tacos and then bury your body."

"You're a hell of a woman, Remi."

"Yeah. Yeah. And you're my big brawny man mountain who had better make Warren Vorhees regret ever laying a hand on a woman."

"I know you're being sarcastic. But I still like the sound of it."

Her flirtatious retort was cut off by the station door flying open. In strolled two scowling suits. The first, a woman, long and lean in a boxy polyester suit the color of horse shit. The second was a baby-faced man who looked like he'd practiced his scowl in the mirror and wouldn't be able to grow facial hair if he tried.

"Who are they?" Remi asked.

"Feds," Brick growled.

According to every cop TV show she had ever watched, a territorial pissing match was about to occur. One that had probably never happened in the history of Mackinac Island.

"Oh, boy," she said.

Brick gripped her arm and steered her toward the side door. "You're going home."

"But I want to watch my mom yell at these guys." Remi pouted.

"I'll re-enact it for you later," he promised.

She heaved a sigh. "Fine. But I want you to do the facial expressions *and* the accents," she insisted.

"God, I love you." Heedless of the audience, he grabbed her by the chin and kissed the hell out of her.

A few of the other officers who weren't staring down the suits whistled their approval.

"Don't forget to come home this time," she said when he'd pulled away and her head stopped spinning.

"I can't go another night without you."

She started for the door, but Brick stopped her. "Turk? You mind walking Remi home?"

"I can get myself home," she scoffed.

Carlos jumped up from his desk. "Sure thing," he said.

"What did we just talk about not even five minutes ago?" Brick demanded gruffly.

"I don't really recall. I was too busy thinking about you naked."

"You're evil."

"Have fun with that hard-on, big guy," she said, tapping him in the balls and breezing out the door with Carlos Turk on her heels.

50

___

S pecial Agent Jana Brice was an ambitious pain in the ass. Her partner, Junior Agent Harold White, was just plain annoying. Fishing for a pissing contest and flashing his Department of Justice badge all over the fucking place. Brick disliked them both on sight.

Fortunately he didn't have to play nice with them. That was up to the chief who, after the first five minutes, looked like she was going to choke on her own tongue from restraining herself.

"I'm guessing since you two showed up on my doorstep eighteen hours after my little report hit your desk that you've already got an investigation going," Darlene mused.

White slouched in his chair as if he were a bored parent at a band concert. Meanwhile Brice sat ramrod straight, flat brown eyes locked on Darlene's.

Brick was used to men's pissing matches. The female element made the contest more subtle and more terrifying.

"We need to speak with Mrs. Vorhees as soon as possible," Special Agent Brice announced.

Chief Ford eyed Brick for a beat. "That can be arranged.

While my sergeant here makes arrangements, you can talk to me about what kind of protection you can offer my witnesses."

There was a special territorial emphasis on the "my" that had Brick's lips quirking. He left the office and dialed his father's phone number.

"Brick!" Once again, William sounded delighted that his son was calling. In the background, he could hear the happy chatter of women. The normalcy of it loosened the knots in his gut. He once again marveled that in the span of less than two months, he'd gone from being a bachelor living alone to sharing his house with so many people they'd blown a fuse with too many hair dryers going at the same time.

"Dad, I'm going to be swinging by the house with a couple of federal agents. They want to talk to Camille and Remi and probably you."

"Okay," his father said, waiting.

"I wanted to give you a heads up in case there's any reason why you wouldn't want to be questioned by an agent."

There was a beat of silence.

"Are you worried about your old man?" William asked.

"No. I'm just giving you an opportunity to not be there if there's going to be some kind of...conflict."

"Son, I've been on the straight and narrow for years now. But I appreciate the concern. I'm more than ready to do my part to bring that son of a bitch to justice."

"Okay then," Brick said, not knowing what else to say. "I guess I'll be by within the hour."

"We'll be ready," William promised.

∾

FORTY-FIVE MINUTES LATER, Brick stood in his own dining room while Special Agent Stick Up Her Ass and Junior Agent

Compensating for a Small Dick faced off against Camille, his father, and Remi. Chief Ford sat at the head of the table.

Magnus and his new buddy Mega had been relegated to the backyard after hissing and barking at the feds.

Remi, an excellent judge of character, was already pissed off at something one of the agents had said.

"I'm sorry. I feel like I missed the part where you expressed concern to my friend here about the abuse she's suffered for years at the hands of a monster. You kind of just jumped straight into the 'tell me about the money' part," Remi said sweetly.

Brick hid his smile as Darlene coughed subtly into her hand.

"Of course we have great sympathy for Mrs. Vorhees's..." Brice's chilly gaze flicked over Camille's bruised face. "...situation. But our agency isn't interested in domestic matters."

"Right, because money is more important than human life," Remi purred.

Like mother, like daughter.

"Mrs. Vorhees," White began, "Chief Ford sent us some interesting information regarding your husband and his use of campaign funds. We're going to need you to elaborate on what you told her."

Camille nodded, the consummate hostess despite her battered face. "Of course, Agent White," she said. "Can we offer you two anything to drink while you're here? Coffee? Tea?"

"A kick in the ass," Remi muttered under her breath.

"Ms. Ford, is it?" Brice asked, arching an eyebrow. "I presume you two are related."

"We are," the chief responded. "Remington is my youngest daughter."

"How does this situation concern her?" White asked

almost flippantly. Brick tensed, ready to take issue with the disrespect, but Special Agent Brice shot her sidekick a cool look that had him shutting up.

"Do you mean besides caring about the violence a man imparted on my friend?"

White was going to get his teeth kicked in if he didn't watch his mouth. And Brick didn't mind letting Remi take her shots at him.

"Do you have any other reason for being at this table other than being a hand-holder?" Brice asked.

"Only from the standpoint that I was in the car he ran off the road and plowed through a guardrail, sending us down a cliff in an attempted double homicide. Or the fact that he's been sending me threats since I came back to the island," she snapped, coming halfway out of her chair.

Camille laid a hand on Remi's sleeve.

White jotted down some notes.

"I see," Special Agent Brice said.

"You bet your ass, you see," Remi said.

"Remington." Darlene's voice was tired.

"This would be the accident on January thirtieth?" Brice asked, shuffling papers in her folder.

"That's correct," Camille said. "My husband hacked my phone and discovered that I was planning on leaving him. That Remi was going to help me."

"The accident that you said occurred because a Ms. Ballard was intoxicated."

"Remi, my friend and Chief Ford's daughter, paints under the name Alessandra Ballard. Much like a novelist would use a pen name. Remi was not drunk that night, nor was she driving."

"But according to the public statement you made—"

Remi stood up fast enough that her chair tumbled over

backward. "Now you listen here. I don't give a shit if you're special agent of god's gift to special agents. This man tried to murder us both. He has nothing left to lose. He's lost his pride, his power, and pretty soon his goddamn seat in the Senate. He skipped out on an arrest this morning. So put your fucking cards on the table, and let's figure out how to make sure this bastard never sees the outside of a cage again."

Brick ached to touch her. To tell her how fucking proud he was of his girl. The urge to hold her in one arm while slapping the shit out of the smug junior agent also ranked up there.

He noticed the smile tugging at the corner of his father's mouth, the straightening of Camille's shoulders. The pride in Darlene's cool gaze. Remi inspired that.

Special Agent Brice expelled a breath and sat back in her chair, steepling her fingertips.

"Our investigation into Senator Vorhees is entering its eighteenth month."

"For fuck's sake." Remi slapped the table. "If you people moved faster, Camille wouldn't have spent three weeks in the hospital, and I could have kept painting without a broken arm."

Brick moved quickly to stand behind her. He brought his hands to her shoulders and squeezed, sending her a silent message.

"What a cozy community you have here, chief," White sniped, eyeing Brick and Remi.

"What a douchebag face you have here, *junior*," Remi snarled.

"Enough!" Brick's voice cracked like a whip. "This is my house. These women deserve your respect."

Special Agent Brice maintained a calculated expression while White looked like he was choking on his tie.

"It started with a complaint filed by a watchdog group with

the Office of Congressional Ethics. Until this," Brice said, tapping a finger on a copy of Chief Ford's report, "all we had was enough for sanctions. But if Mrs. Vorhees has the evidence she says she has, we are looking at prosecution by the DOJ."

Darlene shifted in her seat to address Camille directly. "Prosecution at the federal level carries significantly heavier sentences than spousal abuse. You can nail him for both, which I certainly recommend. But this is how we get him out of your life for years, not months."

Camille took a nearly imperceptible breath. "Let's begin," she said.

TWO HOURS LATER, Brick's back hurt from standing. Remi had a knee pulled up to her chest and was swinging her other foot like a pendulum under the table. He'd never seen her sit still this long, but she'd yet to budge from Camille's side.

"So Senator Vorhees used campaign funds to cover expenses for his family's private jet, for the boat at the lake house, and for personal travel expenses."

Camille nodded. "Yes. There's a flash drive in a tampon applicator in the guest bathroom at home. It has the financials I found as well as copies of his emails and travel records."

Brice shot a look at White, who bounded out of his chair like his ass was on fire. He was already dialing the phone before he ducked out the front door.

Special Agent Brice neatly stacked her papers and returned them to their files. She closed her notebook and turned off her recorder. "Mrs. Vorhees, I thank you for your cooperation. The department appreciates your efforts."

Brice's phone rang, and she rose from the table.

"Seriously? In a tampon?" Remi asked Camille when the agent had disappeared. "High five, girl."

Camille shot her a sly smile. "I learned from the best."

"That's where Remi hid her liquor minis when she was a high school senior," Chief Ford explained to Brick.

Remi gasped. "You knew?"

"Of course I knew. You didn't ever wonder why they were always so watered down? Or why your cheap-ass whiskey tasted like hot peppers?"

"You diabolical woman." Remi shook her head in admiration.

"One day you, too, will ruin your own child's liquor stash," the chief promised her.

Remi's gaze landed on Brick and held for a beat. Her cheeks flushed, and she broke eye contact first.

He wondered what the look meant. Was it something she'd consider? A family? With him? Not so long ago, Brick had assumed he'd live out his days as a bachelor. But that was before Remi warmed his bed. There could be a family filling this house. Little devious redheads running up the stairs. A quiet boy on their heels trying to run herd on his sisters.

The images sprang to life so vividly, he could almost hear the ruckus. There was much he had to discuss with Remi.

Special Agent Brice returned to the room, her lips pursed in a grim line. "Senator Vorhees's plane was met by local law enforcement on the tarmac in Cancun. He was not aboard."

Brick saw Remi take Camille's hand under the table. "Then where is he?" she asked.

"We're following up several leads," Brice said evasively.

"So you don't know," Brick announced, filling in the blanks.

The front door opened, and White stuck his head in. "You got a second?"

Both agents retired to the front porch.

William excused himself to get everyone a round of waters.

Remi wasted no time in running to the window and trying to listen.

"Remington, come away from there," Chief Ford said on a yawn.

Brick stole a seat at the table and pulled Remi into his lap. He breathed in the scent of her hair, letting the warmth of her soft body thaw the iciness that had lodged in his gut.

"I don't like them leaving us out of their stupid plans when Camille is the one in danger."

"You're in this too, missy," her mother reminded her.

"At this point, we all are," Camille spoke up. "William saved me. Remi defied him. Brick provoked him. I left him. He'll come after us and anyone who gets in his way."

Her lower lip trembled, and Brick was struck by just how alone she looked.

"I'm sorry for bringing this to your doorstep," Camille said to Darlene, who was guzzling coffee. "I never meant for anyone else to get hurt."

Remi squirmed in his arms, but Brick held on tight. She turned to him, and whatever she saw in his eyes was enough to make her wrap her arms around his neck and hang on.

"I'm sorry no one did anything a long time ago. You didn't deserve any of this," Darlene said. "No one's in danger because of you. It's because of him. So don't try to take responsibility for his sins. They're his. Not yours."

The words hit Brick dead center, just like they had the first time she'd said them. To him. He'd been busting his ass as a rookie cop like he'd had something to prove.

In his head, he'd needed Chief Ford to know he wasn't like his father. A good-time grifter looking for an easy score. He'd needed to prove that he wasn't going down the same path.

She'd already known it. Strongly hinting that he was being a dumbass if he thought otherwise. And she'd reminded him that on Mackinac, people were judged by their own character, not by those of the people around them.

Remi's fingers toyed with his hair at the nape of his neck. The gentle touch, the weight of her body against his reassured him. She was his. She belonged with him. And no one was going to take her away.

The conversation cut off when both agents returned.

"With this new evidence, the U.S. Attorney is confident she can take this case before the court and win," Special Agent Brice stated.

"We just need the bad guy in custody," White added.

"That is usually helpful," Chief Ford drawled.

Brice gave the room a cool look. "The best move forward at this time is to encourage him to come out of hiding."

Brick didn't like how her gaze lingered on Remi.

She shifted in his lap. "You need bait."

"Essentially yes."

"No." Brick's voice rang out, silencing everyone else.

"Can I speak to you outside, *Sergeant*?" Remi demanded.

"You can't be okay with this," Brick said to the chief as Remi headed for the front door.

Chief Ford met his heated gaze. There was a warning in her eyes and something else. Something like fear.

He followed Remi out into the lousy, damp spring air.

"Absolutely fucking not," he said before she could even open her pretty mouth.

"Hear me out."

"There's no way you're taking their side."

"I'm not taking anyone's side over you," she said, huddling deeper into the coat she'd snatched off the rack inside. It was his.

"You are not to put yourself at risk, Remington. I couldn't take it."

He crowded her against the railing, needing the proximity to her.

"What if there was no real danger?"

He felt a nagging sensation. An irritation between his shoulder blades as if they were being watched.

"It makes sense," she began. "From a big picture level."

"Dangling you in front of a homicidal monster makes no sense on any level," he argued, keeping his hands on the railing next to her. He was afraid if he touched her he'd never let her go.

"I'm saying, we need him to show his grotesque face sooner rather than later so he can be dragged off in handcuffs. He knows that Camille and I defied him. He'd find us here sooner or later."

"What's your point?"

"He knows about the divorce and protective order. He knew about the arrest attempt. Sooner rather than later, he'll track Camille here to a tiny island with a small police force. What he doesn't know is there's a Department of Justice investigation happening. That's a whole lot of law enforcement who could grace our shores in time to nab him the second he lands here."

"You're talking about laying a trap here on Mackinac."

"Can you think of a way to find him faster?"

He wanted to.

"Don't do this, Remi. This doesn't feel right."

"I don't like it either. But this needs to be over for Camille. How long can she hang in there if he's just vanished? How long can she hold it together, knowing that he could be anywhere? Across the country or around the next corner?"

Brick looked over his shoulder, the nagging feeling still

there. But there was no one there.

"Remi, this is asking for trouble. Let the agents handle it. It's their job."

"You heard Dumb and Dumber in there. They've been sitting on this for a year and a half. Do you know how many times he's hit her in eighteen months? How many times he's hurt and humiliated her? There's no way they weren't aware of it. They left her there in that situation because they wanted to follow the money."

"Using you and Camille as bait is doing the same thing. Intentionally putting you in harm's way."

"It's not," she insisted, slipping her arms around his waist and holding on. "Because we have you. Brick, you aren't going to let him get close enough to her. To me. You'll keep me safe just like you always have."

"You don't know what you're asking," he said, feeling broken inside. She couldn't possibly know what she was asking him to do. She wanted him to hold up the single most important thing in his universe and dare a mad man to try to take it away.

He couldn't resist her anymore. He had to hold her. Tucking her into his chest, he rested his head on the red hair that had haunted his dreams for his entire adult life.

"I do. And I know it's not fair. And I swear I'll make it up to you."

"How?"

"I'll spend the whole rest of my life loving you so big that you'll never have reason to doubt it for a second."

"*Remington*."

"Brick. I love you and I trust you. And I've got a whole lifetime planned out for us. I'm not going to do something stupid and jeopardize it. I promise you. I'm just asking you to do what you've always done. Protect me."

51

With the weight of the world on his shoulders, Brick walked in the door after seven to a full house and salsa music. Mega trotted toward him with a welcoming ruff, the cat slinking along on his heels.

He shucked off his coat and bent to pet the welcoming committee. "What's all this?" Neither the dog nor the cat had answers.

The table was set with his grandmother's china, and someone had brought her card table out of the basement to handle overflow seating.

The noise of people, of family, came from upstairs and down the hall. The smells of homecoming wafted toward him, and out of the noise, he zeroed in on Remington's laugh.

And there she was. The flash of red hair. The smile that could thaw the coldest of hearts. She didn't walk to him, she ran. Jumping into his open arms like it had been days rather than hours since she'd last seen him. This was the fantasy. Coming home to *her*. Opening his arms to *her*. Loving *her*.

She kissed him on the mouth, and when it was over too soon for his liking, he fisted a hand in all of that fiery hair and made her kiss him again until he was hard and she was breathless. *His.* The fierce possessiveness nearly choked him.

"I missed you," she said, squeezing his hips with her thighs. "Busy day?"

He stroked a hand down her back to her buttocks, gave them a squeeze. He'd spent all the hours since Camille's interview with the feds, setting up patrols and coordinating the arrival of a dozen more federal agents. They'd be on the island by morning. In the meantime, Mackinac officers were scheduled to patrol past his place, Remi's parents', and Kimber's house every half hour.

"A bit." With regret, he let her slide down his body to the floor. "How was yours?" he asked, tucking a strand of hair behind her ear.

"Good, considering. I declared it family dinner night to welcome Camille. Mom will be here soon. Kyle's coming, too," she said with a wiggle of eyebrow.

"Do we smell a reconciliation?"

"From what I eavesdropped on Kimber's very private conversation today, it sounds like Kyle is changing jobs so he can be home every night, and Kimber is starting her own business. Agnes Sopp hired her to rehab her property by the marina."

"Good for them," Brick said. "I'm going to miss having the kids here though."

Remi smiled coyly and ran her hands down his chest to his belt. "I'm so glad to hear you say that because I volunteered us to take them for the whole weekend next week while Kyle and Kimber go away for a sexcation."

"When can we take one of those?" He skimmed a palm up her side to cup her breast under the jewel-toned cropped sweater she wore. A week away with nothing to do but make

Remington Ford come. He'd move any mountain to make that happen.

"I was thinking. It's been a while since I had a vacation. And it's been *such* a *long* winter."

"Very long," he agreed, thumbing her nipple into a point.

"What would you say to a Caribbean vacation? Maybe a quiet villa with a private pool so I can sunbathe topless?"

He let out a pained breath as his dick throbbed behind his zipper.

"I'll take that as a yes," she said, cupping his erection in her hand.

There was an outburst of laughter coming from the living room, and he heard the oven timer go off. Too many people in the house for him to carry her upstairs and make her scream out his name. "That's a definite yes," he growled. With great reluctance, he removed her hand from his crotch and pressed a kiss to her palm.

"Good. If you hit the shower now, dinner will be ready by the time you get back down."

A shower sounded good.

"I don't suppose you can join me?" he asked wolfishly.

She bit her lip, gaze zeroing in on his hard-on. His cock twitched at the attention.

"Remi, come look at this meat," Gilbert Ford called from the kitchen.

Brick winced.

"Mood killer," she whispered. "Go shower. Oh, and Spence wants to talk to you. I can't imagine about what." She winked.

He paused long enough to dig a small box out of his coat pocket before floating up the stairs, counting his lucky fucking stars.

When he came out of the bathroom in a towel, he found his brother lounging on the bed, looking at his phone.

"What's up?" Brick asked, grabbing underwear and sweats out of the dresser.

"I need to talk to you," Spencer said, jumping off the bed with nervous energy.

"Okay. Talk."

"Well. I wanted to talk to you before something happened. But then something happened and—" He dropped his phone and bent to pick it up, smacking his head off the nightstand. "Ow."

He took pity on his little brother. "You and Audrey," he said.

Spence looked up, rubbing his forehead. "Yeah. How'd you know?"

"Remi saw you sneaking into her room two nights ago."

His brother winced. "I really wanted to talk to you about it before I did any kind of sneaking. Preferably so sneaking wouldn't be required. I've had feelings for her for a long time but I couldn't tell if you were still torn up over the divorce and I didn't want to do anything that would hurt—"

Brick held up his hand. "Spence. Stop. You have my blessing even though neither of you need it."

"Seriously?"

"I think the four of us have wasted enough time, don't you?"

Spencer grinned at him and brought him in for a back-slapping hug. "I love you, man."

"Yeah, yeah. I love you, too. Now stop pretending like you're sleeping on the couch."

His brother paused in the door, still smiling. "This thing with you and Remi. It looks pretty serious from the outside."

With an eye on the hallway, Brick opened his sock drawer and tossed Spencer the small velvet jeweler's box.

"No shit?" Spencer asked, opening it. "She's gonna fucking love it."

"Yeah?" Brick paused to admire the brushed gold band with its scattering of inset diamonds and jewels. He'd known it was hers the second he'd seen it in the shop that afternoon.

"Yeah. It's artsy. It's a little chaotic. A lot cool. Just like your girl. Congratulations, man."

"Thanks." Brick tucked the box back in the drawer.

"Know when you're doing it?"

As soon as he could get her father's blessing and then her alone.

"Soon," he said. "She's a snooper. She'll find it sooner rather than later."

Spencer grinned and paused in the doorway again. "Hey, thanks for letting Dad be here. It means a lot to him. And me."

Brick cleared his throat and nodded.

"And just because I've never said it, and Audrey opened a couple of bottles of wine before dinner, and I've got a happy buzz going, I've always looked up to you, and that's never once changed. You're a hell of a guy, Brick. I hope I'm just like you when I grow up."

His throat tight, Brick grabbed his brother in an affectionate headlock and ruffled his hair. "You're the best guy I know, Spence. Now get the fuck out."

It took him ten minutes to get Gilbert's attention and wrangle the man out onto the front porch away from the pre-dinner chaos unfolding inside.

"If this is about my bar back performance the other night —" Gil began.

Brick hid his smile. "It's not. You were great, and Darius and I are happy to have you aboard."

Gilbert perked up. "Thank God. I thought you were firing me!"

"No. But I do need to ask you something. Something not bar related." Brick felt the words get stuck in his throat. This man had been more of a father to him than his own. How could he ask him to trust him with his daughter's future?

"I'm *all* ears," the man said, straightening his sweater vest and picking up a nearly overflowing glass of wine.

"What's all this?" Darlene Ford, still in uniform, demanded as she trudged up the porch steps. "Ooh! Wine." She took the glass from her husband and drank deeply.

Gilbert slung an arm around his wife's waist. "Well, it's Family Dinner Night. Kimber and Kyle are reconciling. It looks like Spencer and Audrey are finally hooking up. And Brick here is trying to work up the nerve to ask for my blessing to marry Remi."

Chief Ford paused, mid-swallow, to eye Brick over the rim of the glass.

Brick was hot and cold all over. It was like a spotlight was on him, and he'd forgotten all his lines.

Darlene handed the wine back to her husband. She looked Brick up and down and nodded briskly.

"It's about fucking time," she said.

Then she grabbed his face and gave him a smacking kiss right on the mouth. "Welcome to the family." With that, she opened the front door and went inside yelling, "What's for dinner?"

Brick stared after her open-mouthed. "Uh...I..."

Gilbert clapped him on the shoulder. "I don't have much more to add besides I can't imagine a better man for our girl. You've loved her through the bright spots and the dark. You've never once not been there for her. Never once not protected her even from herself. A father can't ask for anything more than that. And I know I've had a *lot* of wine, but I would be honored to call you son."

Brick's throat felt like it was on fire. His eyes watered, blurring everything in front of him. He swallowed hard, barely managing to rasp a "Thank you."

Gilbert gave his shoulder a squeeze. Brick couldn't tell through the blur, but Gilbert's eyes looked a little shiny, too. "Thank *you* for loving my wild child exactly as she is."

He didn't even flinch when Gilbert planted a kiss on him, then slapped his cheek a little too hard. "Congratulations. Now let's eat before we're all shit-faced."

52

$\mathcal{D}$inner with everyone crammed into Brick's dining room felt festive. As if wine, good food, and music somehow managed to block out the bad that lurked just beyond their little island. Camille was deep in conversation with Kimber and their father, filling them in on Remi's gallery exhibitions.

Even Brick seemed lighter than he had when he came home. He ate left-handed just so he could hold her hand under the table, his thumb brushing possessively over her ring finger again and again.

Brick Callan was going to ask her to marry him. And she was going to say yes.

She felt like she was ready to burst. Like it was Christmas Eve, and there was a pile of presents waiting for her under the tree. Only Brick was bigger and better than any present, and a lifetime with him would last longer than any Christmas morning.

Good things were in store for them. All of them, she thought, looking at the way Kyle watched Kimber like he was seeing her for the first time. Spencer and Audrey seemed to be sharing a secret joke at the end of the table. William was answering Hadley's questions about what it was like to be an investigator.

The shrill ring of her mother's phone cut through the chatter.

"This is the Chief."

Remi felt Brick tense next to her as a text came in on his.

Tension replaced the relaxed vibe in the room.

"Pick me up on the way," Darlene said, pushing out of her chair and squeezing her husband's shoulder.

"What's wrong? What's happening?" Remi asked, reaching out to clasp Camille's hand.

"It's a fire," Brick said as he rose, giving her hand one last squeeze. "The Grand Hotel."

He followed Darlene out of the room.

"I can't leave her unprotected," she heard him say to her mother.

"I know. Call Brice. No reason she and White should get any sleep tonight if we're not."

Brick swore, and Remi heard him taking the stairs two at a time.

Darlene was on the phone again, and everyone else stepped out onto the porch. The Grand Hotel was around the bend and uphill, but there was an eerie glow in the night sky.

"This has nothing to do with Warren," Remi reassured Camille. But her friend didn't look so sure.

"Dad," Brick, in uniform again, poked his head out of the door.

William stepped inside, leaving the door ajar. Remi waited a beat and followed. They had their heads together in the dining room.

"This is a big ask. She's the most important thing in the

world to me, and I don't trust the feds. I need you to keep her safe—both of them—until I get back."

William nodded solemnly. "I'll do whatever it takes. You and Remi have something real and right. I won't let anything happen to her. I promise you that."

Remi's eyes misted when Brick squeezed his father's shoulder.

"Thanks, Dad."

"Turk's here with the car," Darlene said, opening the front door.

Brick spotted Remi in the hallway.

"I can't leave until they're here," he said.

Her mom gave him the nod. "We'll see you up there then."

William followed her back out, leaving Remi alone with Brick.

Both of the island's fire trucks screamed past the house, followed by the ambulance.

Her heart thumped.

"You have to go," she told him.

"I can't leave you."

"You're not leaving me alone. There is a house full of people here. You're needed out there."

The island fire department was well-equipped but not to battle what could easily become a 4-alarm blaze. Every available hand was needed to save the landmark. The beginning for so many happily ever afters.

Gripping his arm, Remi looked into those worried eyes. "Go."

"Promise me you won't take any risks. You'll stay indoors. You won't step a foot out the door once I'm gone."

"I promise you, Brick."

He cupped her face in his hand, his blue eyes burning.

"Promise me you'll be here when I get back so I can ask you that question."

She gave him a watery smile. "Yes to tacos."

He brought his forehead to hers and closed his eyes.

She cupped his face in her hands, reveling at the rough of his beard, the smooth of his skin. This face was so achingly familiar to her. He belonged to her. It had been written so long ago, yet they were just getting started.

"I love you. Be safe. Text when you can."

He nodded, then lowered his mouth to hers for one hard kiss. "I will. I love you, Remington."

"Oh, hey. Don't fuck anything up," she called as he started to leave.

He paused and stared at her.

She shrugged. "What? I'm not giving you some kind of romantic last words. I'm giving you something terrible to hold you over until you're home again. Then I'll say nice things."

"I'll love you so fucking much," he said fiercely.

"I'll be waiting for you, big guy."

"Keep your inhaler on you. I don't know how bad the smoke is going to get."

She blew him a kiss as he jogged down the porch steps.

His large form melted into the night as he ran toward the fire.

Remi watched him go with an ache in her chest.

Something tickled at the back of her neck. A nagging sensation that had her turning away from the direction of the fire and looking down the dark street. Neighbors were coming out of their houses to see what the excitement was about. Before long, she was sure there would be a crowd of bystanders at the hotel.

But something out there in the dark made her feel like she was the entertainment. Like she was the one being observed.

William herded everyone back inside and bolted the front door. And while a debate raged over hot tea or coffee or more wine, Remi decided to behave herself and rounded up her inhaler and phone. She had a shit-ton of missed calls and texts. Mostly from Rajesh.

The phone rang in her hand.

"What?"

"Dude," Raj said, "the pics of you and Camille are getting so much play right now. Why didn't you clue me in? I sounded like an idiot when the calls started coming in."

Her heart did a lopsided roll in her chest. "What pictures?" she asked, gripping the phone.

"The ones Camille posted to Instagram. They're freaking everywhere."

"Those weren't supposed to go up until tomorrow morning." Tomorrow morning, when a dozen federal agents and all of the Mackinac Island Police Department were ready to spring the trap.

Ten minutes later, Agents Brice and White showed up. As William shut the door behind them, Remi barreled up.

"Which one of you asshats decided to post the pictures early?" she hissed.

Special Agent Brice frowned and shot her partner a cool look.

Two spots of color appeared on White's cheeks. "What's the big deal? He already knew you were here. He probably guessed his wife would run straight to you."

"The big deal, you stupid, dick-swinging shit, is that the entire police department is on the scene of a fire, and you two are the only federal agents on the fucking island. Why didn't you roll out a welcome mat?"

"Ms. Ford," Brice said.

"Don't fucking 'Ms. Ford' me. If this fire has *anything* to do with Warren Vorhees, if any of my people get hurt, it's on *your* head."

Brice ran her tongue around her teeth. "Stay here and keep an eye on things," she told White. "I'm going to track down Chief Ford at the fire and find out if there's any reason to be concerned."

"You can keep an eye on things *outside*," Remi said, opening the front door for them.

Everyone gathered in the living room for popcorn, tea, and a movie. Her father and Kyle both volunteered to spend the night, telling the kids it was the first big family sleepover. Remi kept her phone on her and waited to hear from Brick.

The tightness in her chest a constant companion as the movie played. As Kimber and Kyle carried the kids upstairs to put them to bed. As one by one, everyone wandered off to bed.

Perhaps she wasn't the only one feeling the tension, she noted.

Her father sprawled out on the couch, a baseball bat on the floor next to him "just in case." Brick's father positioned himself in the dining room with a book, one of Brick's guns, and a line of sight to the front door and stairs.

"You all right in here?" Remi asked, bringing him a glass of water.

He nodded. "I'm right where I need to be."

"I know Brick feels better with you here," she said, brushing her fingers over the chair back.

"He's entrusted me to keep an eye on you," William said. "I'm not going to let him down. Not again."

"Seems like you've been done letting people down for a long time."

"It's nice of you to notice," he said with a soft smile.

"I'm going to marry your son," she said suddenly.

"I'd hoped so. You're just exactly what he needs. A

reminder that life isn't so black and white. That there's a lot of fun to be had with colors."

"It's good to have you here," she said. "I'm going to go back to the studio and see if I can burn off some energy with paint for an hour or so."

He nodded. "I'll be here."

She headed down the hall, wandering past rooms that held so many signs of life now. Schoolwork for the kids. Kimber's makeshift office in the living room. Magnus and her father both snoring in the living room. The popcorn bowls. It felt good, right, to fill Brick's life with just a little bit of chaos.

She stepped into the studio and flicked on the lights. Shaking off the anxiety about what lurked beyond the dark windows, she rolled her work in progress back onto the center of the drop cloth.

She'd finish her painting for Brick later. Right now, she felt like exorcising some demons. With "No Surprises" on repeat, she kicked off her shoes and got to work.

The nervous energy, the sliver of fear that put a metallic taste in her mouth, was exactly what she needed. To create fear and confusion with brush and oil. To bring a desperate drive to survive to life on canvas. As it took shape, as she shaded and scraped and layered, she wondered if anyone else would ever see this painting. Or if perhaps she'd paint it and then burn it. Or maybe she'd sell it. There were collectors out there who would appreciate a moment of fear frozen in time to hang on a wall.

However it ended, she would be free. She, Camille, Brick. They would all be free to go on with their lives, to move forward.

But first, she had to finish.

∽

She didn't know how much time had passed when someone calling her name dragged her from the trance of color and memory. The song was still on repeat, but it felt distant now. As if its hold had been severed.

"Remington?"

She tore her eyes away from the painting and found Camille standing on the ramp. She was dressed casually in borrowed leggings that were several inches too short and a sweatshirt.

Remi snapped the rest of the way out of her reverie and fumbled for her phone to shut off the music.

"Hey," she said. "Can't sleep?"

Camille shook her head. "My brain feels too full. Am I interrupting?"

Remi glanced at the canvas again. "No. I think I'm done," she said, dropping her paint-laden palette on the nearest work table and rolling out her shoulders.

"That song," Camille said, walking down the ramp. "That's what we were listening to in the car."

Remi nodded.

"Are you painting it?" her friend asked.

"I think I painted the song and the accident," she said, again glancing at the canvas.

She needed to step back, to take in the whole picture. After so many hours of detail work, she wouldn't understand the piece until she took that step back and saw the bigger picture.

Camille joined her, and together they stared at the canvas.

"Wow," Camille said.

Headlights and footprints. The colors of the music. Camille's screams. The smell of blood. Everything echoed distantly. Remi felt a strange sense of peace pour over her.

"I can't shake this feeling," Camille admitted. "Like he's coming. I got really good at anticipating when his moods were changing. I knew when he was going to snap, and that's how I feel now. Like I'm just waiting for him to walk through the door."

Remi looked at her friend. "I feel something, too. But remember, you're not alone this time. We're here together and we've got a house full of people who would love to kick him in his balls."

Everything in the world that Brick cared about was in this house. Remi's pulse kicked up a notch. While a landmark burned, everyone that was important to him was gathered under the same roof. It wasn't a coincidence. It couldn't be.

"We need to go," she said quietly.

Camille nodded. "I think so, too. We're putting everyone else in danger just by being here."

Brick was going to murder her. But Freddie Mercury willing, there'd be a Remington for him to murder in the morning.

"Let's grab what we need. I'll talk to that asshat White outside," Remi decided.

Spurred on by adrenaline, they hurried for the ramp when something thumped against the door leading to the backyard.

"Oh my God," Camille clapped a hand to her mouth as Remi jumped in front of her. A hand slapped against the glass. It was impossible to see into the night with the studio lights blazing.

"Let me in," a weak voice rasped. "Hurry."

"Shit. I think it's White," Remi hissed.

"What happened? We can't leave him out there."

"If we get murdered because of this guy, I am going to be so pissed off!"

"Go get William," Remi ordered Camille. "And stay with him."

She waited until her friend was in the main house before

yanking open the side door. White was slumped on the ground. "What did you fucking do?" she hissed as she grabbed him under the arms. "And why are you so sweaty?"

Oh God. It wasn't all sweat, she realized, looking down at his white button-down. A crimson stain was spread in a lopsided circle.

"Did you get your ass shot? I thought you were a big fucking deal, Agent White."

He murmured something she couldn't make out.

"I'm never going to hear the end of this from Brick," she muttered as she managed to drag him halfway across the threshold.

"Remi!" William burst through the door to the house, Camille on his heels.

"He's either been shot or he impaled himself on a fucking garden gnome," Remi said. "Help me get him inside."

William tucked his revolver into the back of his pants and bent to pull the man inside.

"He's heavier than he looks," Remi said, pushing the door closed. But she wasn't quite fast enough. A shadow slithered into her periphery.

"Fuck!" She slammed the door but wasn't fast enough. A black-clad arm slipped wraithlike inside.

Camille let out a sob that broke Remi's heart.

William abandoned the agent on the ground and reached for his gun. But they'd underestimated the enemy. Warren Vorhees shoved the door open with exceptional strength, knocking Remi back so she stumbled over Agent White's legs.

Gun outstretched, he fired one quick shot that sounded like the snap of a firecracker.

William crumpled to the floor next to White.

"No!" Remington shouted.

The gun swung around to point menacingly in her face.

"I wouldn't scream if I were you," he growled.

His handsome face was twisted in a grotesque mask of rage. His light hair had been dyed dark and cut short in a choppy buzz cut. The beginnings of a beard sprouted on his patrician jaw. He wore a cheap pair of sweatpants and a black jacket. His eyes, an unmistakable denim blue, had been disguised by colored contact lenses. He looked wrong, sick, evil. The shine of wealth and breeding had been stripped away to reveal the sickness beneath.

Fear coiled in her chest. Her phone was across the room, next to her painting.

"Warren," Camille said calmly. "Just take me. Leave them alone."

His smile was more a snarl. "You think you can ask for favors from me? You think you can appeal to my generosity after you tried to ruin me?" Gone was the debonaire charm that had seduced Camille and countless voters.

There was no shake in the hand that held the weapon. His rage gave him a chilling calm. "You think you can destroy me? You think you're worthy of being my opponent? You're nothing," he spat.

Camille inched closer toward William, who wasn't stirring on the floor.

"That's what he gets for trying to stop me. For trying to take you away. I won in the end, didn't I?" his laughter was an unhinged nightmare.

He fired another shot into William's leg, the silencer suppressing the noise.

"No!" Remi cried.

"Don't worry," he said, turning to her with dead eyes. "I'm saving a special punishment for you. As soon as I do a little clean-up."

He raised the gun to fire again. But as he did, Camille

threw herself over William. Remi lowered her shoulder and charged the monster. The shot went wide. He laughed, catching Remi by the hair. A thousand nerves shrieked with pain as he twisted and yanked. Still laughing, he hurled her to the ground and landed a well-placed kick to her hip.

"Stop!" Camille begged. But her begging only seemed to excite him.

"You forget your place, wife. You're a possession. A shiny, pretty thing that I take out when I want to and put away when I'm done. Tonight will be the last time I put you away."

"If you lay a hand on her, the entire world will know the allegations are true," Remi said, huffing out pained breaths. The last thing she needed was an asthma attack in the middle of a murderous assault.

"You can't ruin me. Neither of you can touch me. You don't have what I have. The power. The connections. The money. I'll destroy you both, body and soul. And when I'm done doing that, I'll make sure no one ever speaks your names again."

"Delusional much?" Remi wheezed, crawling to her hands and knees.

He landed another kick. This one to her midsection. Camille jumped forward. Warren backhanded her in the face with the gun, and she crumpled like paper to the floor. Remi growled and breathed through the pain.

"Brick is going to kick your ass," she said through gritted teeth.

"I'm counting on him making the attempt. You don't think I'd leave without thanking him for his hospitality to my wife and her friend, do you?"

"What made you such a stupid asshole anyway," Remi asked, trying to buy time. She needed to get help. She needed to get him away from this house.

There was a flash of movement at the top of the ramp, and Remi deliberately drew Warren's attention back to her.

Hadley, in her pajamas, hovered in the doorway.

"What are you going to do with us, Warren?" Remi demanded.

"I'm going to take you two away from here. I have a place we can be alone. Where I can extract my pound of flesh."

"Where is that?" Remi asked. Brick would tear the island apart by dawn once he knew what had happened.

She saw William's hand flex at his side and nearly breathed a sigh of relief.

"It's on the mainland. I'll borrow a boat for the occasion. Don't worry your pretty little head about the details. Just know that tonight will be your last, and if you don't come quietly with me, I'll go upstairs and murder every single person in their beds."

Hadley ducked out of the door.

Remi was going to lodge this man's balls in his skull the first chance she got.

"I'll go quietly," she promised.

"I thought you might," he said with a twisted, triumphant grin.

"I can borrow a boat. My friend Eleanora Reedbottom has one. She won't notice if it's gone."

"There now. It's not so hard to cooperate, is it? Things are so much easier when you accept your place."

When he bent to pick up Camille's limp form, Remi scanned the worktable for weapons. She pocketed a palette knife and prayed for the chance to use it.

"Brick is going to come after you as soon as he finds out you took us, Warren."

Her gaze darted to the doorway. She couldn't see Hadley but knew her brave niece was lurking just out of range.

"Your idiot boyfriend is occupied with an unfortunate fire that started in the hotel's kitchen," he said, tossing Camille over his shoulder like he would a sack of feed.

"Let's go," he said, gesturing with the gun. "You lead the way and keep your hands where I can see them."

With everything at stake and a mad man at her back, Remi stepped out into the night.

53

*B*rick swiped his forearm over his brow as he stared up at the Grand Hotel. She still stood. Just as proud as ever. Maybe a little smoky, and her kitchens a lot worse for the wear. But she still looked out over Lake Huron like a beacon of welcome.

It had taken hours and all hands on deck to get the blaze under control.

Arson. That was clear. An accelerant had been used to start and spread the flames. But the arsonist had forgotten one thing. That Mackinac Island stood up for its own.

There had been a few injuries. Some smoke inhalation. But like the hotel, they'd all survived the night.

No one messed with the lady on the hill. They'd had more volunteers than they'd known what to do with. The hotel guests had been liveried off to other accommodations. Some inns, some private homes. Restaurants and cafes had sent food and beverages up the hill to keep the crews fueled.

Both ferry lines woke up their crews and used their boats to ship firefighters and equipment from the mainland.

And as the promise of dawn began to kiss the horizon,

Brick took his first easy breath. It was a good time to check in at home, he decided. Sinking down into a deck chair, one of the many that some thoughtful volunteer had pulled off the hotel's porch and arranged in the grass for the crews.

He opened his texts when his phone rang. It was his own home number.

"Uncle Brick?"

"Hadley?"

"Uncle Brick, Aunt Remi's gone. Her friend Camille, too. A man came."

Brick launched himself out of the chair. "What happened?" he demanded.

"A man. A man dressed in black. I think Mr. White is dead. He was bleeding really bad. And then the man shot William. I'm with him now. He's breathing, but he's hurt bad. Can you bring an ambulance?"

Fuck.

Brick was in a dead sprint now.

It had been a ploy to get him away from Remi, from the house. He'd just left them dangling like bait. He'd abandoned them when they needed him most.

"Brick?" Chief Ford called from where she was conferring with the fire chief.

"Remi," he said, his voice breaking on the name.

But he kept running down the grassy hill that sloped into town. "Hadley, are you safe?"

"I'm safe but scared. Uncle Brick, he has Aunt Remi and Camille. I think he knocked out Camille. He carried her out, and Aunt Remi looked like she was going to kill him."

"I'm on my way. Is anyone else there? Is anyone else with you?"

"They're all asleep. I couldn't sleep. I wanted to see what

Aunt Remi was painting. Sometimes I sneak down and I peek."

His legs sped up as he passed the school on his left. The houses were all still dark.

He kept Hadley on the line until he burst through his own front door. Kimber and Kyle appeared on the stairs as Hadley ran toward him and threw herself in his arms.

"How long ago did they leave?" Brick asked Hadley.

"What happened? What's wrong?" Kimber asked, running down the stairs to meet them.

"About ten minutes," Hadley told him, ignoring her mother. "I tried calling you, Uncle Brick, and you didn't pick up. So I kept calling while I stayed with William," Hadley reported.

"Ten minutes," Brick repeated. He handed Hadley to her mother and raced down the hall.

It was worse than he feared, the scene that met him. The air smelled of the metallic tang of blood. White was dead. His shirt was saturated dark brown. Glassy eyes staring up at the ceiling, frozen in surprise. A pool of blood spread out beneath.

"Dad," Brick yelled, racing down the ramp. His father sat with his back against the wall. There was more blood there. On the drywall. On his shirt. On his pants.

He looked old, pale, fragile.

"I'm okay," William panted. "Go after your girl."

Brick searched his father's torso, tearing his shirt in two. There was a neat little hole in his chest above his heart.

"Can you breathe okay?" he asked.

"Don't worry about me," William insisted, his voice weak. "I'm sorry I let you down. He got White in the yard, and White came to the door begging to be let in. The girls let him in, and Vorhees got a shot off at me as he came inside. I went down.

Passed out. I think he clipped me in the leg too. I'm sorry. I'm so sorry."

There was a commotion coming from the main house.

"Dad," Brick said again. But none of the rest of the words would come.

"I failed you again. You put your trust in me—"

"This was my fault, Dad. I shouldn't have left. I should have known it was a fucking trap."

"Brick!" Chief Ford's voice cut like a razor blade. "This is nobody's fault but that motherfucking monster. Now both of you get your goddamn heads out of your sorry asses and figure out how to get my daughter back."

Orders delivered, Darlene whipped out her phone. "Yeah, I'm gonna need that ambulance down here ASAP."

Brick picked up the bloody towel he saw next to his father and pressed it to his father's chest.

But his head and heart were already gone. He couldn't stay here. He needed to tear this island apart. He needed to find Remi.

"Uncle Brick?"

"Hadley, don't come out here," Darlene snapped.

"Oh my God," Kimber gasped, coming up behind her daughter and viewing the carnage. "Is he... Is that..."

Kyle grabbed her before she could step into the room.

"Hadley's the one who was holding the towel on me," William said with a note of pride. "Girl's got one hell of a head on her shoulders. Told her I'd hire her as an investigator. After college of course."

"Uncle Brick," Hadley said, stomping her foot. "Aunt Remi knew I was here. She knew I was watching. I think she was giving me a message."

"What did she say, Hadley?" Darlene asked, her voice calm. But her hands were shaking.

"First she said Uncle Brick was going to kick the man's ass."

"That's true," Brick promised her.

"He told her if she didn't come quietly, he'd go through every bedroom upstairs and murder us one by one."

"We're all going to need therapy," Kimber murmured into her husband's chest.

"I'll foot the bill," Darlene volunteered.

"Then she asked him where he was going to take them," Hadley continued.

"Where did he take them, Had?"

"We'll tear this island from top to bottom to find them," Darlene promised.

"They're not on the island. He said he was going to take them to the mainland."

"Jesus," Darlene, looking pale, yanked her phone out of its holster again. "I'll call St. Ignace and Mackinaw City."

"Aunt Remi told him she had a friend with a boat she could borrow," Hadley said.

Brick's attention zeroed in on the little girl. "What friend, Hadley?" he asked.

"Eleanora Reedbottom," she recited.

"I know where they're going," he said, standing up as he heard the wail of the siren. "I need the Marine Rescue."

"Take it," Darlene snapped. "I'll make the calls. They'll be ready for you."

Brick paused and pointed at his father. "Don't die on me, old man. I want you at the wedding."

William's pale face lit up. "Wouldn't miss it for the world."

Without another word, Brick sprinted for the door.

54

$\mathcal{I}$cy water misted over her, soaking her sweatshirt. The dark was losing its battle to dawn, and once there was enough light, he'd know that she'd double-crossed him.

The cold barrel of the gun jabbed at her neck. "Go faster," Warren snarled.

"You got a death wish, jackass? These are the Straits of Mackinac. If I don't pilot us carefully, we'll end up dead on the rocks."

"I don't care. If you don't want me to put a hole in your useless little friend here, you'll go faster."

Grimly, Remi gunned the engine and enjoyed watching him stumble back as the boat picked up speed. The barrel of the gun no longer pressed against the base of her skull.

She'd taken Duncan Firth's boat. The only one she knew for sure that would have a tracking device on it. The entire island knew he kept the key under a life preserver.

Camille had come to just before Warren dropped her unceremoniously in the bottom of the boat. She now sat huddled on the floor of the boat. Barely visible under the orange life jacket Remi had shoved her into as Warren cast off the lines.

Dawn was breaking. She had to time this right. She couldn't get Camille to safety without knowing Brick could get to her fast.

There was a hand in her hair, yanking her head back sharply. She let go of the accelerator, and the boat slowed, knocking his body into hers.

"Don't fuck with me, you pathetic excuse for a female."

"What's with the 'female' thing. You can't say the word woman? Is it too hard for you, you tiny-dicked son of a bitch?"

He hit her in the jaw, snapping her head back and stunning her for a second. But she spotted what she'd been waiting to see, and it brought a wicked grin to her face.

"Where the fuck are we?" Warren growled. "That's not the mainland." The spotlight she'd played ahead of the boat bobbed from water to rock through the fog.

Remi made eye contact with Camille. "Jump," she mouthed.

Camille shook her head.

"Jump," Remi mouthed again.

Her friend shot her a "We are going to have words about this later" look. But carefully slid up onto the bench seat.

"Where's the bridge? This isn't right."

It hurt to breathe. Her airway constricted.

Round Island's decommissioned lighthouse loomed ahead of them out of the mist.

A spotlight caught him in its beam. Red and blue lights flashed out of the fog. The sound of a big boat engine was deafening. Brick. Brick was here.

"Mackinac PD. Hands up, Vorhees."

When he swung his gun hand up and around toward the light, Remi shouted, "Now!"

The second she saw Camille disappear over the side, Remi hit the accelerator, and the runabout surged forward.

Warren was unprepared for the shift in his center of gravity, and his shot went wide as he fell into the bottom of the boat.

Lungs burning, Remi had one last play. She gunned the engine and headed around the rocks toward the beach. If she could keep him off balance, he couldn't shoot anyone. And if she could make it to shore, there was a good chance she could get far enough away that Brick could shoot the son of a bitch.

Sweat and lake water dampened her skin as she swung the bow of the boat around in a tight turn. Warren slammed to the side behind her.

Just a few hundred more feet. Just a little bit farther. Brick had to stop to pick up Camille. She just needed to buy herself a minute, two tops.

But the cold barrel found its way to the base of her neck again.

"I will not lose," Vorhees howled, yanking her hair painfully. Remi released her grip on the accelerator but didn't pull it back. She didn't have any tricks left. It was time to fight dirty.

She let out a yelp as he twisted her hair around his fist. He threw her down on the bench and backhanded her across the face.

She sprawled out on her belly and reached into her pocket for her rescue inhaler.

"Is that all you've got? A little bitch slap?" she wheezed, taking a hit from the inhaler.

She could hear the engine of the Marine Rescue zooming toward them. Camille and Brick were safe. Her family was safe. All she had to do was live through this.

He raised the gun in her face. Behind him, the mist parted.

The rocky outcropping of Round Island loomed in front of them. The beach stretched out to its right. The current worked the bow of the boat toward the little stretch of beach. Any second now. She braced for it.

"You're going to pay for everything," he vowed. "You'll regret ever trying to keep my wife from me. I'll make sure you regret bedding that Neanderthal cop. You'll beg me to end you. And when I finally do, when you're nothing but a stuttering, shuddering shell of a female, I'll do the same to your entire family."

"Fuck. You," Remi enunciated, then dropped to the deck and grabbed on to the base of the bench seat a split second before the boat's bow dug into the rocky bottom.

Vorhees was knocked off his feet. He fell on his back, hitting his head on the boat's wheel.

Her kick landed exactly where it had been destined to. Right in his balls.

"That's for Camille, you stupid son of a bitch." She took his head in her hands and brought her knee to his face. "And that's for me. I'll leave the rest of it up to Brick. And you'll wish you'd never been born."

She sprang out of the boat, landing in frigid waist-deep water. The adrenaline, the fear, the rage, kept her moving toward land as the sky lightened all around her. She heard a splash behind her. Knew he was coming after her. He had nothing left to lose. But she had everything.

Her legs felt numb as she dragged herself toward shore. She couldn't afford to slow down.

Finally, she dragged herself to shore and started a labored jog on numb feet.

"Fuck. Fuck. Fuck." This wasn't a nightmare where she couldn't run. Couldn't scream. This was real life. Light was turning the sky from black to the palest blue. It would be a beautiful sunrise, and damn it, she wanted to see it. She wanted to see a few thousand of them with Brick. Sunsets, too, and everything in between.

She ran as fast as she could even as she heard him closing the gap between them. Even as his ragged growls got closer and closer. She ran even as his hand closed around her hair, yanking her backward.

"No!" Her scream wasn't loud enough. Her lungs burned. Her heart ached. She couldn't see the boat. Was Brick close enough to watch? She couldn't let him see this.

With her last bit of strength, Remi yanked the palette knife out of her back pocket and jabbed it into his leg.

"You bitch!" he howled. "You fucking little bitch!"

He dragged her head back again, and this time, when the barrel of the gun pressed against her cheek, she knew it would be the last. She braced for it.

"Brick," she whispered. If that was the last word she said in this world, it was enough.

She could sense the tension on the trigger and braced.

Two gunshots fired in rapid succession, and the weight on her shoulder lifted.

She stayed exactly where she was for a heartbeat and then another. She was alive.

"*Remington?*"

Brick. Her Brick. She spun on her knees in the sand and stones and watched her hero, his gun drawn, rush forward. He was soaked from the thighs down. The look in his eyes was unlike anything she'd ever witnessed. Blue fire burned from an icy rage.

Warren Vorhees was sprawled faceup in the sand, two neat holes in the dead center of his chest.

Brick was on him in an instant, fisting Warren's shirt

pulling him up. Brick's fist plowed into his face once, twice, three times. Warren's head snapped back limply each time.

"It's enough," she said, grabbing Brick's arm.

"It's never going to be enough," he rasped.

She sprang for Warren's gun and wrestled it out of his grasp. "I've seen too many movies where the dead bad guy comes back to life."

Brick took the weapon from her and holstered his own.

Behind him, three more officers and Special Agent Brice sloshed through the water.

And then he was picking her up and cradling her against him. She broke then. But he only held on tighter. "It's okay. I've got you."

"Did Hadley—"

"She told me," he confirmed, stroking a big hand over her abused hair.

"Is Camille—"

"Camille is wrapped up in rescue blankets and furious with you. I told her to get in line."

"Did I do good?" she asked between sobs.

"Baby, you saved the day."

"You shot the bad guy," she pointed out.

"Yeah, but you got to kick him in the balls."

"You saw that?" She smiled against his chest.

"After I recovered from the heart attack you caused. Hurling Camille overboard. Beaching the boat like that. I saw him hit you, Remington."

She could hear it in his voice. Knew it would be a memory that would haunt him forever.

"I knew you'd find me. I knew you'd get him."

"You're damn right you knew," he whispered against her hair.

"Your dad, Brick," she stiffened at the memory. "He was trying to help me pull White inside, and Warren shot him."

"I know. He's going to be okay. He's being ferried to the mainland for surgery but he's awake and alert."

"It wasn't his fault," Remi pressed. "I'm the one who opened the door."

"Vorhees was preying on your heart. He tried to use your humanity against you, and look where it got him."

"Is he dead?" she asked.

"He is," Brick promised.

She blew out a breath. "Okay. I think I want some breakfast now."

His laugh was a low rumble in his chest. "Baby doll, you're just going to have to let me hold you for a few years first. I don't think I'm going to be ready to let go of you long enough for breakfast."

"I'm okay with that."

"You're a hell of a girl, Remington Honeysuckle."

"I'm your girl," she reminded him as he slowly picked his way down the beach. "Where are we going?"

"Back to the boat so I can examine every inch of you and make sure you're really okay."

"We're not having boat sex in front of a bunch of cops, perv."

55

$\mathcal{I}$t was pandemonium at the docks when the Mackinac Marine Rescue and her flotilla of support boats returned. The crew and its occupants were treated to a hero's welcome.

Remi's dad ran down the dock and picked Darlene up, spinning her around. The kiss he laid on her made Remi realize the thong she'd found in their laundry actually got a workout.

Nothing and no one could convince Brick to put Remi down. So she let him carry her off the boat in his arms without too much fuss as Carlos Turk did the same with Camille, who was looking up at him like he was a fantasy hero come to life.

Her parents approached. Her mom wrapped the rescue blanket a little tighter around her shoulders. "Remi Honey, that was the bravest thing I've ever seen someone do. You saved lives today, and I've never been prouder."

"Thanks, Mom," she said, fighting back another round of tears.

Darlene turned to Remi's own personal hero. "Brick, you

saved one of the most precious things in the world to me. As far as I'm concerned, you're fucking family. You always have been."

By the time they made it home and finished recapping the highlights to everyone there, it was almost eleven in the morning. Brick carried Remi upstairs and kicked the bedroom door shut behind them. He proceeded to strip every article of clothing off her and kiss every inch of her body. After he finished his very thorough inspection, he made love to her until they were both limp and wasted on the sheets.

She woke hours later on her stomach, thirsty and hungry, with Brick's hand possessively curling around her ass. Magnus snored on her right foot.

She managed to slip out of bed without disturbing either one. She pulled on one of Brick's sweatshirts and limped downstairs feeling sore and happy.

The house was eerily quiet, and she found a note in Kimber's handwriting in the kitchen.

At Mom and Dad's for spontaneous celebratory picnic. Show up at 6. Be hungry! Love you!

Remi tucked the note into the pocket of the sweatshirt and took her water into the studio. Ducking under the police tape, she shuffled down the ramp into the room. There were tarps on the floor just inside the door, camouflaging the violence that had taken place there only hours earlier.

Bloodstains would need a scrubbing. Wounds would need time to heal. But for now, she'd focus on the good. She slipped around the tarps to her easel and stood back, taking it in.

The black of night with only the hint of stars was a bleed of black and blue at the top. It faded, getting murkier in the center with the purples and navies from the music. Two pale yellow circles cut through the dark. Headlights askew, highlighting the naked tree that had saved her life. The bottom of the canvas was a snowy white with shades of scarlet scraped and layered. Like bloody footprints walking away from the crime.

In the dead center, right through one of the headlights, was a perfect little hole. Vorhees had put his own mark on her painting by shooting a bullet right through it. Curious, Remi turned around and spotted a piece of tape on the wall marking another hole.

When she turned back, Brick was standing at the top of the ramp. Sweatpants slung indecently low on his hips, his chest bare. Hair standing up in tufts.

Her heart swelled in her chest.

He crooked his finger at her, and she shook her head, beckoning him.

His eyes narrowed at the challenge as he stalked toward her.

He ignored the tarps and barreled into her like a freight train. Bending at the waist, he tossed her over his shoulder.

"Wait!" she laughed. "Look at my painting."

He whirled around, making her head spin and her stomach feel giddy.

He leaned in to examine it and grunted.

"He shot a hole in it," she said, in case he'd missed the tell-tale circle.

"I see that," he said dryly.

"I think I know what I'm going to do with it now."

He grunted again and started for the ramp.

"The painting, I mean," she said, trying to lever herself up.

But Brick merely landed a stinging slap on her ass.

She wriggled against his shoulder, biting her lip as arousal swept through her.

"Where are we going?" she asked, breathlessly.

"Back to bed."

"There's a picnic at my parents'. We're supposed to be there at six."

He didn't acknowledge any of her speech. Instead, he took the stairs two at a time and carted her back to the bedroom and unceremoniously tossed her on the bed. She bounced once, laughing.

And then he shoved down his pants, and she wasn't laughing anymore. Brick grabbed her feet and spread them wide.

She felt alive, excited, adrenalized. Loved.

He climbed onto the bed between her thighs, his erection thick and hard. With one swift thrust of his hips, he slammed into her, holding at the bottom until she writhed and relaxed around him. When the final inches slid into her, he paused, holding himself over her, buried to the hilt.

She locked her legs around his hips as he stole her breath.

When he didn't start to move, she opened one eye and then the other.

"Remington," he said, his voice serious.

"What?"

Grimacing, he went down on one elbow and reached for the nightstand drawer.

"It's a little late for a condom, buddy," she gasped.

But the object he held between his fingers wasn't a foil packet. It was a ring. Stunning brushed gold with the sparkle of multicolored gemstones.

"Marry me," he rasped.

She felt her mouth fall open. "Oh. My God." He shifted his weight, this time moving inside her. "Oh my God," she repeated for different reasons. Her inner muscles were contracting around him, greedy for more. Needing to find fulfillment with him yet again.

"Say yes," he demanded. "Say you'll be my wife. Say we'll

figure out the family thing. That you'll give me a lifetime. That you'll let me keep you safe."

She could feel his cock pulsing inside her, feel the tension in his trembling muscles as he held himself back from rutting into her like she knew his instincts demanded.

She gave him the only answer possible. "Yes," she whispered, closing around his thick shaft as she said it. "Yes, Brick."

He groaned and pulled out before sinking back into her. "Mine," he whispered as he lunged into her. "My wife."

"Yes, Brick!" She dug her nails into his shoulder, trying to hold him closer to her. "Yours."

"Can't hold back," he whispered.

"Don't, Brick. Don't hold back."

His body became a machine that pistoned into her, rocking her into a state of arousal so consuming she didn't think she'd survive the finale.

"Can't stop," he groaned against her neck. "Need you."

She held on tight, and as he powered into her body, she prepared for the detonation. They were so close. So in tune. They could have missed out on this. But they'd found their way to each other.

His grunts, timed with each thrust, told her he was close. And God, so was she.

"Brick. Now! Please!"

He surged into her and held, angling her hips higher. She came apart around him just as she felt him tense. His entire body froze like granite as his release erupted inside her. The heat of it dazzled her. Their orgasms mixing like colors on a palette creating something new and wonderful.

She felt his feet digging into the mattress as he bucked and thrust erratically, trying to ride out both their orgasms.

"My Remi." He said the words over and over again, continuing to thrust gently long after the aftershocks faded. Neither of them ready for it to end.

Long minutes later, Remi tore her gaze away from the ring on her finger. The stones were a delightful surprise. Tiny inset sapphires and fiery rubies glimmered around the diamond in the center.

"Brick?"

"Mmph?" He lifted his face out of the pillow and eyed her with a sleepy-eyed possessiveness.

"How are we supposed to tell our kids how you proposed?"

He gave her a devilish grin.

"I'll ask you again when we're fully clothed. This one was just for us."

She sighed. "God, I love you."

"You better. Because I distinctly remember telling you not to leave this house." He gripped the curve of her ass just above a nasty bruise.

"You can't seriously be ready for another round yet," she said with a laugh. "Where does your testosterone come from? An invisible IV?"

He pinched her skin. "We'll go to your parents. Eat. Tell everyone a G-rated version of the good news. And then when we come back, I'm going to make you apologize."

"You dirty, dirty man." She rolled over him and peppered his face with kisses.

"I'm all yours, Remington. For better or worse."

"I think we just lived through the worse. Let's go enjoy the better."

EPILOGUE

Two months later

*B*rick frowned down at the planks of the side porch, wondering if he was wearing the paint off them.

What if this wasn't what Remi had wanted? He tugged at his collar. A small backyard ceremony had sounded like a good idea at the time. It was easy to throw together. Neither of them wanted to wait, and the reception was at the Grand Hotel so there was still some fuss.

But what if she'd changed her mind? What if between having sex with him last night and putting her dress on this morning, she realized she didn't want to marry him. What if—

"Psst!"

It was coming from above him on the second floor. Brick stepped off the porch and looked up to see Remi hanging out of a second-story window. Her face lit up when she spotted him.

"I'm not supposed to see you," he called back, glancing

over his shoulder toward the backyard where their closest friends and family were halfway shit-faced on Darius's Wedded Bliss specialty drink.

"Then close your eyes."

"What are you doing?" he demanded as she shimmied out onto the porch roof.

"I'm sneaking out," she whispered back. She wadded the dress up around her waist and nimbly climbed off the roof, dangling her legs over the side in search of the porch's banister, before he plucked her down.

She'd left her hair down in wild curls. Her cheeks were flushed a pretty pink, green eyes sparkling. She looked like a mischievous fairy. Her dress was... *Wow*. She'd gone strapless with a fitted corset. There was lace and skin, which he liked very much. The full skirt billowed out in a pinky kind of wash, almost like watercolor.

"Wow," he said out loud this time. There was no way he was lucky enough that this woman belonged to him.

She made a curtsy. "Thank you. You look pretty wow yourself."

"If you run away, I'm just going to drag you back," he warned her.

She slapped him in the chest. "I'm running away *to* you," she clarified. "This is our last chance."

"At what?"

"Unmarried sex."

He relaxed. Only Remington Ford—soon to be Callan— would run away from her own wedding just to have sex with the groom before he became her husband. "You're kidding me right now. I thought last night was our last chance at unmarried sex."

"I figured we have fifteen minutes before the ceremony starts. This is our last last chance. Besides, I look sexy as hell in this dress and I don't want one of your spectacular hard-ons stealing my bridal thunder in all our wedding photography. The flower girl is the right height to lose an eye."

"Jesus, Remi," he groaned. "What am I supposed to do? Pull up your skirts and fuck you right here between the azaleas?"

"Yes."

He was instantaneously hard. It was the spell she had him under.

"See?" she said, pointing at his crotch. "That's exactly what I'm talking about. We're saving a little girl from an eye patch for the rest of her life."

Who was he to argue? If his bride wanted a quick fuck against the house minutes before she became his wife, he would deliver.

He reached for his belt and watched her eyes go glassy. "Turn around," he said. When she complied, he used one hand to hold her against the cedar shake siding while he freed his cock with his other.

"Hold up your skirts," he demanded.

She was already breathing heavy as she gathered the material at her waist.

"You dirty little girl," he said, running his fingers over the sexy, silky red underwear that rode high on her cheeks.

"I thought you'd like it," she whispered, a shiver running up her spine.

He dipped his knees to drop a kiss on her shoulder and then yanked the underwear down so he could line up the head of his primed cock with her entrance.

"Oh, God," she breathed when he settled between her legs.

He couldn't help himself. He landed a short, sharp slap on her ass and felt his dick thicken at her breathy little gasp. Her opening quivered around his tip. He did it again, then growled as she clenched around him.

Without warning, he dipped lower and surged up, fitting himself halfway into her tight channel.

He squeezed her shoulder when she gasped, a warning to stay quiet.

She tilted her ass toward him, welcoming his invasion. It was so fucking hot. Fucking the bride with a few dozen people close enough to catch them.

"Say your vows," she begged.

"What?" He gritted his teeth as his dick pulsed inside her, already close to release.

"Say your vows while you make love to me. We have a secret engagement. I want a secret wedding."

"Remington," he rasped. "You are one of a kind, and I'm the luckiest man on the planet."

"If that's not in the vows it should be," she said on a breathy whisper.

While the band warmed up. While their guests took their drinks to their seats. Brick gave his bride everything she asked for. Dark promises just between the two of them.

"Now you," he whispered, yanking her hips back.

She gave a soft cry.

"Promise me, you'll always need me like this. Promise me that your hand will be in my lap under the table. Promise me that you'll love letting me make you come. Promise me that you'll never let me make you unhappy."

"I promise, Brick," she whispered. He felt her body priming for release. He felt her fighting it.

"Don't fight it, baby. Give it to me."

"I want to give you everything, Brick," she said on a broken cry.

She already had. She'd given him everything he'd been

missing and more. She'd given him light in a gloomy existence. Purpose. A reason to embrace chaos and color. She was the puzzle piece that held everything else in his world together.

He told her so with his words. With fast, hard thrusts that her body accepted with gratitude. And when he felt her let go, he poured himself into her, whispering his vows to her as she trembled around him.

He loved and was loved. They were united, joined, partnered, paired. And that was without the words of the reverend or the piece of paper filed at the courthouse. By the end of the day, Remington Ford would belong to him in every way possible. And his heart would remain in her possession for all the days of his life.

"I love you, Brick. Always. Forever. Fiercely," she promised as their bodies trembled against each other.

He'd never tire of hearing that.

"I love you, Remington."

When she walked down the aisle to him, it was with his pink handprint on her ass.

Brick got a little teary-eyed when she made her promises to him in front of their family and friends and broke protocol by kissing her as soon as she'd said her vows. His father and Gilbert Ford blew their noses noisily from the front row.

"You look happy, husband," Remi said that night as they danced under the stars to "Harvest Moon."

Other couples shared the dance floor with them, Kyle and Kimber, Remi's parents, Carlos and Camille, Audrey and Spencer. But he saw only Remi.

"I'm surprised they let you come back here," Brick teased. "Last time you were at a wedding here, didn't you get arrested?"

"You know, I've been thinking about that," she said

breezily. "I think for this to be a real full-circle moment, you're probably going to have to use your handcuffs tonight."

Her smile was so beguiling he picked her up in his arms and twirled her around. This woman. *His wife.*

"I'm afraid to blink," he confessed.

"Why?" she laughed.

"I'm afraid I'll blink, and the whole day will vanish like the dreams I used to have of you."

"We have a lot of time to make up for," she said, her voice breathy.

"Let's start now," he suggested, closing his mouth over hers.

        ~

Fifteen years earlier...

"YOU DON'T LOOK LIKE A WILLIAM," the tiny redhead mused as she peered up at him. Sixteen and pretty as the little island they now officially called home.

"What's he look like? Do I look like a Spencer?" His brother demanded, hopping from foot to foot on the boardwalk.

Those green eyes flicked back to his brother, and she grinned. "You're definitely a Spencer."

Will felt something warm and *good* when she returned her gaze to him. It was foreign to him. Most people looked at him and saw a carbon copy of his father. William Eugene Callan III most likely had the same destiny as William Eugene Callan II.

Cocking her head, she studied him leisurely as the popsicle stained her lips red. "Brick."

"Brick?"

Her lips spread in a wide, sunny smile.

"As in masonry?" he asked.

"As in durable. Strong. Stoic."

"Our dad's in jail," Spencer announced.

"Spence." Will sighed. How in the hell was he supposed to make a fresh start if his brother was just going to tell everyone all about their past?

"I'm sorry to hear that. I hope it's a nice jail."

He blinked. This girl was something all right.

"Will—I mean, Brick says we shouldn't talk about it because people will think we're tainted or something," Spencer said, shuffling his weight from foot to foot.

"Well, that's just silly," she announced. "How boring would it be if we all just went around pretending to be perfect? It's things like your dad being in jail or me seeing music that make us interesting. *Interesting* is way more fun than perfect."

Spencer looked confused, like he had an inkling he was in the presence of a sage philosopher and had no idea what she was talking about.

"How do you see music?" Will asked, more surprised than she was that he'd asked.

"It's called synesthesia and it's neurological. It means my brain makes extra connections to certain things. So to me, the letter S is yellow, and when I hear music, I see colors moving around like a light show at the same time."

"So, your brain is like broken?" Spencer asked, frowning.

"Spence." Will cuffed his brother on the back of the head in exasperation. Great. Five seconds with a pretty girl and his idiot brother had called her brain-damaged.

"It's okay, Brick," Remi said, waving the offense away. "It's not so much broken as it's like adding whipped cream to a hot fudge sundae. That sundae is pretty great by itself, but add the whipped cream, and now things are getting really good."

His brother managed to wrangle an invitation to Remi's

house for his own popsicle. "You coming, Brick?" she asked, waving to his grandmother on the front porch.

"Maybe some other time," he said. He watched them go, watched the way the sun hit that red hair and made it look like fire.

"I see you've met some of the locals," his grandmother said, handing him the watering can so he could reach the hanging pots of ferns.

"Remington Honeysuckle Ford. She looks like trouble to me."

"Oh, just get to know her. You'll *love* her, *Brick*," his grandmother predicted.

Maybe this place wouldn't be so bad after all.

BONUS EPILOGUE

The Arrest

She had just about had it up to here with Brick Callan's aloofness. It was a wedding, for Pete's sake. At the Grand Hotel. A more romantic setting didn't exist. The man had danced with the bride *and* the mother of the bride. He'd even asked her best friend, Audrey, to dance, but he'd yet to even glance in her direction.

And dammit, she looked good. Older than twenty.

The bridesmaid dress was a sexy, strapless number in navy. Kimber had damn good taste. She also had an open bar that hadn't bothered carding Remi or Audrey, and the two of them were on their way to drunk.

Alcohol made Audrey sleepy. She was sitting at one of the tables, half-asleep on Brick's brother, Spencer. But it made Remi want to find trouble. And she knew just where to find it. With the six-foot-four-inch, size-fourteen-wearing man who looked like he'd rather be anywhere but here.

"Let's dance," she said, grabbing Brick by the tie and towing him toward the dance floor under the tent.

He followed with great reluctance. She kept a grip on his tie just in case he got it in his head to run. As if she'd arranged it, the band slowed it down with "Harvest Moon," making Remi grin at the colors that shifted and shimmered around her. It was the perfect song for their first dance.

She stepped into his arms and slipped her hands around the back of his neck. After a moment's hesitation, his hands, warm and strong, found her hips. He was using them to keep their bodies from brushing. Remi chose to look at that as a challenge.

"You look like you're in pain," she observed.

"I'm fine," he said briskly.

"You looked a lot looser dancing with my sister and Audrey is all I'm saying. Now you look like you're going to barf. You're not going to barf all over my nice dress, are you, Brick?"

The clench of his jaw was a special delight. She'd made it her mission in life to torture him for leaving her high and, well, definitely not *dry* when she was eighteen and hopeful. She'd accepted the fact that there was something about her that revolted him. And she figured spending her return trips to Mackinac torturing him was a decent enough payback.

"I'm not going to barf on anything or anyone."

She rolled her eyes. "Such a sweet-talker." Abruptly, she went quiet to make him nervous. It worked almost immediately, and soon his fingers were tightening their grip on her hips as she swayed to the beat.

"You look...nice," he said.

"Nice? That's the best you can do?" One of her new brother-in-law's law school friends raised an empty glass in her direction and wiggled it. She nodded then winked.

"You're not twenty-one yet," Brick growled.

"What are you? The cops?" she teased. His badge was so new it was blinding with its shine.

"I'm on call tonight. Don't think that you're above the law just because you're your mother's daughter or that we have a history."

"What kind of history would that be, Brick?"

"Christ." He hissed out a breath. "What do you want me to say, Remington? That the time in St. Ignace never should have happened?"

"Believe me, you don't have to say it. You've done nothing since then but make sure I know exactly how disgusted you are by me."

His grip tightened on her. "Disgusted? *That's* what you think?"

"I'm not asking you to like me or want me. I'm asking you to treat me the same as the rest of the women in my family. Is that so *hard*?"

He gritted his teeth. "I treat you the same—"

"Oh, bite me," she scoffed. "Did you ask Kimber to dance? Audrey? My mother?"

The man remained obstinately silent, but there was a tic in his jaw.

"But I had to drag you out here by your necktie."

He took a self-suffering breath. "What happened between us—"

"*Nothing. Happened.* Not then. Not now. Not ever. I get it. I'm just asking for some courtesy. Man up and stop treating me like you're worried I'm going to lead you around by the dick in front of your sweet grandma." She waved to Dolores, who was perched on a chair near the dance floor.

"Jesus Christ, Remington."

His fingers dug into her hips, but instead of pushing her away, he was pulling her closer. Their bodies collided, and they both froze. He was so strong and hard and warm. The forced contact calmed her and excited her at the same time. But it apparently only excited him. She could feel the entire length of his erection pressed against her, but he was looking at her like he wanted to strangle her...or something else.

"You drive me...insane," he said in a harsh whisper against her ear.

She tilted her head to look up at him. "And no one else does?"

His eyes bored into hers with a ferocity that made her knees weak. "No one else."

"And you're not going to do anything about it?" she clarified.

He shook his head slowly. "No. I'm not."

"Okay then," she said, straightening her shoulders and resisting the urge to knee him in the balls. "You should probably take your grandma home. She looks tired."

"Remi," he growled, but she was pushing away from him.

He caught her hand and gripped it hard, but she knew he wouldn't make a scene.

She walked him over to Dolores, looking glittery and sweet in her daffodil yellow sundress and cardigan. "You look tired, young lady," Remi said. "Brick was just saying how he thought it was time he took you home."

Brick's grip on her hand was crushing.

"What a sweet grandson I have," Dolores said, leaning heavily on her cane to get up.

"One of the best," Remi assured her. "Good night, you two."

"What are you going to do without this handsome dance partner?" Dolores asked, taking Brick's free hand.

"There just so happens to be a cute future lawyer with a glass of champagne waiting for me," Remi told her. If Brick's jaw got any tighter, he was going to need a mouthguard to protect his teeth.

"Ah, to be young again," Dolores said with a wink. "Have the time of your life."

"I will," Remi promised her. "Thanks for the dance, Brick."

He didn't make it easy, but she managed to extricate herself from his grip and, without a backward glance, wandered off to meet Kyle's friend.

∾

"Get out of the pool, Remington."

"Holy Missy Elliott," she shrieked, falling off the raft. The warm water closed over her head, sobering her up enough to realize she'd been busted.

After three more glasses of champagne and some cheap bourbon, Remi had been ready to find just a little bit of trouble. She'd danced with three strangers. Not a single one of them made her feel an ounce of the electricity she did when Brick's stupid pinky finger brushed hers. With Audrey sound asleep in Spencer's lap on a porch swing and the wedding party doing drunk karaoke, Remi had decided to sneak off and find some peace and quiet.

The heated pool on the lawn of the Grand Hotel seemed like the perfect spot. So she'd stripped out of her dress and jumped in.

When she surfaced, a towel hit her in the face.

"Get out of the pool."

He stood at the edge of the pool in his uniform and a Mackinac PD sweatshirt.

"Why don't you come on in here and make me?" she suggested sweetly, backstroking to the middle of the pool.

"If I have to come in there after you, I'm arresting you."

"For what?" she scoffed.

"Underage drinking and public nudity."

"They're just breasts, Brick."

With a growl, he sat down on one of the loungers and pulled off his shoes and socks.

Remi snickered, feeling confident she had the upper hand. There was no way he was getting in this pool. He'd have to haul her mostly naked body out, and they both knew he didn't have the stomach for that. She'd just wait him out.

He dropped his tactical belt on the lounger and pulled his sweatshirt over his head.

She was starting to feel a little nervous and a lot sober.

He was unbuttoning his uniform shirt now. "Don't you *dare*, Brick Callan."

"Get out of the fucking pool, Remington."

"What are you doing back here anyway?"

"Making sure you aren't doing something stupid. Guess what? You are."

"You infuriate me."

"Where's champagne guy?"

"Waiting for me in his room," Remi lied.

"Too bad you'll be too busy to go," he said.

"Too busy doing what?"

"Getting arrested. Last chance. If you get out of the pool now, I'll walk you home."

"Oh, like that's some prize." She was so busy scoffing she didn't see him stepping to the edge. He dove into the water like an Olympic athlete and surged toward her.

"Ah, fuck." She dove beneath the surface and tried to swim away, but he was too fast, too powerful. He caught her by the ankle and yanked her back against him. She fought him, but his arms banded around her, his hands everywhere. They broke the surface, still struggling.

"I warned you. I fucking warned you," he growled as he dragged her toward the side.

She gave escape one last try, but the water was too deep, and he was too strong.

"Stop," he whispered harshly in her ear. "Stop fighting me, Rem."

She felt it all then. The hand clamped over her breast. The arm wrapped around her waist, pulling her flush with his chest. His thighs cradling hers under the water. He had her surrounded, supported. With a shaky breath, she surrendered.

"Good girl," he whispered. His hand cupping her breast squeezed a little harder.

"Is that a nightstick in your pants?"

"No."

She went quiet and still against him.

"Put your hands on the side," he ordered.

She did as she was told, gripping the lip of the pool.

"Now just breathe."

Tipping her head back onto his shoulder, she complied. Not realizing until she took a full breath how her lungs ached.

She didn't know how long they stayed like that under the water, taking slow deep breaths with his erection prodding between her thighs. The starry sky above them. It felt like they were suspended outside of time.

But he still made no move to take things any farther.

"You're lucky you've been drinking," he said finally, his lips wet against her neck.

"Why?" Her teeth were starting to chatter.

"Because if you were sober, I'd be inside you right now, making you forget about any guy waiting for you."

Remi's hands slipped off the edge of the pool, and they both went under. She clawed her way to the surface, sputtering and choking. The spell was broken, and as soon as she got some energy back, she was going to *kick his ass*.

Brick hauled her out of the pool, dragged his sweatshirt over her head, and spun her around against the towel shed. When she realized what he was doing, she started to fight, but he was bigger and stronger.

He pinned her there with his own body weight and snapped one metal cuff on her wrist.

"Brick Callan, I swear to David Bowie if you do this, I'll make your life a living hell."

She couldn't be sure in the heat of the moment, but it felt like his lips brushed the nape of her neck. "You already have, baby."

AUTHOR'S NOTE TO THE READER

Dear Reader,

Brick and Remi had two different starts. In 2019, Mr. Lucy and I traveled to Michigan to visit my cousin and his family. While there, they took us on a day trip to Mackinac Island, a charming tourist destination with horses, Victorian homes, and more fudge shops than a candy-lover could enjoy in one day.

"I want to murder someone here!" I announced to Mr. Lucy on the sidewalk. In hindsight, I probably should have either waited to tell him that or at least announced to the strangers around us that I was an author.

A year later, Brick and Remi exploded onto the page while I was busy writing another book. They appeared, nameless and bickering, with a whole lot of sparks threatening to ignite. And then I remembered my murderous Mackinac Island desires. I was so excited about the characters and the idea I sent it off to my admins, Joyce and Tammy. Over the course of two hours we laughed and joked our way through names

("Something manly like Brick but not as porn starry." HA! Brick stuck.), scene ideas, and conflicts.

150,000 words later, Brick and Remi are all yours. I hope you loved them as much as I do. And if you have the opportunity to visit Mackinac Island, I highly recommend it!

As always, if you loved Forever Never I'd be eternally grateful if you'd leave a review and tell 57 of your closest friends! Thank you for reading AND for having great taste!

Xoxo,
    Lucy

ABOUT THE AUTHOR

Lucy Score is a *Wall Street Journal* and #1 Amazon bestselling author. She grew up in a literary family who insisted that the dinner table was for reading and earned a degree in journalism. She writes full-time from the Pennsylvania home she and Mr. Lucy share with their obnoxious cat, Cleo. When not spending hours crafting heartbreaker heroes and kick-ass heroines, Lucy can be found on the couch, in the kitchen, or at the gym. She hopes to someday write from a sailboat, or oceanfront condo, or tropical island with reliable Wi-Fi.

Sign up for her newsletter and stay up on all the latest Lucy book news.
And follow her on:
Website: Lucyscore.com
Facebook at: lucyscorewrites
Instagram at: scorelucy
Readers Group at: Lucy Score's Binge Readers Anonymous

ACKNOWLEDGMENTS

Without the following humans and items, I wouldn't be able to write gigantic books like Forever Never. Please take a moment to salute the following...

- Joyce and Tammy as always for keeping me on track and booting me off Facebook when necessary.
- Kari March Designs for another perfect cover!
- Remi's art and career was inspired by artist Melissa McCracken, who has synesthesia and paints what she sees when she hears music. Melissasmccracken.com
- Fuzzy socks that kept my feet from freezing during my winter marathon writing sessions.
- Full-time Dan for taking a bunch of tasks I was half-assing off of my plate so I could whole-ass this story.
- BRAs, my ARC team, and my Street Team. Without your enthusiasm for my imagination I would have to work a real job.
- Whoever invented the folded-up taco pouches with Doritos in them.
- Book bloggers who took a chance on a book by a weirdo gal in Pennsylvania
- To essential workers, healthcare workers, and teachers. You guys were the real MVPs of the pandemic (when this book was written). I will never again take you for granted. I am in awe of your dedication.
- Jessica, Heather and Dawn for your fancy editorial proofing eyes.

- Kathryn Nolan for being a perpetual cheerleader.
- Succulents because they're super cute and hard to murder.
- Captain Sir Thomas Moore for being the hero we all needed in 2020.
- My Mr. Lucy. I love you SO MUCH! Thank you for making it possible for me to live my dreams!

LUCY'S TITLES

Standalone Titles

Undercover Love

Pretend You're Mine

Finally Mine

Protecting What's Mine

Mr. Fixer Upper

The Christmas Fix

Heart of Hope

The Worst Best Man

Rock Bottom Girl

The Price of Scandal

By a Thread

Forever Never

Things We Never Got Over

Riley Thorn

Riley Thorn and the Dead Guy Next Door

Riley Thorn and the Corpse in the Closet

The Blue Moon Small Town Romance Series

No More Secrets

Fall into Temptation

The Last Second Chance

Not Part of the Plan

Holding on to Chaos

CPSIA information can be obtained
at www.ICGtesting.com
Printed in the USA
LVHW051707110422
715892LV00001B/21